Current Danger

Marilyn Wallace

Current Danger

D O U B L E D A Y
New York
London
Toronto
Sydney
Auckland

PUBLISHED BY DOUBLEDAY
a division of Bantam Doubleday Dell Publishing Group, Inc.
1540 Broadway, New York, NY 10036

DOUBLEDAY and the portrayal of an anchor with a dolphin are trademarks of
Doubleday, a division of Bantam Doubleday Dell Publishing Group, Inc.

Library of Congress Cataloging-in-Publication Data
Wallace, Marilyn.
    Current danger / Marilyn Wallace. — 1st ed.
      p.   cm.
    I. Title.
  PS3573.A4266C8   1998
  813'.54—dc21   97-11721
  CIP

ISBN 0-385-47448-2
Copyright © 1998 by Marilyn Wallace
All Rights Reserved
Printed in the United States of America
February 1998
First Edition

10 9 8 7 6 5 4 3 2 1

For Mark Wallace and Rachael Horovitz.
May the power of love light your way.

Acknowledgments

One of the problems with having a writer for a friend is that you never know when you'll be asked to part with great chunks of your hard-won expertise in the name of fictional authenticity. Many thanks are due to my dear friends Ben Davis and Gerry Hovagimyan for sharing their tales of the New York City renovation scene with panache and with generosity, and for being available to answer questions and make suggestions. Any errors in history and procedure are, of course, mine alone.

Thanks, again and again, to Judy Greber for reading the manuscript; to Sheri Holman for her astute editorial insights; to Molly Friedrich, dream agent; and to Bruce Wallace, for being supportive, funny, smart, and unpredictable.

Current Danger

One

"A million dollars."

Claudia Miller swiveled her desk chair. "Eight units. One hundred twenty-five thousand profit each. A chance to do it my way, and a million dollars to split," she muttered into the late-night silence.

Even after years of deals in which large sums of money were as common as tenpenny nails, the words had a certain cachet, especially now that her own bank account was involved. *A million dollars if they could pull this off.*

The Warren Street warehouse was nothing much to look at: eight stories, brick with stone trim around the windows, twenty-two feet wide, with a rusted fire escape and a corrugated metal awning overhanging the entrance. Because Murray Kurtz couldn't get past the notion that city rooftops might be good for more than keeping out the rain, he needed her to act as designer and developer, to be his partner in alchemy. Together, they'd transform his rectangular, charmless dross into residential gold.

But Murray, who cultivated his cabdriver appearance, whose buying and selling activities made him harried, exhausted, and exceedingly rich twenty years ago, was dragging his heels. They'd danced around the negotiations trading gotchas and gimmes, all the time knowing they'd come to terms. She'd had the contract drawn up, and now he was making her wait for a final response because it amused him.

1

If she couldn't sleep, she might as well get some work done.

Mumbling about the inconvenience of living in a duplex apartment, she climbed the spiral staircase to her living quarters, made a pot of coffee, carried it back down to her office. She burned her mouth trying to drink it too fast, calculated a lumber order twice and got ridiculous figures both times.

At twenty after eleven, the phone rang. Claudia stepped off the distance from her oak desk, liberated years earlier from the office of a bookie on Mulberry Street, to the window, turned and marched back. She stirred a pile of papers, stuffed a pencil into a jar, glared at the answering machine until it clicked on.

After all, God and Panasonic made those devices so people didn't have to talk to everyone with either a problem or a great idea, which, in her experience, often were indistinguishable from each other.

At the end of her message, Bert Kossarian launched into a complicated tale about a delayed order for a dishwasher. "So I handled it," he concluded. "That's what you pay me for, right?"

"We have to find another appliance dealer," she said too crisply, as she picked up the phone and punched the machine's OFF button to kill the feedback. "Sorry. I didn't mean to yell at you, Bert. But this is the second order they messed up."

Her oldest friend and her foreman at the Duane Street renovation job, Bert said gently, "Hey, so patience isn't your strong suit. Maybe you should do something therapeutic, like playing with marble in your studio. Until you hear from Murray, I mean."

"The best therapy would be getting to work converting that building. What do you think, Bert? What's Murray Kurtz up to?"

"Claudia, you've been the man's friend for fifteen years. You really expect him to be rational?"

It was a relief to have it spoken aloud. "You are so right, my Armenian guru. Listen, I better finish working up the specs for that Chelsea townhouse bid and let you get to sleep."

But the numbers wouldn't cooperate and she tossed the Chelsea papers into a file and paced. She tried to forget how much the deal with Murray would mean, beyond the money—a chance to stop being simply a builder and become a developer, an opportunity to

2

prove that simple design and quality materials were timeless, elegant . . . profitable.

To keep from inflicting unintended damage on an unsuspecting world, she pushed open the door to her sculpture studio, flipped on the electric heater, paced while she swore in Spanish, Italian. With both hands clenched behind her back, Claudia studied the block of green-veined marble on the counter.

Cold and slick, the marble had a satisfying solidity, the bones of the earth polished to smoothness. In a trickle of winter daylight it looked ordinary, another object in a prosaic material world. At night, angular shadows etched themselves on the stone, making it easier for her to resist being beguiled into curves when she really wanted planes, a tangle of sharpness, edges.

She drew a line through the dust on the counter, rolled the fine particles until the silken powder made her hands white. The chisels in the tray gleamed seductively, and she selected one. She set the chisel, adjusted it, breathed. Lifted the hammer.

And the telephone rang.

Startled, she jerked her hand back, relieved she hadn't begun the unstoppable arc of her arm, hammer falling onto chisel. It was after midnight, probably a crank call. She stroked the marble again, waiting for the machine to come on.

But the phone kept ringing. Then she remembered: She'd turned the machine off when she picked up in the middle of Bert's message. She'd never reset it. She stomped to the far end of the studio and snatched the receiver from the cradle.

"Yes?" The rough burrs of the chisel left an imprint of regular hatchwork on the pad of her index finger.

"You have to come meet me. This is totally amazing." The voice on the telephone was barely audible, as though speaking an endearment.

"Look, just put it away, joker. Don't call here again." Claudia was about to hang up when she heard a familiar note in the reply.

"I know it's late," the hoarse voice whispered tenderly, "but I want to share this with you. There's all this crystal stuff covering the streets. They're practically glittering."

Tommy. Her half brother, twenty-three years younger and trying on adulthood. Her father's son, juiced and jangling and quivering with adolescent energy. "Tommy? Call me tomorrow. We'll talk then, okay?"

"Hey, I have a better idea. Come walking with me, Claude. It's amazing out here. So many crystals. This time I really think I can write it down before it melts." Her brother's words popped and sizzled like water drops in a hot frying pan, tense, ready to explode. "Come on, Claudia, it's like total shimmer out here."

"Tommy? What did you take? Who sold it to you? What is it, speed?" Two months ago, they'd tramped together through the snowy wonderland of Central Park to catch *Carmina Burana* at Lincoln Center. His arms and legs and his worldliness seemed then to be growing more quickly than the rest of him.

More quickly than his good judgment, she thought sadly.

"Very funny. I'm perfectly straight. Listen, I really need you to meet me. I'm—"

"Tommy, it's late and I'm exhausted. I set framing tracks at Duane Street all day. Go home. Get in a cab and go home."

"Come on, Claudia, you have to—Hold on, okay?"

The sound of a muffled voice raised in anger made her stomach clench the way it used to thirty years ago, when Mrs. Aubrey from upstairs would go after one of her sons with a hairbrush.

"Claudia, listen, I really don't feel so good. . . . It would help me out if you could come and get me."

"What's going on, Tommy? You're not sick, right?"

"I need you to come get me."

He wasn't sick and he wasn't high and he didn't simply want company. Her mind raced, trying to put together pieces that didn't fit. Maybe if she got him talking, she could figure it out.

"If you're in trouble, Tommy, you can tell me. Someone's there with you, right?" A school chum pulling a prank? Or an urban predator who wanted to hurt some skinny, dreamy-eyed high school kid?

"Right."

A sandpaper rasp . . . no, something else. Tight. Tommy's voice was tight.

"That's it, Claudia."

Something was cutting off his breath.

"As soon as you can."

Strangled. That was it. He sounded constricted. *Let me not blow this,* she prayed. "Okay, Tommy, listen, where are you? This other person, is he demanding money? Is that what this is about?"

"No, no, I just need you to come get me."

"All right, I'm on my way." Claudia pushed aside a T square, scooped up her keys, brushed through the welter of catalogs on the file cabinet, fumbled on the desk for her pocketknife. "Tommy, where are you?"

"The street of resurrected dreams, Claude. The avenue of second chances, the bridge over trouble waters, the walkway to the stars, the—"

"Cut it out!" If he'd give her a straight answer, she could do as he asked. She wrestled down her dread and asked, "The nearest street sign, Tommy—what does it say?"

"Can't talk, Claude. It can't say anything. It . . . *Hey!*" Her brother's words were lost in shouting.

"Tommy, hang up so I can call nine-one-one. I can't call the cops unless you hang up the phone!"

A hostile voice yelled an incoherent threat. A series of sickening thumps followed, drowned out by the sound of the phone smashing against something hard, again and again.

"I'll find you, Tommy. I'm coming!"

Through the phone, Claudia Miller heard footsteps clattering on the pavement, fading, and then only a single soft moan.

She flew up the curving staircase, called 911 from the house phone as she grabbed her coat from the closet. Claudia jabbed at the elevator button, jogging in place until the door slid open.

The walkway to the stars . . . She'd better have this right.

Normally, it was a fifteen minute walk from her TriBeCa loft to the foot of the Brooklyn Bridge. Her brother, she knew, might not have that much time.

Two

A gust crossed the Hudson River, honed its edge on the decaying docks, then sliced down the cobblestoned corridor of Harrison Street. No taxi, no car, no intelligent life braved the cold. Tommy had chosen the bitterest night in months to let trouble find him.

She turned south, skirting icy patches and heaped garbage bags as she ran along Hudson Street past the nursery school, Tabak's real estate office, past Duane Park and the grocery store. Except for a yellow square of light in a window above the florist shop, everything was dark.

What was he doing out so late, anyway? Last time they spoke—could it really be three weeks ago?—he'd gone on and on about how he'd discovered the purity of sunrise.

Besides, it was a school night.

At Chambers Street, brighter, more traveled, she headed east toward the Municipal Building and the golden, winged figure looking down from its towering perch. To her left, a ribbon of blacktop pointed north to the Empire State Building, its thatch of St. Patrick's Day lights glowing green against the black sky. The cold made her eyes water. She loped past figures clustered in doorways under cardboard layers, ignoring the voices that called out as she surged past a subway entrance.

Tommy Miller was too damn young, too pampered and protected, too inexperienced for late-night walks on the wild side.

Dark shapes huddled under bare-branched trees in City Hall

Park. Claudia looked away, not wanting to see who they were or what they were doing. She focused instead on every street corner, on each doorway, searching for a pay phone. Midway through the park, she spotted a shadow, legs, a crumpled figure that seemed to sprout from the bushes. Caught in the yellow light, the body lay like a bug trapped in amber, unmoving, indifferent to the cold.

Tommy was curled into a ball, his left hand cupped over his ear. He wore only a pair of jeans, sneakers, a torn plaid flannel shirt, and, improbably, a blue wool blazer with a gold crest on the pocket. Claudia knelt and touched the side of his neck. A pulse beat faintly; his eyelids fluttered open.

"I'm here," she managed. "Who did this, Tommy?"

Dry lips barely moving, he rasped, "Don't know. Swear to God, Claudia. I . . . don't know."

His icy fingers unfurled at her touch, not warming even when she rubbed them. She tried to brush what looked like strands of dark hair from his face, leaned closer when her hand came away wet and warm, sticky with blood from the scratches that ran from his ear to his mouth.

Siren fading, an ambulance screeched to a stop. Doors slammed and footsteps crunched along the street as two men, Mutt and Jeff in medical mufti, skidded toward them.

"Please step aside, ma'am." The slender technician snapped on latex gloves as he knelt beside Tommy. Above the left breast pocket of his Army-green jacket a gold badge announced that he was R. Coreggio. He played a flashlight beam along the cuts on Tommy's face and the bright bruise on his neck. The bloody slashes looked like a truncated music staff—four thin, straight parallel lines running down his smooth cheek. Not a knife, not fingernails that left this delicate tracery of blood. Coreggio frowned, leaned in for a better look, handed his partner the flashlight as he tore the protective paper from a swab. "Weird. How you do that, my man?"

"Some guy was swinging this cable at me like it was a lasso." Each word an effort, he croaked, "Black rubbery stuff stripped off the end so these wires, red, white, black, copper, they were sticking out. Electrical cable. That was what cut me."

"Close your eyes, Tommy. Don't move." Claudia gripped her

brother's fingers as Coreggio dabbed at the bloody mess on his cheek. Talk to him, she told herself, and don't watch. "Sounds like ten-four Romex. I use that cable for clients with heavy equipment."

The attendant tossed the crimson swab into a plastic bag. "My uncles used that stuff to wire up a hunting lodge in the Poconos. So, what about that bruise on your neck?"

"He was choking me with the cable. I pulled it off." Tommy massaged his throat. "When he tried to grab my hands, I kicked him in the nuts. Some taxi passed by and the driver honked his horn and the guy ran away."

"Way to go, bro." Coreggio lifted the tatters of Tommy's shirt and examined the scrapes on his chest, gently prodded his belly. With the help of his burly partner, he lifted Tommy to a sitting position. "His face'll be fine. Thing I'm concerned about is the stuff we can't see. This kid got knocked around, maybe there's internal bleeding or spleen damage or something. We're going to St. Vincent's."

Tommy's fingers clutched hers. "No hospital. I'm okay." He pushed upright, his smile wobbly.

"You can sign this release, says you refused treatment," Coreggio said, turning away from Tommy to address Claudia. "He starts throwing up or gets dizzy, don't wait for no doctor's office. You get your kid to Emergency."

"My kid? I—"

Tommy grabbed her hand, danced from foot to foot like a boxer dodging body blows. "I'm fine, Mom."

At least he didn't say *Mother*. Which was what he called Nora Ransom Miller, three years older than Claudia, her father's wife for the past seventeen years. Claudia scribbled her name on the release form and waved as Coreggio and his silent partner climbed into the ambulance, gunned the engine, and roared into the darkness.

"So, your throat isn't too sore for you to talk?" She threw an arm around his shoulder, flinched at the sight of the raw wound on his cheek as they passed under a streetlight. "I need to know what happened, Tommy."

Tommy glanced over his shoulder, wincing when he turned his head. "All I did was go hear Mako, you know, the poet. The place was cranking. The Knitting Factory. After he was done, I decided to walk across the bridge to see the magic of the city. And then this guy comes up and starts swinging a cable in my face."

She steadied him as he stumbled on the ice. "You want to wait till we get back to my house to tell this story? Because maybe it will be easier then for you to remember the truth. The *whole* truth, Tommy."

"I'm sorry, Claude. This is like . . . shit, I don't know what it's like. A nightmare."

A nightmare that nobody else should have to live through. "We're reporting all this to the cops. Right now. And then I'm taking you home. You're going to explain to Dad what you were doing out so late. I'm not cleaning up after you."

Tommy shrugged off her arm and ran to the corner. "He won't care. He's going to London to see the queen, oi what. Tomorrow. International law, fuckin' ay, that way he can say, Sorry, kids, I have to be three thousand miles away, so I can't come hear you play the flügelhorn in the school band."

"Diversionary tactic. No pouting. First the police, then home," she said firmly.

"Shit, Claudia, Dad's going to ground me until I'm thirty-two."

"With good behavior, maybe only until you're twenty-five." She wheeled and stood in front of him. "Would you recognize this guy if you saw him again?"

"He was kind of tall and he had sort of broad shoulders. But recognize him? I might recognize his ski mask." Tommy struggled to smile again, but his face twisted as a cold sweat beaded his forehead. "And I'd know his lightning bolt in a flash. Ha ha, get it? In a flash—lightning bolt."

Tempted to shake him, she gritted her teeth instead. "Lightning bolt?"

"Yeah. He had a gold chain around his neck with this dumb lightning bolt charm on it. Like that was supposed to scare me, right?" All at once, he looked away, eyes brimming.

"Honest to God, Tommy." She hid her awkward uncertainty as she took his arm. "It's okay to drop the macho stuff. It's perfectly reasonable for this attack to upset and frighten you."

"Sure, just like it's perfectly reasonable for me to write poetry. Except, don't ask Dad what he thinks about that. Shakespeare.

LeRoi Jones. Ezra Pound. Dylan Thomas." With each step Tommy took, another name spilled out, the rhythm shifting from march to dirge to solemn processional. "*They* were men. And they were poets. So what? So fucking what if I write poetry, Claudia? My own father wishes I was someone else, you know? He can't stand that his cousin was a writer, that's his problem. Fuck him, that's all. Just fuck him and his fucking little boxes you have to fit into."

If Tommy wanted help breaking out of the boxes from someone who had already made her escape, he'd have to wait. "You're stalling. The whole truth, remember? You were telling me what happened."

"Okay, okay. He pushed me down and all that, just like I told the nurse guy. But the kicking-him-in-the-nuts part didn't happen until later. First, the guy says to me, 'Here's a quarter. You call your sister and tell her to come meet you. Just be cool and tell her.' Something like that."

Pinned by her shock to the asphalt, she waited for her breath to return. "He wanted *me?*"

"That's what he said. He wanted me to call my sister. I tried to get away from him, but he had that fucking cable wire around my throat."

"Why didn't you just do what he said? You could have been killed." Her disbelief congealed into a knot of anger.

"I figured if you really came to get me, he was gonna hurt you or something so I tried to . . . I guess that was pretty stupid." He grinned. "But, hey, guess what? You're okay and I'll recover, so my little trick worked."

Maybe he had a point, she thought as they approached the First Precinct. Really, that should be all that mattered. But she was filled with fury when she glanced at her brother's blood-streaked face. Sooner or later, the man with the lightning bolt was going to turn up again. Whoever he was, whatever he wanted, she'd make him regret choosing her as a target, and using Tommy to get to her.

Three

He slipped the camera into his pocket and pressed his back against the cold metal of the door. A car approached, the beams from its headlights bouncing against a stained McDonald's wrapper, a kid's mitten lying on a bench, the skinny tail of a rat as it dove into an overflowing Dumpster.

Still. He must be perfectly still, even though the blood in him raced, setting off little explosions behind his eyes and making the breath in his nose feel like goddamn peppermint or something.

She had come out in the middle of the night.

She had gotten out of her bed and run through the streets to help the kid, and she was walking away with him, just like that.

In one impulsive moment, he had abandoned his original plan like it was an old shoe that let in all the cold and the rain.

But it was worth it, the change. Even now, watching them stroll away, he knew the hot, bubbling taste of near-satisfaction, and it made him impatient to work out the details and put a new plan into action.

Finally, he knew what was missing the other times.

Instead of imagining her pain, he had actually seen it. Even though it was only for a few minutes and the light not so good, he had seen the way her eyebrows gathered close in worry as she bent over the boy, had heard her try to get him to talk to her. Could practically reach out and touch that scrunched-up face, lift the trembling chin with his hand and make her look into his eyes and give him what he wanted.

That's what was missing the other time. Christ, the guy in Phoenix . . . he had only imagined what that man's cousin felt. He hadn't actually witnessed it.

He had to slow down so he could use this new information. He had discovered it by accident, but he sure was going to make the most of it.

Accident. No one would say what was about to happen to the old guy on Park Avenue was just a bad break.

The boy was shuffling along, his arm hooked through the woman's, as though he needed her support to keep going. He could no longer see their faces, so he didn't know if she was annoyed or frightened or what she was feeling.

If she felt anything . . .

If she didn't just blow the whole thing off, the way she blew off the black ashes that settled around her head after the fire . . .

It was obvious now, what was wrong the first time, why it didn't feel right.

He hadn't gotten close enough. That was what he now understood, the lesson he'd learned tonight.

He needed to see them, the ones who wept over the bodies. The ones left behind to try to figure out what had happened to someone they loved. The ones who had to live in the deep, black pit of sadness, bottomless and salty with tears. Like the hole they'd left in his life, all those years ago.

If she hadn't made sure there was no escape from that fire, there would be no hole. His own life would be different, better. For starters, his mother would still be alive.

She would have been protected against the man who sent her to her grave a broken, mangled mess.

Well, you learn something every day, and today's lesson was important, that was for sure.

He squinted to keep the two figures in focus, but they were shrinking dots, about to disappear into the yawning black mouth that ate up everything beyond the blinking red light at the far corner.

His hands were cold. He shoved them deeper into his pockets. The coil of cable tugged at his shoulder, and he shifted his weight.

He'd do the Park Avenue guy the way he'd originally planned. And he'd figure out how to make a place for himself in her life.

Somehow, some way, he'd get near enough to watch her as the floating whirlpool swallowed her and poured the heat of rage and sorrow into her, brighter, every day a little hotter, until she became a nova of pain.

He would deliver something to her house, that would do it. When she opened the door, she'd have to look him straight in the eye, and he'd see beyond the businesslike glance that she shot over everything. But that would only be once. He needed to get close to her on a regular basis.

He had to become part of her life.

Some way.

He'd work it out. Because she was the one who would finally give him the satisfaction he longed for.

They were out of sight now, the woman and the boy, but he didn't have to follow them. He knew where they were going. Besides, he had to perfect his new plan. The one he would put into action after they'd gone home and slept. The one he'd be working when they thought they were safe to start a new and ordinary day.

Of course.

Get close to her.

Make a place for himself in her life.

So he'd be right there when she learned the news, when some blue uniform, no expression on his face, just sour breath and fat, rough hands that kept rubbing back and forth as though he was trying to scrape off something nasty, came to deliver the tragic word.

Getting close to Claudia Miller would do the job.

Getting close to Claudia Miller would finally settle the score and give him peace.

Four

Evan Patrick Miller smoothed the collar on his maroon bathrobe, then pointed Claudia to a seat beneath the leaded casement window as he eased himself into his leather desk chair. "You look terrible."

Her father, on the other hand, appeared ready to receive visitors, only one side of his face a little sleep-rumpled.

"And I always thought gray was *my* color." She drew her fingers lightly across the smudges of fatigue beneath her eyes. She might have inherited her father's ability to see around corners, his determination to finish whatever he set out to achieve, but she was definitely *not* heir to that face, impervious to late nights, hard work, the toll of distress. "The paramedic said Tommy would be all right."

"I'm more concerned about you right now. 'Call your sister.' What does that mean, Claudia? What did the police say?"

She smiled ruefully. Without a more precise description than Tommy could provide, police follow-up was limited. Lieutenant Rugowski's apologetic word: *Limited.* "That we were both lucky. Listen, Dad, I'll be fine. So will Tommy. He *knew* you'd ground him. He deserves it."

"I'm glad you agree. I don't want him running to you with every adolescent complaint. And you mustn't do him the disservice of letting him think he has an alternate parent if he doesn't like what's happening at home."

There was something she could do, though, to help her brother's cause. "Maybe he's trying to send you a message. Tommy's choices may not be the ones you'd make for yourself, but they're positive, not destructive."

Evan sat like one of her sculptures, alabaster and immobile.

"You bullied him into Dalton," she continued, "when he wanted Music and Art—the right high school on his résumé when he comes up for partnership at his law firm blah blah. You want a child who'll make you proud? Don't try to squeeze him into a mold. He won't fit. He's got too much heart."

Her father's jaw clenched. The fire crackled. Sparks hit the screen and hissed back onto the hearthstone. "I know heart when I see it, Claudia. *You* have heart and you have *brains*. Yet, you chose to drop out of college and become a laborer. Very good. You broke the rules. You showed me."

"Maybe when I left school it was to prove something to you, Dad. Now, though, it's my life. I love the work." She rose, kissed his forehead, turned at the sound of footsteps in the hall.

Nora Miller appeared in the doorway, the bow at the throat of her demure flannel nightgown peeking from the lapels of the black satin robe that hung from her perfect body. Sheba, coat gleaming like newly panned gold, trailed at her heels, tail fanning the air with delight.

"Hello, Claudia." Nora crossed the room and stood with her back to the fire, hands clasped behind her. The play of the flames sent shimmering lights dancing on Sheba's pelt as the dog circled and sank down, head on paws, to watch the proceedings. "Thanks for taking care of Tommy. Listen, you just spent a couple of hours with him. Did you see any signs of . . . Oh, hell. I think Tommy might be manic-depressive. And ignoring the problem won't make it go away."

Evan recoiled, then dragged his neutral expression back across his face. The minor wonder was that Nora had gone directly to the heart of a difficult matter in her husband's presence. Claudia assumed, because it was all she'd been shown, that Nora was simply a trophy wife getting on in years. Maybe pretty Nora had grown up.

"He *was* agitated and restless," Claudia said carefully.

Nora nodded. She leaned down to stroke the silken fur on Sheba's head. "The depressions are the worst. He lies in his bed and blasts opera on his CD player. Doesn't get up until two, three o'clock in the afternoon. God, I can't bear seeing him like that."

"If he does have a clinical condition, then there's medication, right?" Claudia's heart twisted with the hope that Tommy would be all right. "We all had better get some sleep. If there's anything I can do . . ."

"Don't offer my son an easy out." Her father's spine was stiff, two blotches of red spreading across his face. "I'm sorry, Claudia. I'm upset about this incident. Maybe I should stay home. I could send one of the other partners to London. You know . . . Wait a minute."

She could almost see his lawyer-wheels spinning through a scenario.

Evan's satisfied smile erased the sleep lines from his cheek. "Did the man say your name?"

She frowned. "I don't think so. Tommy said he told him to call his sister. That's all. He was very clear about that."

"It might be random." Her father nodded twice. "He didn't say your name because this lunatic picked on the first vulnerable kid he saw. It just so happened he had a sister. Some other kid, he wouldn't have gotten that far. That's—"

"Don't cancel your trip, Dad." If his random-attack theory comforted her father, she was glad to let him cling to it. "I have to go to Chelsea and to Duane Street later this morning. You make your flight to London and take care of business. We'll be fine here."

In the cab on the way home, she watched the empty streets slide by outside the window and tried to make her mind blank. Exhausted, she fell asleep as soon as she lay down on her bed, rose with a start two hours later.

She gathered papers into her briefcase and rode the subway to 23rd Street. Tommy's bloody face seemed to flash in the window as the train hurtled north. She measured the brownstone parlor floors, flipping through a mental gallery of people she knew who wore gold chains. No one. Not even the guy behind the counter at Two Boots Pizza.

She rode home on a nearly empty subway train with her briefcase pressed against her side. Maybe her father was right. Maybe the event was random, an urban misfortune, and Tommy's attacker didn't know her.

The train screeched to a stop at the Franklin Street station. The platform was nearly deserted, only a bag-toting figure far down at the other end and two whippet-faced women in tight black pants and reefer jackets on the uptown side to hear the echoes of her heels against the tile floor. A steady drip splashed onto the express tracks in the center of the tunnel, creating a puddle between the second and third rail. Two candy wrappers, a comb with most of its teeth missing, and a heart-shaped deflated Mylar balloon floated in the murky water.

Outside, diamonds of blue cold cut at her face. As the wind propelled her across Varick, she glanced back at the glass and iron awning over the uptown subway entrance, as graceful as a classic Métro kiosk in Paris. *Home territory,* it said to her.

But the neighborhood was being invaded regularly these days. A movie location van, tan and brown like a hulking, overgrown family camper, idled at the curb. Stinking up the air with those white-cotton puffs of poison rolling from the tailpipe. Blocking her view of . . . exactly nothing, but she was annoyed anyway as she picked her way along a patch of ice.

She thought of her father's cautions when she struck out into TriBeCa after walking away from her first semester at Brown. "Triangle Below Canal?" he'd said when he first heard the name given to her new neighborhood. "No grocery stores, no amenities, only deficiencies. They should have called it WaSoSo. Wasteland South of SoHo."

Murray Kurtz, though, had the savvy to anticipate the boom in the early nineties. Then the four-star restaurants and the film groups and technology companies and antique sellers moved into the old warehouses. Murray had always known the neighborhood would take off. Murray and his promise to decide about the building this week. What had he said? *I'll call you by five on Thursday . . .*

It was Murray who had decreed they should meet outside the building on a dark, sleety morning so he could complain about how he needed time to find a place for the balance scale and glass display cases he'd hauled out of the basement. Claudia had watched with fond amusement as he worked his strategy, aware that anything in the underground vault, with its dirt floor and a sump pump that hadn't worked since one of the Roosevelts was president, was only good for the trash heap.

He didn't really care about all that moldering memorabilia. He was piling up points, squeezing her for a concession. She'd agreed to help him arrange for storage. That piece of business off the table, it was time to stop dicking around.

"Murray, Murray." The wind drove needles of ice into her skin, but she'd turned away, peeled a fleck of brown paint from the carved wood pillar beside the front door. "You underestimate how much work it's going to take to do something with this piece of . . . *history*. I want the contract signed in forty-eight hours."

Murray's ruddy cheeks sagged as he brushed ice crystals from his eyebrows. "I know, but I haven't had a minute to think. Two hours ago, I got back from Boca. My granddaughter's bas mitzvah, the last one, thank God. Seven grandsons, five granddaughters, twelve ice swans, twelve chopped livers shaped like fishes. Eleven. Mindy's they made into a turkey. What's the matter with *mounds*, for crying out loud? I gotta talk it over with my wife and my lawyer. Gimme a week, say. I'll have it to you by five next Thursday." He'd extended his hand and she'd taken it.

Well, in two days Murray's time would be up. If the signed contract wasn't delivered by then, she'd start looking at other properties after the weekend.

Without warning, Claudia Miller was hit from behind. She scrambled for a foothold on the ice, but her legs flew out from under her and she landed on her bottom with an unceremonious thud.

The face peering down at her was young, concerned, and more than a little confused. Blond hair pulled into a low ponytail, blue eyes glittering behind wire-framed glasses, a straight, nearly perfect nose, high cheekbones: he'd be pretty, if not for the angular jaw.

"Oh, Jeez, are you okay? I guess I was going too fast. I was trying to get to the corner to catch a cab and I slipped on that ice, and, well, Jeez, I'm really sorry. You're all right?"

During his speech the young man, who had somehow ended up in front of her, stuck a paperback book with a nondescript gray cover into his pocket, then dabbed at the slushy mess on Claudia's coat. His cheeks were tinged with pink as he brushed the hair away from her eyes, a gesture of reassurance and comfort—or of uninvited intimacy. She waved away his offer of help and rose, wiped off the wet pebbles of grit that clung to her gloves.

"I'm fine. No damage done to *me*." But the battered cordovan leather of her briefcase looked like a skinned knee, scrapes and scratches turning dark and wet. One of the fittings that held the handle in place was missing; the bag dangled sadly.

He knelt, scooping items that had spilled from her briefcase, straightening papers, shaking moisture from everything. "Let me buy you lunch, Claudia." His earnest blue eyes and the relaxed set of his mouth were friendly, unfamiliar.

She tensed. A blue scarf, tucked into his coat and reaching all the way to his chin, made it impossible to tell whether he was wearing a gold chain. "Do we know each other?"

"Well, now we do, isn't that right? You're Claudia Portia Miller, builder." He tapped a finger under her name in the center of one of her business cards. "I'm Charlie Pastor. You mind if I hold onto this card so I know where to send the new briefcase? And, really, I'd like to buy you lunch. A late lunch, but it's the least I can do."

What she wanted was for Charlie Pastor to get out of her way so she could get back to work. "Don't bother. No new briefcase and no lunch. Thanks anyway, but I have to go now."

"Portia. Bet your father picked Clarence for his son's middle name. As in Darrow. His children were going to be lawyers, the family business, a long line of distinguished jurists going back to Cromwell's England and carrying on in post-Mayflower America. That's where the Miller part comes from, right?" He handed her a lipstick and a tape measure, then bent to pick up a color card from Pearl Paints. "So, like any modern woman trying to live larger than the stereotypes, you went into construction. This is more than amazing. Not ten minutes ago I conjured up a tall, dark-haired woman with an intriguing past and you just appeared. It's—"

"—not the story. Although my father wouldn't mind if it were." She laughed, gently tugged her business card from his hand, and stuffed the items he handed her back into her case. "My father was too busy trying to live down his blue-collar origins and the fact that Henry Miller is his second cousin to worry about his daughter's middle name. My mother gave me that particular burden. What's it called, sublimation? Transference? She dropped out of law school when she became pregnant with me. She died when I was twelve, but she always wanted me to live her—" She reeled herself back in, annoyed that she'd dropped her guard. "Mr. Pastor, I'm going to work now."

"Okay, not a whole lunch. The third cousin of Henry Miller? Or is it second cousin, once removed? *The* Henry Miller? The writer who drank his way through the brothels of Europe and taught Anaïs Nin how to write dirty stories? Surely you have enough time for a cup of coffee."

He was glib and he was cute, but she was in no mood for banter. "Time isn't the problem. Good-bye, Mr. Pastor."

"Guess I'll try to find another cab. You think they're all keeping warm in a cozy huddle near Penn Station? Maybe we'll run into each other another time." Grinning, he saluted, straightened his coat, and strode away.

Get over yourself, she thought as she watched him turn the corner. She tucked her injured briefcase under her arm and continued past the noisy hum of the Western Union Building to Duane Street.

Five

A figure huddled in the bit of shelter provided by the barely recessed building entrance. She recognized the white kinky hair above the creased brown face: Ike Hitchens, her summertime pal.

Still sober at lunchtime and flush with funds, Ike had talked her into a couple of beery hours swapping stories in the hot July sun. They'd sat by the river and discovered common ground: a love of music, a conviction that the new American separatism was unhealthy, and what was worse, boring. She helped him out with clothing, money, odd jobs whenever she could, but she hadn't seen him all winter.

Head dangling, Ike looked like a thick question mark covered by layers of found garments. "I do pretty fine till the sun don't shine," he sang. He swayed as he riffed in a minor key, scatting the alto sax line. Beside him on a crust of clouded ice lay a strapped-together suitcase and a paper bag, the top twisted to give him a better grip on the bottle inside. "But I feel real, real bad 'round midnight."

"What you really feel is *cold* 'round midnight. I thought maybe you went down south for the winter."

Ike stumbled toward her, head bobbing. "You want to be careful, running around the street late at night. Ike watches out for you when he can, you know that, but I ain't always gonna be there. So you be careful, hear?"

"Ike, did you see the guy who attacked my brother the other

night?" She watched as he swigged again from his bottle, then said gently, "Tommy was very frightened."

His face dissolved in indecision, and he looked down at his neatly wrapped bundles. "That was your brother? I didn't know you have no brother. Someone attacked him?" He dipped his head, eyes closed. "Turrible. A turrible world this is turning out to be."

Maybe later she'd walk him over to the Franklin Square Diner and buy him a bowl of soup. For now, Ike was safe in his warm world, the embrace of cheap wine more comforting than food or company. She pressed a ten into his hand, and dug in her purse for the key ring.

Without a key, the elevator wouldn't go anywhere. A necessary security precaution in buildings like this one and her own, where each floor was a separate living unit and the elevator opened directly into the apartment. Not so convenient when the damn key decided to play hide-and-seek. Finally, her fingers closed over the ring, and she unlocked the outside door and crossed the small lobby to the elevator. Inside, she inserted the key, pressed four, turned the key to lock it again, so that no one else had access to the apartment.

When the elevator door slid open, she headed toward the sound of a circular saw biting through a board. Work, Bert's ready and familiar smile, the smell of new wood—they would all help last night's adventure fade from her memory.

Bent over his task, Bert hadn't heard her come in. When had his hair gone so gray? Why hadn't she noticed before? He straightened, wiped his forehead with the back of his hand, looked up and waved.

Claudia pointed to the cartons in the middle of the floor. "This says birch. They're supposed to be—"

"I already called the factory in Canada and told them we needed the cherry cabinets this week. The guy promised. Listen, I ran into this fellow I met a couple years back." He nodded toward the rear of the loft, to the figure kneeling beside a pile of sheetrock. "His name is Gary Bruno. He's between jobs. We could use an extra hand for a couple of weeks."

"Fine. Maybe you know this guy from Adam, but have you ever

worked with him before? You don't know if he can . . . oh, shit. I'm sorry." She caught her breath, started again. "What do you know about his work?"

Bert leaned against the cartons and brushed a tiny cloud of sawdust from his hands. "I've heard his name, you know, here and there. Good things. I want you to see him do his stuff. Gary, come meet Claudia Miller."

Gary Bruno emerged from the shadows and walked toward them with a rolling gait, like a sailor on shore leave. Dark hair combed back almost into a pompadour, dark eyes, a nose with a minor bump—he looked like a too-tall Neapolitan who should be sitting at a sidewalk café toying with a glass of house red and a cigarette. His hands were jammed into his pockets; a smile tugged at the corners of his wide mouth. "Hey, nice to meet you, Claudia. Like I said to Bert, I'm really a master rock finisher, you know what I mean, but I can handle this framing. I did it around. Out on the Island. Washington Heights. I already told Bert I'd get him references. You don't have to take my word. I got people who'll tell you what a good job I do."

"Show me. Finish framing that wall." She nodded at the stack of lumber.

He measured the height between floor and ceiling twice. Strong and deft, he ran a steel tape along a two-by-four, measured again, then made a single clean slice with the crosscut saw at his mark.

Call your sister. A man with a gold lightning bolt had sliced up her brother's face and forced him to phone her. What did he want with her?

The blat of the screw gun startled her, and she watched Gary Bruno fix the stud in place.

"Yeah, good," she said as he turned. "But two things you should know. First, you earn laborer wages for laborer's work. Including Saturday, no double time, no time and a half, just straight pay. Second, since I don't want you walking away until the job's over, I'm holding back the extra four dollars an hour I pay for taping until you're done."

He folded his muscular arms across his chest. "You mean three things, right? You also mean I shouldn't try to steal your equipment or I'm outta here on my ass, that's what you forgot to say.

Bert told me how much you hate that shit. Well, don't you worry. I didn't take this job to steal from you, Claudia. We got a deal." He shook her hand hard, then started restacking the boards near the window.

From the back of the loft, Bert applauded. "See, I told you it would be okay."

Whether he was talking to her or to Bruno, Claudia didn't care. "Fine, it's okay. Now, why are you running the computer wire through the bathroom wall? That's an extra twenty feet. Just take it over the doorway. Your way, the signal's more likely to degrade."

For ten minutes, she and Bert wrangled over how to install the computer cables the owner wanted threaded through the new walls. She was tired, wound tight; besides, both options had merit and it was easier to grant Bert his victory.

"Whatever," she said. "Just make sure Bruno doesn't cut the wire when he's putting up a stud."

Bert grabbed her elbow and steered her toward the front windows. His blue eyes were shaded with concern. "What's pushing your buttons, Claudia?" he whispered. "You can't let Murray do this to you."

"It's not Murray." She told him about the attack on her brother, the paramedic's ministrations, the visit to the First Precinct. "Tommy was trying to protect me. Do you believe it? The guy said, 'Call your sister,' and Tommy gets all brave and takes one in the face to protect me. My father thinks it was a random attack, that Tommy just happened to have a sister to call. The cops kind of shrugged off the whole incident, too."

"Definitely a bad night." Bert's hug was strong and reassuring. "Look, don't get mad at me, but I kind of agree that you shouldn't make too much of this. Bottom line, your brother will be all right, and so will you if you don't go running out in the middle of the night alone. Listen, Bruno's going to pick up his Durabond and some tools from another job later, but he'll be here for a while. Don't, I repeat, do not scare him away. We need him for the taping."

"*You're* not going to take off on me, are you?" Bert's frustration level was high, she could tell by the way his gaze jumped around the room. If he left on one of his rambles right now, that would ice this particular cake. "You won't have enough money to get to Paris or Rio or wherever until this job is over, will you?"

Bert smiled down at her. "Have I ever walked out on you in the middle of a job? I always give you a month's notice. Kyoto. I want to be there before summer, but I won't mess you up here. Besides, I need to keep working so I can buy a new camera, too."

It was her turn to offer a hug. "Your travel muse makes me nervous sometimes, that's all. I know you won't walk out. Meanwhile, we've got Bruno and everything's going to be fine, right?"

"I promise." He kissed her cheek and stepped back. "One way or another."

Only the fictions that allow you to carry on are worth believing, she told herself. And Bert delivered them so well.

Six

There will be others.

Detective Mitch Russo pulled on his latex gloves and pushed through the noise—med techs clattering down the hallway with the gurney, beat cop using his best manners to quiet the curious, chatty, bathrobe-clad residents and get them back behind their own doors—to the far end of the neat, chilly foyer and into the master bedroom.

On the bed, a queen made up with plaid flannel sheets and a down quilt like the ones advertised in the Macy's Sunday circular, his first body of the week lay, wrapped in a shiny carapace of black electrical tape.

Russo's throat tightened. Carefully, precisely, someone had unwound spool after spool of the inch-wide tape until the upper portion of the body on the bed was insulated, all right, from air, from light, from life. Wrists bound together by a wide bracelet of tape; ankles, too. Did he start just above those wrinkled, age-spotted hands first? How long did it take to do the job? How many minutes of terror for the poor fuck on the bed?

Russo remembered seventh-grade first aid class, practicing bandage wraps, giggling to hide the nervous thrill of actually touching each other, recalled, fleetingly, Angie Ciccarella in her wallpapered bedroom, pressing her breasts flat with a roll of the white gauze she stole from Sister Domenica's desk.

Why was this old man turned into a black plastic mummy?

Only the eyes remained uncovered, and the bags of soft flesh around them. The eyes reminded him of his father's: sad, resigned to the shuffling routine of killing daylight hours in the park, waiting until dark and the reward of cheap chianti to get him through the endless crap the television spilled out into the room. This man had ten times more money than Leonardo Russo ever imagined, but there was something familiar in those eyes.

What a goddamn dismal existence. A four-bedroom Park Avenue apartment, all this fancy, curlicued furniture painted white and gold, pictures on the wall of a life gone by, a television in every room—but he died alone, and horribly, anyway. He'd tried to hang on to a life that was emptying quicker than a flushing toilet. According to the neighbors, the wife spent her winters in Florida with one of the daughters. The son lived in New Jersey, the other daughter in California. This old man, rattling around alone, his steps muffled by the wall-to-wall carpeting in these overstuffed rooms, ends up like this. Dismal.

Two floral upholstered wing chairs and a table with a faded white water stain marked a separate space in the corner of the bedroom. On the table, a chessboard, the game three moves old, standard king's pawn opening. Most likely, the old man played both sides himself, but he'd ask around to see if anyone knew of a regular chess player who visited.

Two dressers, one tall with doors and gold knobs. Surely not real gold. Russo leaned down; Cissie would know, would smile that he couldn't tell right off. Not much dust under the lace runner or on the leather jewelry box or the gold-framed photograph of some family outing, Central Park in autumn, eight or nine little kids dressed in fancy outfits, three couples in expensive suits, all of them beaming at the camera. In the middle, an older man and woman, arms around each other, heads touching.

Russo choked up, cursed himself for letting it get to him, looked around the room to see if anyone noticed. His transfer from Brooklyn, where they knew him, knew how he worked, meant he had to establish himself all over again with people who might pass wrong judgment, but the two techs and the uniform were busy, not paying a bit of attention to one middle-aged cop with a weakness for pretty family scenes.

"A neighbor woman called this in?"

A bald guy dusting the dresser top for prints turned, his brush poised midair. "Screamed it in. We had to get a doctor to give her Valium. Man, this handkerchief has more color than her face. She was coming home from the theater, noticed the door open. You ask me, she was probably a little drunk, one of those expensive brandies these people love. Anyway, this widow, she's a friend of the wife's, she thought maybe the guy had a heart attack or something, and she came back to the bedroom and found him and screamed. Another neighbor heard her, called us. Mrs. Bender, the widow, she's waiting in a cruiser downstairs. You'll enjoy that interview."

Russo scanned the room again. Under the window, the bed, one of those white iron-frame jobs with brass balls skewered by the spokes of the footboard, neatly made except for the corpse in the center. A skinny-legged bedside table held a clock, a telephone, a blue box of house-brand tissues. A photograph on the wall above the bed, the same man and woman standing proud and straight in front of a car, maybe from the fifties; big hair, big skirt on the woman, one of those tropical flower shirts and white shorts on the bowlegged guy.

"Park Avenue guy like this, he really needs Social Security checks? Bleeding the system, these rich guys. Anyway, he won't be cashing this." The uniform, a kid with a shaving cut on his Adam's apple, waved a paper in the air, shook his head. "This for a month or week, do you think? They really think old guys, I mean in the Bronx or something, can actually *live* on this?"

"Hey, you wanted your government to cut taxes and balance the budget. Or maybe you didn't vote so someone else decided for you." Russo snatched the check from the kid's hand and bagged it, refusing to look at the amount because he knew it would depress him for weeks thinking about all the people who had to live on the pittance of a failed government retirement system. "All right, you know the rest. Dust for prints, see if you can find an appointment book, a phone book. Get in touch with his place of work. Let me know when you have the phone book so I can call the wife in Florida and the kids, too. We need to get someone in here to see if there's something missing, to give us some indication of what this guy's life was like. The co-op board's gonna croak when they find out about this. The commissioner's not gonna like reading about this with his morning Wheaties, either."

The building's security, a uniformed doorman complete with gold braid epaulets, cameras everywhere, had been useless. The sicko who did this old man might be someone the guy knew, someone he approved entry for when the doorman buzzed. But the doorman claimed no one had rung for apartment 12-F on his watch, and this body, still stiff with rigor at midnight, was a fairly fresh one. Okay, so a delivery person might have claimed to be going to a different apartment. That was the next step. Get a list. Check out all the deliveries in the past twelve hours.

Russo leaned down and examined the body, took out his flashlight and ran it along the seams where the black tape met. One stray hair, that's all he needed. It wouldn't help him find the perp but it sure would seal the case when they did catch him. A loony like this, Russo thought, and shook his head.

He'd make sure a report circulated to all the boroughs. Maybe there was another poor slob out there already, one they didn't know about yet, who'd been suffocated under a wrapper of electrical tape. Sure as shit, there would be. The person who did this enjoyed himself too much to stop here.

Seven

"Okay, the figures work out for the glass-paned pocket doors. The Chelsea budget survives." Bert poked at the jumble of lighting brochures on her file cabinet. "You really should throw this stuff out. You don't use most of these things, right?"

"But when I need them, I have them." She scanned the figures. "This looks good. So, one of us should pick out the new porcelain door pulls from Simon's. And I have to get the little man at the bank to agree to early payoff of the Duane Street loan."

"Simon's. They're closing at three today for inventory. Go to Yaffa's instead. Have a cappuccino. Because if you don't take time off, and on a regular basis, you know what's going to happen to you. All the 'W' words. Worn out. Weary. Worse for Wear."

"Oh, sure, you just want to keep me away from Duane Street so I don't scare Bruno off," she said, grinning.

After two nights of fitful sleep and two days of constantly looking over her shoulder, her life had assumed a pattern. Work, work, sleep, and work again. And phone Tommy at least once a day. And listen more alertly whenever the telephone rang.

"You hear from Murray yet?" Idly, Bert turned pages in a flooring catalog.

Claudia shook her head. Things really were back to normal. "Why don't you enter those figures and print out the estimate for the Chelsea renovation? I'll see if I can get Murray on the phone."

Bert slid his chair to her desk; the notebook computer chirped as he put it through its start-up routine.

Claudia pulled the Rolodex toward her, squinted at the cards and realized that the sun, after its brief emergence, had disappeared, swallowed by low clouds that looked as if they would linger all day. She reached for the table lamp, turned the switch.

A crackle startled her onto her feet.

A momentary flash left a bright afterimage, and then they were plunged into darkness, a thin, acrid stink rank in her nostrils. Heart banging, she peered down at the outlet. A frayed wire near the plug—that was the culprit. She yanked it from the wall.

"Not too bad." Bert stood beside her, assessing the damage. "One lamp with a plug that needs replacing, one black smudge on the outlet plate, and two racing hearts. I didn't open any files so I didn't lose anything on the computer."

"I'll reset the juice and then fix this sucker." She grabbed the lamp, groped her way to the hall, flipped the circuit breaker to restore power, then hurried up the spiral staircase.

She rummaged in the kitchen utility drawer for wire cutters, electric tape, a plug. As she set them on the counter, the buzzer blared and the phone rang at the same instant. Whatever had caused the lamp to short seemed to have set the world into crazy motion, like a child's movie where the appliances suddenly start dancing to a demonic symphony.

Frowning, she reached for the phone.

"This is Kitchen Magic. Those cherry cabinets should be delivered in a week. We—"

The buzzer sounded again. "Hold on a second, would you?" She checked the monitor and found herself looking past wire-rimmed glasses into familiar blue eyes. The young man in a hurry to catch a cab, the attractive, clever spinner of tales who'd sent her sprawling on the icy street. "Listen, if you don't get those cabinets to me by then, forget it, understand?"

She slammed the phone down, lifted the intercom receiver, and said, "Yes? What is it?"

"Charlie Pastor." He smiled into the camera's eye. "I have an appointment uptown in an hour and I don't want to carry this around with me all day when it really belongs with you. Can I

31

come up for a minute and drop it off?" He held up a cordovan briefcase, its tags still dangling from the handles.

She buzzed him in the front door, then pressed the elevator call button to bring him directly into her apartment. She would accept Charlie Pastor's apology, allow him his closure, and send him on his way.

The elevator deposited him inside, his face glowing with cold, his eyebrows rising in surprise.

Charlie Pastor stamped his feet to shake bits of dirty snow from the tips of his shoes. He unbuttoned his coat and set a green shopping bag on the floor beside the coir mat. "Wet shoes," he said, explaining his reluctance to step on her gleaming wood floors. "This is . . . not exactly Kansas, Dorothy."

"It's not *Architectural Digest*, either." This smart young man was taking his impressed-as-hell business a bit too far.

"I'm not used to all this New York elegance," he said, rubbing his hands against his thighs. "I arrived a week ago from Los Angeles. I'm hoping to find great wealth, true love, and a job writing for one of the soaps. A friend from California set me up with an interview. Tomorrow, and I'm not ashamed to say I'm a little nervous. A *lot* nervous. I mean, what do I know about illegitimate children and long-lost brothers and political rivalries that lead to mutilation and murder? My Lord, this loft is spectacular."

"You should have seen it before I got my hands on it." Layers of grime, concrete floors, the dank, airless feel of the place—she could hardly believe it was the same space.

"*You* did this work?" His wave took in the oak bookshelves, the curve of the marble counters, the glass doors set like echoes of light between the open living space and her bedroom. "What's the view from that window?"

Amused by the wonder in his voice, she folded back the iron shutters and clicked the light switch. As always, the mural behind the window glass, sentinel poplars standing watch above vineyards climbing a Tuscan hillside, coaxed a smile from her. "Years ago, this used to be a real window. When they put up the building next door, I decided I'd have my coffee in San Gimignano every morning. Better than staring at a blank wall."

Charlie Pastor laughed softly, leaned forward to peer past the kitchen toward the spiral staircase. "I'd love a real tour, but honestly, I don't have time. Now that I've murmured duly appreciative comments about the wainscoting, I want to ask you something, Claudia Portia Miller. And I want to give you this." He pointed to the bag at his feet.

Nothing in the loft even resembled wainscoting and he knew that very well. "I told you the other day it wasn't necessary to do anything about it."

"I really did feel awful about ruining your briefcase," he said. "Sorry I interrupted your morning, but I—"

"Charlie, the scratches can be covered with good shoe polish and I can get the handle replaced." She watched as he ventured off the mat, took a step into the kitchen, and held the bag out to her.

"Please take it, Claudia. One of the things I learned in college— Rice University, maybe someday I'll tell you about my rodeo experience—anyway, I learned about Texas style. You can't go to Harvey Keitel's penthouse loft and hand him a bid on redoing his kitchen—would Harvey do it all in black Italian marble?—anyway, you, a lady of obvious class and quality, can't carry a disreputable briefcase. And I couldn't live with myself knowing I was responsible for that shabby state of affairs."

His grin turned into a puzzled frown when she didn't reach for the bag right away.

He caught her arm gently, studied her face. Charlie Pastor stood so close she could smell his minty breath. "Please. I want you to have it."

Claudia looked down at the shopping bag. It would be stupid to make him take the briefcase back when all he was doing was trying to apologize. Accept it, she told herself, and send him on his way. "All right, Charlie. It wasn't necessary, but thanks. And now—"

"You have to get to work. Me, too. I guess I could have been more graceful about this. I didn't mean to bother you. Can we meet for coffee sometime? I really am new to New York, and I'd love it if we could . . . I guess that look on your face is not an enthusiastic yes." His forehead wrinkled in confusion. He patted the pockets of his coat, glanced around the kitchen. "You see my leather gloves?"

Before she could answer him, the phone rang. The Kitchen

Magic salesman launched into a convoluted explanation for the delivery delay.

"I told you. I don't really care why they're going to be late," she said, keeping her voice low and controlled. "I have deadlines and other projects. You should have told me the truth when we made the deal. Now, if you—"

He dangled the possibility of a deep discount to make up for the inconvenience, tried to jolly her into a playful exchange, but she wasn't in the mood. "Just fax me a note with the new terms and make sure those cabinets get here in four days."

When she hung up and turned back to the room, she saw Charlie Pastor, head bent, coat collar turned up, blond ponytail falling over his shoulder, deep in concentration. She approached him, curious to see what was claiming such rapt attention.

"Hey!" The lamp in his hands almost crashed to the floor as his head whipped up. Her wire stripper lay in his lap. The old plug, blackened where the frayed wires had shorted, rested atop the folded newspaper in the center of the table. "You scared me. Do you always sneak around like that?"

"This is *my* house, remember? I happen to live here. What are you doing?"

"A smart woman like you has to ask a question like that?" He twisted two exposed wires together, snipped a length of black tape from the roll and wound it carefully and tightly around the splice, then pushed the wires into the plug receptacle. He held up the old plug for her inspection, then tossed it in the basket. "I'm proving what a practical kind of guy I am. I'm finished, *and,*" he said triumphantly, holding up the missing leather gloves, "I found these in the shopping bag while you were on the phone. If I don't leave right this minute, I'm not going to make my appointment. Have a truly wonderful day, Claudia. Whoops, I forgot. Not only are we not in Kansas, we're not in California either. Bye."

She watched as he stepped into the elevator, grinning and saluting as the door rolled shut.

Glad for the quiet, Claudia pulled the briefcase from the shopping bag, set it on the counter and studied it. It was, after all, a nice gesture Charlie Pastor had gone out of his way to make. She started to fold the shopping bag, frowned and pulled out a paperback book. In the center of the gray cover, a stand of slender white-barked trees rose like antic spires in a city skyline.

The Works of Robert Frost.

Tommy wasn't the only the guy in the city who liked poetry. Claudia tried to remember: Wasn't this the book Charlie Pastor had in his hand the other afternoon when he ran into her on the street? He might have left the book behind as another excuse to see her, but that wouldn't work. If he rang her bell again, she'd bring the damn thing downstairs, hand it over, and let him know just how transparent his disingenuous tactics were.

Eight

Bert was right. If she didn't pay attention, she'd wake up one morning depleted and indifferent. She wouldn't see the burnout coming until she'd jammed herself into an impossibly tiny space, like one of those enormous earth-boring machines that sends its giant screw spinning implacably into the hard-packed soil.

Call your sister. Not *Claudia*. He didn't say *Call Claudia.*

Maybe, for fifteen minutes, she should pretend she had a life. Some distraction, a drink, a little meaningless conversation would do her good.

She pushed open the Greenwich Street door to Yaffa's and inhaled the rich bouquet of cigarettes, coffee, and Moroccan spices. Behind the bar, one of the waitresses slipped a Melissa Etheridge tape into the machine, heaped foam-crusted cappuccino cups into a plastic basin, and disappeared into the kitchen. Claudia had always imagined the kitchen looked like the rest of the place—quirky, warm, declaring itself by virtue of its hard whimsy.

The bar was filled with the usual weekday crew: conceptual artists disdaining the canon; secretaries, plumbers, graphic designers, filmmakers; guys in black sweaters assuring every willowy young thing that they *are* filmmakers.

"You think I can serve bouillabaisse on the Ides of March?" Yaffa squinted her date-colored eyes as she removed bunches of yellow plastic bananas from the chandelier, where they'd been hanging since last St. Patrick's Day. "It's kind of Roman. Besides, it's Friday. I have to serve bouillabaisse today."

"Beware the tyranny of traditions," Claudia warned as she retreated to the relative sanity of the Tea Room in back. That separate universe never failed to soothe her. The tables, except for one, were empty. Irina Orlov, seated next to a man with his back to the door, toyed with a glass of white wine as she eyed the red velvet curtains that created a tiny vestibule between the restaurant and the door to Harrison Street.

Why Irina had chosen this place was a puzzle to Claudia, who would have guessed she'd be more drawn to the tony glitter of the Bubble Lounge. But they'd become friends here. Because Irina was so determined to learn about her adopted city, Claudia taught her to scan for bold-type mentions of people and places in the *New York Observer* and the *Tribeca Trib*. Since Claudia hated shopping, Irina passed on some of the more wearable clothing she'd been given on modeling assignments.

The man beside Irina turned, and, unexpectedly, Claudia was pinned in place like a butterfly on display.

His eyes, glinting black coals set in soft flesh, seared her face. His gaze slid past her shoulders, as though he were intent on devouring her.

"Come sit with us, Claudia. Have a glass of wine and a good gossip." Irina's dimples flashed. "And I want you to meet Mikhail Chernin. Mike."

Mike. An indigo sweater stretched over his broad shoulders. Brown hair streaked with gray curled in fierce disarray on his head. He clutched a tumbler of clear liquid.

Claudia set her new briefcase on the floor, shrugged out of her coat, and settled into a wrought iron chair painted the verdigris of a New Orleans veranda and outfitted with plush cushions. The waitress asked if she wanted her usual and she gave a thumbs-up in reply.

"Mike's from Kiev and Paris." Irina seemed proud of these facts, as if they reflected well on her somehow.

"And New York. Eight years I live here. A blink. A lifetime. Depends on my mood." A smile lit Mikhail Chernin's face. "Today, a blink."

"That must mean things are going well for you."

Irina slapped the table in enthusiastic endorsement. "Mike just sold one of his businesses to my uncle. A car service in Brooklyn. Now he's trying to decide what kind of business to—"

"Video rental. TriBeCa population explodes, everyone educated, professional. Working long hours, but having to keep up with all the films. Exhausting, no? And in this whole neighborhood, only one video rental store. Big prices, small choices. So I need a space." Mikhail glanced at his watch, his eyes so large and luminous she wanted to be swallowed up in them. "I have to call my investigator. One must learn about one's rivals in business, no? You'll excuse me, please."

Mikhail Chernin certainly caught on quickly to the ways of American business. Hiring a private investigator to check out the competition . . . definitely a shrewd move. He walked past the espresso machine and disappeared into the narrow corridor leading to the front room.

"I have a shoot next week in Miami, maybe. Resort wear for winter, my agent said." All at once, Irina's face sagged like a heap of unsorted laundry. "Too bad."

"Bad?" Amazing—even a model with a late-winter job prospect in Miami could find something to complain about. While Claudia was looking elsewhere, Irina Orlov had become a true New Yorker.

Dreamily, both hands around the glass as though it were a steaming mug of cocoa and she'd just come in from an afternoon of sledding, Irina drained her wine. "Maybe you should fly south to the sun with me."

"Miami's coming back, you know," Claudia said. "A seedy old hotel near the beach . . . I've never worked on anything like that."

And wouldn't now, despite the relentless grip of winter. Maybe it had been fun getting started twenty years ago, feeling her way around the maze of city regulations, but it had taken years to get her contacts in place—workers, discount supply houses, bankers, her buddy Phil on the Historic District board, Building Department clerks, fire inspectors. She didn't even know whose pockets had to be lined before anything got done down there. Still . . .

"So, what's bad about having a job in Miami?"

"*Maybe*. Maybe is what's bad. I won't know for sure until

Monday. But at least I'll be here next Saturday. Oh, Claudia!" Her hand flew to her red mouth in mock horror. "I told you about the party, didn't I?"

A vague memory floated up as the espresso machine hissed and spat steam. Irina's agent, perpetually posing, something about Irina's birthday, a bash at Rasputin, the Russian nightclub in Brighton Beach. *A bash.* People only spoke that way when they were sure they were being watched.

"Yes, you told me. I . . ." Hell, why not? By then, she'd either be celebrating her deal with Murray or in need of consolation. "I'll be there."

Maria—the one from Prague or from Australia, Claudia couldn't remember—waited for Irina to move her newspaper aside. "Here you go, mates." Maria from Perth smiled as she set down another glass of wine and a bowl of steamed vegetables, laid the soupbowl-sized cappuccino cup and the brandy on the table.

Irina poked at a serrated carrot disk, her hands almost translucent, almost lost in the long sleeves of her white sweater. "So, what, your day is going well?"

"Oh, sure, great. I watched Bert and another guy work, and killed a bunch of time trying to get the right cabinets for a client who thinks big and spends small. Plus, I haven't heard about my big deal." Claudia took a slug of the brandy to ward off her annoyance.

Irina sipped her wine, patted the sleek ballerina skein of blond hair at the back of her neck. Her violet eyes darted from the glass tabletop to the door as she straightened the little blue packets of sweetener. "So. It's not so bad if you don't get this deal, yes?"

"Not the end of the world. But, damn, it's a great opportunity." Better than any she'd seen in a long time. Almost as good as Mercer Street. She pushed the thought away. She needed to keep in the present. "I could do the floors in wide-plank hardwood, turn the building into something special," she said longingly. "The owner doesn't have the eye."

"He wants only a simple business transaction." Irina's voice was edgy; her face shimmered as the setting sun glanced off the window and sent shards of light into the room.

"The man who owns that building is hungry, and I have to feed his ego. No such thing as a simple business transaction with wheeler-dealer real estate moguls."

"*Not* your moguls." Irina waved away the word. "Mikhail called me this morning and we started talking. Business, TriBeCa, this and that. And then he says he wants to meet this Claudia, this beautiful, smart—"

"Come sit with us and we'll drink wine and gossip." Claudia pushed the half-full brandy glass away. "That's what you said. But it was a setup, Irina, and I don't like it."

"Wait! Don't be angry. Come on, Claudia. Okay, so he's divorced and clever and handsome and knows how to make the best blinis in New York. But how can I set you up? I didn't know you'd be here."

"I have to go." She stuffed her arms through the sleeves of her coat, gathered her purse. "Don't lie to me, Irina. I expect it in business, but not from friends. Besides, you know as well as anyone—I'm not a good candidate to be fixed up with someone."

Fixed up. The words jerked around in her brain, as though she were one of her own renovation projects, something to be repaired, restored, and sold for more than it was worth.

"I'm just seeing that a friend gets what he wants, help getting started with his video store. Anyway," Irina said gaily, her cheeks pink with the bloom of conspiracy, "it's too late, isn't it? He needs a smart American and that's you. Don't bite my head off."

"Sorry." Her anger was passing, a little curiosity creeping back in but still under control. "It hasn't been a good day. If your friend wants to talk business, he can call me."

The music and the conversation dribbled into silence, an anxious, shifting energy gathering at its center.

"At least you don't get wrapped in tape until you can't breathe." Irina shivered and rattled the *New York Post* that lay on the table beside her bowl. "Electrical tape, yes? This is something you would ever in your mind think to do to another person?"

Claudia's throat tightened and her breath caught as she scanned the caption. Her eyes wouldn't focus, print danced and swam in a hailstorm of black and white. *Murray Kurtz, dubbed the Park Avenue Mummy . . .*

The grainy photograph wasn't terribly clear. Claudia forced herself to examine it. To look at the uncovered eyes, at the gray flesh around them. Eyes that told stories, mischievous, a little greedy, a little careless. Murray's eyes, staring out from a swaddling of black electrical tape.

"Are you all right?" Irina's hand covered hers.

Claudia looked away, trying to dispel the image of Charlie Pastor working the roll of black tape, wrapping it around and around the frayed wire. She swallowed hard to push down the lump of anger and sadness that swelled in her throat.

"He was a friend," she said when she could speak again. She tore the page from the *Post* and folded it so it fit into her pocket. "I have to go."

She didn't break stride, stepped past the bar and parted the red velvet curtains covering the doorway. Irina's voice followed her.

"I'm so sorry about your friend. I hope I'll still see you next Saturday."

As Claudia released the curtain, Mikhail Chernin filled the space beside her. Caught between the heavy velvet and the frosty door, he smelled of whiskey, tobacco, and something cold and piney, like winter forests. "You'll come with me in my car to Irina's party next week. I'll pick you up at nine and we'll talk, yes? Business."

When he gripped her shoulders, she tensed. He touched her right cheek with his, a continental leave-taking, was about to complete the gesture on the other side. Claudia pulled back involuntarily. No way could this thick Ukrainian gallantry be anything but dangerous. No way.

"I can see something has upset you. You go home and drink hot tea with honey. Meanwhile . . ." His lips brushed her temple. "There. An old Russian remedy."

A gust tried to pull the door from her grasp, but she held on, stepped to the sidewalk, and then, without looking back, pushed the door shut behind her. Outside, cold night air pressed damply toward the rooftops and misted the lamps with irregular halos. Dark shapes, still hunched against a wind that had already died, scuttled by on the other side of the street.

Nine

If Bert were around, she'd sit beside him in the comfort of shared silence until they figured out what this news meant.

Maybe he was still at the Duane Street loft. If he wasn't, she could wander among the sidewalk vendors of Canal Street, wend her way between the cheap tape players and the canvas backpacks and the knock-off halogen lamps, see if he was at the hardware store.

Or she could go home. Heaven was starting to look like a can of lentil soup, a glass of merlot, Vivaldi. And home was only down the block.

Her loft wasn't much warmer than the street. Glad she'd had the sense not to wander around the city in the cold dark, she pushed the thermostat higher, pictured Murray lying on some steel table as they cut him out of his black-tape shell, plopped his organs into stainless-steel basins, whirled his no-longer-vital fluids in centrifuges.

Murray wouldn't ever again have to worry about whether the heat was working properly.

He had a wife, a son, two daughters. Claudia had never met them, but she knew from his stories which one had been promoted to a managerial position at Healthcare USA, which one returned dresses to Saks after wearing them to weddings with the tags tucked in. A man who'd been married to the same woman for more than forty years had family stories to tell, and Murray told them with glee, ending his tales so the joke was always on him.

She dropped the mail on the table, stripped off her coat, and pressed the NEW MESSAGES button on the answering machine to stop the blink that punctuated the dark like a silent, throbbing heart.

"Claudia? I'm sorry if I overstayed my welcome this morning. Maybe we can have coffee soon. Did I leave a book in that shopping bag? Oh, and, really, I'm *still* sorry for upending you that way."

Charlie Pastor. Not quite so glib and entertaining on tape, although in person he *was* cute, she had to give him that. She fast-forwarded through his contrition to the next message.

After the beep, Bert's voice. "Hey, Claude, pick up if you're there."

She kicked off her shoes and tossed them in the closet, waiting for him to stop whistling "Ne Me Quitte Pas" and realize she wasn't home.

"I have to tell you something important," he said finally. "And if you're not there, don't call me when you hear this. I won't be home. I mean, that's a conundrum, right, if you're not there don't call me because how would you hear this at all if you're not there so that's not what I mean really but that's how it came out. Anyway, I guess you're not there waiting to decide if you're in the mood to talk now so I'll hang up before I run your message tape into oblivion. See you later, sweetie."

As she was reaching for a brandy glass, the buzzer sounded.

No way. She was in no mood to chat civilly with the person on the other end of that insistent noise.

When she heard the buzzer twice more—Bert's signal, her prayers answered—she nearly cried with relief. She checked the monitor, saw him take his keys out, waited for the elevator to deposit him in her kitchen.

She set out two brandy glasses as Bert peeled layers, one by one, until scarf, gloves, knit cap, parka, and snow-crusted workboots lay in a heap on the mat in front of the door.

"I hear Murray Kurtz went ballistic yesterday because you were supposed to call him at five or something. I forgot to tell you."

Bert examined the Martel label, pulled out the cork and sniffed it. "I ran into his secretary on my way to work this morning. She was like a puppy dog, worrying about were you really still interested. I went along with it, told her I knew you had a full schedule of meetings, that you were running late all day. Anyway, that was a brilliant move on your part."

Either Murray had been maneuvering for another concession, or he was suddenly worried about the depth of her interest, or he'd just plain misremembered that *he* was supposed to call *her*. He was her friend but he'd always been exasperating. Even dead he was infuriating.

"Murray's dead, Bert. They found him late last night. Oh, shit." She handed him the page from the *Post*.

Bert's twinkle faded as he scanned the article. "Murray wouldn't take elevators. Said they made him choke because they were confining. Did you know that, that he had claustrophobia? Shit. *Shit.*"

She poured two brandies. "It was so spooky reading about Murray suffocating under all that tape. Charlie Pastor sat right in my kitchen, fixing my lamp. With my very own roll of black electrical tape."

Bert gulped his drink in a single swallow, shook his head. "Unrelated. An unlucky coincidence. Assuming he's not stupid. Because if he killed Murray, he's not going to come to your apartment so you can watch him play with what amounts to a murder weapon. Hey," he said, suddenly pale. "You remember Leroy?"

Stupid was not a word she'd use to describe Charlie Pastor. Arrogant, maybe, facile, even self-promoting, but he *was* intelligent. "Leroy, Leroy. The dancer with the little sports car? What are you talking about Leroy for when Murray's dead?"

"Stay with me, okay?" Bert shook his head. "He always pretended he didn't have a last name. Like he was Liberace, right? Or Charo. One name, toothy smile. That's Leroy. Last name is Jefferson. He moved to Arizona a while back."

"So, now I understand why I got a card from Phoenix two months ago about a performance piece at some art gallery. What does this have to do with Murray?"

"I swear to God, Claudia, I'm not making this up. I heard Leroy was murdered. Someone hooked up a hot electric line to his water pipes, the ones in his bathroom. The guy's standing in the shower,

pipes, the ones in his bathroom. The guy's standing in the shower, which is really a cast-iron tub. He gets wet, right? He's standing in the water. And when he grabs the metal handles to adjust the water he gets zapped. Heart stopped, just like that. Last month. In Phoenix." Bert tossed down the second drink she handed him, his face still chalky. "If you ask me, it's bizarre."

"What is? The electrical connection?" A cold, dark shadow stole toward her; she forced herself back to the conversation. "Why didn't you tell me before this? About Leroy, I mean?"

Bert traced tiny circles on the speckled surface of the counter. "Because Ellie told me."

Ellie was back. "I'm not your mother, Bert. If you want to run around saving twenty-five-year-old women who're looking for Daddy, you go right ahead. I won't pick up the pieces when they dump you but I'm not going to tell you I told you so either. Ellen Stern is your business, honey pie. I have nothing to say about that."

Silently, they drifted to the living room and sat side by side on the sofa.

"Here's to Murray." Claudia clinked her glass against Bert's. "And, I guess, to Leroy."

This time, Bert sipped his brandy, held the liquid in his mouth a long time before he swallowed. "Here's to having your worst nightmare never come true."

In the dim light and in silence, they drank. Framed by the living room window, fat flakes of lazy snow drifted by.

"You remember Spring Street, that time we worked with Murray?" Bert's socks gleamed white against the Shaker table as he crossed his legs at the ankles and pressed back into the sofa cushions. "You saved that fucking job."

Claudia elbowed his ribs. "You're getting tight too fast. You never use that kind of language."

"Fucking Murray," he said. "Fucking Murray got himself fucking killed. And he was the one, right? He owned that building on Spring Street, right? He was the one who looked around at the sorry assholes after Parrillo took off. You remember, the king of the down-payment junkies. Sure, Parrillo says, I'll do your job but I need money up front. A down payment to hire people and get the materials. And the next thing you know he's sitting on a beach in Jamaica or something, smoking a spliff, and the money's gone. But Murray said, okay, he did that to me, I still need the work done and he pointed his finger and said you, you took over Mercer Street when Amos Fischer got sick. You got the job done on budget, even with all the problems, so you get to be the boss."

His finger had pointed at Claudia Miller.

Her stomach clenched, and her chest swelled with boozy gratitude. "We both made out okay on that one, right? Me and Murray, I mean. I got to prove I could be trusted after Mercer Street, and Murray got his job for half what anyone else would have charged."

Bert was silent, drawn to his glass, fallen into his memories.

The brandy hit the back of her throat, and she knew with blinding clarity that by morning she'd regret every drop past this one. She didn't care. The momentum of their private wake was not to be denied. "You see Murray's brother lately? Jack, that was his name, right? Murray set him up in the window business, you know that? Jack Kurtz. Jack, the window man."

"Yeah, Jack. The guy who called you about the trouble on Mercer Street." Bert pushed the bottle to the edge of the table, just out of her reach.

She leaned forward, poured another shot, gazed at the golden liquid. "Mercer Street. That was the worst. That was *my* nightmare come true. The cops were sure we were all guilty." She drank it down, shivered.

"Everyone who worked construction in those days was suspect. There we sat like ducks lined up on the barstools at Puffy's Tavern. Nine at night, bam, the door opens and it's some builder who needs four, five workers. He's promising to pay in cash at the end of the day, so we work our tails off and for that, the cops label us con men and crooks. Con *people*, excuse me. That was some crew on that job." Bert rattled the bottle, made a great show of pouring each of them two inches. Some of the brandy sloshed onto the table and she mopped it up with a napkin.

"How did we ever get anything done? All those egos, all that artistic ambition. Good thing a couple of us were in it because we wanted simple, honest work." Work, she understood from the start, that would send the message to her father that she was choosing her own life. Work that asked few emotional commitments, made no promises, and left her physically exhausted at the end of every day. "Those painters we never got around to hiring, what were their names? They were dancers, right?"

"Judy Lamson. Trudy Jones." Bert nodded dreamily. "Judy used to go with Jefferson."

"Jefferson?" The name meant nothing to her. "Okay, which one is Jefferson?"

"*Who's* tight?" Bert frowned and splashed more brandy into their glasses. "Laverne Jefferson, Leroy's cousin. He was in charge of the demolition. Did you know Murray hired Leroy to be a bartender at his daughter's wedding? Because he found out Leroy needed money for payments on his Porsche."

This was getting maudlin. Pretty soon they'd be celebrating every human gesture Murray had ever made. Steadying herself against the edge of the table, she picked up the stack of mail, tossed bills and ads into an untidy heap.

When she came to an envelope the size of a slender volume of poetry with her name in block letters in the center, she frowned, held it close to keep the print from running together. No return address. A New York City postmark. Claudia undid the metal clasp, turned it upside down and shook out the contents. Four color photographs slid out.

Tommy.

Her throat swelled. A flush of fear and anger rose up her arms and flooded her chest.

Tommy, standing alone on a corner, his blazer collar pulled up to his neck.

Tommy, surrounded by a gaggle of schoolgirls sporting Kipling backpacks.

Tommy, dodging cars at Columbus Circle.

Someone was trying to tell her something. If only her head was clear . . . She turned over the last photograph.

A nighttime shot. Tommy, no longer enchanted with the night, leaving City Hall Park beside her, her arm wrapped firmly around his shoulder.

Call your sister.

Tommy's attacker had known exactly who would be on the other end of the phone.

"Jesus, Claudia. This is . . ." Bert stared at the pictures and shook his head.

It was scary. Infuriating.

She didn't have the whole picture yet, but these pieces were related. Eventually, the whole puzzle would come together. When she hadn't had so much brandy . . . When she could speak without sounding like she had sand in her mouth. But, damn, the pieces she had did fit.

"Okay, okay, listen, Bert." He'd be her reality check. "Murray and Leroy were murdered. And the murders both had something to do with equipment an electrician might use, right?"

Bert's forehead wrinkled. "Yeah, I guess. But so what, Claudia? You know what it means? Nothing. *Nada*."

"Wrong. One was suffocated with electrical tape. The other got zapped because his plumbing was hot-wired. So the murders both had something to do with electrical stuff. Which would be strange enough all by itself. Except, they have something else in common. *Jack* Kurtz and *Laverne* Jefferson worked on the Mercer Street renovation with us. Members of their families were murdered. With electrical equipment. Pass me that pencil, would you? Who else worked with us on Mercer Street?" She turned the photographs over so she wouldn't have to look at them, then scribbled and mumbled. "Jack Kurtz installed the windows. Laverne Jefferson was in charge of demolition. Ann Magursky did the framing and Dave Benedetti was the plumber."

"Sure, Benedetti, the guy who was so cool he left Taos just when everyone else was discovering it." Bert raked his hair with a trembling hand, then slugged down another belt of brandy. "The victims are related to workers on the Mercer Street crew. Not any other job. Mercer Street."

Her father was in London, so it was Nora she'd have to tell. Tommy had to be protected. From what, she didn't yet know. The attack on Tommy had to do with Mercer Street, she was certain, but that was all she was sure about. Nora was a night owl who read until two or three every morning. Claudia reached for the phone, praying as she dialed that Tommy was in his bed asleep and safe.

48

"Claudia? Is everything all right? You sound funny."

Oh, great, down four brandies—was it five? more?—and then try to talk about this weird, nightmarish theory to the quintessential ice lady. "I was worried about Tommy, Nora. Is he all right?"

"He's fine."

Which was all her father's wife was going to say, she could tell.

"Listen, can I see you in the morning? Early. Before Tommy leaves. It's important."

"You've been drinking, haven't you?"

"Nora, I'm a big girl. I have had a couple of drinks. What does that have to do with whether or not I can see you in the morning? I need about half an hour of your time."

Nora sighed. "Eight o'clock. At the house. He leaves at eight-thirty for his SAT class."

Claudia agreed, hung up, flipped the four photographs over.

How dare he . . .

She didn't have to sit here and let some maniac with a camera invade her life. "I'm going out," she said, weaving toward the closet, frowning when she realized she wasn't wearing shoes.

"Never mind the icy streets, you can't walk a straight line in this apartment." Bert shook his head. "It's late. Let it be until tomorrow."

"I have to get these pictures to the cops. I have to make sure they protect my brother." The old snow boots in the back of the closet would have to do. She pulled them on, jammed her arms into the sleeves of her jacket, stuck the photographs into her backpack.

"And why do you think the cops will care? You think they'll pay attention to a drunk with a story they won't understand and a couple of pictures?" Bert giggled and slapped his knee. "Sure, lady, that makes sense. Some swishy dancer dies in Phoenix. A rich geezer buys the farm on Park Avenue. And you get pictures of a kid in the mail. Must be a conspiracy. Sure, lady, and what drug did you say you were on?"

Maybe. A cop might blow her off. Her hands curled into fists.

"Sarafino," she whispered.

"Enrico Sarafino?" Bert repeated. "I thought he retired."

"Not yet. He's still at the First. He was on the job when Mercer

Street happened. He'll understand the connection. Brilliant." She pulled her beret over her ears, stuffed her keys in her pocket. "Be there, Rick. Be on duty."

"Enrico Sarafino. I'm coming with you. Maybe we can keep each other upright until we find him." Bert tapped the paper on the table and nodded. "Hey, we've got quite a little list here. Definitely, there's something going on, and for sure it's got to do with Mercer Street, with what happened sixteen years ago. But if we want a complete list of everyone who worked the Mercer Street job, we have to include one Bert Kossarian, and a certain Ms. Claudia Miller."

"Who happens to have a brother."

"Whose pictures appeared like magic in her mailbox."

She nodded. "A brother who was cut on the face and nearly strangled."

"With an electrical wire," Bert said as he struggled to zip his jacket. "Ten-four Romex. A fucking electrical wire that sliced up the face of the brother of the lady in charge of the Mercer Street renovation."

"Woman in charge," Claudia muttered. *"Person."*

Ten

1981 / Mercer Street / The Threat

She stepped from the overheated building onto the sidewalk, her boots tapping *clack clack clack* on frozen asphalt as she avoided the hardened mound left by a medium-sized dog. The twitchy, yapping terrier, maybe, who always ran half a block ahead of the scrawny twelve-year-old who'd helped her carry gallons of paint up three flights of stairs the summer before.

James, whose eyes had danced when he saw the pile of wood. "I don't want money. I want that, and I want to use them tools," he'd said, pointing at scraps of three-inch molding and plywood subflooring and a foot-long sample of hand-turned pine trim, then at the saw, the hammer, the plane. He'd bounded up the stairs to her loft every morning for five days, built a doghouse—to keep in his bedroom. James, precise and grave, cleaned up after himself at the end of each work session. Would have cleaned up his animal's mess. Not James responsible for that particular crusted pile.

"Claudia Miller?"

The voice startled her, and she whirled around, ponytail swinging. "What? Who are you?"

She found herself looking into the green eyes of a broad-shouldered six-footer with hair cut so short his ears looked like they were pasted on two inches too low. Under his wool jacket, unbuttoned and fraying at the lapel, the stitching on the pocket of his blue coveralls identified him as BIG RED.

"Kevin Mahoney. IBEW. International Brotherhood of Electrical Workers, in case you didn't know. My friends call me Red. We met last year, must've been July. At the bar in Puffy's." He pointed east with the black stem of his pipe, its pearly bowl clasped by scarred, chapped fingers. "You're doing work on that building on Mercer?"

Amos had told her this might happen. But knowing it was coming hadn't prepared her for the way her throat would close up and her heart would pound when she faced a union official. She took a deep breath, squared her shoulders. *You will not flinch,* she told herself. *You will not let him get away with anything just because you're a woman and he thinks that means he can push you around.*

"I'm helping a friend, you know." She smiled, all innocence and openness.

"Yeah, sure, I know. Whose job this is, I think I know."

She grimaced. "And I have promises to keep before I can call it quits for the day. So long."

"Aha, a lover of poetry." The smile Kevin Mahoney returned chilled her. His teeth, large and white and jammed into his small mouth, glistened. "What's important is that you've got all union electricians helping this friend, right? Anyone who touches the wiring, the boxes, the lines that come in from the street, they're all union, aren't they?"

Damn. She was so close to pulling this off, and without going late, or running over budget, or ignoring the client's specs. Bad enough she had to prove to every macho day laborer, and a few of the women, that being female and being twenty-three didn't mean she was soft and stupid. Mahoney must have known that she was running the job until Amos recovered from his appendectomy, must have decided she'd roll over for his demands because she was a *girl.* He'd never even think to call her a woman.

"Look, cut to the chase here, all right, Mahoney? The guy doing the electrical is licensed. This isn't a union job. He doesn't have to be union. So, what do you want? You didn't come out in this weather to see if I'm doing okay. Just say it right out."

A bead of moisture hung on the tip of his nose. Mahoney swiped at it with a handkerchief, blew his nose loudly, said, "No, really, I just wanted to make sure your people are union. I told my boss, hey, that's a smart girl. She knows it's better to have union on the electrical. Rest of it, maybe you can get away with, you know, casual labor, but not on electrical."

"Fuck you, Jack." She started to walk away, felt a hand grab her elbow.

"The name is Kevin, little lady." He pulled up beside her, then stood in front of her, blocking her way. "You're new to this neighborhood. It would be a good thing for you, for your health, you understand, to find out how we do things around here."

She watched his lips form the words and she thought about kneeing him, about how this thin mouth would contort with pain. Instead, she pried his fingers from her coat. "In case the cold did something to your hearing, I repeat: Mercer Street isn't a union job."

His eyes grew wide with rage. "You don't want to act like this. We don't need no good fences to make good neighbors. There's a simple solution. We're just concerned about safety, you understand. Something happens, wiring ain't done right, breaker box is installed wrong, well, you can see we can't be too careful about safety issues. So that's why we insist you hire union."

She walked away. He kept up with her, huffing to breathe and talk at the same time. "Now, before you tell me what to do again, I'm gonna offer you a solution. The one less traveled, maybe, but it will make all the difference," he persisted.

"What, you're gonna stop mangling poetry and move to Burbank?" She swung north onto LaGuardia, wished she were headed for Bleecker Street, for the Figaro, wished she were meeting Amos. Mahoney was scaring her; a little support would be welcome right now.

"Easier." He smiled. "You need a foreman, you know, for the electrical stuff. Someone who comes in and makes sure everything's done to code, to the high standards the City in its wisdom has set for these buildings."

"A union foreman, right? Someone to collect a couple hundred dollars a week. Not going to happen, Jack." The light changed, and she hurried across the street. "Not on this job. There's not enough margin here. Go bother the people working in midtown or wherever. Leave me alone."

For the third time, he grabbed her arm.

"Get your hands off me, Mahoney, or I'll have you busted for assault."

After an instant, he let go. "Don't make it hard," he said between gritted teeth. "I got a lot to do, miles to go before I sleep, you know what I mean, so let's settle this. It's much better, much safer if you have a union foreman. Period. I'll come by next Friday and do the inspection myself. That position's normally three hundred dollars a week, but since you said you weren't getting paid so much, for you I'll make it two. Every Friday."

"First of all, don't ever touch me again." She strode past him as though he weren't there, stopped ten feet away. "And second of all, fuck you, Jack."

She kept moving, feeling his gaze boring into her as she marched down the street, uneasy in the knowledge that he was standing there trembling with fury. A man like that, maybe nobody had ever said no to him before. Well, he'd have to get used to it. He'd have to adjust.

At Mercer Street, she took out her keys. One thing at a time. Today the new elevator was going to be installed. As she let herself in, she heard voices, two men, but she couldn't make out the words.

They'd used the old freight elevator to haul the new housing to the rooftop hut. The pulleys that would lift the new cage were in place. A bare lightbulb hung in the old cage; she could tell that it was at the second floor.

She whistled the four-note signal to let Bert know she was waiting at the ground floor. The conversation stopped.

"One minute." The voice echoed down the brick walls.

Damn Kevin Mahoney. Amos Fischer, the foreman she'd replaced, treated his workers well, paid them well, too. Not by union standards, but then they didn't have to pay union dues that went to make sure corrupt bosses got to take February trips to St. Thomas. Maybe everyone wasn't as generous—well, that was their problem. Tapping her foot, she watched the freight elevator descend, groaning and creaking.

Besides, she didn't get into this business to have someone else tell her what to do. She certainly wouldn't let the union dictate who she could and couldn't hire, even if she were only in charge for a month. And, in any case, it wouldn't be Big Red Mahoney giving her orders, not with his barely concealed contempt for her. "Not because you're a woman," he'd said that day in July when he sat down on the stool beside her at Puffy's. "But because you all think you're hot shit. Because you all think calling yourself artists makes you better than anyone else."

She hadn't bothered to answer.

She wasn't an artist, or a musician or an actor or a writer or a photographer or any other damn thing. She was a woodworker temporarily in charge of a renovation, and she liked her work. No uptight jerk was going to tell her how to do it.

"We're nearly done," Bert shouted. She waited beside the gate as the elevator rumbled to a stop on the ground floor and Bert stepped off. "The only thing left is the final signal decisions. Guy says you have to decide if you want to use this fancy gizmo that automatically sends the elevator back to the first floor after sixty seconds. You think people would appreciate that? Or would it be too much wear and tear on the equipment?"

The tenants of the building might disagree after a while, but an elevator that was always waiting on the first floor would be an advantage while they were hauling materials. They could leave the batting on to protect the walls and floor. The freight elevator was so slow, such a pain in the butt. "Can it be reset easily?"

"Piece of cake, according to the Otis guy. He says even I will be able to change it." Bert wiped at the back of his neck with a blue neckerchief. "What does that look mean, Claudia? This isn't such a big-deal decision, you know."

How did he do that? It was as though Bert Kossarian had the ability to see into her mind. "It's not the elevator. Yeah, let's try the automatic return and see how it works. At least for a while. I ran into Kevin Mahoney on the street just now."

Now, it was Bert's turn to frown. "The electrician?"

"The *union* electrician. First he spouted poetry at me and then he said we had to hire a union supervisor for two hundred a week.

55

Shit, Bert, that's pure and simple blackmail. It's protection money, no different than the mob."

"Except, on union jobs it's legal. We're not a union job. You ever hear Amos talk about what happened when he said no to the electricians? You ever hear him tell about the fire that burned down the building he was working on? As if we don't all know who was responsible. So, maybe you ought to think really carefully about this, Claudia."

She frowned, trying to remember the details. "Someone said the wiring was bad."

Bert shrugged. "Well, Amos said he did that job personally and he knew it was right. That's the deal, that no one can prove it. Amos swears on his life that Mahoney was responsible for that fire."

"You're right, he always said the way that building burned was fishy. Of course that fire was set." Claudia lifted a scuffed yellow hard hat from the nail where she'd hung it the night before. "Sure, gasoline tossed around the ground floor—I'd call that fishy. And the boys in blue saying it was probably the result of improper safety procedures, that was even fishier."

"So now Mahoney tries to claim that every work site that doesn't have union oversight isn't safe. And for only two hundred a week, they'll take care of it. Safety—yeah, sure, that's why he demanded you put him on the books. Not because he's on the take, nah, not Kevin Mahoney. His mother's sainted lad, busy keeping the world safe from incompetence. What're you gonna do, sweetie?" Bert tapped her hard hat and smiled.

"Nothing," she said as she stepped into the freight elevator. If Mahoney accused her of trying to prove she had *cojones*, that was fine with her. What he was doing was despicable. If none of the *guys* would stand up to him, she would.

Eleven

Cramped and thirsty, legs dangling over the arm of the sofa, Claudia Miller forced her eyes open and stretched her hand into the dark void for a clue. Her own living room came into focus as the smell of brandy made her gag. She stumbled to the sink, let the water run cold, drank two glasses without coming up for breath, then fell onto her bed and pulled the covers around her fully clothed body to stop the shivering.

Fingers of light pried her eyes open, and she padded into the living room. Everything was fuzzy—her mouth, her vision, the cottony mass in her head. A brown and white pigeon waddled along the railing of the fire escape across the street, pecking at the bright orange paint as though it were littered with seeds. Claudia watched in silence, then glanced at the clock. Ten to seven. She needed a double dose of caffeine, had to shower away the desire to roll herself into a ball in the center of the bed until the world became a kinder place.

Maybe she'd do better in the light of day. God, she was glad she had thought of Sarafino. Bad enough trying to explain to Rick Sarafino about the attack on Tommy, the apparently accidental death in Phoenix, Murray; about how those events all tied in to a job renovating an old warehouse years ago. He'd listened without saying a damn thing, even after she laid out the photographs on the table in the interview room. Then he'd gone into action, scooping the pictures into a plastic bag, scribbling notes in a small spiral pad.

"I'll deal with this," he'd said, finally. "Meet me at Walker's at eleven tomorrow morning and I'll fill you in. Meanwhile, you two better go home before you hurt yourselves. You sure you can make it without falling on your faces?"

Bert had risen, had said gravely, "Thanksh, Sharafino."

Now, she had to tell her father's wife that she had reason to believe that her brother wasn't the victim of some random street mugging, had to pass on Enrico Sarafino's suggestion that Tommy go away for a while. She would raise some consciousness on the Upper East Side and then go to Duane Street and see how the work was progressing.

Claudia was enveloped in a cloud of rolling steam before she realized she had no idea whether Bert was still in her apartment, or when they had finally finished the brandy.

Her *Times* was waiting on the table in the downstairs lobby. She turned pages until she found the obits. Murray's funeral would be family-only, date undetermined. No mention that his wife and children were violating Jewish custom, postponing his burial so the Medical Examiner could complete an autopsy. At least today she wouldn't have to face his grieving widow and children, all those lovely grandchildren.

The image of Murray, bound, a mummy, made her choke. She untied her wool scarf, beset by memories: Murray's delight as he played sidewalk supervisor at a demolition site, his relieved laughter when a cast-iron bathtub didn't fall off the dolly on its way out the door.

The connection between Murray's murder and Leroy's Jefferson's shimmered elusively as she stepped from the warmth of the small foyer onto the street. How much simpler if she could believe Leroy's death was gossip some twit kid told Bert. But that wasn't the explanation. Someone had gone to the trouble of finding family members of two people who had worked on the Mercer Street renovation sixteen years before.

Get real, she told herself as she headed for the corner. *It's three people, and you know it.*

Except for Bert and Jack Kurtz, she'd lost touch with the others from the Mercer Street job, but she would care if any of the people on the list were murdered.

That wasn't exactly right.

It wasn't the people on the list who were being killed. It was their relatives: a cousin, a brother.

A brother.

Talking to Nora Miller was going to be about as much fun as sitting on a splinter.

When the elevator door opened, Bert and Gary Bruno, perched on the top steps of metal ladders set eight feet apart, both turned, startled by the sudden sound. They were bathed in sweat, scowling, balancing a ceiling panel and obviously struggling under the load.

"I knew we should have cut it into sections before we tried to take it down. This is heavier than a pregnant rhino. Uplighting, my ass. This panel is an instrument of torture. Oh, man, it must be made of stone or something." Gray grunted as they eased the panel lower. "Okay, one step at a time. Drop this and we're pancakes."

"Christ." Bert was ashen, shaking under the weight. His foot explored the air until he found the ladder rung. With both feet planted, he crouched and let the weight of the panel rest on the ladder. Gary did the same, and they both climbed down to safe ground, licking dry lips and looking up.

"That panel isn't going anywhere for a while." Bruno smiled and pointed with a metal tape measure at the ceiling. "Even without the support of those Chicago bars, the ladder will hold the weight. Four pieces, cut it up, we can handle it better." He dug into his shirt pocket, thrust a paper into Claudia's hand. "I took my measurements. This is the stuff I need for the taping."

"Fine. I'll order it for delivery in two days. Which means we'll be lucky if we get it in four. Thanks, Gary. Anything else you need, let me or Bert know."

"Round two coming up. I'm going out for coffee. Bring you something?" He acknowledged their refusals, saluted and hit the elevator call button, knelt to drop the metal tape into the nylon duffel bag resting at his feet. "Stay warm, kids."

Keeping warm was the least of her problems. When the elevator door rolled shut, Claudia turned. "Got a minute, Bert?"

He patted his pocket for his cigarettes, extracted the pack, led her to the French doors that opened onto the fire escape. "Step into my parlor," he said as he unbolted the door. "How did your stepmother react to the news?"

"I wish I had the pictures to show her, even if they would have half scared her to death. Nora said she wasn't ready to even think about sending Tommy away. She has to get through this medical labyrinth first. The tests, the shrink, and then she'll see. I think she was kind of relieved that the attack wasn't something Tommy made up or brought on himself. I told her I'd find out about a bodyguard. She's keeping him home today. Maybe I can put some pressure on Sarafino for police protection."

"My dad, he's pretty easy to get to in that nursing home. And I have two cousins in Trenton. One of them, maybe I think he'd be better off if someone did cover his flapping mouth with electrical tape." Bert inhaled, then blew a pungent stream of smoke across the rusted railing.

She peered over the edge of the fire escape at Bruno's receding back as he turned the corner. "At least Sarafino didn't blow us off completely when we told him about how we thought Mercer Street tied in. I got the feeling that, up until the very second when I pulled out the photographs, he was getting ready to tell us to go home and sleep it off."

"It *was* a good thing Rick was there last night. I can't imagine what one of these shiny new cops would have done with our story." A gust carried the ash from the tip of Bert's cigarette to the hem of his jeans.

"Sarafino's been on the street for, what, maybe twenty-three, -four years now, and he's still out there without his detective's shield. Last fall, I remember, he was counting the months until he could move upstate and open what he called his bait-and-doughnut shop on Copake Lake. Maybe this will help him get a commendation on his way out."

"It's not just Tommy, Claudia." Bert leaned back against the railing. "The guy made Tommy call his sister, remember? You want someone to keep an eye on you, you call me and I'll—"

"No way. I mean, I appreciate the offer, but I can handle my own life." She looked away from Bert's concerned gaze.

"Fine, okay, keep your appointment with Sarafino. I guess I don't have any new ideas." Bert crushed the flame end of his cigarette against the sole of his shoe and tossed the butt into an overflowing mayonnaise jar.

"That's truly disgusting. The health department's gonna get you for that." She pulled open the French doors and stepped inside as Gary Bruno emerged from the elevator. He set a cardboard coffee container on the counter, tossed his jacket to the floor, knelt over a stack of wood. "Keep up the good work, guys. See you later."

Bert ducked out of the way as Gary carried four boards to the rear of the loft to be measured.

The two stooges, and she was in charge. Great.

The old-timey, dark wood bar smelled of cigarettes, despite the city's no-smoking ordinance. Off-duty cops, two couples armed with the *Times* real estate listings, and several neighborhood regulars filled the front room. The sight of Sarafino's distinctive slouch made her smile.

"Black coffee."

The bartender, who looked as though he'd recently hung up some kind of uniform and still missed the action, nodded and poured a mugful from the Bunn carafe.

Rick Sarafino looked at her over his shoulder, winked. "Hey, that you, Miller? You ready to come out and fix my deck like you promised? Hempstead isn't so far, you know."

She threaded her way to the other end of the bar. "Soon as your wife goes to visit her mother I'll come take care of it. Hey, Rick, what's news?"

He glanced away, as though he'd seen enough of the world. "Nothing. I thought maybe I'd have something to tell you but the lab's backed up. I turned that stuff over to the detective in charge of the Mummy case. Hey, I'm sorry." He shook his head. "I mean, the Kurtz case. They're working on it."

Claudia hooked two fingers through the mug handle and lifted it to her mouth. "I knew Murray a long time. Fifteen years."

"Yeah, that was real ugly." Sarafino squinted through the steam. "Listen, I will definitely call you when there's something. But I'm not in that particular loop, if you know what I mean, so you see what you can do about getting the boy out of town. And you should keep a low profile yourself. Sounds like this guy's main business might have been with you. Look, if that's all, I really gotta get going. *Hasta la vista,* buddy."

"Actually, there is something else," she said as the couple beside her broke into raucous laughter. "*I* want to tell *you* something. You walking downtown?"

Rick pulled on his gloves and adjusted the earflaps on his hat. "Up. To Canal. Gotta check out a complaint against a luggage store owner. Something about cutting up the seats of a cab because the cabbie dumped him at Lincoln Center when he insisted on going up to Hunnert Twenny-Fith Street at ten-thirty. Something crazy like that. You want to walk with me, that's okay."

Claudia tossed two dollars on the bar and followed the big man out the door. Enrico Sarafino might be as strong as a tow truck, but no one ever accused him of hiding his rocket-science talents under any bushels. She did a quickstep to catch up with his long stride.

"Hey, Rick, you've been around the neighborhood a long time, right? What is it, eighteen years now?" The air stung the exposed flesh on her face.

Rick frowned. "Eighteen, right. I got assigned to the First after I said no to the Bronx because I needed to be near home because of my kid. That was when I was still living down on Mott. So, yeah, eighteen years."

There'd been talk about Sarafino's son having a congenital heart problem. She'd always liked him a little better for wanting to be close to home. "Your son's okay?"

"Sure, he's about to graduate from NYU." Rick Sarafino turned bright red, and he shook his head in slow amazement. "You ever hear of anyone studying hospitality science? The kid's dying to go into hotel management. He wants to work on an island some-where. The tropics, Hawaii, the Caribbean, you know. Maybe it's not such a bad idea, right?"

They'd reached the precinct building. In the midday gloom,

Claudia looked through the wide doorway of lower Manhattan's only police stable. A row of iron stanchions curved to match the swell of round, muscular haunches protruding into the aisle. Feathery white breath rose from the first stall and a restless tail twitched. The warm smell of oats and hay, saddle soap and horse piss wafted out as she waved at the woman in the back pitching straw into a golden heap.

"Let me get to my point. Somebody beat up my brother the other night. Tried to strangle him. Whipped his face with an electric cable with the wires exposed. Tried to make Tommy get me to come out in the middle of the night and meet them near City Hall." Keeping up with Rick's stride was making her breathless, but at least her toes weren't numb anymore. Ahead, the sea of noisy, late-morning traffic that was Canal Street loomed.

Enrico Sarafino looked puzzled. "Right. You told me that."

"And then yesterday, those photographs came in the mail. Of my brother. At school, walking around the streets. I'm not sitting around while my brother gets killed, you understand? You know how Mercer Street was such a big deal, I mean, when it happened. Someone could have been nursing a grudge all these years. I want your help getting a police guard assigned to my brother right away."

Rick Sarafino stopped walking. His face squinched into a skeptical bunch. "Whoa, Nellie. I told you last night, that's not gonna happen. Word came down from City Hall a week ago. No overtime. Your old man's got money, let him either send the kid away or hire private muscle." Sarafino cocked his head. "Hey, I can maybe suggest a name, someone for you to call. I got a cousin in the business. Let me check with him and get back to you. Best I can do."

"You'll take responsibility if my brother gets hurt? And you'll convince the brass they have to notify the rest of the people on the list?"

He wouldn't make eye contact, so she marched around until she was blocking his path. Finally, he looked down at her. "I can't just go and put in a requisition for a personal guard for your brother. I *can* get you in touch with a private firm. I told you last night I'd do my best to find the people on your list. If it'll make you feel better, I'll let you know when I get a line on Benedetti and Magursky, okay? That I can do. And I'll call you when we get a hit on any prints the lab pulls from those pictures." Rick Sarafino shook his head. "But you have to do your part. I don't go putting up walls, because maybe the way I'd do it, they'd fall and hurt someone. And you, Miller, don't go around playing Dick Tracy, okay?"

Twelve

If she kept moving, she thought as Sarafino lumbered to the corner, bad news couldn't find her.

The notion constituted a surrender to safety she found both sad and comforting. She wandered the streets until she was drawn by the hanging displays in brick and teal, wine and maize into a gift shop on West Broadway. Alive with fields of color and pattern, rich with the perfume of incense clinging to the rugs and the pottery, the cheerful space held her in its thrall.

"Muslims weave intentional mistakes into their rugs. Only Allah, they believe, can be perfect. The weavers prove their humility by incorporating a noticeable defect." The shape in the rear of the store resolved into a small, nut-colored woman, seated just out of the light on a high stool.

"Allah has nothing to worry about from me," Claudia said. And Tommy had nothing to worry about from a jealous Allah; her brother's face bore witness to his mistakes, and to her own. "How much is this rug?"

"Not for sale." The proprietor shrugged apologetically.

Claudia was relieved. The bright oblong with a central design that looked like a harp would always make her think of Murray, who was surely no celestial musician. He'd worn his imperfections proudly, defiantly, as though they were the handprint left after he was sent into the world with a slap across his face instead of his bottom. He'd flaunted his flaws, disdainful of the god who gave him a congenital limp, and of the people who underestimated him because of it. "What you really get good at if you're a kid whose body is God's idea of a bad joke," he'd once told her as he wolfed down the last of a pastrami sandwich, "is hunger."

Claudia walked, without direction or volition, wandering toward open spaces until she found herself at West Street. She'd been seeking the river, her peaceful place, the backdrop to let her mind spin and bump and finally to empty.

The Hudson River Park felt like a movie set, the Statue of Liberty guarding the river, the Verrazano Bridge forming a distant marker. She leaned against the railing and watched a water-swollen stick as it rode the turgid chop, thought about Tommy's fierce, protective streak, admitted to herself that she really admired his brave foolishness.

Pigeons clamored for the crumbs two blond toddlers tossed onto the playground stones, and she wondered how the work was going at Duane Street, decided Bert was seeing to it, was glad to be away from it for a while.

With Murray dead, she mused, she should start looking for another project. She couldn't, wouldn't ask Murray's widow about the property, not until some decent mourning period had passed. A ferry made steady progress as it pushed its way toward the low clouds tumbled behind the buildings lining the New Jersey waterfront, and she wondered when Sarafino would call her with news from the lab.

"A bagel for your thoughts."

She whirled around, startled by the voice behind her. Charlie Pastor. How long had he been following her? He closed the gap between them, held up a white paper bag, turned a brilliant smile in her direction. Her jaw tightened. If she played this right, maybe she'd find out more about Charlie and his dexterity with electrical tape.

When he pointed to the benches along the west-facing promenade, she followed.

"I stopped by a while ago. At your apartment, I mean. You weren't there, but I've found you anyway, so it must be fate. Now you can sit with me and look at New Jersey and share a little conversation." The river glinted with the afternoon sun. A gull posing on the curved arm of the next bench flapped toward the water as Charlie set the paper bag on a hexagonal paving stone.

Charlie Pastor's blue eyes glittered with mischief; Claudia looked away, reminding herself that she had an agenda regarding this handsome young man that he probably didn't imagine.

He reached for the bag. "Celebration time, ma'am. Bagels and lox and coffee."

Cawfee—he wouldn't play Stanley Kowalski anytime soon, but his try at a Brooklyn accent was credible enough to make her smile. She asked, "Is it belly lox or Nova?"

"Belly lox? Sounds like a medieval chastity device. So, can I share my good news and my very late breakfast with you? It's terrible to have dreams come true if there's no one to share the excitement with."

"No apologies, no briefcases, no cream cheese?"

"On the side. I wasn't sure about your allegiance to the food police. Actually, this is all in the name of research. I'm studying the ethnic culinary history of New York, and I thought you'd be a good source of information. You look like the kind of woman who's had personal experience with calzone and samosas and camarones criollas and dolmas and borscht."

His smile was broad and unaffected, but the chill of suspicion lingered in her bones. "You hunt me down for a little food chitchat when there are ten million other possibilities in the city of New York? Tell me, Charlie, is that really why we're sitting here?"

"Now, that's what attracted me to you in the first place, Claudia. You're so trusting." He grinned and watched a lanky teen struggling to control a tiger-striped box kite. "Okay, you got me. We're sitting here because I'm mad about you. Wait, no, make that desperate to be with you. Hold on, let's try, I don't know any women in this town and I like you and I think I can learn things from you, about the city and about life, and that's a nice way to spend a semi-cold afternoon in March."

"Try again, Charlie." She watched the kite swoop on the currents of a breeze.

"Actually, this really is a celebration. Of what, you might wonder." He beamed down at her and flipped his hair off his shoulder. "Only the magnificent start of a brilliant career. But if you're too busy to join me in a moment of thanksgiving, I'll understand."

Even trade—my company for the history of your prowess with electrical tape, she thought, running her finger along the barely warm edge of the coffee container. "Tell me your good news."

"I just got a great deal on a long-term sublet. Great apartment on West Tenth Street. And," he said, beaming, "I'm one of three writers in the running for some big indie producer's attention."

"In the running?"

He smiled sheepishly. "When I get the contract, I'll bring champagne. You're the only one in New York I care to celebrate with, Claudia. When I met you, I knew you were destined for a special place in my life."

"You just saw some old Jeanne Moreau movie, right? Or are you making this up as you go along?" Surely this pleasant young man knew better ways to meet people than to knock them over in the street. Unless the meeting wasn't accidental . . .

"These feelings are too complicated for me to make up." He shrugged and grinned and pointed to a barge heading upriver behind a red tugboat. "Sometimes I envy those guys. Their lives are so simple. Get up in the morning, see if it's snowing, raining, whatever, dress for the weather, work your buns off, then collapse in front of the tube with a beer and your woman and wait for morning so you can do it all over again."

"That's incredibly patronizing. People who do physical work have lives that are no less complicated than yours. If you can't see that, you'll never be a real writer." Annoyed, Claudia tugged her jeans down over her boots. She was tired of people making assumptions about worlds they could only imagine, tired of people like Murray getting cut down before they should, tired. "Where'd you learn to fix lamps, Charlie? Did you study to be an electrician and then decide you'd rather drink Brut than Bud?"

He frowned. "I *love* Budweiser beer. Doesn't every red-blooded American boy—I mean, *child*—learn to fix things by watching dear old Dad? It's just like I sort of know it, the way you know how to take apart an Oreo and eat the white stuff first. Why do you ask?"

He sounded convincing, but that was apparently one of his special talents. She slid to the edge of the bench. "Just curious. I better go."

"Now that you got what you wanted, it's only fair that I get the same." He bent his head toward her.

For an instant, she imagined his mouth, warm and firm against hers, sliding down to her neck, igniting little fires. Summoning her will, she pushed away. "Don't do that," she said.

"I'm sorry. No, I'm not." He shook his head and looked at her over the rim of the coffee container. "Yes, I am. Sorry that my timing or something seems to be off. This is new to me."

"I have a feeling this is anything but new to you." *Pay attention,* she warned herself. *He's cute and clever and hiding something.*

"No, not that. Not wanting to kiss a smart, sexy woman. Not even," he said with a self-deprecating nod of his head, "being told to stop when I'd rather not. What's new is the feeling that I'm completely willing to wait, because the unfolding is so rich. I guess I really am smitten. Is that sappy or what? Listen, there's something I want to ask you."

That wasn't going to happen. She wouldn't let him turn the spotlight on her. "Sappy. That's a pretty good word for that little speech."

"Dazzled," he said. "Any better? Or is that sappy, too?"

She slipped the strap of her purse onto her shoulder.

"Bewitched," he said, and she nodded. "Captivated. Mesmerized."

"Exaggerated. Overstated. Hyperbolic." She watched him unwrap the bagel. "Enjoy your research."

"Wait! Can I see you when I get back from California? I'm making a very early flight tomorrow, God, six A.M. from Kennedy, so I have to get up at, what, four. The City Flickers guys want to talk to me about my script this week. Amazing, right? Just when I'm grooving on New York, they crook their little fingers and I have to come running."

"Maybe you should pitch your idea to De Niro," she said brightly. "He's just down the street."

His hand brushed against hers. "I want to spend my New York time wisely. Gathering memories. Making pictures I can keep with me when we're apart."

"We're going to be apart for a very long time, Charlie. The rest of our lives." This had gone far enough. Claudia gave him one last appraising look before she rose and walked to the park exit.

"Hold on a second." Breathing hard, Charlie ran up beside her. "I know I'm the victim of an incurable romantic vision, but don't let that get in the way of whatever might develop between us. I'm sorry, I really am."

"Have a good life, Charlie." She strode down Chambers Street past Stuyvesant High School toward the old West Side Highway, now a six-lane roadway hugging the riverfront. Some people fell into a pattern: transgress, apologize, transgress again. Charlie Pastor was sure to have his own variations on that theme.

If she ran, maybe she'd beat the traffic to the intersection. The footsteps behind her stopped when she did.

"I guess I shouldn't be surprised at what's happening here," Charlie shouted above the rattle of a Federal Express truck. "After all, we started our relationship with me apologizing."

Her eyebrows shot up. "Our relationship? That's a pretty pompous name for an accident on the street, a repentant gift-offering, and twenty minutes watching tugboats." The light changed, and she walked briskly to the corner behind a clutch of women pushing baby strollers.

"And I don't want it to end on a cold street corner. Please don't shut me out, Claudia. I can't stand the thought of you being angry at me."

"Forget it, Charlie. I'm going home and you're going wherever you go. My anger is quite irrelevant." They passed clusters of chattering students on their way to the subway.

"Whether you care or not, I'll let you know how things go in California." Charlie Pastor knelt in front of her, took one of her hands in his and placed it above his heart. Two of the students giggled, staring with open interest. "How many general contractors does it take to change a lightbulb?"

"I don't know, Charlie." Annoyed, she pulled away.

"I don't know, either. But maybe next time I'll get you to smile." He rose, bowed, and headed for the corner.

Charlie Pastor: gone with the whim. Maybe there was a sinister reason he seemed to keep turning up, but she hadn't ferreted it out. He looked, sounded, smelled genuine. Odd, intense, but writers were like that. Still, this wasn't the time to start believing everything her senses told her.

Two messages.

The first was from Lazlo Sarafino, Rick's cousin, the security expert. He was out of town, the nasal voice declared, but someone was already on the job. He'd send her a bill, but it wouldn't be anything she should worry about. And he repeated Tommy's name, his address, the description Rick had passed on.

The second was from Rick himself, asking her to call him at home before five. When Sarafino answered the phone, she loosened her grip on the pencil, aware for the first time that she'd been jabbing at the notepad while the messages played. "Hi, Rick. This is Claudia Miller. I just got in. You said to call?"

"My cousin get ahold of you?"

"Yes, thanks for getting on it right away."

"Sure, yeah. One other thing. Dave Benedetti, you were asking about him and Ann Magursky, right? Magursky I don't know about, but Dave's in Montclair. I spoke to him half an hour ago." Sarafino recited a New Jersey telephone number. "Listen, you stop getting all obsessed about this. The department is on it. You do what you know how, and so will we. I don't want anything to happen to you. So you take care, you got me?"

"Thanks. Really, I appreciate everything you're doing, Rick." She broke the connection, the receiver still in her hand. If only someone else would volunteer to call Tommy and tell him about his bodyguard . . . She sighed, dialed his number, told him about Sarafino's cousin. "I didn't want you to think there were two guys following you around," she said lightly. "Everything's going to be all right."

Tommy was quiet. Finally he said, "I'll tell my mother. Do me a favor, all right? Don't make this, like, a bigger deal. She's crazy enough with worry. Please, Claudia. Don't get her all nuts with the details, okay?"

Reluctantly, she agreed. "You be careful, Tommy. I'll talk to you later. Love you."

When she hung up, she paced the length of her office, looked at the catalogs on her desk, the paid invoices that should be filed away in a folder. Pencils—she should sharpen those pencils, check to see if the pens still had ink. No, she shouldn't. She should just get the damn call over with.

She dialed Dave Benedetti's number, realized with a pang of sympathy for Sarafino that he had to explain this strange situation not only to civilians but also to fellow cops. Despite her fears, the preliminaries were quick and painless.

"I know Rick Sarafino went over this, but I have to be sure you understand. Murray Kurtz was murdered a few days ago," she said. "Someone wrapped him in electrical tape and suffocated him. Leroy Jefferson was electrocuted when someone hooked a power line to his bathroom plumbing. Then my brother was almost strangled with ten-four cable. Bert and I got to thinking these things were connected. We think someone's going around killing relatives of people who worked the Mercer Street renovation. So I'm checking in to tell you to be careful."

"Hey, you were always real good at delivering bad news. Like it was your special thing, you know?"

Leave it to Benedetti to respond with a non sequitur. "What? What does that mean?"

"It means, didn't you love telling me I had three days instead of five to do the job? Didn't you love firing Bridgeman's ass when he didn't show up after he went on a bender? It's pretty clear. You get off on this, don't you?"

No apologies, no explanations. She wasn't going to be drawn into Dave Benedetti's carefully nurtured resentments. "Do you know how I can reach Ann Magursky?"

Dave hesitated, as though he were deciding just how helpful he wanted to be. "No," he said, and then he hung up.

She sat for a long time watching darkness carpet the rooftops before she pushed open the door to her studio and sought the comfort of working her marble.

Thirteen

The movie last night wasn't nearly as good as he'd hoped. All those old war movies were actually kind of stupid if you really thought about it, full of that buddy crap, one-for-all garbage that went out with Audie Murphy. At least it had gotten him through the dark hours, the time when he couldn't sleep for remembering, for planning, the time when he would wake up bathed in cold sweat. A year. Since his mother died. It had been like that for a year.

He lifted the binoculars, watched the lights go out behind the sheer curtains in the front bedroom of the two-story frame house. The van was an icebox, but if he drank any more coffee he'd explode. Ten more minutes. Then the woman would step onto the porch in her dumb fake fur jacket, turn to check if the door was locked, and half run to catch the bus.

Five minutes after that he'd be inside, where it was warmer. Less than an hour to do the whole job. That's all it would take.

First, though, he'd take the longest, most careful piss of his life.

He'd flush, because who knew what they could do these days with a couple of drops from a toilet bowl.

He looked in the rearview mirror at the shaving cut on his upper lip, squinted, wondered if that woman from Cleveland he met two years ago would notice it. Sitting there those mornings in her bathrobe, her skin still pink from the shower, trying to get a rise out of him just by walking around like that, with her fine boobs swaying and her butt kind of rolling along as she walked to the counter to get a cup of coffee. Sharon, that was her name.

Coffee.

If he ever decided to do another early morning job, he'd be more careful about what he drank and ate. Funny, he'd spent so much time sitting quietly in the dark room, waiting for advice, getting plenty, but never a warning about drinking too much coffee. He smiled.

From the corner of his eye, he saw the front door open. The woman shifted her shoulder bag, ran back into the house, leaving the door ajar. Probably forgot her commuter ticket or some letter she planned to drop in the mail on her way to the bus.

Save himself a lot of trouble if he just slipped in now while no one was looking and hid in the coat closet until she left. But the woman stepped onto the porch again, adjusted the bag with the same motion she'd used just a minute before, checked the lock, and ran down the steps. She didn't even bother to look at the Therma-Care van with New York plates parked across from her house as she hauled the empty trash can to the driveway, teetering in those stupid high heels. She pushed back the sleeve of her fuzzy jacket to look at her watch, then, high heels, ice, and all, she headed to the corner at full clip.

Don't slip, lady, he prayed. *Don't fall and rip your stockings and have to go back home and change them and make me wait out here in the cold an extra ten minutes.*

When she disappeared around the corner, he checked his watch. Three minutes. The express bus would pull up and she'd climb those steps and find a seat and read the paper or whatever she did all the way into the city.

Two men approached the van, noses red from the cold, their conversation dribbling to a stop and their eyes narrowing as they came closer. But they kept walking, didn't even slow down or look over their shoulders after they'd passed. He controlled his desire to whoop with victory.

It was an omen, that's what it was. This one would be easy, unlike the last one, which was so complicated, so nearly out of his league that he almost gave it up. But he was glad he'd gone through with it, because it meant he really could run down the list, finish this business once and for all. From the second he first thought about it, it had taken a month to decide to do it, another half a year to track them all down. He wouldn't stop before the job was done.

He lifted the black tool bag from the floor and set it on his lap, looked up just in time to see the bus drive by. Good. He couldn't sit around with his legs crossed forever.

He pushed open the van door, grabbed the case, and walked to the other side of the street. No one stopped him. No one asked why the man in the Therma-Care coveralls and jacket was going down the driveway to the cement slab that was her backyard, past the wood picnic table and the benches turned upside down.

Maybe she thought that would save them from the winter cold, from the ice and snow. Woman like that living alone, she needed someone to teach her about protecting the yard furniture from the elements. The wood was going to crack in a year if she didn't take care of it. Her son really should check on her more often.

Up two steps to the aluminum door. Even that was a sign—the screen door still on at the end of winter. She was a real target. A pro would take the yard furniture and the screen door as signs of a woman living alone, would watch the house for a while to make sure he was right, and then figure the good time to hit it. Women stuck to their schedules, came and went regularly. At least this woman did, more regular than the other one he'd been watching for the past two weeks.

He opened the screen door, slipped a plastic card between the lock and the wood frame. His gloves made the operation a little awkward. After several tries he got it, turned the knob, swung the door open into what his mother used to call a mudroom. On an old green towel, folded in half and pushed right up to the wall, next to the snow shovel and a nearly empty bag of Qwik-Melt, a pair of fur-lined boots stood. The woman sure did have a thing for fur. He took off his galoshes, left them upside down on the towel beside her boots. No wet footprints in the house—that would be too careless, too easy for someone to trace.

The door leading inside was locked, a surprise, but he worked it open in half a minute and stepped inside in his dry shoes. The kitchen still smelled of her breakfast. Toast and coffee, a single crumby plate and a half-full mug in the sink. He stood in the sunny room, listened to the hum of the refrigerator, noticed that the paint on the cabinets, probably once a bright yellow, had turned grayish and streaked with repeated washings. Flat paint, not the semigloss she should have used. The paint job looked to be five, six years old, about what he would expect for a woman whose husband had died eight years ago. A couple of years to mourn and then a couple of months to change things so they didn't remind her of the old life. Work she probably did herself, to save money, and to keep busy.

He tiptoed to the second door.

All *right*.

The bathroom.

He took care of business wearing one glove, so he wouldn't leave prints anywhere. At least now he could think instead of having all his attention on his damn bladder.

The basement door, next to the broom closet at the far end of the kitchen, stuck when he pulled at it. He put his weight on the knob, pushed down, yanked at the door, nearly lost his balance when it flew open. God, he hated these wet, moldy holes, hated going down the stairs, hated the spiderwebs that would brush his face.

But this was where he would find the circuit breaker box and the pipes. The box would be somewhere near the street, easy for the utility people to get to, not so hidden that a widow living alone couldn't find it if something blew.

There, to the left of the window, the metal box gleamed. A Square D, one of the brands he knew. He crossed the dirt floor, pulled the door open, and smiled at the little adhesive tape labels that were stuck onto each breaker.

BR1, BR2, LR, DR, APP, W/D, K/R, K/D, K/O.

APP had to be appliances, maybe her air conditioners, but it didn't matter. The K's were the only part of the code he cared about. One for the refrigerator, one for the dishwasher, one for the lights and the wall outlets.

She would come home, let herself in the back door, take off her shoes and set them on the towel. Next, she'd unlock the inner door and turn on the lights. And that would be that.

He flipped the main, then turned each individual breaker to the off position, just to be sure. K/O controlled the toaster. The coffeemaker. The kitchen lights. He tugged at his gloves, gripped the nylon handles of his tool bag, then sat down on the bottom step to catch his breath.

One spark from the shorted wire in the gas-filled basement was all it would take. And then her son, who lived two blocks away, would know what it was like. The pain, the nightmares. Dave Benedetti would spend the rest of his life with that black hole inside him.

He trudged back up the stairs to the kitchen. If he made it through the next twenty minutes without his heart bursting out of his chest, he'd be home free.

Now, to work. Using a screwdriver blade, he pried off the baseboard, sighted straight down from the light switch, picked up the drill. He pressed the ON switch and the drill whirled through air. *Keep the angle clean,* he reminded himself as the drill bored through molding, then air, then floor.

He dumped the drill into the bag. Concentrating, he unscrewed the light switch cover plate, set it on the floor beside him, then snipped the wires that she expected to send juice to the kitchen ceiling lights. He stopped to mop with his handkerchief at the river of sweat that streamed down his face.

And after the explosion, then what? So, Benedetti would feel bad. Would he grow thin and wrinkled because he couldn't eat or sleep? Would he get a little crazy every time he saw a TV show where a grown son rolled his eyes because his mother was being overprotective?

He would never know. That was what was wrong. But he'd fix that with the Miller woman. Next time, he'd do better.

When he could breathe without a ragged pain biting at his chest, he cut the sheathing away from the first six inches of the cable on his spool, twisted it onto the snipped wires that no longer connected to the ceiling fixture. Carefully, gingerly, with sweat still pouring into his eyes, he ran out the spool until the length of cable was three times his height. Eighteen feet. Two more than he needed, just to be safe. He cut the cable from the spool and fed it down to the hole, down past the floor, down to the basement.

He replaced the cover plate, then the baseboard, and tossed his tools into the bag.

Almost done.

Going back down those steps would be easier this time. He clutched the bag in one hand, his flashlight in the other, and descended into the basement again.

From his bag, he pulled out a cordless screwdriver and picked his way to the center of the dark space, tapped the pipes. Water, sewer line, exhaust from the furnace, ducts into the house; the gas pipe, the last one, right up to the kitchen. First to the water heater, then up the cracked gray basement wall to the kitchen stove.

He hummed as he set the screwdriver to reverse and positioned it on one of the screws holding two sections of pipe together. He dropped the screw into his pocket, removed another, stepped back and blinked when the pipe sagged and the sections separated.

Gagging at the sweet-ugly smell, he forced himself to build a tower of cartons just below the separated pipes. He dragged the cable that dangled from the hole in the kitchen floor and set it atop the carton marked XMAS, the black letters faded from years of handling. With care, he laid the exposed end-wires a quarter inch apart, just enough to create the arc. The arc that would ignite the gas. That would blow up the house that Benedetti built.

Fine. Everything was going just fine.

It was the next step he dreaded. First the individual switches, everything but K/O. He swallowed hard, jerked his hand when he had reset each one.

When he flipped the K/O switch, he inhaled, grinned, and then threw the master.

He hated it; no matter what he did, electricity still made him nervous. He could stand up against three drunken sailors trying to pick a fight in a bar, could drive ninety miles an hour on some deserted road just for the fun of it. But electricity, something he couldn't see or smell or hold in his hand, scared the shit out of him. He knew all you had to do was remember a couple of important cautions, but it was like the stuff had a life of its own.

He'd thought about the words of it for years. Surges and charges, crackles and sparks, discharges and resistance, power—sometimes they sounded like words about sex and then he felt he understood it a little better. But mostly it was mysterious and scary, and he hated it when he had to work with it.

Now he was done; better to leave quickly, not call attention to himself or the truck.

Even if he timed things right, he couldn't risk sitting in his truck across the street when Dave Benedetti arrived. He wouldn't see his face or watch his body curl up with the pain of knowing someone he loved had died. And that was the shame of it, this old and useless plan of his.

Definitely, he'd do it differently next time.

Fourteen

The bar at Yaffa's was quiet. The lunchtime crowd had thinned, and the television was tuned to NY One, the city news channel, where a reporter was fueling the controversy over which groups would have official sanction to march in the St. Patrick's Day parade.

The Czech Maria smiled at her, asked if she wanted her usual, stopped midstride when Claudia shook her head. "Just a mint tea."

Maria brought the tea, and Claudia turned her attention to the news. The sweeping second hand began its journey around the clock face on the television screen, a warning that the one-minute news recap was coming up.

The first shot was of a garbage scow and a group of angry, placard-waving protestors.

"You are a student of the nautical?" the voice beside her asked.

"The political." She set the wicker tea strainer in an empty glass, and turned to face Mikhail Chernin as the announcer's voice droned on. "Every time there's a story on garbage, the haulers offer special deals, lower prices, extra pickups. Commercial garbage is still run by the old families, and it's still three times more expensive in New York than anywhere else in this country."

"Ah, I see why Irina says you know this city."

But the sound of a name made her turn away from him and face the screen. *Benedetti.* Was that what the announcer said? Claudia was riveted to the image of firefighters directing a stream of water onto the smoldering remains of a single-family home. In the background, an ambulance pulled away as the camera followed it down the tree-lined street.

"—*in New Jersey are investigating the possibility of foul play in yesterday's Montclair fire. And now it's time for weather on the ones, and a check of the readings in your neighborhood . . ."*

Did Charlie Pastor like to play with matches? If someone in Dave Benedetti's family burned up in that fire, did the earnest young man with the wire-rimmed glasses have anything to do with it?

"Did he say someone died?" Mikhail squinted in concentration.

She stood beside the stool, gathering her coat and purse. "Sorry. I have to go."

"Something's wrong." Beneath the heavy brows, his dark eyes crackled. "Is there anything I can do?"

Perhaps Mikhail Chernin *could* help. "You left the table the other day to call an investigator. You're pleased with his work?"

"Her." Mikhail nodded, reached across the bar for a napkin and a ballpoint pen that lay beside an order pad. In European script, he scrawled a name and telephone number. "She is very good. Thorough. Fast," he said as he slid the napkin to Claudia. "You still look upset. Do you want company for a while?"

Despite his gentle voice, Mikhail Chernin's intensity burned too brightly. She found it more unsettling than intriguing. "Thanks, but I have to go. It's kind of a family emergency."

"I understand." He helped her into her coat. "Maybe you will tell me about it next time."

"Next time?" Her scarf had fallen to the floor; she stooped to retrieve it.

"At Irina's party. I'm picking you up, yes?" He adjusted the ends of her scarf so that they were even, held onto them as he said, "If you want company, you call me, Claudia."

She murmured her thanks and stepped outside, dug a quarter from her purse, and walked to the pay phone on the corner of Greenwich and Franklin, across from the TriBeCa Grill. The mild breeze felt almost springlike, mockingly hopeful. She dialed the investigator's number.

Maybe Charlie Pastor was exactly what he appeared to be: a fast-talking, attractive newcomer to New York with a moral code that required him to make amends for even his accidental sins. If he was something else, she wanted to know.

"Laurette Lacroix?" Claudia held her finger just under the name Mikhail had written on the napkin.

The voice on the other end was musical, light. "Yes. Who are you?"

"Claudia Miller. You did some work for someone I know. Mikhail Chernin."

"Right, sure, the guy with the car service. What can I do for you?"

"I need a background check. His name is Charlie Pastor. Charles, I guess. He's about twenty-nine, maybe thirty, blond, blue eyes, wears glasses. A graduate of Rice University. He sublets an apartment on West Tenth Street. He's from Los Angeles originally. According to what he told me, he's there right now trying to sell a script or something, but I'm not really sure about anything he's said. If you need cash or a check or something before you get started, I can have it messengered right away."

"That's fine. I'm a little backed up with a big job, but once I clear the decks it won't take long. Five hundred dollars for the first round. If you want more information after you read that report, we'll talk about it."

Claudia scribbled the investigator's address, then fished another quarter from her purse, caught Rick Sarafino at the First Precinct, just as he was going off duty.

"Meet me in five minutes at the Square Diner," she said when she heard his voice. "It's important."

Sarafino's groan sounded heartfelt. "What? I told you the lab is all jammed up with that Chinatown sweatshop murder. You have to get real, Miller. This isn't the only thing going down in Manhattan."

"And New Jersey, right? Surely you already know, Rick. Get your detective's shield yet?"

"Gold shield, my Sicilian butt. I'm no frigging hero. I spent five hours yesterday in court with a crack bust from last Memorial Day and then chased that cabbie thing. Tomorrow I gotta do a double shift because there's flu going around and every damn one's calling in sick, so I want to go home while I can."

She slid a carefully folded newspaper across the table. It fell to the vinyl booth-seat and landed beside Sarafino's hat. He glanced at it and nudged the coffee cup away, sloshing pale liquid into the saucer, avoiding her gaze until she rapped the folded newspaper on the table. Discomfort deepened the ruddy color on his face.

"I don't want my brother to become a headline," Claudia said. "Carla Benedetti, whose loving son David was the plumber at Mercer Street sixteen years ago . . . She's what, homicide number one hundred? Two hundred? So far this year, I mean."

"Now you're talking like I have some special power around here. You're aware that I'm still on the street? You have any idea what it's like to be weeks from retirement? When I became a cop I thought I'd save the world. Now I just want to get outta here with my arms and legs in one piece, you know what I mean? I wish I *could* do something."

"Try this, Rick." Her voice was soft, and he leaned forward to hear her. "Try getting a cop assigned to protect my brother. Twenty-four hours, no lapses, no harm comes to Tommy."

They both jumped when the phone beside the pastry display case rang, didn't speak until the counterman shouted something in Greek into the receiver.

Sarafino's Adam's apple bobbed. He nodded, sighed. "Sure, Miller. And then I'll fly to the moon and win the lottery and invent a cure for cancer. I can't do it. Probably even the commissioner couldn't do it. Look," he said as he examined a speck on the back of his spoon, "if the bodyguard doesn't make you feel safe, maybe you should send the kid away for a while until this blows over. It wouldn't be the worst idea in the world if you went with him. Think about it, Miller. The man who hurt your brother wanted you, right? You got relatives out of town, maybe that's the ticket. You both go away, you both stay safe."

She stabbed at the list. "See that name? Laverne Jefferson. Whose cousin Leroy was murdered in Phoenix. That's pretty far out of town."

But, already, a plan was beginning to form in her mind.

For all his lugubrious reluctance, Sarafino was probably right. Tommy's safety was all that mattered. Keeping him tucked away for a while might be the only sane course of action. She dropped her last quarter into the phone outside the diner and dialed her father's house. "Nora, hi, it's Claudia."

"Claudia, how odd. I was just about to call you. I—"

"Listen, I need to talk to you and Tommy. Can I come over? Now, I mean."

"Don't you ever listen to what other people say? Did you hear me tell you I was just going to call you? Tommy's out. I'll be here, though, if you think you want to face me right now. I'm extremely angry with you, Claudia. Suit yourself."

Dressed, coifed, and made-up as though she were about to serve tea to the ladies' auxiliary, Nora Miller led the way to her living room, sat in the center of the sofa, waited while Claudia settled into an armchair. The ubiquitous winter fire crackled in the fireplace, and Sheba warmed her hindquarters in its heat. "You're doing a good job of scaring me, Claudia," Nora said.

"Well, that's not inappropriate. We need to proceed with caution. Caution and positive action." She'd had time in the taxi to get calm, to confirm to herself that, above all, she wanted no harm to come to her brother. The rest of it—the discovery of the truth, the reparations for any of her sins that might be the source of this trouble—would come later.

"Positive action? You've taken that already. Without bothering to tell me. Just before Tommy left for his SAT class, he told me you already hired the guard." Nora glared, her face twisted with anger. "What right do you have? What goddamn right do you have to hire a bodyguard and then not tell me? I regret every argument I ever had with Evan about your good intentions. You need good judgment to go along with it. What you did was a breach of common sense and decency. Now, you will please leave my house and stay out of Tommy's life."

"It's not like we hadn't talked about the possibility. Maybe I didn't use the best judgment, but I was keeping a promise I made to Tommy." Claudia didn't say it as calmly as she'd hoped. "Teenagers need to keep some things from their parents, as a way of easing out of the safety of the nest, you know? Well, Tommy asked me not to say anything to you on the phone. He was worried about upsetting you and he wanted to tell you himself. It would have been a violation of—"

"You get in the middle of things, Claudia, and Tommy has no chance to work them out with Evan and me." Hands pressed in her lap, Nora squared her shoulders. "Stay away from him for a while. You want a child so badly, have one of your own. Stay up with him nights when he has an earache, wipe his puke from your living room carpet, explain AIDS and racism and plane crashes to him. Figure out whether limiting his television is punishment or reward. You want a child, you better be ready for everything that goes with it, not just the rescuing and adoring part."

"I made my choices years ago. I wouldn't be a very good mother, I knew that. But I decided I could be a really good sister." Claudia took Nora's silence to be an invitation to continue. "If you're jealous of my relationship with Tommy, maybe you ought to look at that. I *do* see your point, Nora. I should have told you right away, and for that I apologize. But we can't get sidetracked by this stuff. We have a problem to face. It's a problem I brought into your life, I understand that. Three people are dead. I don't want Tommy to be next."

Her mouth drawn into a thin, harsh slash, Nora stalked to the doorway, then whirled around. "If anything happens to my son because of something you did to prove you were some hotshot feminist carpenter or whatever it is you were trying to prove, I'll kill you."

"You're forgetting something, Nora. I'm not going around killing people. I'm not responsible for what's happening here. Blaming me isn't going to make things all right for Tommy. I really think he should go away until this monster is caught." Clearheaded now, impatient to implement her plan, Claudia traced the seams of her wool slacks with restless fingers. "What makes sense to me is sending Tommy to Ted's. My ex. Ted Stavros. He's got a weekend place in a little town called Taconic Hills, about a hundred miles north of here. You and Tommy could—"

"We already discussed that. I don't want to pull him out of school. This is the last half of his junior year. I can't jeopardize his final chance to raise his grades, the ones that count for college entrance."

"But you can sit back while someone tries to kill him?"

With an exasperated sigh, Nora slumped into a chair. Claudia knelt and stroked Sheba, running her fingers down the flat bone between the dog's eyes, smiling as the animal sighed, blinked, and snuffled out a wet thank-you.

"I have to think about this. What if someone follows him up there?"

They should prepare for that; Nora had a point. "I'm sure we can figure something out. I don't know, maybe someone wearing Tommy's clothes can go off in one direction while we get Tommy out of the city." How ironic—Charlie Pastor would do just fine. About the same height and build as her brother, a little broader through the shoulders, maybe, wrong hair, but that could be hidden under a hat. "Wait a minute. This new guy who's working for me, he's about Tommy's height, maybe a couple of pounds heavier, but not that anyone would notice under a coat."

The circles under Nora's eyes darkened as she bent her head. "I'll talk to Tommy and Evan. You give me some space, Claudia. Let me breathe and let me think. I'll call you when I've decided.

Fifteen

1981 / Mercer Street / The Crisis

"Why does he do that?" She jabbed her fork into the pasta bowl, speared a clam, shook her head and took another swallow of wine. "He waited two days to tell me about the baby. My father's child bride gives birth three weeks early and he waits two days to call me. What's that about, Amos? Why does he need to hurt me that way?"

"You hear how you talk about the whole thing—calling his wife his child bride? Doesn't that give you a clue to how hostile you are about his marriage to Nora? Put a little extra garlic on the pasta, Claudia. It's bland." Amos Fischer passed a shaker across the table, waited while she sprinkled the fine powder onto her spaghetti. "Did he get you to pay attention? Yes. Did he force you to think about him? Certainly. Did he give you a dose of how it feels to be left out? You bet."

The waiter, a dark-eyed young man who held her gaze too long when he asked for her order, stopped beside their table, frowning. "Is everything all right?"

"No, it's not. But it's not the food." She looked away, annoyed at his attention, and at Amos's response to her question. "You don't think he was being a class-A prick?"

Amos held his hand up, finished a mouthful of pasta. "Oh, yes, a world-class prick. But you asked me why, so I told you. You should have the lemon ice for dessert. It's the best thing they make here. You want espresso?"

He was wonderful, smart, no, wise, and she knew exactly what she wanted for dessert. "Let's skip the ices tonight, Amos, and just go home. You think your stitches are healed enough for a little physical activity?"

He smiled, waved for the check, nodded. "The good doctor gave me the go-ahead this morning. He assured me my appendix hasn't grown back and my scar is healed enough for unathletic sex. Unfortunately for me—and luckily for you—I can't go back to work for another week, and even then I have to lay off the heavy stuff for another month and a half. Ready?"

"I've been ready for two weeks, Amos. Let's go home."

Amos Fischer snored gently beside her.

In the dim light, watching the rise and fall of his chest, she felt a surge of gratitude that he'd showed up in her life in time to teach her some important things. Amos didn't follow other people's rules; instead, he created his own, this man who crafted his life with the same care he lavished on the built-in cabinets and library walls he made.

She shut her eyes and tried to stop her thoughts, but he filled them, as he had for the past three months, and she shifted her arms so they were clasped behind her head.

At forty-one, Amos seemed to be enjoying the fruits of his labors, and if he were sometimes too eager to play the role of teacher, that was the trade-off for what she learned from him.

Despite her restless movements, he slept on, his leg curled around hers. She tried to ease herself away, but he stirred, snuggled in closer. She was already almost at the edge of the bed; her choice was to try again to induce the semihypnotic state that sometimes passed for sleep these days or to get up, find a spot on the sofa, read until she fell asleep with the lights on and the afghan pulled to her chin.

Claudia shifted again, gave Amos a gentle shove and scooted to the middle of the bed when he rolled toward the far edge. A foghorn moaned in the darkness; she pulled the pillow over her head and repeated her new mantra: *Courageous and elegant, free and authentic. Courageous and elegant, free and authentic.*

The idea was so simple and yet so obvious that, when he explained it to her, she wondered whether he really shouldn't give up woodworking and become a teacher of this new system of meditation. He had instructed her to think of four qualities she wanted to cultivate, and then find an arrangement of words to represent them that sounded pleasing to her. By repeating them to herself silently when she got into bed, she would call these concepts into her life, absorb the apparent contradictions, and lull herself to sleep all at the same time.

The words blurred into sounds. Her jaws unclenched, the small muscles at her temples let go, and she felt herself drift down toward sleep, when the telephone jolted her awake.

"Yes?" she said, pulling the sheet to her neck.

"Claudia? Sorry to bother you. It's Jack. Jack Kurtz." He whispered into the phone, as though he were trying not to awaken someone beside him. "Listen, there's been a fire at the Mercer Street loft. The whole building's gone. I mean, ashes, that's all that's left. I can see it from my bedroom. Man, the fire trucks woke me up and I rolled over and thought I was dreaming but the sirens just kept on, I mean, there must be eight, nine trucks down there."

The whole building . . . gone, he said. And she still owed some of the workers money. "Shit, my tools were in that loft." Her father would have called her tone snippy, but she didn't care if Jack Kurtz thought she was a flaming bitch. *Flaming.* Her jaws clenched as she envisioned fire destroying all the months of work on the Mercer Street apartment. She wondered if Edward Molino had insurance.

"Listen, the body they found inside is in the ambulance. That's the part I thought you should know about. I guess there's nothing you can do, but I thought you should know."

With cold detachment, she watched her anger rise, watched herself grapple for control of the fury that made her want to throttle Jack Kurtz so he'd never do this to anyone ever again. "The body? Is that what you said? Who is it?"

Kurtz's long silence gave her time to go through a catalog of all the people who had keys to the building. *Please, God, let it not be Bert,* she prayed silently. *Let it not be any of them.*

"They don't know yet. Or at least, they wouldn't tell me. But they did say they pulled it off of the fifth floor."

"Shit." The tears that sprang to her eyes turned quickly to ice as her anger grew to rage. "The goddamn electrical union. If Kevin Mahoney hurt any of my people with his goddamn fire, I'll kill him. I'll fucking kill him."

"If that's what happened, I'll help you. Maybe it was one of those junkie kids been hanging around."

Now she could hear it in his voice: Jack Kurtz was stoned, drifting in his marijuana dream, getting his courage in a hit of smoke.

"The firemen, they're still there?" She watched Amos stir beside her, and she reached over to cover his back, bare to the unheated night air, tugging gently at the blanket where it was caught beneath his body.

"Oh, yeah, it's gonna be a while before that sucker's cold."

Her toes curled involuntarily as they hit the chilly floor. "I'm coming down there, Jack. If you find out anything else, watch for me in the street, okay? Thanks for letting me know."

As she gathered her clothing with one hand, she dialed Bert's number. The phone rang and rang; she pictured his studio apartment, the bed neatly made, the table stacked with papers and books in piles beside his typewriter, and a sharp pain swept through her. He's with one of his dollies, she thought, and congratulated herself on being sensible and calm as she raced out of the building, leaving the keys to her apartment on the dining room table.

By the time she reached Mercer Street, a crowd had gathered in wide-eyed wonder. The blaze lit the sky with a neon-green glow. Something about the chemicals in the paint turning the flames that color, a soot-covered fireman explained as he eyed her appraisingly.

"Look," she said, pushing her way past the police cruiser to talk to the fire lieutenant, "I know you pulled someone out of there."

Stoically, he said, "Right in front of the elevator, it was. Must've tried to get out that way instead of the fire escape."

"I'm the contractor in charge of the fifth-floor job. I want to

90

know if any of my people . . ." *Don't let it be Bert.* She swallowed back her fear. "Take me to the ambulance. Maybe I can tell you who it is."

The man, beefy and square-faced, peered at her skeptically through smeared bifocals. "You ever see a crispy critter before? I don't think that's such a good idea."

Crispy critter. Her throat closed up against the sour rush from her stomach. Dead—whoever was in that ambulance wasn't waiting for medical attention. "Well, I don't think it's a good idea to let that body be anonymous if I can tell you who it is."

Wordlessly, she followed the lieutenant to the ambulance idling at the curb. Two teens with shoulder-length hair watched, started to follow them, retreated when the fireman growled something menacing. He undid the latch, swung the door open, nodded to the attendant to unzip the body bag.

A stench, like rotted fish, rose from the black plastic.

She gritted her teeth, stepped forward, and forced herself to look.

The shoes, intact and a little sooty, seemed to be the only thing to have escaped the fire's wrath. Black flesh hung in strips from the hands and arms of the man in the bag. His coveralls were melted to his skin along the thigh, and the face of his watch was embedded in his arm like a macabre, free-form sculpture. The nose and the flesh on his cheeks were nearly as disfigured as his hands.

The shape of the chin, the high forehead, the close-set eyes gave her enough to fill in the blanks.

"Kevin Mahoney," she said before she turned away and vomited onto the cobblestones.

No ice for him. His world had ended in fire.

She wiped her mouth with a tissue she dug from her pocket, took a couple of shaky breaths, and prepared to face what she knew would be a very long day.

Sixteen

She tossed her coat atop the sealed cartons, impatient to get Bert alone. She was right, she felt it. The idea had come to her five seconds after she'd spoken to Tommy. She'd marched around her studio muttering until she decided she couldn't wait.

At Duane Street, Bert greeted her with a barrage of construction news. "We have to have the walls done in a week. That's when the floor guy is scheduled to come in. So, it means the walls have to be not just rocked and taped, but primed, too."

Gary Bruno helped Bert set the drywall in place, then resumed his own task. "Too bad we can't use steel studs for everything. The metal ones are lighter, they go up quicker, and they're fireproof."

"You know you have to use wood studs when you frame doors." His complaints were trying her patience. "And you need them for hanging cabinets." *If they were ever delivered,* she thought angrily. *If they arrived in this century.*

Claudia glanced at Bruno, who was measuring boards in the back of the loft, then steered Bert to the window. "I thought of something that might explain what's going on, but I don't know if it's anything more than my own obsessive rambling. Maybe having this confirmed will help me get a grip. I'm so weirded out I've even been considering carrying around the gun that old Cuban guy left in the cigar box."

The wrinkled old man who'd left the gun in one of the lofts on Prince Street had called it his payroll insurance. So much cash on

Fridays, he'd said, that he didn't want anyone to feel tempted to try to rip him off, so he took out a little payroll insurance in the form of an old Glock nine millimeter and kept it on the table as he counted out piles of twenties at the end of the week. When he called Claudia and asked her to do the Friday chore, she'd found the gun in the same lock box as the cash. He'd never returned, and she'd quietly stashed the pistol in her closet in a box, under her rarely worn silk scarves.

Bert scowled. "You still have that gun? You're not serious. You're not going to drag that old thing out. It hasn't been fired in years. The way you've been so distracted, you'd probably shoot off your big toe if you ever tried to use it."

"Distracted? Okay, but I still take care of business."

"Mostly. Except," he said, pointing with his head to the front window, "the Hockmans won't like it if you keep leaving the fire escape window open. Any old guy with a ski mask and a lightning bolt around his neck could get in here, you know. Just promise me you're not going to walk the streets with that thing in your handbag."

"Of course I'm not going to start carrying a gun." She *had* been the last to leave last night, would have yelled bloody murder if Bert or Gary or anyone else had left that window open. "This may seem like I'm trying to change the window subject, but it's not. I got the message. Okay? Now I *will* change the subject. Tell me if this makes sense. We know this guy is killing the *families* of people from the Mercer Street crew, but the question is, why? I've been walking around asking myself that. And I got an answer, three in the afternoon, clear as that blue sky.

"Because it's pay-back. He thinks we set that fire deliberately, just in time for Mahoney to show up. To get Mahoney off our backs because we didn't want to hire union electricians. We rigged the elevator because we wanted Mahoney to be stuck on the fifth floor is what he believes. He suffered all these years because *his* relative died and now he's making us suffer by killing *our* relatives. The guy is a relative of Kevin Mahoney."

Bert patted his shirt pocket, took out his pack of Pall Malls, tapped the pack against his palm. "He's administering his own perverted justice. A kind of biblical vengeance. He's making sure we feel the same pain."

So, it sounded right to Bert, too. Claudia nodded, said, "I made up my mind to stop letting this roll over me. I'm going to see Deirdre Mahoney. Maybe she can tell me something. I hardly know the woman but I remember her face. She wouldn't want anyone to suffer. She wouldn't believe you could ease one person's pain by hurting another."

"You hear how terribly noble that sounds? Don't be surprised if Deirdre Mahoney doesn't exactly welcome you with open arms. Only a saint would be capable of passing up an opportunity to get in a few choice words to the woman she probably thinks had something to do with her husband's death. Don't be surprised if she says something to hurt you."

Claudia Miller wasn't worried about being hurt by the truth. She was more concerned about recognizing it when she heard it.

"Please, not Mrs. Mahoney. Deirdre. The first time Kevin heard of *Deirdre of the Sorrows*, he went out and saw that play. He must have seen it five times. He used to say the sound of my name made him think of rain on the green hills of Ireland. Sit down, would you?"

Her delicate hands fluttered like white birds at the belt of her dark skirt. Deirdre Mahoney, aglow with natural color, waited until Claudia lowered herself to the ivory brocade sofa before she perched on the pale chair beside the coffee table. The room smelled of apples and old leather, and Claudia flashed on Deirdre's husband in his Sunday church clothes waiting for his in-laws to finish their tea so he could change into his sweats and go down to the basement to work on his model trains.

Not sweats, she reminded herself. *Sixteen years ago, to someone like Kevin Mahoney, only athletes and models wore sweats.*

"I am sorry to bother you, Mrs. Mahoney. This isn't . . . I guess I better just start. Interrupt me if I don't make sense."

The woman pushed back a strand of wiry gray hair that had worked loose from her tightly rolled French twist. The expressionless face dissolved into a forest of fine lines branching from the corners of her eyes and her mouth. "One thing," Deirdre said crisply.

"I never did believe you were responsible for my husband's death. I just thought you were a hotheaded, insensitive girl who shouldn't have been going around making rash statements about a man who wasn't there to defend himself."

"I do wish things had turned out differently." Claudia was chagrined at the lame sentiment, relieved to have said anything at all. The silence stretched on. Finally, she said, "The reason for this visit is a little complicated. It has to do with some recent murders that I think might be connected to Kevin."

Her restless, unmanicured hands resumed fidgeting with her belt as Deirdre Mahoney shook her head. "You are, you know."

"I am what?" Claudia felt as though she was being chastised by a prim, self-satisfied aunt.

"You are an insensitive girl. You speak plainly now so we can get this over with. Every time you say my husband's name I want to throttle you. Get on with it, would you?" Spine rigid, she stared hard into Claudia's eyes.

"In the last six months, three people have been murdered. First, I found out that Murray Kurtz was wrapped in electric tape until he suffocated. He's the man the newspapers call the Park Avenue mummy. Then, I heard about someone in Phoenix, Leroy Jefferson, dying of a heart attack when he touched his shower handles, which had been hot-wired. And now Carla Benedetti. A spark from a rigged electrical short ignited her basement, which was full of gas. Her house exploded. That was that Montclair fire that was all over the television yesterday.

"The thing is, Mrs. Mahoney, every victim had a relative who worked on the Mercer Street job with me. And all the attacks involved electricity or electrical equipment. I believe a single person is responsible for the deaths of the relatives of the Mercer Street crew. I think it's someone trying to achieve some kind of personal justice."

Deirdre Mahoney paled, the high color bleached from her cheeks and lips. She slumped in the chair and buried her face in her hands, then shook her head. "I can't help you, Miss Miller. I can't think of anyone who would do these terrible things. Certainly not anyone in my family, if that's what you're getting at. I have a son who lives near Los Angeles. His name is Sean and he's a pediatric oncologist." She offered up each syllable with obvious pride.

"And he's not here on a visit or anything like that, right?" There must have been a more tactful way to say that, but directness was a virtue with this woman, who laughed bitterly at the question.

"Visit? Sean calls me religiously on Christmas, Easter, Mother's Day, and my birthday. He deposits a thousand dollars a month in my checking account. He even sent me tickets to come to California. My son hasn't set foot in Queens for ten years. My daughter Fiona, on the other hand, does come in the summer and during semester break. She weighs about ninety pounds and has nothing on her mind but making straight A's in the mathematics program at MIT where she's finishing her master's degree. That's all the family I've got. Kevin was an only child and all my people stayed in the old country. We have no other relatives. So you take your sad story elsewhere, you hear me? I have nothing to say that would be of any use to you."

Deirdre Mahoney, living alone among her memories and photographs, waiting for her children to feel guilty enough to call, wasn't telling her everything, Claudia was certain.

"I have a sixteen-year-old brother, Mrs. Mahoney. Someone cut his face with exposed electric wires and tried to strangle him. That same person followed him around and took pictures of him, then mailed them to me. I'm afraid for him. He shouldn't be involved in this business. He wasn't even born when that fire happened."

"What, and my Kevin should have burned up in that slum you were trying to turn into an apartment?"

"You know I'm not saying that. But whoever's killing these people appears to be doing it out of loyalty to your husband. Anything you can tell me, anyone you can think of who might go this far to avenge Kevin's death, please tell me. I'm not a crackpot with some harebrained theory about Martians trying to take over our minds or something. You must see the connection between these victims."

Deirdre Mahoney's head whipped up and she held Claudia's gaze long enough for Claudia to confirm her own belief that the woman knew something, or at least had a suspicion. But then she looked away. "I want you to leave now, Miss Miller."

Claudia added her home phone and the number of the Duane Street loft to her business card, set it on the coffee table, and got her coat from the closet. She felt silly saying it, like some old disheveled detective in a television movie, but she had to do it. "You can call me anytime if you think there's something I should know."

"I told you to go, Miss Miller." A tic jumped below Deirdre Mahoney's left eye as she waited for Claudia to cross the threshold onto the fieldstone step. The door slammed, rattling the air, echoing like a gunshot down the quiet street.

Seventeen

Someone was in her kitchen.

Claudia jumped up from the sofa, grabbed a marble gargoyle from the shelf, and shouted a war cry as she groped for the light switch.

"Whoa, don't shoot. You looked so tired before, I kind of figured you might be out. Sleeping, I mean. That kind of out. So I used my key to deliver these. Dead flowers aren't much of a gift, you know."

Bert stood at the kitchen sink, a bouquet wrapped in silver and white florist's paper in one hand and her fluted glass vase in the other. She must have been in worse shape than she thought: in all the years they'd known each other, he'd brought her flowers twice, once to celebrate her divorce from Ted Stavros, and then four years later, just six months ago, for her thirty-ninth birthday.

"Have to protect the turf," she muttered as she set the statue on the table. "Sorry. I heard this noise and I figured some madman was out to rob me blind."

Or do me harm. The possibility had always felt so remote, until the night Tommy phoned. *Call your sister.* Everything was different since she'd heard those words.

Bert stuck another green stalk under the stream of running water, made a diagonal slice, set it in the vase. "Maybe you should take some time off, Claude. Isn't Irina going to Miami or something? You could tag along, hang out in the sun for a few days. It would do you good."

She wasn't going to be lulled by Bert's soft voice and lovely flowers, although he was arranging the tulips and freesias into a spare, deliberate study in white and pink.

"I have work to do. That's very pretty."

"*Gracias*. Now read the note that came with them when I found them on the lobby table."

She reached for the small card he handed her, jumped when the phone rang. Claudia set the card on the counter and snatched the receiver from the cradle.

Nora's voice trembled with alarm. "I started to tell Tommy about your Taconic Hills proposal," she reported, "but he never let me finish. He grabbed his coat and said he couldn't stand being cooped up and he was going out to hear some poetry. That was hours ago. I'm worried. I do think it's best to take him to Ted's. The sooner, the better. But I don't know where he is."

"I'll find him." This time, she prayed, we won't need the ambulance crew. She fingered the edge of the florist's card. *Nine o'clock Saturday*, it said. *I count the hours.* "I'll bring him to your house and we can work out the details."

Claudia bent to find the shoes she'd kicked off when she'd plopped onto the sofa.

"Secret admirer?" Bert's shoulder touched hers as he turned the card over, turned it back. "Who? Tell, Claude."

"A friend of Irina's. I have to find Tommy." She yanked her jacket from the closet, searched the counter for her keys.

"That guy with the curly hair I saw her with last week? If you ask me, he looks like a hit man for the Russian Mafia. I'll come with you."

"I better go alone. Tommy's pretty weird these days about other people knowing his business." She pulled on her gloves. "Mikhail Chernin. That's the guy's name. He wants to talk business or something."

Bert grinned. "I think it's probably more *or something*."

Claudia pulled the crumpled newspaper from her pocket and scanned the entertainment listing. A chill wind knifed at her exposed skin; wherever he was, Tommy was probably dressed for May, not this bone-chilling cold. She pushed open the storefront door, stepped into a warm, book-lined cave of a room, heard a droning, amplified voice.

"I walk not run to the edge of life and hope, another four-letter word, another disappointment, another blossom in the lonely desert, that my time will come before it's up."

The woman at the microphone, a round-faced, gray-haired cherub in a faded denim skirt and thermal undershirt, bowed her head, waited for the perfunctory applause to die, and then stepped down. The air in the Biblios Café was hot and dry, the scent of cigarettes and coffee heavy in the air.

"That's three dollars."

Claudia looked over at a woman with a roll of tickets in her hand and a beatific smile on her face.

"If you're planning to stay for the poetry, there's a three-dollar admission charge," the woman repeated.

"I'm just looking for someone. Give me a minute."

After an appraising glance the woman waved her inside. Claudia took a hesitant step into the room, her gaze pausing at each table only long enough to determine that Tommy wasn't there. A stocky man with a knitted cap pulled down close to his eyebrows looked up at her with apparent interest; she checked his open collar, exhaled with relief when she saw the glint of gold at his neck was a large, plain cross.

She was about to leave and look for a cab to take her to the East Village when the door opened and Tommy stepped inside.

He was shivering, his head bent so that he looked like a child playing *El Toro* in a bullfight game. He flapped his arms against his sides as though that might help him warm up. When he saw her, he groaned. "I have a life, you know. All by myself, I have a life I like, one I'm working at. One I would like to keep to myself, if you don't mind."

"And that life may not last as long as it should unless you get a little smarter, Tommy. Sit down. We have to talk." She started to move toward an empty table in the middle of the room, but he grabbed her arm.

"Not here. Come out with me. Tell me while we walk." He was

already half out the door; she had little choice but to follow him into the crisp night. In contrast to the smoky café, the cold actually felt good, clean, despite the trash blown by the wind into the middle of the street.

"I know, I know. My mother's frantic, so you were headed for Alphabet City, no less, hoping I'd let myself be taken prisoner by your rules instead of by the man with the gold lightning bolt. Well, in case you didn't know, I started taking lithium today. The tests came back and, surprise, surprise, I'm up or down, high or low, hot or cold, manic or depressed. I'm about to experience a chemically induced cure, so I wanted to say good-bye to my old life." He stuffed his hands in his blazer pockets as he stepped off the curb in the middle of the block, oblivious to the panel truck barreling down the street.

She grabbed the back of his jacket just in time, and stood shaking with anger as the truck rumbled by. Nora hadn't said a word, not a single damn word about hearing from the doctor, about Tommy's starting treatment.

"You're not going to lose the poetry, Tommy. Only the pain. See that place down the block?" She pointed to the corner, to the psychedelic sixties mural, complete with half a Volkswagen bus that looked as though it had just rammed into the wall above the door of the Burrito Bar. "We're going inside. We're going to sit down where it's warm. You're going to have something nonalcoholic to drink, and I'm going to have a single malt Scotch, neat with a soda back. You're going to listen while I tell you why I came out in this freezing night to find you.'

Tommy grimaced. "Big Sister is watching you. Watching *me.*"

But he followed her into the restaurant and slid into a booth facing the door, ordered a Coke, sat in stony silence, head bent so the injured side of his face was hidden. He pleated his paper napkin diligently. His eyes, when they met hers, narrowed. "I'm sorry. I guess I've been a bit of a jerk."

"No, I'd say you've been a *big* jerk. Now, stop apologizing and start paying attention. This guy with the lightning bolt . . . Have you seen him again?" *Say no,* she urged silently.

"How could I see him? I don't go anywhere but school." A frustrated sigh escaped in a hiss. "I'm thinking of taking a camera and a tape recorder wherever I go. You know, something like this, it can be a new art form, see what I mean? Here's Tom Miller, folks, being scared witless by the man wearing the lightning bolt around his neck. Watch Tom turn himself inside out to show how brave he is. Watch the man keep to the shadows, watch him stick like dog shit to a rubber-soled shoe. Watch—"

"Have you seen him? This is important." She leaned across the small glass-topped table. "If you can look at me and not get what I'm saying, Tommy, we have a real problem here."

His eyes filled and he wiped at his tears before they could spill over. "I get it. Okay?"

She nodded. "Good. So, has he been around?"

"So, everyone needs darkness. We seek out the shadows so the light is brighter, so the calm, windless day can carry the birdsong on unseen currents, so the sun, the river of light and life flowing from a burning star, can—"

"Is that a yes or a no? I feel like I need Cliff Notes to have a simple goddamn conversation with you." She pushed her glass away, and when she looked at her brother, he was grinning.

"He gives me something to hold onto. He's real, Claude, not like all this bullshit stuff about school uniforms and extracurricular activities. Yeah, I think I saw him from my window, standing at the corner and pretending to wait for the light to change. He wasn't there when I came out, though. I have to test him, you get it? If he can find me all the places I go, he's real."

Behind his eyes, a flicker of heat burned brighter than his curiosity, hotter than the challenge of the chase. Tommy was excited by his own fear. Trying to talk him out of it would only strengthen that stubborn resolve to hold on to what was uniquely his, his shadow-buddy.

He fiddled with his glass. "So, how do you tell the good guys from the bad guys?"

"That, my friend, is a life's work," she said. "The cop who arranged for your bodyguard did it as a personal favor, but he says his hands are tied, that he can't do anything else. Even unofficially."

Tommy nodded and winked and stirred the soda with a straw. "Come on—favors and stuff, you can make anything happen.

Wheeling and dealing. I've been watching all my life, Claudia. You're good at that. Almost as good as Dad."

"From you, I'll take that as a compliment. Except, this time, I really can't. Listen," she said, "there's been another murder. Which means the cops are working hard to get this cleared up. That'll be soon, I hope, but I can't promise, Tom. Nora and I think you should go away until they catch this creep."

He frowned as he stacked sugar packets. "What about school?" he asked quietly.

"We'll arrange for you to get assignments and do them on your own. Maybe some kind of computer hook-up, I don't know, or maybe you'll have to do a session of summer school. But that's better than being dead."

Tommy's eyes glistened. "Where?" he asked in a voice so small she could barely hear it.

"Ted's weekend place in Taconic Hills."

The smile he offered her was sardonic. "This is the ex-husband Ted, who's about half an inch taller than you, right? The one who weighs maybe a hundred and fifty pounds and is losing his hair. This is the Ted who's going to protect me from the big bad evil out there?"

"What's going to protect you is that you'll be where the lunatic can't find you. If it makes you feel any better, Ted has a rifle and he knows how to use it. So, what do you think?"

"What does my mother think?" He fidgeted in the seat, toyed with his straw.

"Nora's willing to take Sheba and a suitcase and some books and go along with you. She's convinced this is a pretty good solution."

Tommy rose so violently that his chair flipped over with a noisy crash. "No way. No. I won't do it." He tried to unhook his jacket from the tangle it had made in the legs of the fallen chair.

Claudia sat back and watched his struggle, restrained the impulse to leap up to help him. "What just happened, Tommy? Will you tell me that?"

"Look, I love my mother. But not to spend twenty-four hours a day, seven days a week with. Not to have her on my case all the time. Not to be trying to get inside my head and find out what makes Tommy run. I'll go, Claudia. But only if she doesn't."

103

Eighteen

A battered black bicycle pulled up at the curb, the rider balancing an insulated pizza carrier on the wire basket as he maneuvered between two cars. He swung one leg to the ground, head down and face hidden beneath the rim of a Mets cap, then pushed the bike onto the sidewalk. He chained it to the NO PARKING sign, his gaze darting from the trio of women and their tiny, scampering dogs to the taxi that idled halfway to the corner of First Avenue.

"He's here." Claudia turned away from the living room window as Nora looked at her son, a fleeting, solemn longing shadowing her face.

"You promised, Mother. You said that once you made your decision you wouldn't give me any grief about it. I'll be all right, I swear. You'll come up on the weekend, unless they catch this jerk before then." Tommy wrapped his arms around Nora and pressed his cheek against her hair, his too-big hands covering half her back.

Juggling the pizza and a large paper bag, the rider yanked at the frayed waistband of his Giants jacket, pulled a receipt from the pocket, checked the house number, difficult to see because the light above the entrance was unlit. He headed for the steps confidently, pressed the bell, stepped into the dark hallway when the door was opened.

"You think it was easy to keep my face covered?" Gary Bruno set the paper bag and the pizza case on the floor and stripped off the jacket and the cap, tossing them onto the straight-backed chair and nearly knocking over a gilt-edged porcelain plate and its ivory stand that occupied the center of the elaborate inlaid tea table. "Claudia says it's this big secret, but, hey, good luck wherever you're headed."

"Out of town, that's where." Tommy winked, pulled on the jacket Bruno handed him.

For a second, Claudia thought she read on Nora's face enough doubt to call off the ruse, but Tommy jammed the Mets cap on his head and looked in the mirror appraisingly. "Six more months, we couldn't do this. I'm gonna be at least two inches taller by then. See you in five minutes, Claude." He offered a thumbs-up, kissed Nora's forehead, and then dashed to the doorway.

"Wait!" Pale and tense, Nora shook her head, held the insulated case out to her son. "You forgot this."

Grinning, Tommy took the pizza case and let himself out.

"Shit, did I give him the key to the bicycle lock?" Gary dug in the pockets of his jeans and his shirt, muttering, until they saw Tommy extract a key from the jacket pocket, unlock the bike and toss the chain into the basket, then pedal calmly and deliberately toward Second Avenue.

Nora let out her breath. "I didn't see anyone follow him. I hate this, all of it."

According to her watch, one minute had passed since Tommy walked out the door. Claudia would wait another minute, then retrieve her car from the parking garage on 68th Street. Fifteen minutes after that, a nylon backpack slung over his shoulder and wearing Tommy's parka with the hood pulled up, Gary would walk downtown and buy a ticket to whatever was playing at the Third Avenue movie theater. In a men's room stall, he would exchange the parka for his own ski jacket, which had been stuffed into the backpack. Then he'd return to his apartment.

"You'll let me know when you get there. And remind Tommy I want him to call me every morning, nine o'clock." Nora looked down at the shredded tissue in her hands. "This better work, Claudia. It had better work."

She'd never used the word before, in her thoughts or in conversation, but when she finally pulled her big white convertible onto the

Henry Hudson Parkway, Claudia Miller felt as though she'd been skulking.

Tommy slouched in the seat beside her, his baseball cap pulled down over his eyes, his sneaker laces sprawling like sinuous white worms on the dark floor of the car.

"Are we there yet?" Tommy grinned, sat up, and threw his cap onto the large carton crammed with books, CDs, clothes, hand weights that covered half the back seat. "On the road. I'm going to do it, right after I graduate. Buy a classic car like this one. Get up at four and hit the blue highways in the dark. Watch the sunrise colors glorying up the morning, then stop for breakfast with the truckers and drink coffee and listen to their stories."

If she could keep him safe, he'd have the chance to go for his dream.

And then, if everything fell into place, he'd have his own adventure. Hers had begun when she bought the 1966 Oldsmobile in the late seventies. The red leather seats and the ragtop were in good shape, and the car made her feel like she might meet up with James Dean at the next gas station. Instead, she'd met Bert, for which she was grateful.

The road ahead was dark, no other midweek travelers on their own late-hour journeys. Good—no cars following them. But that didn't mean she could stop checking mirrors, could forget to watch for headlights approaching from feeder roads and on-ramps.

Tommy would *not* be the next victim. Unless Nora let slip to the wrong person where he was. Unless her brother couldn't stand the isolation and called one of his friends, who spread the word that Tommy Miller was skipping school and hanging out with some product designer in a tiny little town no one had ever heard of. Unless, unless . . .

The operative word must be *until.* Until the murderer was caught.

They celebrated the magic of trains and cars and boats, and never mentioned why they were speeding north up the Taconic State Parkway in a darkness so complete she wondered where the earth ended and the sky began.

Eyes burning, Claudia cut the engine and the lights and flexed her fingers when, at last, she pulled into Ted's driveway. The constant vigilance of the drive had exhausted her.

Something scurried into the bushes when she opened the car door. The rustling stopped, and silence poured like a ribbon of silver over all the low places she knew were out there, the fields and lanes, and tree-bordered streams she couldn't see. The night crackled with cold, the air so clean she wished for a full moon to light up the white rime slicking the tufts of dried weeds across the road.

"Either this is heaven or it's a scene from some horror movie, I can't decide which." Tommy sounded awestruck.

"Not everything has only two dramatic possibilities. It's just a weekend cottage on a country road, and we're going inside so I can get some sleep before I drive home. Ted said you should take the bed in the back room. I'll be on the sofa."

Tommy bent to grab his bag, instead stood empty-handed beside the car. "You don't have to, you know, not *be* with him because of me."

She suppressed her laugh. "Sorry to disappoint you. These days, Ted and I are friends." She added under her breath, "Just barely."

They stepped into the warmth of the cottage, pleasant and welcoming compared to the blasts of dry heat that greeted visitors to New York City apartments.

"Back here," she whispered as she led him past a player piano and down the center hall to the room off the kitchen. She flipped on the light, smiled when she saw a note resting against the wool blanket.

first one up turn on the coffee maker.
sleep well.
t.

The essentials, and a welcome she appreciated. She set Tommy's suitcase on the braided rug, pointed to the towels Ted had left on the Morris chair and then to the door across the hall. "Bathroom. Ted only flushes when it's necessary, to save water and to protect the septic system. He'll tell you the rest of his rules tomorrow.

Today, I guess it really is. I have to close these tired eyes and lay this weary body down, kiddo. See you in the morning.

When she leaned over to kiss Tommy's cheek, she was startled when he grabbed her, held her in a trembling hug, whispered, "Thanks, Claude. I know I've made things hard for you and for my mother. Maybe the drugs will change me, maybe they won't. I hope the poetry *does* survive. Anyway, thanks."

Embarrassed, she restrained herself from putting a finger to his mouth to stop his speech. He needed to say those things; maybe someday she'd learn how to be gracious about hearing them. She patted his back, then tiptoed to the dark living room, where she stripped down to a T-shirt and panties and crawled into the sleeping bag Ted had left for her. The sofa was comfortable and she was exhausted, but she twisted and flailed, finally sat up and watched the first streaks of pink, pale and washed with gold, spread on the horizon.

So close she could touch him if a wall weren't separating them, Ted Stavros slept. He was supposed to be the love of her life.

That had been his view of things. She'd been thirty-two when they met, still contemptuous of the deals people expected her to make. Ted was to be her proof that life could be lived without compromise. He was her companion in stubbornness, her accomplice in rebellion. And the most varied and considerate lover she'd ever known.

He was also, like the other men she was drawn to, pathologically incapable of keeping his opinions to himself, which meant he had something to say about everything from how she nailed a stud to a header to the way she set a dinner table to the music she chose when they were making love.

Determined to break the pattern with irrevocable finality, she'd sent him away.

Or was his leaving his own choice?

The distinction was rhetorical. Even if she were given the chance to play it again from the top, the grand finale would surely be the same, a quietly discordant fade that would leave her wondering when the music had actually stopped.

The trees along the roadside began to acquire definition, thick trunks boled and twisted with knots she hadn't been able to see in the dark. A tractor lumbered by, and in its headlights she noticed that patches of snow lingered in the low hollows and in the north-facing crotches of the tree limbs.

"If you leave the bottom of the sleeping bag unzipped, your feet won't get so hot." Ted stood in the doorway, a red-checked flannel shirt hanging open over his sweatpants. In the early morning light, his eyes looked steady and watchful.

He seemed solid and rooted, like something that simply belonged to the earth instead of having to try so damn hard to figure out its place. *Like a tree,* she thought when he came closer.

"You know what they say about hot feet." She smiled, stretched her legs. "I'm really grateful, Ted. We'll all sleep better now that Tommy's out of the city."

Ted sat on the sofa beside her, his scent unfamiliar but comforting, a mix of wood smoke and soap. "I'm glad you said that, Claudia. That's why I'm doing this, because I hope it will bring you a little peace of mind."

"You know what? That's about the best thing you could have told me. I'm sorry I've been out of touch." She folded the sleeping bag, eyed the pile of clothing on the floor and realized she was practically naked. She tugged on her sweater, frowned because she couldn't find her jeans.

"Here," Ted said as he moved the sleeping bag aside and handed her the jeans. "I'm going to bring in some wood and get the fire going. Before you leave, I have to say my little speech again. It's my work space I'm concerned about. Sometimes I don't come out of that studio until nine or ten at night. I turn off the telephone, ignore dogs and horns and everything short of flames licking at my toes. If Tommy can stand it here alone while I'm working, we'll be fine."

"And if he can't?"

"If he can't, which really means if he won't, you'll have to make other arrangements." He shrugged and grabbed the log carrier from beside the wood stove.

A blast of cold air rushed into the room when he opened the door to the shed where the winter's wood supply lay stacked and dry. Claudia shivered before she tied her boots and rose to help with the wood chore.

Nineteen

"You miss me?"

Teresa.

Detective Mitch Russo laughed so hard into the phone, he nearly fell out of the chair. "You bet your buns, lady. What's it like out there in the wilds of Brooklyn without me? You getting any action lately?"

"Not since you transferred to Manhattan. I'm downstairs, Mitch. You have a couple of minutes, maybe we could have coffee or something."

"Absolutely. I'll be right down."

The sky outside his barred window had gone purple while he wasn't looking, but a lot had passed his notice since he caught the Mummy case. He took a last look at the list on his desk, grabbed his coat from the rack, and headed downstairs, glad for the break. As she'd done so many times in the past, his former partner was about to rescue him.

He straightened his tie, rounded the corner, smiled with pleasure.

God, she looked good, Teresa Gallagher with her warm grin and her wild hair and her smart, miss-nothing eyes. Under the watchful gaze of a trio of Vice cops, Russo hugged her and led her to the street, his arm hooked through hers, her familiar scent making its way from his nose to his brain.

"You really like it better here than in Brooklyn?" She looked a little pale to him, but as soon as they'd gone half a block, two bright spots of color bloomed amid her freckles.

If he tried, he could picture her as a kid with her nose pressed against the window of some store where they sold . . . what? Not candy, not dolls. Teresa Gallagher made a point of letting him know once that she never fell for any of that girly stuff when she was a kid.

"Just different. My new partner's a grizzled old coot who thinks Joey Gallo was a prince and Frank Sinatra should be president. It's okay, a little slow compared to the 'hood. What I miss is the old-timers on the street, the shopkeepers and the grandmas who sweep their stoops. Hey, listen to me getting sentimental." He pushed open the coffee shop door, led her to a booth in the back. "So you got my message, right? About Therma-Care? No listing in the phone book, but the doorman said some repair guy wearing Therma-Care coveralls came in with a work order. Said the company was in Brooklyn, in Park Slope."

"Doesn't mean a thing to me. I checked it out, asked around, but nobody ever heard of them. Anything else I can do?"

"No, it's just, I feel like I'm thrashing around here. Forensics turned up zilch so far. The dead guy was this landlord type who was selling off his property, one building at a time. His wife says he wanted to do things with the money before he died instead of letting the state take half of it in inheritance tax."

"Something you and I stay awake nights worrying about, right? How's Cissie? The kids?" Teresa draped her coat over the back of her chair and sat, green eyes sparkling.

"Great. Everyone's great. Cissie's studying like mad for her broker's license. She's talking about working out of the house for a year or two until she builds up a customer base. She can't sit still, that woman."

"Send her my love, okay? And tell her that as soon as I move, you two have to make the trip to my new place."

"Move? Trip?" They hadn't been partners for a year, but the thought of Teresa Gallagher going far away made Russo feel as though a piece would be missing from his life. "What's up, Doc?"

Pencil in hand, the waitress, a cheerful brunette whose crackling dark eyes reminded him of his Aunt Guilia handed them menus.

Teresa shook her head, ordered coffee and wheat toast, waited while he wrestled down his desire for the key lime pie and finally ordered black coffee.

"So?" He cocked his head, cupped a hand over his ear. "I didn't hear an answer yet."

The smile she'd been trying to suppress broke into a grin. She lifted her hand, placed it on the table, fingers spread. A gold ring with a modest, square-cut sapphire in the center shone on the fourth finger of her left hand.

"I want you to give me away."

The breath caught in his throat until he felt Teresa Gallagher's hand close over his. His heart bumped noisily in his chest. "Oh, wow," Russo said, and then he laughed and his amazement turned to pride and pleasure. "This is terrific. Terrific. Who? When? Tell me."

"His name is Jay Goldstein. He sat next to me at that seminar I went to last year, the one on using the Internet for homicide investigations. When?" She smiled and shrugged. "Maybe in the fall, we think. It depends on how soon this big case he's been working on comes to trial. The Coit Tower case, you've heard of it, right?"

Coit Tower. *San Francisco.* Was Teresa Gallagher going all the way to California? The woman who had season tickets for the Knicks, who endured standing room at the Met whenever Jessye Norman sang, who knew every hole-in-the-wall place in the city of New York that served authentic egg creams, whose idea of a luxury cruise was an evening sail on the Hudson on the *Clearwater* when Ian, her boatwright friend, could get her aboard—this woman thought she could be happy three thousand miles away?

"Aren't you going to say, 'That's wonderful, Teresa. I'm so happy for you, Teresa. I'd be honored to walk you down the aisle, Teresa?' You forgot how to talk, Mitch?" Her eyes twinkled with mischief. "Oh, wait, I probably should tell you—Jay's giving up a promotion to captain in the SFPD to start a doctorate program in philosophy at Fordham. He'll be teaching undergraduate classes. I found an apartment on Seventeenth Street, near Loehmann's. He can get the C train to the Bronx, and I can walk to Seventh Avenue and get the subway right down to the First Precinct. To which I am officially transferring tomorrow."

"Holy shit, that's *wonderful!*" He leaned across to hug her and almost knocked over the waitress, who grinned and stepped out of the way. "I'm not only happy for you, I'm busting with pride and I'm thrilled and I'm honored, I mean it, awed, to be asked to walk with you down the aisle. Of course I'll do it. I need to lose ten pounds to fit into my tux, but hey, there's time."

She reached over and broke off a corner of her toast and set it on the plate. "His father is upset that the only son won't be married by a rabbi, but Jay promised to break the glass anyway. All right, enough of this wedding stuff. I get a little nervous when I think about forever, so let's talk about something else. What about this case? Therma-Care sounds like a heating or air-conditioning company, right?"

Forever—at least Teresa Gallagher wasn't going into this marriage with the idea that it was something she could discard like last season's shoes.

"Yeah. The doorman swore the guy gets out of this van with the words 'Therma-Care' on the door, but no address. He's wearing coveralls and a jacket, has a baseball cap and sunglasses on. He's carrying a clipboard and a toolbox and he says something about having to do a maintenance check on the central air unit. Shows him some work order. Turns out nobody in the co-op management company ever saw it, nobody authorized it, nobody knows nuttin', as they say."

She nodded and sipped her coffee. "And the guy? What're his stats?"

"White guy, in his thirties, tall to medium height, light brown hair. Doorman says he never took off the dark glasses. Doorman also says maybe he's wrong about all of it because he was baby-sitting this little poodle for one of the tenants, you know? And the dog starts whining and yanking at the leash to get to the door, so the guy thinks he's gonna have to clean up some mess from the carpet and he's trying to get the dog to the curb, at least, before it loses it. So he tells the Therma-Care guy to sign in and he gets the poodle outside just in time for it go in the middle of the sidewalk." Russo grinned, shook his head. "Doorman had to go back and get newspaper and pick it up. He groused for twenty minutes to me about the dollar tip the biddy gave him. All of this to try to explain why he couldn't give me any more information."

Her spoon tapping against the saucer, Teresa Gallagher stared off into space. "Okay, so this Therma-Care guy comes in to Kurtz's building with a clipboard and a toolbox. Maybe he's your man, maybe not. No address on the van, phony work order, all that sounds promising. The other side of this thing is, why the mummy routine? What does that mean?"

"I have someone checking out Egyptology departments all over the city. Seems far-fetched, though. And it doesn't have anything to do with Murray Kurtz's life and his interests, not that I can see. Not yet. One thing you could tell, though. Whoever did all that wrapping was real patient, real careful."

Gallagher's eyes widened. "Not Egypt. That's not what it's about. If it was Egypt, he'd have done the guy in some kind of gauze like they used on the real mummies. Christ, that's easy enough to get ahold of, but he made a choice, right? He didn't use gauze. He used electrical tape."

Russo beamed. "Absolutely. I taught you well. *Electrical* tape. That's the key item. Good, Ms. Gallagher." He grinned. "You don't even have to change your monogrammed towels."

Teresa Gallagher frowned. "I'm keeping my name. I love Jay Goldstein and I plan to spend the rest of my life with him, but I think Teresa Goldstein sounds like the daughter of some confused hippie flower child."

"Electrical tape. Used at every construction site, in every renovation in this damn town. And Murray Kurtz bought and sold buildings, and fixed them up, presumably. I'm looking into that angle, too. Thanks for checking on Therma-Care. I owe you one, Teresa."

"Just make sure I don't trip over my own feet before I get to say 'I do.' You know how I hate to look stupid in front of a bunch of cops." She pushed her chair back and laid three dollars on the table. "You know, Mitch, I never thought marriage was a good idea. Not until I met you and Cissie. I've seen other people who made me think it was possible. But you and Cissie make it seem . . . like a blessing."

He rose and peered under the table, shook out the paper napkin and examined the table surface, pulled one of his pants pockets inside out. "Hey, lady," he said as he tapped Gallagher's shoulder, "you see my friend Teresa anywhere? Pretty lady with red hair, one of the toughest broads I ever met. You see her anywhere lately?"

Teresa Gallagher shook her head slowly. "You don't get off that easy, Russo. I'm trying to thank you here, okay?"

"Okay, okay. I gotta get back, Teresa. I have to see my man in the electricians' union. And work my way through the list of buildings Murray Kurtz owned, the supers, any workmen he might have had a dispute with. Really, thanks for talking the case out with me. Hey, when your guy gets to town you call me. Cissie's looking for an excuse to make up a batch of her mama's tagliatelle. You call me, okay?" Mitch Russo gave his former partner another hug and made his way to the front door.

Teresa Gallagher, getting married.

Russo said a prayer for her future happiness, which he hoped would include the desire to stay on the job.

Twenty

Laurette Lacroix had left two messages, asking when she should messenger over the Pastor report, apologizing for taking two full days to get the work done. Time, Claudia realized, had turned elastic. It was hard to believe that mere days, not weeks, not months, had passed since she first asked the investigator to check out Charlie Pastor.

If that's his name, she reminded herself sternly as she peered into the monitor at the messenger, hatless and red-faced, standing on the street and looking into the security camera's eye.

"I'll be right down," she said into the intercom, shrugging off his snarl of complaint at being left outside in the cold. "Sorry— building rule. No unaccompanied delivery people inside."

Warring feelings accompanied her as she rode the elevator down. Laurette Lacroix's report would be enlightening, yet Claudia found herself hoping that Charlie was just what he claimed: a lonely young man who talked too much and too fast when he wasn't sure of the rules.

She signed the receipt, then accepted a large manila envelope from the messenger. A momentary chill chased down her spine, a memory of the feel of the packet of photographs she'd taken from her mailbox days earlier. Taking a deep breath, she unwound the red string, drew the top page up as she rode the elevator back to her apartment.

Fifteen minutes later, with the help of Laurette Lacroix's report, she'd strung together little beads of facts that formed a necklace of deceit. "Shit," she muttered under her breath.

Charlie Pastor was a wisp of smoke, a cotton cloud, a mist.

Born in Memphis, July 4, twenty-seven years ago, to Elizabeth and Charles Pastor, the youngest of three children. Attended Memphis private schools. Father a businessman who eventually owned several shopping malls, mother active in the local Methodist church. A brother ten years older, a sister eight years his senior. Attended but didn't graduate from Rice University. Earned beer money in college by selling papers to fellow students on topics in English and American literature, arrested once on campus for possession of amphetamines, charges dropped, moved to Los Angeles at the end of his sophomore year.

Married a year ago to Analise Gladding Butler Chilton in Pasadena, California.

No mention of a divorce. No children, no legal separation.

Obtained a loan of thirty thousand dollars three years ago from a California bank to start a restaurant in Santa Monica called Diversity, with a partner named Miguelita Jacinto. Five months in arrears on the payments. Business apparently limping along.

A study of the ethnic cuisines of New York, wasn't that what he'd told her when they were sitting on that bench in the park? She shook her head. Charlie had his share of secrets, deviations from a straight-and-narrow that people observed more in theory than in practice. Far from grand, his deceptions were the petty stuff of an incomplete education, a faltering marriage, a comatose business. Charlie Pastor seemed perfectly capable of waking up one morning, seeing the baldly depressing truths of his life, saying, "This isn't working," and then heading to the Greyhound terminal and buying a ticket east to try again.

But murder? Wrapping an old man in electrical tape? Garroting a gangly, dreamy-eyed kid with Romex cable?

Eight hundred dollars in a Manhattan checking account. No other visible assets. No history of any personal IRS filings, in California, Texas, or New York, although Diversity had filed corporate returns for the past three years.

She smiled to herself. The cops might bust big-time racketeers on income tax evasion, but no one would prosecute Charlie Pastor, since nothing in the pages before her offered proof that he had any income to report.

No medical insurance, no life insurance, no disability insurance, no homeowner's insurance. A California driver's license, issued ten years earlier, a speeding ticket two years ago, various vehicle registrations, and, yes, auto insurance.

None of the history so carefully noted in the investigator's report had even a shred of a connection to Mercer Street, to Kevin Mahoney, to Murray Kurtz or Tommy Miller. None that she could see, she reminded herself.

She should let Bert know about this dead end. If she hurried, she might still catch him at work.

She pulled on her coat, tucked the envelope under her arm, and marched the two blocks to Duane Street, aware that she was more eager than she'd expected to prove to Bert that nothing sinister or even significant had turned up in Charlie Pastor's slender dossier.

Where building superintendents had tossed salt to melt the ice, patches of white covered the sidewalk like some hideous winter disease that required a protracted dose of spring rain and sun before the city would be healthy again. A clutch of Con Ed hard-hats, faces red and fists thrust into the pockets of their down vests, stopped their conversation and looked up as she passed. In their expressions she saw a trio of naughty boys caught with their hands in the Twinkies box. Claudia marched past them, the two-block walk from Harrison to Duane suddenly an endless trek past urban obstacles.

Even the elevator seemed to take forever to carry her upstairs. When the door finally slid open, a frigid breath blew in the window, swirling wood shavings and plaster dust on the floor in random eddies. A clanging, mindless noise blared from the radio—didn't anyone believe in melody anymore?—and she shouted over the din, waited to feel the vibrations of Bert's step as he crossed the floor.

Nothing. Only a screw gun spitting steel through sheetrock.

"Bert! It's me. I have to show you—" In the sudden silence, her words bounced back at her from the hard surfaces, tile and wood and metal, in the loft. From the rear of the eighty-foot-long space, a grinning Gary Bruno waved.

Claudia clutched the envelope and dropped her coat on the stacked two-by-fours as he approached.

If there had been a doorway in the rectangle of space, Gary, relaxed and confident, would have been leaning against it. "Sorry about the music. I just figured, no one's around. It's not bothering the neighbors and it helps me work faster."

"No one's around?" She peered into the loft, looking for Bert, seeing only a forest of studs waiting for sheetrock.

"He left about an hour ago to meet a friend. Something about catching an early movie. I said I'd clean up and get out of here when I was done. That's all right, isn't it, Boss Lady?"

"Claudia," she muttered. "Sure, fine. How's it going?"

Gary rolled his shoulders, rubbed his neck, stretched. His forearms glinted in the silver light. "Back wall's framed out and I hung one section of rock just to get a feel for those new screws, *Claudia*. What did you say this building used to be, a food warehouse, right?"

"Butter and cheese." The mottled colors that spread like a sprawling Rorschach over the brick walls, a faded cheddary yellow, a green like Tuscan olives, had always reminded her of TriBeCa's not-so-distant past as a wholesale food market.

"It's wild, you know? A hundred years ago—all that cheese, wheels of it covered in black wax, tubs of it sitting in the dark. This building, I mean, same bricks and all, carts and horses parked out front." His expression grew dreamy. "I like that, picturing those horses. The sound of their hooves on the cobblestones. Steam rising up from their flanks in winter, those powerful chests."

"The stink of all that cheese in the summer. Hauling it up four flights of stairs on your back." Gary's glossy picture of the past conveniently overlooked nonexistent plumbing, rampant disease, rigid social structures. Claudia preferred the present. "*Any*way," she said, riffling a mound of materials invoices, "you go ahead with what you were doing."

Lithe and easy, Gary sauntered to the rear of the loft, as though he wanted to impress her with the possibilities in steaming flanks and powerful chests. All she cared about was that he worked sober, took half-hour lunches, didn't make mistakes. She picked up two coffee-stained invoices; Bert was getting careless about the paper-work. She hated scolding him, wondered whether this past week and a half might have been harder on him than he let on.

"You run into that old musician guy with all those shopping bags when you came in?"

Startled, she looked up into Gary Bruno's scowling face.

A thin sheen of sweat glistened along the cords of his neck as he pressed the button to call the elevator. "Man, that guy gives me the creeps. I hate the sight of him, all boozed up like that. You never know what an old alky like that's gonna do."

"No need to worry about Ike." Something was making Bruno uncomfortable. She studied his awkward stance, the way his elbows pressed against his sides when he folded his arms across the knitted waistband of his leather jacket.

"Well, anyway, I'm outta here. See you in the A.M., Claudia." He winked and cocked a finger toward the open window, pecs stretching the leather as he lowered his arm. "Cold's gonna be a bitch tonight. Don't let the new pipes freeze and bust, right?"

And then she understood his discomfort: she couldn't let him leave. Not yet. She leaned against the two-by-fours, looked down at the stitching on her boots, then back up at Gary Bruno.

"Hey, Gary. Come here a minute." She ran her fingers through the fringe of hair on her forehead, licked her lips.

"What? You said I could leave, remember?" He jabbed at the call button again, weight shifting uneasily.

"Just for a minute, Gary. I have something to show you."

His nervous laugh gave way to head-shaking. "Nah. Tomorrow, Claudia. You can show me tomorrow. I really gotta get outta here." He glanced over his shoulder, looked imploringly at the indicator light.

"The guys on the third floor must be holding the elevator while they move their equipment out. Well, then." Claudia pushed away from the wood and ambled toward him. Languorous. Half-smiling. "I'll just have to come to you."

He paled and backed against the newly hung sheetrock with a thunk.

"Watch your jacket, Gary. Sheetrock's not taped yet, screws could tear that leather, you know." She was close enough to count every thick, curled lash above his coffee-colored eyes. Close enough to see the twitch at the corner of his full mouth.

He sidled toward the window. "Hey, what're you doing, Claudia?"

"I'm the boss lady, right, Gary? Humor me, okay?" His damp breath chilled the side of her face. Arms open, she pulled him to her.

"Claudia." He tried to break free, and she enjoyed the shock on his face as her breasts pressed against his chest.

"Oh, my, Gary. What's that in your pants? Or are you just happy to see me?" She slipped her hands under his jacket. The screw gun was pleasantly warm from the contact with his body. "Ah, Gary, you got it all wrong. That's the way a wiseguy carries his *piece*."

"Hey, you're the one got things wrong here. What are you doing?"

"Don't whine, Gary. It's unattractive." She set the screw gun on the boards and pulled four twenties from her pocket, counting them out deliberately, giving Gary time. Time to say he'd made a mistake, to apologize for trying to rip off Boss Lady. Time to offer some reasonable explanation, so she wouldn't really have to fire him, because replacing him would be a royal pain right now. Mute and glowering, he backed away stiffly.

"Don't come to work, Gary. Not tomorrow, not any day." She held out the money, still praying he'd explain himself.

His cheeks flamed, blood-red, a livid stain of fury and confusion. The elevator door slid open but Gary stood frozen. Finally, he forced out a breath, said in a strangled whisper, "Bert told me it was okay to borrow it. I promised a friend I'd put up some book-shelves this evening. I was gonna bring it back tomorrow and—"

"If Bert told you it was all right, why were you hiding the damn screw gun in your pants?"

The muscles along his jaw worked, tightening as he exhaled. "I don't have gloves with me," he said deliberately, "and it's fucking freezing out there so I wanted to be able to put my hands in my pockets."

Lord, she'd really blown it this time. "I . . . I'm sorry. I guess I'm wound a little tight these days. Please, take the gun. I really am sorry."

Gary Bruno wheeled and stepped into the elevator, the screw gun left behind on the boards. A tiny smile quirked the corner of his mouth for a second; then the mask was back in place. "Forget it. See you tomorrow?"

Claudia nodded just before the elevator door slid shut. When she heard it descend to street level, she watched him from the window, a small figure storming along the street forty feet below. If Gary Bruno had Bert's permission to borrow the equipment he should have just said so instead of setting them both up for this unnecessary confrontation. When he disappeared around the corner, she pushed the heavy window down and locked it. Wind whistled through a quarter-inch gap.

Better pick up some weatherstripping to keep the cold out.

Better yet, she should go home and stay out of trouble. If she kept pissing off the workers, they'd never get the job done.

"Claude?"

His voice was tentative, fragile, unlike the too-bright, breathless clamoring she'd heard when he'd called from the Brooklyn Bridge. Claudia Miller gripped the telephone in one hand, laid the chisel on the workbench with the other. "Tommy, what's up? Everything all right?"

Silence.

"Tommy?" She closed her eyes, preparing herself, imagining.

"Right, yeah, everything's just honky-dory. Isn't that what they say in those old black-and-white movies you watch all the time? Well, sure, hanging out with the trees and the bugs, it's just great. I'm having a great time counting how many different kinds of weeds grow between the back door and the studio where Ted holes up to get away from me."

His well-chosen words rang with deep sadness, not fear. "You've been taking your medicine, right, Tommy? Every day?" Damn. Where had *that* come from? Making accusations, getting all maternal were the last things Tommy needed from her now.

He laughed. "Yes ma'am, Mizz Miller. Sure enough, Mizz Miller. I wouldn't disturb the best-laid medical plans of my elders and wisers. I would hate to do anything that might make you feel you failed in your duty to keep Thomas Evan Miller on the road to

122

a right and proper adulthood. You can substitute prison for that last word, if you have half a mind to." The laugh turned into a cackle. "Or, simply, if you have half a mind. Which is all it takes to see what's going on here, the pharmaceutical alteration of one—"

"Tommy, stop. Listen, you're in a tough situation, but you have to deal with it." He should do something to work up a sweat. Run a mile—except that might expose him to Lord knew what dangers. Split wood for half an hour—but an ax was a lethal weapon that might be turned against him. "You ever do push-ups? Do fifty, eighty, whatever, as long as it's more than you've ever done in your life. And then when you're done try to tell yourself it's only for a little while longer. You can do that, can't you, Tommy?"

"You know what, Claude? I can. Sure I can. I don't want to, but I will. Here, Ted wants to talk to you."

She listened to Ted's cheery description of the new wood-stacking skills Tommy had acquired, offering his quiet reassurance that her brother was fine, safe.

Tommy had a protector, she told herself after she hung up, and she would go to Irina's party tomorrow night and not worry.

She was going to play dress-up, put on mascara and lipstick and a little black dress and laugh and drink champagne and celebrate and forget.

Twenty-one

At nine o'clock exactly, Claudia's buzzer sounded. She gathered her things, glanced in the mirror, and then rode the elevator to the ground floor. A hulking, stone-faced driver scurried in front of her and opened the rear door as Mikhail, coatless, his curls tamed tonight, offered his hand and rearranged his long legs so she could join him on the spacious leather seat of the car.

"You don't look like construction worker." The door slammed and the light went out but his eyes lingered in her memory, powerful enough, she was sure, to follow the shifting shape of her thoughts and the irregular contours of her feelings. "That's what I love about American women, this changing from one thing to another with such ease. You would like a glass of champagne while we ride?"

After the brandy debacle with Bert last week, a little restraint wouldn't be a bad idea. "Later. What I'd really love is club soda, if you have it. For the moment, I'd like to keep my champagne and my business separate."

The car swerved as it pulled away from the curb; her shoulder bumped against Mikhail's. He pulled away from the contact, the complete gentleman.

"In Ukraine, the business comes after the drinking." He poured water from a sky-blue bottle into two crystal glasses and handed one to her. "In Ukraine, everything comes after the drinking. But, all right, I'm in Rome so I'll play Romans. Business. So tell me—how did you learn construction? In the old Soviet Union, we have

124

women driving tractors, operating bulldozers, making buildings. But in Manhattan?"

"I got lucky. And then I worked smart." She sipped the water. Through the smoked window glass, the lights of oncoming cars became bright smudges as they drove onto the Brooklyn Bridge. "When I was eighteen, the idea of wearing a suit to an office and playing lawyer every day like my father did sounded like a life sentence to hell. I quit college and ended up in Albany. Got a job waiting tables at a place called the Gemini Jazz Cafe. Except I wasn't very good at being nice on demand, so my friend Bert hired me to do some framing. There were two other women on the job. I'm not such a pioneer."

"But you learned fast. How to hammer a nail. How to make the permits and the papers. This Bert, he was the mad affair of your youth?"

Bert would laugh at the thought.

"No, we've always been friends. We still work together. I get three or four big jobs a year and try to put him on. He works until he has enough money to go off traveling for a few months and then he comes back and I'm glad to have him around."

"You're the big boss, yes? You decide what job to take."

"I decide." Overhead metal bridge struts flicked by like a hypnotist's swinging watch. "I don't lowball, and I *do* bring in my jobs on time and on budget. I've exceeded my estimate only twice in the past nine years. I can help you create the best video rental store in the city."

"You do know someplace, yes?" Mikhail's broad forehead creased. "I don't trust this."

She bristled. "Trust? What don't you trust?"

"Talking business without champagne. I don't trust this." He produced a bottle and two graceful champagne flutes, tore open the gold foil and untwisted the wire from around the cork. The pop, properly festive, startled her into a sudden smile. "To many good deals we make together."

She was struck again by the intensity of his gaze, by the heat that drew her into a space only large enough for two. Wordlessly, she took her glass, raised it to his, and then touched it to her lips without drinking as the yeasty aroma spread pleasantly through the car.

"A video store." He nodded. "You know what else TriBeCa needs? A bookstore. There are good ones on Chambers, for business and for mysteries. But not a great one that sells everything. Or a cheese shop. Or a fancy kitchen gadget store. Someday . . ." Something in his tone had lightened, and she was reminded of how Tommy sounded when he talked about poetry. He downed his champagne and poured another stream of golden bubbles. "I want to buy a building, to not worry about the owner deciding he doesn't like the color paint I put on the walls. To not worry if I get enough heat or fixing the leaks or whatever. Especially, to not worry about throwing rent money away when I could be watching my property grow in value."

She toyed with the stem of the glass, twisting it in her fingers, part of the familiar ritual of celebrations and seductions, the champagne occasions in her life. "Spoken like a born capitalist."

"Ah, a *poor* capitalist. Your banks don't trust me yet. I don't have enough to buy building *and* start business *and* send money home."

She quirked an eyebrow. "Home to your wife in the Ukraine?"

His laugh was hearty and immediate. "Home to my father. He's eighty-one, too stubborn to let me bring him here so he can be comfortable, too smart not to take the money so he can get the things that make his life easier in Kiev. My *ex*-wife lives in *Brooklyn*. She's so American she needed a divorce two years ago."

She released her held breath softly, surprised herself by telling him about her six-month marriage to Ted Stavros. They drove past the attached single-family houses and six-story apartment complexes of Brooklyn, finally pulling up in front of a cinderblock building set amid low storefronts. A fur-hatted doorman guarded an ornate doorway under a canopy emblazoned with the name *Rasputin*.

"We talk business another time. Now we celebrate." Mikhail reached across the seat and hooked the clasp at the throat of her cape. Warm fingers brushed her skin. "We enjoy Irina's birthday and toast to her health."

Like a George Raft movie.

Damn, if that wasn't what it felt like.

Glitter and vodka.

Booming laughter and sad balalaikas and bad food carried on metal trays by phony Cossacks and rivers and rivers of vodka downed by stocky men in dark suits and women with hair the color of fresh egg yolks. Irina's party was wrapped in a haze of cigarette smoke drifting above clinking goblets and candles that flickered in hobnail glasses on white-draped tables.

They tried to talk property values and pedestrian flow theory, but the music and the merriment were too loud. Claudia was relieved when Mikhail excused himself to huddle with two burly men who looked like they needed smiling lessons. Yaffa flitted by in a red and black bodysuit, then drifted away into the crush of corporate types and EuroPunk jeans-and-leather beauties.

A stoop-shouldered man approached her table, his features rising from the dim pool of her memory. He pushed his way across the dance floor toward her; she didn't remember his name, but the face was memorable. Dark eyes set close together. A jaw with a correctable underbite. Ringlets Bert used to swear were permed.

"You're the floor guy, right?" she said in answer to his outstretched hand. He stood in front of her, fiddling with his sequined bow tie. "Now I remember: Al Candelaria. We worked together a couple of times."

"Except, for business purposes I'm Alan Carter now. You know how it is for photographers on the Coast. Yeah, we did work together. Until I messed up on the Broome Street job."

Messed up: Candelaria had gouged a fourteen-hundred-dollar groove in a new wood floor when he dragged a screw for five feet with his sander. He'd paid for it by working overtime. "You're living in Los Angeles?"

With a red toothpick topped with cellophane curls, he fished for the olive that lay at the bottom of his glass. "I just got into town to do some publicity stills for Spielberg."

Her glass, still full of champagne, sat on the table. "Listen, Al, you might think this is strange, what I'm about to say. There've been three murders in the past two months."

His gaze was steady as she went through the details. By the time she came to the Montclair fire, she had his full attention. "So the way I see it," she concluded, "someone's after the families of the

Mercer Street work crew. I really need to warn Ann Magursky, but she must have gotten married and changed her name. I was thinking—she used to hang out with John Bridgeman. Maybe he knows—?"

"John Bridgeman's dead." Candelaria's cocked eyebrow made a sharp vee. "Fell off a scaffolding in D.C. Drunk as a skunk and trying to sit in Abe Lincoln's lap when the guys who were cleaning the monument took a lunch break. What was it, ninety-two? Ninety-three maybe, I don't remember. This is weird, Claudia, really fucking incredibly weird. I might be able to find Ann. I'll let you know." He was still shaking his head as he disappeared into the crowd.

"You're Irina's agent?" A woman popped a cracker into her mouth and perched on an empty chair. In the dim light, her face looked like damp clay supported by the armature of perfectly curving bones.

"No, not her agent. Just a friend."

"You should try the caviar. It's not bad. For America." The blonde licked an invisible fish egg from the corner of her mouth. "A little salty, maybe. And maybe a little old. But not bad, really."

Before she could reply to the woman's dubious recommendation, Mikhail Chernin appeared beside her, smiling as he held out a hand.

"This is the only dance I do. Please."

The music was a slow fox-trot, something Johnny Mathis might have recorded forty years earlier. Claudia rose and followed as Mikhail worked his way through the crowd, nodding, shaking an occasional hand as though he were a politician stumping for votes. Everything about him suggested solidity, directness, gravity. When they reached the floor, the band segued into another ballad, and she stepped into his arms.

Whatever she imagined about Mikhail Chernin as a dancer, the reality was better. Everything fell away but the insistent rhythm and their bodies, his breath moving her hair.

When the music stopped, she noticed Irina, halfway across the room, waving energetically, nodding yes when Claudia pointed to herself. Glad for an excuse not to be pressed against Mikhail in the sheltering darkness, she took a step back and said, "I'm going to wish Irina a happy birthday."

He frowned, reached for a vodka from a passing waiter. "Of course. The band doesn't stop for hours, we will dance later."

By the time Claudia made her way through the crowd, Irina, her dress the color of little Italian plums and her hair cascading down her back in a golden sheet, was surrounded by three lovely boys in tight black pants and white flowing shirts. She turned from them, midsentence, and whispered to Claudia. "Come with me, yes? I have to get out of this noise." She pulled Claudia through the crowd to the ladies' room.

Inside, Irina sank onto the gold chaise, closed her eyes, sighed. "Oh, God, all this sentimental crap." She reached up and pressed two fingers to the bridge of her thin nose. "You know Alan Carter? You two had something very intense going on. Mikhail was watching."

Exasperated, Claudia examined her reflection, replaced the lipstick that had come off on her champagne glass. "So, now I can't talk to other men? I don't owe Mikhail any explanations."

"I heard something tonight. I don't want to interfere, but you should know this. About Mikhail. They say that when he was in Kiev, he—"

A trio of hefty, overdressed blondes crooning a minor-key lullaby, stumbled in and stood with arms around each others' shoulders in front of the gilt-framed mirror.

Irina rose, patted cold water on her throat, let it run full force against her wrists.

When he was in Kiev. They say.

He what?

Irina patted herself dry, hooked her arm through Claudia's, and led her back into the dark party room. "I get so dramatic sometimes. It's not such a big thing. Just be careful, yes? You're my friend and I thought he was, too, but I hear this talk tonight. About how Mikhail tricked his business partner out of a lot of money. Be careful."

And then Irina was gone, swept into the crowd. Dramatic, indeed. Claudia was about to go off in search of a glass of club soda when warm hands pressed lightly on her shoulders and a kiss brushed her hair. Mikhail Chernin leaned down and whispered, "You come with me now. Another dance. I've been waiting."

They wove their way past dancers too hypnotized by the music or too drunk to care when Mikhail jostled them aside. He drew her close, banishing thought, molding himself against her as they danced. This time, he was a little unsteady on his feet, the dance no longer a flowing, liquid glide along the polished floor.

His hand firm against her back, he guided her to a dark, deserted corner of the room, far away from the frenetic party chatter and the syncopated wriggling of the other dancers. When he pushed her against the table, her first thought was that he'd stumbled. But he pressed against her and said her name and she knew this was no accident. His breath was damp and boozy, the kiss he planted on her neck shockingly tender. One hand trailed up the back of her thigh, under her dress, warm fingertips tracing the top of her stocking.

"If you want me to stop I will," he whispered, his fingers working their way to the edge of her panties, alternatively insistent and teasing.

She allowed herself a second of pleasure, then yanked at the hem of her dress and twisted away from his embrace. "I don't want to do this here," she said when she could breathe.

She tried to lead him back into the crowd of swaying bodies, but he stopped at the edge of the dance floor, set his hands on her shoulders. "You can see my eyes, yes? I've been thinking about you since you walked into Yaffa's."

Suddenly, she wanted only to be in her own apartment, to visualize it in sufficient detail so that she would be transported there, so she could avoid having to fend off his hands and his lips and the lure of his body on the long, awkward ride home.

"I don't want to ruin your good time, Mikhail. Please, you stay and enjoy yourself. I'm tired and I have a lot to do tomorrow. I'll call a car service."

Without waiting for a response, she headed for the heavy doors leading to the entrance hall.

"Claudia! You can't leave until I open my presents!" Irina parted the crowd as she sailed toward her. She clasped Claudia's arm, leaned close and whispered, "Be careful, okay?"

Mikhail appeared out of the swarm that buzzed around Irina, kissed her on both cheeks, beamed. "Happy birthday, Irina. I'll talk to you soon. *Das vedanya.*"

When they reached the empty foyer, he muttered, "Silly goose." He laid the coat-check tickets and a five-dollar bill on the counter, watched the woman disappear among the furs and wools. "Don't call a car, Claudia. I'll take you home. You don't have to worry."

Mikhail was exactly right. Another time, a different state of mind, and she would have stopped him on the dance floor with a laugh and a promise. Instead, he was tainted by the dark prism of her suspicions.

With his accent and his dark, brooding air, he was an exotic variation on a very old theme in her life.

Sweet, beautiful, self-obsessed Ted Stavros, who paid for dinner the night their final divorce papers arrived; Amos Fischer, who stepped graciously out of her way when it became clear that their working relationship was healthier than their romantic connection: They retreated into good manners when rejected.

Mikhail Chernin, she trusted, would do the same.

Twenty-two

Claudia woke as the sun stole into her uncurtained bedroom. The smell of cigarette smoke lingered like a vile cloud that had permeated her hair and the dress she'd tossed onto a chair.

She had slept, but not long enough. Sunday, a day of rest, closed banks and hardware stores. For once she was glad for the enforced stillness. She showered, pulled on old gray corduroys, a black sweatshirt, and the moccasins she kept threatening to throw out, and then padded to the living room and made herself comfortable on the sofa.

She drank coffee and read a story in the *Times* about yet another deputy mayor caught in a web of feudal fiefdoms and reluctant allegiances. Catlike, a sliver of sunshine crept across the floor, and she imagined a silken creature curled in her lap, drowsing and letting her stroke its head. The impulse, she knew, was a wish for contact, for warmth.

Scenes from the tumult of Irina's party interrupted her reading, replaying in her mind like a movie clip. Irina's whispered warning. Mikhail's head tossed back in laughter, his graceful fingers wrapped around the stem of a champagne flute. He had no idea just how bad his timing really was.

What did it matter? The vanished opportunity of his video store business wasn't all that big a loss, and until this Mercer Street madness was settled and over, she didn't have the energy for a new, complicated relationship. Curling up in the big chair with the crossword puzzle in the amber light that spilled from the table lamp might smooth out the edges and jangles of this strange, unsettling week. Winter used to be a time of quiet decadence, the luxury of silence and early darkness, as though nature compelled her to lose herself in books, to stare out windows at the lights of the city, to lie on the sofa and drift. There had been no such indulgence since Tommy called.

She reached for the magazine section, uncapped her pen, hissed a sigh of frustration as the telephone rang.

Ted's shaky hello ripped her out of her daydream.

She waited for her heart to stop slamming against her chest before she said, "Start again. What's wrong?"

"Tommy's got a concussion," he said matter-of-factly.

Whatever she'd done to protect her brother, it hadn't been enough. She slumped into the chair. "What happened?"

"He's resting. It's all right, Claudia. It was a snowmobile accident."

"Snowmobile? When we were up there—"

"It snowed last night. An inch. Tommy sat by the window for hours counting the damn flakes."

"But he's never driven anything more complicated than a ten-speed Schwinn. You let him take the snowmobile out?"

"No, I did not let him take it." Ted paused; his voice seemed to drop an octave and a decibel. "I woke up really early and spent an hour in the studio. When I went back into the house to make coffee, I noticed Tommy's door was open. He wasn't in the house and there was no note on the refrigerator."

"No note on the refrigerator? That was the rule, right, that if he was going out for a walk he'd leave a note on the refrigerator."

Ted sighed. "That was your rule. He agreed to it to keep you quiet. He told me it made him feel like he was eight years old."

She should have seen it coming, a reminder that her brother still needed to test the boundaries and free himself from the constraints of childhood.

Unless Tommy had been lured outside . . . Someone might have tampered with the snowmobile. This was her best shot at keeping him safe? What she'd done was set him up so someone could deliberately create a hazard and— She slammed her hand against the arm of the chair. Speculation and guilty projections weren't going to keep her brother safe.

"Okay, all right, I'm sorry. What happened?"

"I found a note on the hall table, under a pine cone. Something about needing to face his own darkness. So I went to get my car to go look for him, and I noticed the Skidoo was missing from the garage."

Tommy, courting his fear on a blade-runnered vehicle—another predictable piece of business. "You didn't hear him start it up?"

"I told you, I was in the studio working. A truck could have driven through the door, I probably wouldn't have heard it. Anyway, I found the snowmobile overturned about fifty feet from the house. Tommy was out cold in a snowdrift. He must have hit a concealed rock and flipped the damn thing. I wasn't sure what to do, so I got Doc Everts to check him out and then I called Riley Hamm, to be on the safe side."

"Riley who?" The pounding in her head grew sharper.

"Riley Hamm, the sheriff. He stomped around in the snow, said it looked like a case of a boy who didn't know how to drive, that he didn't see anything suspicious. Listen, I'd like you to call Nora. I really can't deal with her maternal panic, not now."

Wonderful—now *she'd* have the honor of listening to Nora Miller alternately blaming and blubbering.

Immediately, Claudia repented her reaction. She had to assume Nora would be rational. She couldn't continue to treat Nora as though she were incapable of having a coherent thought.

"I'll phone her. Please, Ted, I know this is asking a lot, but please keep my brother in your direct line of sight until we figure out what to do."

Ted sighed. "I have to finish that design by tomorrow morning, Claudia. Best I can do is drag Tommy out to my studio, and try to keep him comfortable while I finish my work. I'll plug the phone in. You can call whenever. We'll be there. Together."

She hung up, dialed Nora's number, told her what happened.

Without a pause, Nora said, "I'm going up there to get Tommy. First, I'm going to call the sheriff and ask him to check Ted's every half hour. Then I have to call that doctor and make sure it's safe . . . make sure Tommy's up to a two-hour drive home. And then I have to prepare for bringing my son back to the city. That's where the real danger is."

"Prepare?" Claudia heard the challenge in her voice, struggled to change it to a simple inquiry. "How will you do that?"

"By convincing someone at my local precinct that my son is in danger. If the cops won't listen, I'll make sure the commissioner knows what morons they've been. I'm not going to ask for the moon. A beat officer to keep an eye on my house. One of those devices that would allow Tommy to call for help if there's a problem. And I want the arrangements in place by tomorrow morning. I'm going to make these calls now, Claudia, and then I'm leaving for Taconic Hills. We'll talk in the morning."

The performance was amazing, the lines delivered with unexpected bravura by her father's second wife.

"You sound completely in control."

"Oh, I learned how to hit my marks when I need to. I played Emily in *Our Town* in high school, did you know that?" Nora's voice was tremulous. "Fuck," she said softly, and then she hung up.

The low clouds looked as if they would linger all afternoon. Claudia reached for the lamp, then, angry at the momentary hesitation that stopped her hand midair, twisted the switch until an eruption of light flooded the room.

He wasn't going to win. She might not be able to stop thinking about Tommy and his snowmobile mishap and his concussion, but she wasn't going to start fearing every lamp or toaster or drill that was part of her ordinary life—she couldn't, wouldn't let that happen.

Where's your wife today? she wondered, remembering the young man sitting at the table with a roll of electrical tape in his hand. How's the bankruptcy procedure going?

No rule of decency decreed that Charlie Pastor should have offered up the details of his life. She was the one who had made it clear they had no future; he owed her no explanations.

If he hadn't waltzed into her life at precisely the wrong time, she might have enjoyed playing out their pas de deux to see where it might lead. On the surface, he was so very different from the men she'd been attracted to in the past, more playful, freer, and most

obvious, younger by decades. Even in her twenties, she found herself connecting with men who were what her friend Judy called
"previously road-tested."

She had behaved toward Charlie the only way she could. Still,
something about him made her wonder what she might have been
missing all these years. She glanced over at the little table beside
the elevator door, at the gray and white paperback book he'd left
in the shopping bag.

For days, she'd circled around the book, touching it, moving it,
wondering what it meant to its owner. *The Works of Robert Frost.* A
volume of poetry. She reached for it, caught the fleeting scent of
something spicy and warm as she opened the book.

Birches. She read the familiar lines and smiled at the notion of
catapulting into the heavens from a supple tree, no longer bound
by earthly cares, by what Frost called "considerations." But she
was, and she'd do well not to forget it. In fact, a little earthly con-
sideration of the materials list for the Chelsea townhouse would be
a good thing for her to get to right now.

Absently, she stretched her arm to set the book down, missed
the table, looked over, annoyed.

The book had fallen to the floor, splayed open. A piece of paper
the size of a folded dollar bill lay beside it on the carpet. Something that dropped from between the pages of the book? She bent
to pick it up, read the precise printing, was suddenly rigid with
shock.

MAGURSKY

BENEDETTI

MILLER

JEFFERSON

KURTZ

KOSSARIAN

All in a row. The crease, neat and sharp, like a knife blade. She
turned the paper over, then opened it, smoothing the ridge with
trembling fingers until she realized with a start that she might be
obliterating fingerprints, a watermark, some mysterious forensic
evidence that would nail Charlie Pastor to the legal system's wall.

Carefully, using only the tip of her fingernail so her flesh wouldn't touch the paper, she slid the note and the book into separate plastic bags.

Ann Magursky. Dave Benedetti. Claudia Miller. Laverne Jefferson. Jack Kurtz. Bert Kossarian. The Mercer Street crew, names printed in precise letters in blue ink on a piece of paper folded in half and then in half again, and stuffed in the pages of Charlie Pastor's book of poetry.

My God, how could she have missed the significance of the book? Kevin Mahoney had spouted Frost to her that day. One of the newspaper articles had quoted his wife as saying he kept a book of Robert Frost's poetry by the bed and read from it before he went to sleep every night.

Liar. Damn deceiving and conniving liar.

Charlie had sweet-talked his way into her life so he could get to Tommy.

She was going to stop him, the lying bastard, one way or another. Sarafino would have to be told about this list. Alone or with help, she would stop Charlie Pastor.

If the note wasn't something Bert had written and she'd picked it up without thinking and stuck it in the pages of that book.

Reeling with shock and indecision, she sat heavily in the upholstered club chair, hoping for comfort and clarity, finding none. She rose and paced the apartment, felt as though she might, for the first time in her life, explode with anger and with hurt. Thoughts roiled through her mind too quickly for her to sort things out. Help—she needed some real, objective help to figure out what this meant.

She flew down the spiral staircase to her office, ran the list through her fax machine and slipped the copy into her purse, then pulled the papers from the clasp envelope that lay on her desk, and dialed the number at the top. "Ms. Lacroix? This is Claudia Miller. I know it's Sunday, but I need to talk to you about that background check you did on Charles Pastor. It's urgent. Can you see me?"

After a brief pause, the soft voice replied, "Of course it's urgent. Can you be here in thirty minutes?"

Twenty-three

It wasn't Charlie.

Something about the tilt of his head was wrong, the chin buried too close to his neck, the hair too dark, too short, and too sculpted, as though he'd positioned it just so on his forehead. The man who had bumped into Claudia Miller on that icy street would never spend time perfecting an intentional curl.

Would he drive up to Taconic Hills and rig Ted's Skidoo and make sure Tommy took it for a drive?

The fellow in the blue peacoat pulled up his collar and squinted at the pears spilling in bright disarray on the stand, then chose one and strolled into the crowd as a red-faced woman who resembled a cinnamon bun yelled after him that they didn't give samples.

Claudia continued down Broadway, turned at West 84th Street, and then searched the numbers on the even side of West End Avenue. A sliver of sunshine lit the stone facets of a building down the block as she tugged her purple beret down over her ears and walked faster, the wind pushing her from behind, damp and gritty.

The buzzer next to the L. LACROIX nameplate squawked loudly when she pressed it. A woman came to the door, a slender silhouette who beckoned Claudia inside, led her down the dim, narrow hallway to a small reception area with a coat rack and three wicker chairs lined against a wall. On the opposite wall, bookshelves were stuffed with paperbacks, everything from *Coming of Age in Samoa* and *The Catcher in the Rye* to *Chaos Theory* and *Snow Falling on Cedars.*

The rest of the apartment, prewar and solid, conveyed the sense of someone having taken care to leave out the things that were unnecessary. Laurette Lacroix, however, looked as though she'd created herself according to different principles. Tall and thin, she wore a long, sheer skirt blooming with scarlet peonies over a black bodysuit. Instead of walking, the woman seemed to flow through the white and tan living room into a large, brightly lit office.

"Thanks for seeing me on such short notice." Claudia lowered herself to the chair beside the desk. "What did you mean when you said of course it was urgent that I wanted to see you about Charlie Pastor?"

"Everything's urgent. At least everything people come to me about." Laurette Lacroix tossed her braids and the beads at the ends made a pleasant, tinkling sound. "Someone canceled. I had free time."

Haiti, Claudia thought, or some other Caribbean island once ruled by France where the beaches were long ago overrun by American tourists.

"You did a good job on this." She slid the papers across to the woman, who glanced at them, expressionless. "I have a couple of questions about Charlie Pastor that aren't answered here."

The investigator pinned the papers in place with a single brown finger laid emphatically across the top. "I prepared this report to your specifications."

"I know. I didn't realize what all the questions were when I called you. I'm willing to pay for your time, of course."

Two computers hummed side by side on the desk. A third, on the credenza behind Laurette Lacroix, was dark. She sighed. "Okay, Ms. Miller. Terms are still the same. Seventy-five an hour. You've already satisfied my four-hour minimum. If there are other expenses, I'll clear them with you first. But you should understand. My specialty is background research. I don't do domestic photo work and I won't take cases that have anything at all to do with drugs." She shrugged and smiled. "My time, my call."

The rules made her curious about the woman's past, but Claudia could live with them. "First of all, I want to find out whether

Charlie's really in California. Then, I need to know if he's related to a man named Kevin Mahoney. His widow lives in Queens. I need to know if there's any family connection between the two men. That's all."

Laurette studied her. "That's not really all. What you want to know has as much to do with this Kevin Mahoney as it does with Charles Pastor, right?"

If Claudia Miller was going to pay good money, she might as well get her nickel's worth. "Exactly right. So, in addition to checking out what Charlie's up to in California and seeing if there's a Mahoney connection, I want you to find out about Kevin Mahoney's family. His children, primarily, but also nephews, nieces, cousins, siblings. His wife says there's no one, but I want *you* to tell me."

"Whoa, this is starting to sound big-time. I have to put someone on in Los Angeles, that's a thousand dollars a day. You're a bank, or do you want me to put some kind of limit on this?"

A thousand dollars a day—what would her investment give her that she couldn't find out by simply phoning Charlie Pastor and asking him what the list meant?

Laurette Lacroix straightened a pile of papers on her desk. "While you're thinking about that, let's look at this other piece. You're going to tell me why I'm checking out this Mahoney family, aren't you?"

Was a murder investigation one of the things on the investigator's list of forbidden topics? Claudia explained about Mercer Street and the recent murders.

"You're looking for someone who was so upset over Mahoney's death," she said, "that his life is consumed by hurt and anger and maybe a need for revenge. You're looking for a link between Charlie Pastor and Kevin Mahoney."

Laurette paused, then said, "Families can be such a mess. If there is a family tie, that won't take long to find. Maybe a day. But if Charlie Pastor and Kevin Mahoney aren't related, it could take longer to reach that conclusion, you understand. It's like trying to prove that white people have no rhythm. You can show that some of them do easily enough, but it's the negative that's hard to prove."

"One day in California. Then, after I get the report, I'll re-evaluate, see if I think more time will serve any purpose. But go as far as you can in, say, six hours with the Mahoney family."

Claudia wrote out a check, passed it across the desk, then shook the other woman's hand. With proper framing, she thought, this could be an ad for one of those clothing companies that thought it sold concepts instead of sweaters.

"Nice hat," Laurette said as Claudia pulled the door shut behind her.

"I have to talk to you." She waited for Bert to look up from the task of marking out the place where kitchen cabinets would be hung. "Is Gary Bruno in the back?"

Bert shook his head. "Bruno asked for a couple of hours off. He's been working pretty hard, and he's still a little pissed at you for accusing him of stealing your tools, so I told him to go ahead. Something's wrong here."

"The ceiling's not level, that's what's throwing you off. We may have to shim one end of the cabinets, hide the problem with the splash guard." The upper left-hand corner of the cabinets would be too high, she could tell from the lines Bert had drawn on the unpainted plasterboard wall.

She squinted, held the level parallel to Bert's line, checked the bubble. "Drop the mark on the upper left by a hair. Less than a quarter inch. We better snap a chalk line."

Grumbling, Bert walked the metal ladder along the wall, climbed to the top step and held the end of the cord against his mark. He handed the other end to Claudia, who pulled it to the second mark, nodded that she was ready. Bert snapped the line and a faint blue chalk mark appeared on the plasterboard.

She stepped back, shaded her eyes with her hands. "That's better."

Bert set the level along his mark, tapped the corner, smiled with satisfaction as the bubble came to rest in the center. "You're right. It's okay. Now, what's going on? You look mad at the world."

She thrust the paper at him. "Do you recognize this handwriting? You didn't write this, did you?"

Bert glanced at the paper, shook his head. "You know I didn't." He slipped a piece of door trim into the chop saw.

She closed her eyes, her breath ragged and her mind threatening to hurtle into panic again. "Shit, Bert. That's the wrong answer. I found it in a book Charlie Pastor left in my house. Robert Frost poetry. Kevin Mahoney loved Frost, remember?"

"Wow. Well, what do you think *this* means? That he saw your list, the one we made the night we found out about Murray, and he copied it? Maybe he thought these people were all old lovers and he wanted to ask you about them. Maybe he's got an old brownstone in Brooklyn Heights he wants restored and he's gathering the names of people who can do the work." The blade sliced through the diagonal guides. Bert selected another piece of wood, set it in the chop saw.

She knelt and traced a question mark in the pile of sawdust on the floor, wiped her finger on her jeans. "Just for discussion, say the list is his. So the real question is, what does he have to do with Kevin Mahoney's death in eighty-one? How is Mr. Pastor connected to Mercer Street? I asked that investigator to try to find out, but no matter what I do, Bert, I can't turn him into a killer. I don't see it. Just to be safe, I asked Laurette Lacroix to check on him in California. Maybe she can help us get to the truth. We need answers here."

"We?" Bert cast a skeptical frown in her direction. "You mean the cops, right? You're going to give Sarafino the list and then get out of his way, right? Lives are at stake here, Claude. This is not about you, sweetie."

"I know what's at stake. Nora left a couple of hours ago to get Tommy. He drove a snowmobile off a rock and ended up with a concussion." She held up her hand to stop Bert's questions. "Don't ask. Bottom line, it looks like an accident—no electrical shorts or wires or tape or anything, just a rock that popped up when he didn't expect it. I have a hard time believing there's a connection between Charlie and the murders and Mercer Street. He seems so gentle. What I can't get past is—"

"—the lie. The deception. Don't you get it yet, Claudia? People lie all the time. It oils society, keeps things running smoothly. You lie and everyone knows you're lying and they lie back and you get some practice reading what it means. It's just code. That's your problem, sweetie. You never learned the code." Bert patted her hand. "I swear, Claudia, you set yourself up for so many problems with this thing. No way you won't get hurt if you expect people to be honest with you. No way."

Maybe, after all, tact was simply another version of deceit.

If she conceded that, she'd have to assume that everything might be only somewhat true. Which sounded a little like being somewhat pregnant or somewhat dead.

"I'll think about it. Did the cabinet guy call? Because if they're not here soon, I'm going to have to kill someone myself."

"I was going to tell you. The truck should be here later this evening. Problem is, I have an appointment with Maria. The one from Prague. She's making me dinner. Bruno says he's coming back by four, but who knows if he'll make it. Besides, he shouldn't have to take responsibility for okaying the shipment after all the problems we've had. You think you can be here to take the delivery?"

"Sunday. They mess up and then they're late, and then they want to deliver on Sunday. Early evening, furniture time, means they might pull in by nine or ten on anyone else's watch." She sighed. "I'll be here."

"Good. Now that that's settled, what are you going to do with that list? You can't do that, Claudia, go and change the subject and think the problem's vanished."

Clearly, Bert Kossarian wasn't about to let it go away. She was tired and confused, resentful of the forces that were batting her around like a kitten's rubber ball. "I feel like I should give Charlie a chance to explain the list to me before I drag him into a police investigation."

Bert shook his head gently. "No, you don't. You just don't want to face the truth. It's not only up to you. I have family, Claudia, people who are in danger until this creep is caught. You should have turned that list over to the cops hours ago. If you don't do it, I will." Bert poked at the plastic bag with the handle of a screwdriver, then pushed it toward her. "You take this list to Sarafino, tell him how you found it, make sure he knows all the details. It's going to feel like hell because you're going to have to say that you were tricked, and not only that but by a man twelve years younger than you."

"Hey, fuck you, Bert. This isn't the time to get back at me for busting you about Ellie." She grabbed the bag and stomped to the window.

"You can lash out at me if you want to but facts are facts. It's a bitch, sweetie, but you found the list in *his* book. What would Pastor be doing with that list?"

Twenty-four

The First Precinct entryway was a welter of signs and handwritten notices taped up opposite the front door, a flurry of static, crackling sounds. At the foot of the stairs, two men and a woman, out of uniform, hair still damp from showers, conferred in hushed voices.

"So when I got there," the taller of the two men said, "it was like, you know, she was out of it. I mean, this guy rammed her car and took off and left her there with her head bleeding and her fender pushed up against the tire. She couldn't do nothing, I mean, not a fucking thing to get the car moving. And the traffic's skidding all over the place, all the way down Hudson in the goddamn snow and nobody can see her, her lights are out and I can see she's gonna get creamed again unless I do something but then if I do maybe I'm gonna get creamed, you know what I'm saying?"

They nodded encouragement, but before he could go on, Claudia stepped into the silence and said, "Can you tell me where I can find Officer Sarafino? It's really important."

Sighing, the storyteller pointed to the desk behind the glass window. "Someone'll be out in a second. She'll take care of you, ma'am."

Claudia approached the desk, waited as a woman, her blond hair pulled in a tight bun, Evita lipstick glaring bright and scarlet, smoothed her blue shirt and settled into her chair. "I have an appointment to see Officer Sarafino," she said, controlling her annoyance. "My name is Claudia Miller."

The woman flipped pages in a directory, pressed buttons on the phone, fingered the top button of her shirt. "He'll be down in a minute," she reported, a sweet smile softening her face.

Claudia watched the stairs, trying to catch the ending of the automobile accident story, until Sarafino appeared, gray hair slicked back behind ears that were tipped with pink.

"Hey, Miller, how things going?" Sarafino steered her through a door to the reception area. "I haven't called you because the lab got only a couple partials on those pictures. They're still trying to match them, but so far, nothing. I'm sorry. I was gonna call you tomorrow to tell you."

She handed him the plastic bag that held the paper that had fallen from Charlie's book.

A dull patina seemed to wash over Sarafino's face. "You already gave me a copy of this list."

"This is a different one." Claudia sighed, wishing again that she had some other explanation for that little piece of paper. "I found this stuck in the pages of a book. The book was left in my apartment by a man I met right after Tommy was attacked. His name is Charlie Pastor."

Rick Sarafino nodded, turned the plastic bag over. The light, yellow and dim, fell like a tired theater spot on his chapped hands, and she stared at them as though they had some meaning beyond their attachment to his body.

"Who's this Charlie? And where did *he* get it?" Sarafino coughed, pulled a neat handkerchief from the pocket of his pants.

"I told you: I met him a week and a half ago. He ruined my briefcase when he bumped into me on the street and then he bought me a new one to replace it. I saw him a total of three times. The list fell out of this book. He left it in my house."

Sarafino's eyes widened as she handed him the book.

"Frost," she said. "Kevin Mahoney's favorite. Charlie forgot the book when he brought me the new briefcase. He was in my dining room a total of eighteen minutes. During which time, if you remember, I told you that he fixed a lamp of mine. With black electrical tape. I have no idea what the list means or how it got there. I just know it was in that book in my loft." She paced to the window, but there was nothing to see except darkness. "He told me all this stuff about being a writer, about coming from California and being new in the city, and that he had to go to the Coast to pitch a script."

Sarafino frowned. "Pitch a script?"

"Pitch as in a sales pitch. He's trying to sell a script he wrote to some movie producer. That's what he told me, anyway." At this point, everything Charlie Pastor had ever said to her was suspect. Until proven otherwise he was a liar.

"Huh." He tapped the plastic bags, nodded his head. "All right, I'll take care of this. You call me if you hear from this guy, you understand? You stay away from him. Until we can track his movements when all the murders took place, we—*you*—have to be careful. Smart and careful, right, Miller? You let me know if you find out where he is."

"Sure," she said wearily, "I'll call you."

"You're not holding back or something, are you, Claudia? You're not, like, protecting your boyfriend or anything like that?" Color flooded Sarafino's already beefy face. "You don't do anything about this, you hear me? I don't want you getting hurt, Miller. You go home and you take care of your job and I'll take care of mine. And you call me if you hear from this Charlie Pastor. *Hasta la vista,* buddy."

Finally.

"That's it, lady, that's the last carton." The deliveryman mopped sweat from his mahogany forehead, ran the red neckerchief over his tight curls, held out a paper. "I need your signature and a check and then I'm out of your hair."

"You believe this? On-time delivery only eight days late? Sheesh, for a truck that supposedly left Quebec four days ago, this sure took long enough." Gary Bruno spread a line of compound along a seam, knelt, and scooped another load onto the trowel. "People didn't use to do things that way. There used to be respect and honor and . . . Well, at least they're here."

The receipt looked right, all ten cartons looked right, but that wasn't enough. "I paid you an extra twenty bucks to get these cabinets up here instead of leaving them on the sidewalk. You really think I'll sign this before I see them with my own eyes?"

The deliveryman grumbled, pulled the staples from the top of the first carton, ripped off the flap, continued on down the line, grunting as he yanked at each piece of cardboard. From the bathroom, she heard water running, Bruno humming to himself as he cleaned up his equipment.

"Lady? You want to look, so look."

The flashlight beam lit up the interior of the first box, the second, and as she continued her inspection the breath flowed more easily in her chest—this phase of the job was nearly over.

"I gotta get out of here or I'll miss my movie. See you tomorrow, Claudia. Looking good around here." Bruno pointed to the last box, then reached back and pressed the elevator call button. "You better check this one. Carton's turned on its side," he said before the door slid closed.

Only pine backing strips were visible when she pulled aside the flap. "Open another side, *any* other side."

Muttering and scowling, the deliveryman wielded his screwdriver and approached the carton again.

"Hey! If you scratch the wood, you're taking it back. Just watch it, okay?" This was beyond nightmare, too painful to be a dream. But the surface of the last cabinet in the last carton was the same rich cherry as the others.

Claudia applauded and handed the deliveryman another ten for taking away the cardboard.

If Gary Bruno were still around she would buy him a beer. Even small victories were precious these days, to be celebrated when the rare opportunity permitted. Irina was in Atlantic City on a shoot. Maybe Bert would join her for that beer. She dialed his number, let the phone ring until his answering machine came on.

Okay, if not Gary Bruno or Bert Kossarian or Irina Orlov, she'd see if Nora and Tommy had come back from Taconic Hills. That wouldn't be quite as much fun—but at least it would be good for family relations. She dialed her father's house and launched brightly into her opening. "Nora, I'm glad I caught you. I wanted to check in, see how you and Tommy made out."

"Things are just wonderful, grand, terrific. Your father's coming into JFK tomorrow night at nine-thirty."

So much for celebration. "My father's coming home at nine-thirty tomorrow night? I thought he had meetings all week in London. If you give me his number, I can call him and explain about—"

"Evan says he can't concentrate on his work because he's worried about Tommy. He's furious at himself for saying yes to that Taconic Hills plan."

"Listen, Nora, give me his flight information. I'll go out there and pick him up."

"Your father is arriving on flight nine-two-six, British Airways."

"Nine-two-six. British Airways," Claudia repeated as she scribbled on a hardware store receipt.

"But he specifically said I should arrange for a limo to pick him up. And that's what I've done. Don't go out to the airport."

"At least if I have forty-five minutes alone with him, I'll have a chance to explain so he understands why we took Tommy to Taconic Hills, why it seemed to be the right thing to do. My relationship with my father has had its share of bumps, but this is a huge one, and I want to take care of it before it gets bigger."

"No, you listen, Claudia. I have to make sure my marriage survives this crisis. Let him come home in peace, as he requested."

Before Nora could hang up on her, Claudia said a soft good-bye. Her father's aborted trip spoke volumes. Evan had never come home early to deal with a family situation before. He'd simply phoned in his instructions, carried on with business, made statements about his priorities through his actions.

She glanced at her watch, grabbed her coat, rode the elevator to the ground floor, swung open the outside door.

A chaotic, five-foot high heap of cardboard spilled from the loading dock onto the sidewalk like hurricane debris.

"Sonofabitch took my ten dollars, too," she muttered, as she kicked at the torn cartons.

Twenty-five

He checked his watch for the hundredth time, patted his overcoat pocket, and wondered if the handcuffs made a noticeable bulge. Nine-seventeen at night, and Kennedy Airport was busier than most big cities in the middle of the day. So many people scurrying like frantic ants to their gates, rushing with their bug-eyes to the baggage claim, sitting in those sad, smelly bars trying to make themselves believe they really had fascinating lives and were only perched on those stools so they could be observers. Talking—everyone chatting up the person next to them as though what they had to say about Aunt Martha or the weather in San Juan or how many fucking units they needed to move of shoes or teddy bears or whatever they sold in all this flying around the world was oh, so important.

The drivers waited patiently. Mostly short, all dark-haired, they held signs with the names of their fares printed neatly, placards they'd raise when the doors opened and the arriving passengers stepped into the terminal blinking and squinting. He clutched his newspaper, made sure the square of cardboard on which he'd carefully lettered the name was safely tucked away.

Outside, a mechanic with ear protectors tossed a patched-up canvas suitcase onto an open truck, his breath white puffs in the clear air. It was cold out there, cold as the ice that ran through Claudia Miller's veins. No blood, not that woman, no real feelings as far as he could tell. Well, she was in for a surprise. A surprise that was bound to crack that hard surface. Tears, a little wretched agony, something visible to confirm her pain—that was all he wanted.

He scanned the walls, the ceiling, looking everywhere to find the speakers where the pagings were announced, noticed a blob of a brown stain across the acoustical tile. Before he could finish his examination, he heard a crackle from a round perforated disk set high in the wall. A nasal female voice intoned, "Will the Eagle driver for Mr. Evan Miller please come to the white courtesy phone for an important message?"

Smiling, he watched the primmest of the waiting drivers, a mustached man with dark eyes and high-polished shoes, frown and look around for the phone. When he found it, he pushed his way through the crowd to the far wall, his sign flapping against the leg of his blue suit. The driver listened, blew out a breath, then nodded as he hung up the phone.

Good—the limo driver hadn't argued with the person on the other end telling him to go to the American terminal, that Mr. Miller's flight had been changed. He watched as the man disappeared in the direction of the parking lot, and then he pulled the sign from the envelope he'd held under his arm, and took his place among the other hired drivers.

Maybe she'd fall to her knees, hold her head in her hands, beg for understanding from God, who would turn a deaf ear to her pleas. It might take weeks, months, maybe years if he did his job properly, for her to realize her life would never be the same, that it was just some broken picture of what might have been, that she was the star of a movie that would never have a happy ending.

He shouldn't be so greedy. That was one of the answers that came to him when he asked for guidance. Well, he couldn't help it. Her suffering should be endless, as his was.

He looked over at the gate. The first of the arriving passengers started trickling into the waiting room. Evan Miller probably traveled first class, but he had to go through customs anyway. A woman with a fur coat draped over her shoulders juggled an armload of books and three shopping bags until she spotted a uniformed man leaning against the wall. Two tired-looking businessmen approached.

This could be it. He didn't know what Evan Miller looked like, but judging by his children, the guy would be tall. And he was a lawyer, so he wouldn't be wearing any L. L. Bean flannel shirts, more like the tweed suits the guys on those British cop shows wore. He held the sign, chest high, and looked them in the eyes, but the two men kept walking.

A family with two sleepy kids, an old woman wearing a veiled hat, a guy in a black overcoat, an expensive-looking garment bag slung over one shoulder.

Tall, white-haired. A serious face and eyes that took in everything. Like Claudia Miller's eyes, arrogant and maybe even a little bored. This was it. He tugged at his shirt collar, took a step forward. "Mr. Miller?"

The man nodded. "I only have this one bag. I'd like to just get home. Family emergency."

"Sorry to hear that, sir. We'll be on our way. It's pretty cold out there. I can bring the car around, if you want to wait inside. I'll pick you up at—"

"Don't bother. I'll come with you to the lot." Evan Miller didn't slow down, despite the heavy bag he carried. "It will be quicker that way."

A driver was supposed to act like a servant, wasn't that the way it worked? Evan Miller probably wasn't used to carrying his own fucking bags. "Can I take that for you, sir?" he offered.

"I'm fine. Exercise, you know. When I travel, walking and carrying my own bags are my only form of exercise." He plowed through the crowd as though he were the only person in the airport with something important to do, didn't stop when the automatic door slid open and the cold air hit him with a wintry punch.

You had to give the old geezer credit. He wasn't just a soft rich guy who paid other people to take care of him. Even if he did hire a limo to drive him home from the airport. That Town Car had cost plenty to rent for the evening—Evan Miller had better not complain that it wasn't a limo.

The parking lot was quiet, every space occupied. He could do it here, right between a Mercedes and a Honda, he could do Evan Miller. But it wouldn't be as good as going through with the plan. Take it slow, he warned himself. Get it right.

"This way, sir." He inserted the key in the trunk, smiled when Miller handed him the garment bag so he could put it in the compartment. Wouldn't want to take the chance that you might touch an old rag or some oily wrench that might be on the floor of the trunk, he thought angrily.

Evan Miller waited for the door to be opened, slid into the backseat, and pressed two fingers against his pursed lips. *Don't get too relaxed,* the driver advised silently, not bothering to hide his smile of satisfaction. *We got things to do, you and me.*

He settled himself behind the steering wheel, turned on the low beams, and twisted the ignition key to the start position. Engine purring, he maneuvered out of the parking space and then to the exit lane.

The man in back was quiet, as though he had a lot on his mind. Well, let him do his thinking, let him worry about his precious little son and what had happened to that snivelly kid in the country. It wouldn't do him any good. He pressed a button and slipped a tape into the slot, lowered the volume. As the music swelled, some classical piano thing he picked up in the bargain bin for three bucks, he negotiated the turn onto the Belt Parkway.

He drove in the center lane, heading west at a steady fifty, eyes watchful for the gas station. Fifteen minutes away. Headlights reflected in his rearview mirror stabbed at his eyes like bright, sharp knives. He crossed over to the left lane, passed the Canarsie exit, slowed a little when he saw the Flatbush Avenue sign. Ahead, in the center of the roadway, the lights of the gas station beckoned. He tapped the brake, then the gas, repeated his actions so the car bucked a little, tossing Evan Miller against the seat.

"Sir," he said as they pulled off the road and came to a stop in the darkest corner of the gas station parking lot. "I need to check something."

He got out, went around to the rear of the car, knelt down and counted to twenty. "I think we're going to be all right, sir." He fastened the safety belt and pulled into the streaming traffic.

Mr. Sharp Lawyer didn't notice, he gloated to himself. *He doesn't know we're headed in the wrong direction.* They rattled over the drawbridge, the car juddering as they hurtled over the metal roadway. The driver tapped the brakes, the gas, the brakes again.

153

Evan Miller sounded annoyed. "Is something wrong with the car? I'm in a hurry to get home to my family, so if there's a problem, I'd like you to make a call and make some other arrangement for me."

The car nosed into the exit lane, made the right-hand turn, and rolled down the isolated road, stopping in front of a huge metal shipping container with the name Sea Box printed on the side. The driver stepped onto the blacktop, made a show of looking around the car, opened the passenger door. "I wonder if you could give me a hand, sir."

Miller frowned, shot him an angry look, then slid across the seat and got out, bending to keep from hitting his head on the doorframe. "What seems to be wrong?" he asked in that grumpy, why-didn't-you-take-care-of-this-yourself voice. "How can I help you?"

The driver wrenched Evan Miller's right hand behind his back, slipped the handcuffs onto his wrist, then reached for his left hand.

Miller swung his free arm and caught the driver just below the ear. Dazed, he grabbed the swinging arm before it could connect again and snapped the cuff over it.

"See, we stopped because I want you to call your daughter. I want her to come and meet us here. So, you're going to call her and tell her just what I say and we'll all be much happier. You're going to tell her to come get you, and then you're going to tell her exactly where we are."

He shoved Evan Miller to the blacktop, set one foot squarely between the man's shoulders, grabbed a handful of Miller's pretty white hair and yanked his head back. "You call her," he growled as he pulled a cellular phone from his coat pocket.

"Kill me," Miller rasped. "I'm not calling her."

"Okay, Mr. M. Have it your way." Surprise, surprise, the guy had balls. "I'll call her."

He wrapped a handkerchief around the mouthpiece, dialed the number he knew by heart, waited to hear her voice on the phone. The pleasure of anticipation coursed through him. "Pick up the phone," he muttered as he increased the weight of his foot against Miller's squirming back. "Pick up the fucking phone."

And then he heard her voice. Annoyed. Pissed off that someone dared to interrupt her in the middle of her quiet evening at home. "Yes?" she said, like some fucking Queen of the Amazon.

"You want to see your father again, you listen to me very carefully. You don't call the cops, you don't tell anyone, you come alone. Otherwise your father doesn't make it to eleven o'clock. Come to the parking lot off the Jamaica Bay Riding Academy exit of the Belt Parkway. Leave your car at the third lamppost on the right. There's a path across the way. You walk down that path. Half an hour. You be here in half an hour." He was about to hang up, when he heard her shout.

"Wait! Put my father on. I'm not coming out until I know he's all right."

The driver smiled, lifted the handkerchief, grabbed a handful of Evan Miller's hair and yanked and twisted. Miller screamed. Panting, the driver replaced the handkerchief, said, "That's it, that's all you get. Your choice. Jamaica Bay Riding Academy in half an hour."

Twenty-six

The lights of the Verrazano Bridge glittered against the black sky, blurring as she pressed harder on the accelerator. She felt around on the seat beside her, relieved when her fingers closed over the gun.

That had been her father, screaming. Without question, it had been his voice; as muffled and distorted as it was, she knew that much. She'd been so busy arranging for Tommy's safety, she never saw it coming.

Or maybe it was just that Evan Miller seemed so untouchable, all her life the one constant. Resolute, firm, the unwavering certainty of his convictions had made him seem invulnerable. Yet, someone had done something awful to generate a scream like that.

Coney Island loomed ahead, the top of the parachute jump a glinting scalpel piercing the air. Shivering, she turned the heat up, then cranked the window down and let the cold air rush over her face. She had to stay alert, couldn't let herself get drowsy. The bobbing masts of the Sheepshead Bay marina flickered to her right as she sped east.

What did he want?

It wasn't about Evan, had nothing to do with his international law practice, she was sure of that. This was about Mercer Street.

A sign announced that Jamaica Bay Riding Academy was the next exit. She cut across three lanes of traffic to get to the right lane, took her foot off the gas, coasted onto the ramp. Whatever he wanted, she'd give it to him—money, an apology for something he imagined had happened all those years ago, whatever. Her throat was dry, her hands slick with sweat as she pulled into the parking lot and counted lampposts. Third on the right, he'd instructed. She pulled up in front of a rusty shipping container, left the headlights on and the engine running as she looked around.

Ahead, the drive looped around a small island of grass. Opposite the island stood a low, boxy building with a long canopy awning over its entrance. Spotlights on the corners of the building pooled on patches of stubbly lawn.

Between her lamppost and the building, at the far end of the blacktop parking area, a large, dark car sat beside a space marked with a stenciled blue wheelchair. She squinted, but she could see no one inside. The only car in the lot, a late model Lincoln. She fumbled in her purse for a pencil and paper, got ready to scribble the plate number, walked with careful steps toward the car.

The license plates had been removed. Front and back, they were gone.

She pulled her collar up, listened to the hum of traffic as it passed on the parkway behind her. She turned off the engine and the lights, patted her pocket, willed herself to open to the sounds, the smells, the details of the place. A puddle, the edges freezing little sticks and seashells into place, crackled under her feet. Stunted sumacs rose up between horsetails, which parted to create an entrance into the looming darkness.

The path was sandy, firm enough to show a jumble of footprints. She stepped onto the matted grasses along the edge of the path instead. Better to preserve any existing shoe prints than muddy the scene. Wasn't that what one of those television cops would have done?

The gun in her pocket felt heavy, cold, and she took another step forward.

This was a mistake.

She should never have come here alone. Should never have let herself be ordered around by some disembodied voice on the telephone.

But really, what choice did she have? It wasn't as though he'd left room for negotiation.

157

She should have called the cops.

The path veered to the left. The sea grass, taller and denser here, scratched at her hands. The smell of salt air brought a rush of memories, childhood excursions and teen romances, but she pushed them out of her mind. She had to pay attention. A crackling sound in the brush behind her made her turn her head; something chittered, then ran away, and she took another step forward. Thick clouds had hung low all day, and now blocked whatever meager light the half moon might have offered.

She pushed forward, pausing every fourth step to listen, to peer into the darkness to see what awaited her.

Claudia made herself as small as she could, still, quiet, the sound of her heart loud and overpowering. A cluster of trees formed a dark blot on the horizon, like a silhouetted hand reaching from the earth toward the sky. Like the cover of that book, she thought, except the trees weren't birches but sumacs, ungraceful and low to the ground. Her pace picked up, the grasses worn down here, progress easier to make. She stumbled, kicked a stone with her toe.

She whipped her head around at the sound that seemed to come from the trees. A choked, wordless protest, someone struggling to warn her of danger.

Suddenly, bright light flooded the area twenty yards in front of her, illuminating the clump of trees like a bizarre stage set. She gasped, stopped in her tracks. Her father, hands secured behind him, a gag stuffed into his mouth, hung by an orange noose from a branch of the tallest tree.

An extension cord. His noose was fashioned from a long electrical extension cord.

She started to run toward him, her breath painful in her chest.

"That's far enough."

She screamed, whirled around to see who had shouted the words. Only the blinding light in the middle of a black void, no looming figure, no movement. The voice sounded muffled. Her father, twenty feet away, glared in the direction of the voice.

Her hand in her pocket, she unsnapped the safety on the gun. Claudia Miller didn't pray. Her resolute will to keep her father safe was as close as she could come to spiritual appeal.

"What do you want?" she shouted, drawing her hand slowly from her jacket, her gaze fixed on the figure beneath the tree. Her father's eyes flitted wildly from the source of the lights to her, flickered away, then lingered on her face. She thought she saw in that look an apology, not a warning or a threat, but an expression of regret.

"Don't move, Dad. I love you. Just don't move." She took another step forward.

He seemed to nod slightly and she noticed for the first time that his feet rested on a rope-secured log. In the bright light, his shoes gleamed with a high-buffed shine.

"I want you to watch," the muffled voice demanded. "You like to watch, don't you, Claudia?"

He's talking through a ski mask, she thought. She didn't recognize the voice. If she had more practice with the damn gun, she could shoot at the orange cord, sever it, and her father would drop harmlessly to the ground. But that wasn't an option. She must get her tormentor talking so she could hear him again, so she could keep him from—

Oh, God, she knew what he was going to do.

She wheeled, fired two shots in the direction of the lights, then started running toward the trees. The log supporting her father was yanked out of place. It tumbled from under him. His feet kicked out frantically once, twice. Then they were still.

She ran forward, willing the air to move into his lungs and keep his heart pumping. She crashed through the brush, stumbling once, picking herself up and pushing on. Ten more feet. From here, she could see his eyes, wide with fright, as though they were asking for her help.

The branch was nearly seven feet from the ground. She would need something to stand on. As she set the log in position, she was plunged into darkness. Her father's body swayed against hers as she set his feet on the log. She jammed the gun into the waistband of her jeans, pulled the pocketknife out, and began to saw at the orange extension cord.

Something knocked her hand away. She whirled around, flailing in the dark, seeking connection with whatever had struck her. A guttural grunt gave her just enough warning to duck; cold air breezed by her face as a fist smashed against the tree.

Her attacker screamed and shoved her aside.

She reached back and grabbed a handful of rough wool—a coat?—and tried to swing around. Off balance, she stumbled, felt something hard smash against her arm and break her grip. She fell backward, crashing against the rough bark of the tree, her forehead scraped above her left eye. Blood ran warm and sticky down the side of her face.

She drew the gun and struggled to turn, to catch a glimpse of shoes, pants, anything that would make a target. Was that a jagged glint of gold below her attacker's ski mask?

Claudia Miller was struck on the back of her head with something hard, sharp. In a blur, a hand reached past her and grabbed the gun. Blood seeped from the cut above her eye, her palms were scraped raw where she'd tried to hold on to the tree for support. The last thing she saw before she slumped to the ground was the scuffed sole of one of her father's shoes.

Something ran across her hand.

She blinked, felt the sand in her mouth and in her eyes, raised her head. A string of lights on the water cast merry reflections on the glassy surface. The clouds had disappeared, and the moon hung in the sky like a fat, half-eaten pudding. She turned slowly, hoping the clutch of trees she expected to see was a dream, a figment of her imagination. But they were real, sharp limbs poking upward, and from one of them, the body of Evan Patrick Miller twisted in the gentle breeze.

She pushed herself to a standing position, took a tentative step forward, afraid, hopeful. "Dad? It's me, Claudia," she whispered.

Where it wasn't mottled with purple contusions, her father's skin was white, doughy, a cold film glistening on all the exposed flesh. Claudia longed to press her hands to his face until the color returned.

Instead, she stumbled back toward the lights of what she hoped was the parking lot, panting, dizzy, disoriented as she crashed through the clawing brush. Her car stood waiting beside the Sea Box, and she pulled the door open with hands slick with her own blood. She fumbled in the glove compartment, found the cellular phone, punched out 911. She managed to give her location and tell the dispatcher to call for an ambulance.

Then, darkness closed over her and she collapsed, hands tucked beneath her like a sleeping child, in the front seat of her car.

Twenty-seven

Bright lights, noise, a flurry of purposeful activity surrounded her. A draped gurney clattered past her down the hall, pushed by two expressionless attendants. Claudia didn't know if the corridor was brightly lit or dim, didn't notice whether people were milling about, wouldn't remember later whether it was a short distance or miles to the emergency room.

She struggled to keep her eyes open, nodded at a sullen young woman with lips the color of her tangled, raven hair who had settled into a chair, hugging her spangled denim purse to her chest. Instantly, she fell into an odd, jerky sleep that was neither healing nor restful.

She saw Bert's face swimming above her, Tommy's, Ted's, saw her father's dark eyes and knew that whatever drugs they'd pumped into her arm had sent her visions. She tried to close her eyes, realized they were already shut tight, worked hard to open them, failed.

She was moving again, rolling down a hallway, sliding past swinging doors. She stopped, blinked back her fear as she was carried forward. Her brother was standing in front of a bulletin board, his foot tapping. His face, when he turned, streamed with tears that flowed from his swollen eyes. He looked away, then tried again to focus on her. He moved closer in slow, even steps, clasped her hand.

It was as though she could feel his shuddering breath in that gentle touch. "Shh," she said, tapping her lips, "take it easy, babe. It's gonna be okay."

Tommy exhaled noisily. "It was supposed to be me." And then he closed his eyes and his chest rose and fell, and Claudia bit her lip and stared at the wall to keep from screaming.

The voice was unfamiliar. When she managed to open her eyes, she saw a doctor in green scrubs, mask dangling below a face that seemed far too young. He stood beside two chairs pushed against the wall, reached past Tommy, and touched Nora's arm gently.

Her throat was so dry, her limbs heavy. She tried to turn her head, to reach for the water glass on the table beside the bed. Nothing. She couldn't move.

"She's doing well," the doctor said, "but I want to keep her here for a while. I gave her something so she can sleep. Her face and her arm are pretty raw and she has a really bad bruise from the brick that hit her on the back of her head, but nothing else seems to be wrong. We did a battery of tests—MRI, CAT scan—to make sure we didn't miss anything." He shrugged, smiled, patted Tommy's arm. "Your sister's going to be fine. I promise."

No pain. That was something, anyway. She couldn't tell whether she had all her parts, but none of them hurt. Evan—could he have survived? She knew the answer. A tear leaked from the corner of one eye, but she couldn't wipe it away.

Tommy nodded, his glassy stare unchanged even when Nora pressed his hand with hers. She released him and rose, her posture straight and her voice controlled. "Thank you, Doctor. Thank you for everything."

"You can stay and talk to her now, but just for a minute. Talk to her, touch her, but softly, everything softly. I know she looks terrible but that will only last for about a week. It's good for her to hear your voices."

They appeared behind a nurse, a woman whose hair seemed intent on escaping the pins trying to hold it in place.

"No, don't talk, Claudia. Not yet." Nora stroked her hand.

163

Her eyelids fluttered, her mouth struggled to form words, but her throat felt as though it were filled with cotton.

"Hey, something's wrong!" Tommy grabbed the nurse by the sleeve.

Frowning, the young woman turned and glanced up at the monitor. "She's thirsty, that's all." The nurse lifted Claudia's head, held a straw to her lips. The water rose slowly, slowly, in a tiny dribble that trickled down her throat like a slide of cool spring air. More. She wanted more. She reached up, but the nurse moved the glass away. "Not too much, dearie. Sorry."

Claudia's head sank back into the pillows.

"Claudia." Tommy bent close and said something she couldn't make out. The faint pressure of his fingers against hers made her smile.

The nurse went about her business silently, set up another IV bottle, attached it to the tube taped to her hand, and Claudia tumbled into the darkness that had somehow stolen into the room.

Her mouth felt like she'd been chewing sawdust and her head ached from shouting to her father. He wouldn't listen, didn't seem to be able to hear her as she warned him about the red-eyed snake tightening itself around his neck.

She touched the cold metal of the hospital bed slats. Tingling pain started in her wrist and spread to her hand as sensation returned. In two chairs across the room, Tommy and Nora Miller sat, slack-jawed and pale.

Her father was dead. Her body felt broken. Her mind slithered into warm darkness every chance it had.

Nora appeared beside her bed, held the glass so Claudia could take in a few more sips of the precious water. "Try to stay awake for a little while, Claudia. There are a couple of detectives in the hall. You think you're ready to talk to them?"

She struggled to keep Nora in focus. "Sure. If I can make my mouth work right. Send them in."

She heard the door open, heard footsteps. One of them was a smoker, she could tell by the smell that filled the room as he approached. When she looked up, she saw a hand, a leather jacket, unfamiliar eyes peering down at her.

"Thanks for talking to us, Mizz Miller. Whatever you can tell us, we appreciate it. Did you see another vehicle in the parking lot?"

She blinked, told them about the Lincoln. Her voice was so low, they bent near enough for her to smell the fruity chewing gum and see the yellow ridges on the teeth of the man closest to her.

"Who knew when your father was coming back from London?"

Her head ached. Who? Nobody. She blinked away her tears. "Me. Nora. Tommy, I guess. But no one else I can think of."

They asked more questions. Frustrated, she told them about Murray Kurtz, about Leroy, about Carla Benedetti in Montclair, but she wasn't sure she was making sense. Didn't they know all this already? But they continued to probe, and she answered them until, finally, the nurse returned with a pill for her to swallow. Once again, Claudia Miller slipped into darkness that descended like a soft cloak over her.

"Miller?" Earnest brown eyes peered down at her, and she glanced at the stadium jacket slung over his shoulder, at his cuffed brown pants, at the crepe-soled shoes. Rick Sarafino sat beside her, folded his hands on the arm of the bedside chair. "How you doing? You need anything?"

She knew better than to shake her head. Sudden movements sent sharp pain piercing her skull. "Thanks. They tell me I can go home as soon as the doc gets here and signs me out. I'm surprised to see you, Rick. You know they have a task force now, working my father's case? I heard about it this morning. Seems like there's been a parade of detectives rolling through this room. More cops than nurses," she said weakly.

He looked pained. "That's why I came by. To tell you how bad I feel that your father . . . well, that you lost him."

Like a shoe she'd misplaced? She started to say something, stopped when she noticed Sarafino's chagrined expression.

"I'm sorry, that's all. I'm sorry he's dead. What happened, Miller? Maybe there's something I can do. You tell me what happened, okay?"

She wanted to tell him it wasn't okay, that she was exhausted and needed to forget for whole minutes at a time, but she shook herself gently and sat up in the bed.

165

"So, did you recognize the voice?" Sarafino pushed up in the hard chair, his trousers rumpled and the cuffs of his shirt rolled partway to his elbow.

"I told the other cops already. The guy was wearing a ski mask. He said I shouldn't call the cops or stop anywhere and that I should come alone. I did what I thought I had to." But it had been the wrong thing, an awful hubris that had cost her father his life. The lump of sadness in her chest rose to her throat again.

Sarafino patted her hand, held out the water glass with the plastic straw.

"When I pulled into that parking lot, there was one other car. A Lincoln Town Car with the plates removed. Rick, would you tell them I think the car was rented? It was so . . . *clean*. Maybe they can check with the rental agencies in the city. I don't know if that would do any good."

"It might." Sarafino nodded. "You're real lucky, you know. This guy, what did he look like?"

"Don't you think I would have told the detectives right off? I never saw him. I only heard his voice, and that wasn't very clear. He was wearing a ski mask. I have to tell you, I was paying more attention to my father." Claudia pounded the thin mattress with a curled fist. "I should have called the cops. I was so determined that I was going to take care of this, that it was something I could do on my own. I was the one who made this happen. Me. I should have called the cops. I killed him, just about."

Sarafino shook his head. "No. You did what you thought was the right thing. This is a crazy person doing crazy things and it's his fault, not yours." He took a breath. "I'll check in with you when you get home. Meanwhile, if there's anything you need, you call me, all right? And you remember: This is the fault of the man with the ski mask. Period."

"You really want to do this? Maybe it's better if you go home first, get settled, listen to your telephone messages. You have about ten billion of them. The people at the hospital may think you're ready for real life but *I* sure don't. Okay, okay, I won't argue with a woman in your condition." Bert offered his arm and helped Claudia from the car. "Nora's been kind of out of it since they told her about the autopsy. They say they're not going to release your father's body for four more days. The doc has her pumped full of sedatives. It's going to be . . . I don't know what it's going to be."

Amazing, to stand on the sidewalk, with people going about their lives untouched. Claudia inhaled the city air, glad not to be smelling the reeking, antiseptic breath of the hospital. "I can handle it. I have to be in the same room with her and with Tommy. I don't even want to say anything. I just want to be in the same room." She rang the bell, stepped back, and nodded to the woman who opened the door. One of Nora's Junior League friends, no doubt; she could tell by the string of pearls and the gracious, impersonal invitation to come inside.

Claudia clutched her coat to her chest as she walked upstairs and knocked softly on the door. Her father's widow lay like a zombie atop the bed she and Evan had shared for seventeen years. Claudia stood beside the bed, held the woman's hand, and then turned around and closed the door behind her.

Her brother's room was two doors down, and she knocked, thought she heard a grunt of answer, and stepped inside. Tommy, his head drooping, slumped in a chair in the corner of his room and stared at his hands. When Claudia perched on the corner of his bed, Tommy looked up.

"Would you leave me alone, please," he said in an adamant whisper.

She didn't argue or ask her brother's forgiveness. Instead, she made her way downstairs, sat in her father's leather chair, looked up at the leaded glass window, and wondered whether he'd really understood what he meant to her.

She tried going over the telephone call in her mind, wondered at what point she should have known that this wasn't something she could face alone.

Finally, she let herself cry.

At least some part of her realized she couldn't keep running away from her sadness forever.

Twenty-eight

1981 / Mercer Street / The Complication

"Claudia! Claudia! Open the door! Hurry up, goddamn it, let me in!" The frantic pounding on her door stopped, but the shouting continued. "Claudia! Open up! Claudia!"

Through the tiny peephole, his image distorted in the fisheye of the lens, Amos Fischer's disheveled hair and wild eyes, his loosened necktie and his heaving chest made him look like an escapee from some institution behind very high walls where burly attendants in starched white jackets kept order.

"All right, okay, hang on." She undid the top lock and released the chain.

He shoved her door closed, flipped the locks, sank into a chair with his head in his hands, panting as though he might never catch his breath. "I'm screwed." He clutched at his shirt like a character from a Greek tragedy.

A dusty bottle of Chivas had been stashed in the back of her closet since her father's last visit. She poured a hefty shot and handed him the glass. "They indicted you?"

He threw back his head and downed the Scotch in a single breathless gulp. "Arson. Murder. The whole incredible nine yards." He refilled his glass, took another swallow, coughed, and shook his head. "I have to disappear. I swear to God, I won't make it if I have to sit through a trial and wait for some jury to say the evidence was overwhelming and I have to die. I won't make it."

This couldn't be happening. Amos Fischer had been with her when the blaze was set. Hadn't he? *Hadn't he?* The D.A. had argued that she was either protecting her *boyfriend*—when he said it the word sounded oily, slimy, and she wanted to shower off the taint as soon as she could get back to her own apartment—or Amos had stolen away while she was sleeping, set the fire, slipped back between the sheets without her knowing he'd been gone.

"I thought they weren't going to get to the decision until tomorrow." It was the best she could do. She needed time, time to get calm and figure out what to do about Amos's frantic behavior.

And suddenly, she understood.

"Amos—you ran away. You ran out of the courthouse, didn't you?"

He could only nod, his haunted eyes closed against the memory.

This time, she filled a tumbler with water, drank half of it, refilled it, and then handed it to Amos. He drank greedily, as though he were starving and she had provided manna. Finally, he set the glass on the table and rose, speaking in a frantic rush.

"The judge kept looking at me over those glasses, those little half glasses sitting on the end of his sharp nose, as though I were some kind of bug he wanted to squash with his shoe. The prosecutor kept calling me a hippie and my lawyer kept jumping up to object and I'm sitting there thinking, how did my life turn out to be a Kafka novel, you know?"

The same creepy sensation had overwhelmed her when Amos called and said he needed a lawyer because the police, armed with a search warrant, had discovered the receipt for a five-gallon can of gasoline in his apartment. And they'd carted away a pair of Amos's shoes, later claiming they matched marks left in the hall. When an old snoop of a woman who lived on the other side of Mercer Street absolutely identified Amos as the man going into the building, she'd felt like an untrained acrobat participating in a circus of injustice.

Amos stalked the perimeter of the room. "So, there I am, in the hall, and the grand jury is off in their chambers or wherever it is they go, and I hear two reporters. 'Five to one, he goes down,' one of them says. 'Nah,' says the other, 'more like two to one. They got his shoes and the receipt for the gas can in his apartment and they got an eyewitness who saw the guy go into the building carrying the can and a roll of rope. Two to one.' And I knew he was right. But I also knew *I* was right.

"I'm innocent, so how can they indict me? Very good, Amos, being an ostrich is just what you need to make you feel safe, Amos. And then I think back to the case I read about where some poor slob spent eighteen years in jail for a murder he didn't commit. When the grand jury came back and the judge read the indictment and set bail at three hundred thousand, *three hundred thousand,* I lost it, Claudia. Something inside me just broke, you know what I mean? Snapped."

He groaned.

"I jumped over that railing and ran down the hall and kept running. I heard all this shouting behind me, but there were a lot of people in the hall so I just kept running through the biggest crowds I could find until I got here. I had nothing to do with Mahoney's death. Nothing. I'm not going to jail for doing nothing. You have to help me, Claudia. I have to get out of here."

Amos Fischer, the most organized man she knew, meticulous, with a rule that governed every action, had leaped from the clutches of the law right into the bogus safety of her apartment.

Probably dragging half the cops in the city of New York behind him.

The next knock on the door might well be accompanied by drawn guns.

"You can't stay here, Amos. Even if no one followed you, they'll come here to look for you."

"I don't know what came over me. I didn't plan to do it, Claudia. I just know I won't live to see forty-two if I go to jail. I had nothing to do with that fire. You believe me, don't you?"

His face was lined with worry, gray with fear, and she knew she was going to help him. *How* was another question. She could save Amos Fischer from life as a prison inmate only by turning him into a fugitive, but the choice would have to be his. "I believe you. The question is, what now?"

"I can't think, Claudia. Help me. Help me think." He stumbled to the chair and sat, head in hands, breathing noisily even when she stroked the back of his neck.

Comfort wasn't what he needed. Amos Fischer had to disappear.

She scrabbled through her purse, came up with ninety-three dollars in cash. "This is all I have. I can get more, we'll figure out something. But you have to get out of here. For your sake and for mine."

He grabbed the bills and stuck them in his pocket, his expression dazed.

"Look, you go to that bar in Times Square, the Blarney Stone. Sit in the back in one of the booths, get yourself calm, and figure out where you're going to go. No planes, no borders to cross, just somewhere you can get to by walking onto a bus at Port Authority. Buy a toothbrush and a change of clothes. I'll get together some money and meet you there in an hour and a half. Go, Amos."

"Go? Go where? What do I do?" The light of comprehension made him shake his head. "Leave my work, my apartment, everything? Leave who I am and just go away and become someone new? How do I do that? Oh, shit, Claudia. Maybe I have to just face the—" Ashen, he clapped a hand over his mouth and ran to the bathroom, slammed the door.

The sounds of his retching stopped, and then she heard running water, the toilet flushing. Amos Fischer stepped back into the room, wrapped his arms around her, and then pulled back. "I'm okay. You're right. I have to leave. Listen, if you ever get a letter or a phone call from someone named—"

"Don't. Don't tell me. And don't get in touch. It's too dangerous. I'm going to miss you, Amos. I have two thousand dollars I can get my hands on. I better get to the bank before it closes. I'll meet you at the Blarney Stone."

Kevin Mahoney had reached out from the grave to keep the battle going. Amos Fischer had become Mahoney's hostage, but she wouldn't let him become a permanent casualty.

Twenty-nine

Because of the public notice her father's murder had generated, more people called or wrote to offer sympathy than she thought she knew. Some of them, she was sure, she'd never met, like the lawyer offering to bring suit against the riding school and the accountant who promised to guide her family through the probate process for a hefty percentage of the estate. Others, like Mrs. Hockman, offered not only condolences, but also the gift of time, an assurance that Claudia shouldn't worry about the Duane Street loft until she was ready to return to work. She was touched by the eloquence of some, and comforted by the sheer number of good wishes; they had accumulated into a buffer of kindness whose power to heal surprised her.

She could take her time returning most of the messages that had accumulated on her machine, but one in particular caught her attention.

Laurette Lacroix's quiet voice left a message offering her condolences, and asking what she should do with the information she'd collected.

She dialed the investigator's number. "I'm sorry it took a while to get back to you," she said. "I've been—"

"I know. I'm sorry about your father. I thought you should have this information. You up to hearing it? I can messenger it, if you'd rather."

Claudia let her eyes fall shut. "Tell me."

"My guy in LA tracked this Charlie for one day, like you said. Pastor stayed in his motel room most of the time, had food sent in from a deli down the block—turkey sandwich on some healthy hundred-grain bread, hold the mayo, and a carton of *milk*. Made three phone calls to his wife—and that's it. Except for his one foray out of the motel, an afternoon visit to some sleazy divorce lawyer in Venice, a block from the beach."

"That day . . . when exactly was it?"

Laurette paused. "The day after you gave me the green light. Which makes it the day before your father was murdered. After I read the papers, I had my guy check. Pastor's still out there. There's no evidence that he ever left California. Which isn't the same as saying that's where he's been all this time, you understand."

If Charlie Pastor never left California, he couldn't have found out when her father was coming home, and couldn't have met him at the airport. But then why did he have the list? It didn't make sense. Unless Laurette's associate had been fooled.

"Seems like Charlie's wife is soon to be ex. Working on her third alimony at the tender age of twenty-nine. A smarmy little black-widow type, except she doesn't kill them physically. Only financially. Husband number one is a movie executive who, it is rumored among sources who usually know, introduced our girl to cocaine, which she held over his foolish head when she declared she wanted out. Number two is a boy scout who happens to be a mathematical genius who grew up to be the brains behind some hot new Internet security software."

"And number three," Claudia said, frowning, "is Charlie Pastor. He doesn't fit the pattern. No money, no influence. Am I right?"

"Ah, but that's where I needed to do a little extra homework for you. Charlie Pastor's mother was Elizabeth Hadley. That much I knew from the first set of reports. The name kept echoing in my brain. It finally came to me while I was watching the news. Unless you read the agribiz columns in the papers, the name won't mean anything, but his mother's family owns approximately a gazillion acres of California's Central Valley. Spinach, broccoli, beets, soybeans, boy's a veritable vegetable king. Vegetable *prince*. That sent me digging in some new places. Took me a while to find out that his money's all in a complicated trust. It's in his mother's name until he turns thirty-five. I guess the little wifey was hoping to hang on until then, only Charlie gave her the boot."

Claudia's head spun with the new facts of Charlie's life. If he stood to inherit a fortune in eight years, then maybe he really was living his life fully, *free and authentic, courageous and elegant,* following his passion, trying to make his mark at something his family probably thought was useless and even a little suspect.

But that didn't change the fact that he had the damn list. And it didn't change the fact that he appeared to have been in California the night her father was murdered.

"The rest of the report isn't going to help much, either. I didn't turn up anything remarkable about the Mahoney family. A son in Pasadena, a doctor. Working with kids who have cancer. Wife, two kids, house with a pool. The American dream, complete with golden retriever and Land Rover. An overachieving daughter at MIT. Nobody else. No one. If there is a connection with Charlie Pastor, I didn't find it." Laurette paused, then said, "Listen, if you ever just want to have coffee . . . you call me, all right?"

Claudia murmured her thanks and hung up.

For the first three days after she was released from the hospital, Claudia felt helpless against the compulsion that made her look into every mirror, every window or other reflective surface, to stare at the bruised, scraped skin above her eye and try to see a glimmer of life in a face she wasn't sure she inhabited.

By the day of her father's funeral, a morning of fitful showers that gave way to glorious sunshine as the cortege entered the cemetery drive, as though heaven itself were welcoming Evan Patrick Miller, she could barely see the scar. It had become a fading pink reminder that would disappear long before the vivid pain that stabbed at her whenever she thought about her father.

"It's really tough to lose someone you love, especially that way. I'm sorry for your loss," Gary Bruno said, the first day she returned to work. She barely had enough energy to thank him before she turned her attention to the living room walls.

She woke early, went to bed before ten, slept with the help of the little blue pills that Irina said she kept for traveling to a new time zone where people were going to sleep just when she was ready to eat lunch.

"Hey, Claudia, how many screenwriters does it take to change a lightbulb?"

She almost dropped the phone.

Anger, hot and liquid, began in her center and spread to her limbs, and she leaned against a wall to support herself.

"That was your father's obituary I read in the paper?"

She held the receiver at arm's length and took a breath. "Yes, Charlie, that was my father's obituary in the paper."

"I've been so busy I kind of fell behind in my reading, but as soon as I saw the article, I felt so bad. I wanted to tell you how sorry I was to hear about it. Is there anything you need, anything I can do to help?"

Not on your life, she thought, or mine. "It's just going to take time."

"If I rubbed a bottle and my special genie appeared, I'd make a wish that I could do something to help you get through this. I feel awful about the way things ended between us. I can't even comfort you. I'd like to do that, I really would."

Like a self-centered child, he was trying to make his distress one of her worries. All the Charlie Pastors in New York and Hollywood would never be a match for her father. If only she'd responded differently to that phone call . . . He'd still be putting on one of those damn blue suits every day, haranguing the world with his righteous lectures.

Evan would have scolded her for that maudlin bit of self-flagellation. Evan, with his superb timing and his supreme confidence, would have gotten Charlie to explain the list by now.

She closed her eyes, let a deep breath fill her lungs. When she exhaled, she felt calmer. "Charlie? What's it like in California now?"

"Well, I'm sitting in a turquoise and orange motel room with a spectacular view of a parking lot. Venice Beach, rollerblade capital of the Pacific Coast. Claudia, something's going on with you. I heard it in your voice." His breathing, quick and a little too loud, rattled in her ear.

175

The facts in Laurette Lacroix's reports careened through her mind. A life of lies and deceptions, and his sympathy the biggest one of all. Good—anger was what she needed to pull this off. She steeled herself and said, "It's work. We're way behind on Duane Street. Bert's threatening to make me hang sheetrock."

He laughed, too hard and too long. "You had me worried. I thought maybe you were angry with *me* for some reason. Anyway, after I read about your father I wanted to hear your voice, make sure you were okay. And tell you that I'd like to stop by and see you when I get back. I have a few more appointments with some good people."

To get advice from the best electricians about how to fry some relative of Bert's? Either Charlie was telling the truth now, or believing him would be the worst wishful thinking she'd ever done in her life.

"That's great, Charlie. I'm glad. Listen, I'm sorry I'm not more enthusiastic right now, but, as you can imagine, this is a bad time. Good luck on your meetings, okay?"

"You can talk to me." His voice grew tender, soothing. "I want to be there for you."

"How about if I make a little list of everything that's bothering me? Then maybe you'll understand." Annoyed, she started to hang up, but his shout made her stop.

"Hey, what's that supposed to mean? Claudia?"

"Which part didn't you understand? A list. Of things that are bothering me."

"As in Santa Claus, right? He's making a list and checking it twice, gonna find out who's naughty and nice. That list?"

"More like Gilbert and Sullivan. How does it go? Something like, 'I've got a little list of society offenders who might well be under ground and who never would be missed.' That list."

"*The Mikado.* You found it."

What had she done?

She had to be crazy to banter with the man who had tricked his way into her life, the man who might be responsible for several murders, including her father's.

"Yes, I found it. Why did you write down all those names, Charlie?"

She could practically see him push his glasses up on his nose, could envision him pulling his hair back and wrapping an elastic around it. "Oh, God, I knew I should have told you. I found the list in a book. A bunch of names on a piece of paper in a book I found that day I met you. When I knocked you down."

She closed her eyes, brought up the image of the ice-slicked sidewalk, Charlie brushing slush off her coat, helping her retrieve the items that had spilled from her briefcase. Yes, she could see him slip the book into his pocket.

"I remember," she said softly. She'd gone this far; now, she might as well finish the job. "Where did you find it?"

He blew air three thousand miles across the telephone lines. "My turn to ask the questions. What's so important about that list? What's it a list *of*, for Chrissake?"

"Oh, good, play stupid. It's not going to get—"

"I'm coming back as soon as I'm done with those meetings. This is too strange. I'll tell you, Claudia. I'll tell you about the book. I'll explain everything. When I get back."

"I have to go now, Charlie." She laid the receiver in the cradle and didn't answer when the phone rang and rang and rang.

Thirty

She was through playing detective. Let Rick Sarafino and the entire NYPD investigate, let Laurette Lacroix play her little computer games. Claudia Miller was a builder, and that was what she'd confine herself to from now on.

She'd gotten through the funeral with her dignity and her sanity intact; now, she'd be glad to make it through her father's memorial service in one whole and recognizable piece. She was on time and properly dressed, and she would act the part of the civilized mourner. Maybe this ceremony would, indeed, slow down the grinding media machine, as Nora had hoped when she first planned it. Perhaps, two weeks after Evan Patrick Miller's funeral, the symbolic gathering would mark the first step in a return to normal life.

Mercifully, Bert and Irina and a couple of other friends had offered to come back to Nora's house after the service. She'd need help facing all those grimly positive memories everyone was sure to drag out.

The table gleamed with platters of smoked salmon, sliced ham, cold asparagus, caviar, baskets of bread, bowls of potato salad, crackers covered with artfully swirled spreads garnished with olives and pimientos. On the sideboard, crystal glasses and decanters of amber and garnet liquids sparkled on silver trays. Nora looked

178

around, grabbed three salt cellars from the china cabinet, set them on the table.

Even without makeup, her hair pulled off her face into a French twist so that she resembled a grief-ravaged Audrey Hepburn, Nora Miller was beautiful, dignified, steady. Only her gaze, alternately unfocused and jumpy, betrayed her.

"Everything looks wonderful. My father would approve. All his favorites. You'd think the food was chosen because the colors go so well together." Claudia lifted the cover of the sugar bowl, saw the pile of dainty cubes, realized that Nora had seen to every detail. This was the rightful province of the wife of the deceased, not his daughter. Not Evan Miller's builder daughter's job to see to a proper party celebrating his life.

"You think the flowers are too showy?" Nora stood back, hands on hips, head cocked. In answer to her own question, she took a cut-glass vase from the sideboard, pulled eight carefully selected stalks from the floral arrangement in the center of the table. "There. That's better. He left you some stocks, you know. He never told you about it, but they're worth a nice sum. Tommy *did* get more because he said his education needed to be—"

"It's all right, Nora." She had expected nothing, or at least not very much. Ironic if her inheritance turned out to be what she needed to buy Murray's building on Warren Street. "You know I'm not one to measure things that way. Is it all right if I go up and see how Tommy's doing?"

Her cheeks hollow and her eyes without luster, Nora nodded. "He's going to need both of us."

Claudia squeezed her arm and flew up the stairs, knocked softly on her brother's door. "Tommy?"

When he didn't answer, she knocked again, waited with her fingers closed over the cold brass knob, wondered why she heard no sounds from inside the room. No, nothing could have happened to him. She mustn't let herself get carried away. But she pushed the door open, and Tommy Miller whirled around.

"I didn't say you could come in." A black T-shirt and jeans hung from his lanky body; he looked like a child playing dress-up. He shot her a glare and tossed his hair out of his eyes, then dumped black Go stones from a glass jar, rolling them in his palms so they made sharp, clicking sounds.

"Quit that." She grabbed his shoulders, then took his face in her hands and looked into his eyes. "I love you, Tommy, but I can't get through this afternoon for you. You have to figure out who you want to be, and then you have to act that way. It's your life. You're in control."

"Yeah? What about the guy with the lightning bolt?" Tommy shoved the stones into a pile, divided the pile in two, then in four, then scooped them all into the jar and stalked to the far end of the room.

"You have a point. I guess I should have said, you're in control of your own responses. Tommy, I don't have any more energy for wisdom. I just wanted to give you a hug."

He flopped into a chair, his face dark and tight. Arms folded across his chest, he buried his head, then burst out of his seat, an angry geyser erupting into the quiet of the room. "Maybe I should go to California. My friend Rob can get me a job at ILM doing special effects."

"Industrial Light and Magic? The floor sweepers have more movie experience than you. You never even made paper airplanes. I think what you should do is get changed," Claudia said gently. "People are going to start showing up in about ten minutes. Anything I can do to help you get ready?"

"Leave me alone, all right? That's what you can do for me, just leave me the fuck alone, Claudia." His voice was wet and throaty from crying and from lack of sleep. "I don't care who's coming. What's the difference what I wear or who I talk to or who I ignore? You tell me that. What's the difference? And don't say I should do it for my mother. She's just sleepwalking through this whole thing. And so are you, if you really want to know the truth. You hate lies, right? Well, here's the fucking truth, Claudia." He spun around, eyes burning. "It was supposed to be me. That makes more sense, you know? I'm just this zero and he was important. It was supposed to be me. And you messed up the plan, and he's dead."

Reeling, she clung to the doorknob.

"Tommy," she whispered. "It's not true. Some deranged person killed him. It can't make sense. Nobody was *supposed* to die. Please try to see that. Please—"

He ducked past her into the bathroom, where he slammed the door, turned on the shower, sent her a clear signal. This interview was over.

A buzz greeted her when she started down the stairs, and she took a deep breath, preparing to be the daughter of the deceased. How ironic that in his death her father was getting the daughter she thought he wanted years ago, the well-mannered reflection of his good breeding, good taste, good sense.

Don't go getting all sentimental on me, old girl, she thought as she looked around the clusters of people gathering in the corners of the sunny room.

Someone touched her arm. She turned and found herself looking into the myopic gaze of Nancy Weston.

"Claudia? I can only stay about two minutes. There's some state inspection thing tomorrow, well, you know how it is. But I wanted to stop by and tell you if there's anything you need, well, you call me."

Claudia recalled the day Nancy had said, "I need something steady and soothing." Everyone had assumed she meant Valium, but her vision had been broader. She took a loan from her parents, went to pharmacy school, came out the other end a bespectacled pill-dispenser.

"Thanks for coming, Nancy. How are things going?"

"I still don that white coat six days a week so I can rollerblade and go to Broadway matinees and dine at Lespinasse on the seventh. It's the kind of trade-off I never thought I'd make when we were humping sheetrock, but it works for me. You take care of yourself." She pressed Claudia to her in a great, enveloping hug and then disappeared into the crowd.

This wasn't going to be so bad. Claudia moved toward Irina, who stood talking to Nora, stopped when she saw Mikhail Chernin deep in conversation with Bert.

As though he knew by the reflection in Bert's eyes that she was near, Mikhail turned and approached her. He kissed her cheeks, stood back, said, "I am so very sorry about your father. Irina told

181

me, and I felt sad for you. I hope you don't mind that I'm here. I wanted to tell you in person I'm sorry."

His hand was warm on her arm, and she realized she was glad to see him, a person so visibly and forcefully alive. "Thank you for coming, Mikhail. We're all still in shock. Excuse me," she said, looking down at her arm, waiting for him to let her go. "I do have to talk to Nora for a minute."

Was he the one who had met Evan at the airport?

"Before you go, I tell you one thing." He released his grip but held her gaze. "I promise I won't try to change you or fix anything for you, but if you just want company, you call me, yes?"

She searched the crowded room looking for Tommy, stared at the tallest heads bobbing among the chattering group, didn't see her brother's shock of fine brown hair.

Standing alone and uncomfortable beside the dining room windows, a man with a jowly face and alert eyes sipped from a glass of club soda. Russo. The cop heading the task force investigating her father's murder, and Murray's. He nodded, then shifted his position so that he stood behind a trio of white-haired men in dark suits. There were so many business acquaintances, golf pals, corporate board buddies . . .

She needed a drink of water to take away the awful tightness in her throat. She remembered the nurse in the hospital, holding her head and warning her to take small sips. Claudia reached for a glass, poured water from a crystal pitcher, lifted it to her mouth.

Russo, she noticed, had moved on to another group.

The man surveying the humming, swirling throng wasn't here because he felt a social obligation, or because he thought he could offer comfort to Nora or to Tommy, or even to the daughter who had made a deadly decision the night Evan Miller was murdered. He was here because he might find something that would help him solve the case and add a gold star to his record.

She turned away, tears in her eyes, and almost bumped into one of her father's partners. "I'm so sorry about Evan," the man said, his tone serious and his eyes unable to meet hers. He looked past her to assess the room. "You know you can call on me, my dear, if you need anything. Nora is being so very brave but she'll need support. I'm glad you'll be there for her."

She murmured something unintelligible, then slipped out of his grasp. Enduring the canned inanities was going to be harder than she thought. They were, as Bert had said, part of the code that guided people through life's awkward moments. But in order to do a proper job, she needed a moment to gather her public self from the well of her anger and her sorrow.

She ducked into Evan's study, sat in the leather chair behind the desk, glanced at the pencils, blooming like a tidy bouquet in the squat ceramic vase, noticed for the first time the small framed picture on his desk. She'd never seen it there before.

How long, she wondered, had Evan Patrick Miller kept a photograph of his only daughter, smiling from under a yellow hard hat, front and center on his desk?

Thirty-one

He closed his eyes, folded his hands in his lap and exhaled. He needed an answer, and he needed it now, before he did something he shouldn't, before he messed up the whole plan by making a wrong move. He emptied his mind and then carefully, with his heart ready to receive whatever words would be sent, he formed the question.

What should I do about her?

She was really getting on his nerves with her smart-ass ways. Not only did she have to be right about everything and have the last word, she had to play this goddamn soldier game. Marching on no matter how many bodies fell around her. She had to prove she was smarter, braver, tougher than everyone else.

It was all an act and he'd prove it.

A tic pulled at his eyelid when he realized he'd had no response to his question. His heart and his head weren't quiet enough, that was the problem, but how could they be with all this damn noise about her going round and round in him? Better let it run out, like a tape that would later be rewound, and try again.

Maybe if someone had taught her a lesson years ago . . . But as far as he could tell she'd never learned a thing from anyone else. If she stuck to things a woman was supposed to do, she wouldn't be in this mess. In a way, whatever he might do, she had brought it on herself.

He wasn't getting calmer, wasn't approaching a state where he could receive the answer. Then, he'd have to try harder.

Or get help. His heart banged against his chest as he let the idea slip in. Yes, it helped him make that first decision to take action, hadn't it, so why shouldn't he do it now? That's why he had *his* things, so he could have *his* help when he really needed it.

He opened the closet door, reached for the zippered garment bag, the pounding of his heart louder, faster as he ran his finger along the collar of the blue coveralls inside. He pulled out the hanger, hooked it over the top of the door, eyes glazed as he kicked off his jeans and began to unbutton his shirt. His fingers slipped, trembled when he tried again to grasp the tiny buttons. He swallowed hard, took a deep breath, undid his shirt and dropped it beside his jeans.

Shivering despite the dry heat in the room, he stepped into the coveralls, one leg at time. Twisting his torso until he found the armholes, he pulled the garment onto his shoulders, his skin so sensitive, so aware of every seam, of the elastic waistband, of the way the second button pressed against the tip of his penis.

Shoes: this was the part that worried him, because he couldn't wear *his* boots. He reached into the back of the closet, feeling around past the sneakers and both boxes of dress shoes until his fingers closed on the steel-tipped toes of his own work boots. At least they were the same brand, even if they were a size smaller. He sat gently on the edge of the bed, pulled on the boots and tied them the way *he* used to, wrapping the laces around the top of the boot once before he made a neat double knot in front.

When he got up, he turned and straightened the wrinkled quilt, checked the mirror, compared what he saw to the image in the photograph.

His sideburns were a little too long, but that wouldn't matter much. His eyes traveled back and forth between the mirror and the photograph hanging over the bed, and he reached down and unbuttoned the breast-pocket button on the coveralls. There. Now everything was perfect.

Excitement swelled inside him, a flutter in his stomach that, when he first felt it, months ago, he thought of as a nervous tickle. Eventually, he realized it was a sign that *he* was nearby.

From the top drawer of the old mahogany dresser, he pulled out the green wood box, set it exactly in the middle of the little round table, on the doily. With held breath, he slipped the latch, pushed up the lid, stared for several seconds at the white handkerchief that lay in graceful folds inside. He closed his eyes, inhaled, lifted the handkerchief.

Every time he saw it, it took his breath away.

The pipe, a bone-pale meerschaum bowl with a cherry stem, gleamed up at him, and instantly, all his doubts, all the pulsing pain behind his eyes disappeared. He reached for the box, prolonging his anticipation by moving like a cat, quietly, steadily toward the round swelling of the bowl.

When his fingers closed around it, he half expected angels to burst into song, but instead, he heard only the sound of the kids upstairs rolling across the floor in their rubber-wheeled bikes. He waited for his annoyance to go away, then sat in the chair, in the sunshine that fell into the room from the lace-curtained window three feet away.

With the pipe cradled in his hand, he leaned back so the nape of his neck touched the top of the backrest. He tried to find exactly the right words.

I'm sorry I was so careless with the book. That was what he needed to say. *I considered getting another one but it wouldn't be the same.* He sent the message out, then thought again about how to frame his question.

What was he going to do about her, about these feelings of wanting to make her sorry she was such a know-everything show-off? Wouldn't it mess up the original plan if he let himself act on those desires?

Too many thoughts at once. Have to keep it simple. One question. He sighed, smiled, closed his eyes and concentrated.

What should I do about her?

You know that's not your real question. You want to know if the time has come to make her pay personally.

A burst of gratitude swelled in him. They would work this out together, and when he got up from this chair he would know what to do. He no longer had to squeeze his eyes to keep them shut, and he ran his hands along his thighs, rubbing them against the

186

fabric made silken by countless washings, years and years of Deirdre Mahoney's care.

A whispery breath touched the side of his face, and he reached up to his cheek, but it was gone, whatever it was.

Approval, that's what that was.

He didn't have much time left, had better get in one good, clear question right now, before *he* slipped away.

How should I . . .

What should I . . .

They were wrong, based on assumptions. He had already asked his first question and gotten an answer.

She would be next. But he needed to know how. When.

The radiator hissed, clanked, gurgled. He wanted to get up and turn the thermostat down but he didn't dare move. A car alarm went off on the street below his window.

This had never happened before, not when he was trying to talk to *him*. Would it send *him* away? The noise was such a pain in the butt, so distracting that it would probably chase *him* right back where he'd come from. A shiver of fear shot up his spine. Don't go until you've given me an answer, he pleaded silently. Tears pricked his eyes but he turned his head to the side and waited.

Bitch never did know her place. Maybe you need to scare her good first. Maybe she's not exactly next.

Grinning, he nodded, his shoulders relaxed, and he let a single tear, this time one of happiness, slip down his cheek.

When he opened his eyes, he knew, *he* would be gone. He offered his thanks for the visit, and promised to finish the job. "Before May," he said under his breath. "It'll be done before May."

When he hung the coveralls in the closet, he noticed an oily smudge at the top of the left cuff. That wasn't there before, was it? It was proof, that's what it was, that *he* had really been here.

Thirty-two

Work. The harder, the better. Despite Mrs. Hockman's assurances that she shouldn't rush back to the job, Claudia needed to work.

Hour by hour, she moved from one task to another, sometimes going back to sort through the same box of nails a second time or restack boards because she needed to keep moving. She cleaned windows, knowing they would have to be done again before the job was over. If she was numb for now, that was better than total catatonia.

She zipped her jacket, frowning because she could barely remember what season it was, never mind the day of the week. Still not the heart of spring, she thought as she stepped onto the dark street. She hurried the two blocks home, head down against the strong wind blowing salt air from the river.

Wearily, she waved to Nancy Weston as she passed, then turned when she reached her building. All at once, she felt as though she'd run out of gas. She was almost too tired to pull the heavy front door open, except that the promise of kicking off her shoes and watching the local news with a glass of wine in her hand enticed her to keep moving. A glass of wine—who was she kidding? It had become more like three or four before she could sleep. She grabbed the mail from her box, rode up to her loft. Piece by piece, she tossed the mail on the counter.

Four condolence cards. Three magazines. Two bills. And a wheat-colored envelope about the size of a paperback book.

Exactly the same size and the same color as the one that had arrived all those long weeks ago.

A New York City postmark, yesterday's date. How very efficiently the postal service brought unsolicited complications into her life. Claudia picked up the envelope by one corner, slit open the top, shook out the contents.

Four photographs. Not Tommy. The subject this time was a tall, slender woman with short, dark hair.

Going into the hardware store on Canal Street.

Her palms slicked with cold sweat and she wiped them on her jeans before she pushed the top picture aside.

Getting into a car parked in front of a townhouse on East 68th Street, her gaze distracted and her black pumps about to kick a stone on the sidewalk. Vacant—had she really looked like that at her father's wake, her eyes so glazed and empty?

Emerging from the Franklin Street subway station, her purple beret pulled down over her ears.

Lying in the weeds, arms reaching, reaching, blood trickling down her forehead.

Stuck to the last picture was a note, black letters on yellow paper. The message, typed neatly in the center, made the bile rise in her throat. KEEP AWAY FROM THE COPS. Like the warning he'd whispered over the phone.

That time she'd listened.

He hadn't yet made the entire Mercer Street crew pay a debt of grief, so what did this mean? Bert Kossarian's family had managed to escape unscathed so far. How had that happened? Unless . . . No, it wasn't only Bert. There was Ann Magursky, too.

Maybe, she amended. Maybe she simply hadn't read about some cousin of Ann's in the papers. Bert's family, though, was still untouched. She shivered with doubt.

This was a price she was not willing to pay.

She would not allow her friendship with Bert to become another casualty; she was not going to turn over everything sane in her life to this monster.

Besides, the person who'd sent these photographs, who had killed her father and three other people, who had so far been able to get away with all these things, wasn't a *monster.* If she started

189

thinking that way, she'd be giving him mythic powers. No, he was a man, someone without ordinary feelings who operated from his own distorted logic.

Inevitably, he'd make mistakes and he'd be caught. He had tricked her once, but she wouldn't make the mistake of trying to deal with this on her own, not a second time.

She would turn the pictures over to Enrico Sarafino.

She examined the last photograph again, gathering her anger, strengthening her conviction. If only she had called the police that night . . .

She had never been given a telephone number for Tommy's body-guard, had never gotten a bill.

She'd wondered about that once or twice, but her concern had gotten lost in the aftermath of her father's death. She felt as though she were awakening from a long, drug-induced sleep.

Why hadn't any of the detectives on the task force asked her about Charlie Pastor and his list?

She'd handed the list and the book to Enrico Sarafino, and she'd assumed he had turned them over to the appropriate people in the police department. And she'd given him the photographs of Tommy, too.

Maybe the wheels of justice really were grinding away, inscrutably, methodically, persistently, proceeding along pathways unfamiliar to ordinary working stiffs. Surely, all her questions had answers that didn't lead back to Rick Sarafino.

Trembling with anger, she phoned Bert.

When he arrived five minutes later, his face bright with the exertion of running, she nudged the photographs across the countertop to him. "Something's wrong. I mean *really* wrong. These came in the mail today."

Bert stared at the images, his chest heaving, his mouth open. "You got these in the mail? I'm sorry, that's stupid. You wouldn't have said it if you didn't. You think he's going after you? I guess that blows our theory of . . . oh, shit. You don't think I—"

"No." If he were lying, he wouldn't hold her gaze, would avert his eyes. She trusted those baby blues—they'd seen her learn how to hang a door, had watched her drive her Volkswagen off the road so she could help an injured rabbit, had witnessed the six-month-

190

wonder that was her marriage. "I don't think you have anything to do with this."

Bert exhaled noisily, patted his cigarettes, chewed on his lip as he poked at the photographs with his fingertip. "You're going to take these right down to the First Precinct and give them to Sarafino, aren't you?"

"Try this on, Bert." The lights of the Twin Towers winked at her across the rooftops as she looked out the window. "I think Rick Sarafino is dirty. I don't think he ever turned those pictures of Tommy or Charlie Pastor's list of names or that book over to anyone. I never heard from a single other cop about them. And Lazlo, that bodyguard cousin of his, I never got a bill or anything. Why, Bert?"

"Because he's not too smart?" Bert shrugged and shook his head. "Even Sarafino must realize that if he held on to the list and someone found out about it he'd be in deep dog-doo."

"How about a cover-up?" Her heart pounded. "Maybe he knows who's responsible and he's covering up, stalling."

"You think he's protecting someone? Maybe . . . Oh, Jesus, there's a *really* terrifying possibility."

She frowned and studied her friend's face, wondering what he was seeing, knowing it wasn't going to make her happy to find out. "What are you talking about?"

"Suppose Sarafino's not in it alone?"

"Dirty cops, *plural*? That's what you mean?" It didn't make sense. Unless they were all shielding one of their own . . .

"From where I sit, anything is possible. Which doesn't change what you have to do."

"I know." Her stillness was complete and deep, like a forest after a snowfall. "I'm turning these pictures over to the guy who's heading the task force. I'm not making the same bad call twice. The cops come in on this and do their jobs so I can do mine and you can do yours. I'll call right now. You go home, Bert. I need to do this alone."

Bert swept the pictures into the envelope. "And you'll tell them about Sarafino and the list. No holding back, right?"

She nodded.

"And you'll tell them about your screenwriter friend? This

Charlie, he's in California, right? So, if he comes around, he's going to have to ring the bell, and you're going to see who it is by checking the monitor, and if it's Charlie Pastor, you're not going to let him in."

The voice of reason. "Not on purpose."

"That's good, sweetie. You have to swear to me that you won't see Mr. Wonderful." He handed her the envelope. "In fact, I have a really terrific idea. Why don't I just stick with you? I can stand anything for a while. I can sleep on the couch downstairs in your studio. But you have to let me up here to shower. No shower, no bodyguard."

"You just miss my cognac, that's all." The tightness in her chest loosened its grip a little at the thought of having Bert nearby all the time. "That would be good. For a couple of days. If you promise not to talk to me until I've had my second cup of coffee."

"If you promise not to make snide remarks about how long it takes me to finish the crossword puzzle."

She hugged him, then sat back in her chair. "I feel better already. Maybe you should go ahead and get your clothes, books, music, whatever you need. I'm going to call that cop and ask him to come see me here. I don't know, maybe it's stupid, but if we're right about Sarafino being dirty, I want to keep this little talk with Russo as low-profile as I can. I'll see you back here in a couple of hours, all right?"

"My God, woman, you understand what's happening here? You just asked me to move in with you. What *will* the neighbors say?"

She smiled. "They'll probably say your girlfriend threw you out and now you have nowhere else to go."

Thirty-three

"Mizz Miller? I got here as fast as I could."

She held out her hand to the stocky man with the buzz-cut hair and the tired eyes, then took his coat and hung it in the closet. "Thanks for coming by, Detective Russo. Can I get you a drink, some coffee?"

When he pointed to the coffeepot, she filled two mugs and then led him to the living room.

"You mind if I tape this interview?" Russo sat on the edge of the club chair. "I'm pretty bad at taking notes and, well, you know how the memory gets when you pass . . . thirty."

She settled herself on the sofa. Rick Sarafino had never taped a bloody thing. "No problem," she said.

Russo set a tape recorder the size of a box of playing cards on the end table between them and pressed the record button. "I was going to call you tomorrow, to fill you in. We found out where the Lincoln was rented. Some place up in the nineties on the East Side. Renter gave them an out-of-state license that turns out to be a phony. Nobody remembers what he looked like. We've done over a hundred interviews with construction people, but they all can account for their time when your father and Murray Kurtz and Carla Benedetti were murdered. Oh, and one of my cops found a couple of good shoe prints in the sand on that path. Work boots. Worn on the outer edge of the heel. Pretty distinctive pattern, my shoe expert says. But we don't have our guy yet. I'm sorry I don't have more to tell you."

"That's not why I called. I got these in the mail today." She handed him the envelope.

Russo's reaction was hard to read. His face emotionless, he tilted his head, turned each photograph sideways, upside down, stared silently at the spread on the coffee table for a long while, and finally said, "I'm going to keep these and send them up to the lab."

Having them out of her sight was just fine. "What's your take on this? What do you think they mean?" she asked quietly.

A grimace twisted Russo's mouth. "Hey, if I knew that I'd be as crazy as this sick bastard. Sorry. I don't know. This is a new move, zeroing in on you. I can think of two things. The first theory you told me about when you were in the hospital—you know, some guy going after the families of those workers—that was wrong. Or else it's right, but for some reason he, like, changed his mind midstream."

It was reassuring to have her own reactions mirrored by this man, to listen to him grapple with his thoughts and try to fit something so illogical into a pattern of reasonable, coherent thought.

"Good," she said, ruefully acknowledging her agreement, "I see it that way, too. Now, the question is, does this change anything? What next?"

Russo hesitated, then leaned forward in the chair, elbows resting on his knees. "I want to go over some of this background with you again. Maybe we'll see something we missed before."

"Whatever it takes."

"Murray Kurtz was a friend, isn't that what you said when I first spoke to you? I know you told me his brother was one of the people who worked on Mercer Street with you, but you seem to have had a separate relationship with Murray."

He was going to back her up all the way to there? "I've known Murray seventeen years. I worked with him on a couple of projects," she said, uncomfortable with the severe scrutiny of the man who sat across from her. "He gave me a break early on. We've done business from time to time ever since we met."

"And you said you were working for Mr. Kurtz when he was murdered?"

"I was negotiating with him to go into partnership on a building on Warren Street. He owned the building and would put up most of the money. I'd put up the rest and have complete control of the work—design, permits, hiring, everything." She watched Russo's face for reaction, saw nothing but the patient skepticism of a man accustomed to withholding judgment.

Finally, Detective Russo nodded. "This building, did you and Mr. Kurtz have a contract?"

He was fishing, and she didn't like the way he looked at her with those unblinking brown eyes.

"With Murray, until he decided he'd played the game to his satisfaction, there were always details to be worked out. It was how he entertained himself. No, we had one or two things left to settle."

"You sound a little bitter, Miss Miller." Russo made the observation and leaned back in his chair. "So, he played with people. Do you know anyone who was, let's say, especially annoyed with Mr. Kurtz, with his *games?*"

She laughed. "At one time or another, anyone who's done business with him was annoyed. I mean, the New York real estate scene is full of characters. It's changing a little now. The new players are much more businesslike, things are a lot more civilized than they were when Murray and I started out. A sign of the newly conservative times, I suppose. Not everyone loved Murray. Not everyone loves me. The same goes for any landlord or contractor or construction worker. Comes with the territory. If that's all, there are a couple of things I want to ask you."

Russo spread his palms. "Go ahead."

"Do you think these photographs were taken by the same person who mailed me those pictures of my brother?"

Russo frowned.

"And did you find out anything about the list and the book I found?"

"Book? Refresh my memory, would you?"

"The book the list was in," she said, hoping he'd nod and tell her not to worry, that the entire NYPD had copies of Charlie Pastor's list and the handwriting experts were hard at work narrowing down the responsible party. "You know, the one I found in the shopping bag."

He shook his head, puzzled. He really didn't know. He had never seen the photos of Tommy. The man heading the investigation into her father's death had never been told about the list.

"Weeks ago, before my dad died, I found a scrap of paper in a book," she said. "Someone left the book in my apartment. It had the names of all the people in the Mercer Street crew. I turned that paper and the book over to a cop the day I found them."

Russo met her gaze.

For a single horrifying moment, her only thought was that Detective Mitch Russo was in Sarafino's pocket. But the decency apparent in his concerned expression banished the thought.

Claudia Miller reached over and snapped the recorder to PAUSE. "When my brother was attacked, we made a report to Lieutenant Rugowski in the First Precinct. Several days later, I gave another cop four snapshots of Tommy that came in the mail. I thought maybe he could help me get some protection for my brother. This was before the fire in Montclair. He told me the police lab got some bad partial prints from the photos but no matches. When I found that list, he was the one I gave it to. Then my father was murdered and it took me a while to remember everything that had happened before that night. These photographs kind of jarred a couple things loose for me. If this cop turned everything I gave him over to the right people, I'm sure you know exactly what I'm talking about."

"And if he didn't?" Nothing in Russo's face told her whether or not he'd heard the story before.

"If he didn't, then I have to believe he's either dirty or really stupid. Look, I don't know what it means. I don't want this cop to get hurt if he hasn't done anything wrong. But I won't play the sucker anymore, either. For all I know, you're covering for him, you're all covering for each other. I figure I have to take that chance now. What happens next, Detective?"

Russo unfolded his fingers and picked up the pen, rolling it back and forth between his hands. "You don't want advice from me. You want some kind of assurance that you can name names safely. You know something about a dirty cop, you tell me. Tell me or tell someone else, I don't care. Frankly, it's no picnic for me to go to Internal Affairs with this stuff, so if you want to make that contact

196

yourself, be my guest. Here, I'll even tell you who to call." He lifted the pen, pulled a piece of paper from his notebook.

"Never mind." She hit the RECORD button again. "His name is Enrico Sarafino. First Precinct. I gave Enrico Sarafino those pictures and the list of names I found in that book of poems. Robert Frost, did I say that already?"

"And the name of the person who left the book in your apartment?" Russo studied her face.

She looked away. "Charlie Pastor. He called me yesterday. From California, he said. He claimed the list was in a book he found. I only know it was stuck in a book of poems by Robert Frost. Mahoney adored Frost. Quoted him all the time."

"Tell me about this Pastor guy." Russo folded his arms across his chest and leaned back in the chair, as though he were settling in for a long, gossipy chat with an old friend.

And she told him. About the chance meeting on the icy street, about how Charlie had made a visit to her loft to bring her a new briefcase and ended up fixing her lamp with electrical tape, about her belief that Charlie was in California. She handed him the reports Laurette Lacroix had put together.

Russo scanned the first page. "I'm going to keep these, too. As far as you know, this guy is on the West Coast right now?"

"As far as I know. He told me he had several appointments in Los Angeles and then he was coming back to the city. He's subletting an apartment somewhere on West Tenth Street. That's all I know."

"We'll check it out, Mizz Miller. Meanwhile, if you hear from him again, you'll get in touch?"

Claudia Miller gathered both coffee cups and carried them into the kitchen. "I'll let you know."

"I can't say what these pictures mean, but we both know it's not good news. You want to be careful. I'll have the cruisers keep alert on your block. I'll call you if I find out anything. You did the right thing by telling me, Mizz Miller." Russo accepted his coat, picked up the two envelopes, and stepped into the elevator.

Claudia Miller wanted to believe him. As much as she could summon the energy to care about anything, she needed to trust someone right now.

Thirty-four

You walk in, the new kid on the block, and you tattle on the favorite uncle who takes everyone to the ballpark. You know it's wrong that he's diddling one of the little kids, so you holler bloody murder. And then you find out you're the one who's screwed, labeled a snitch, and your life is a periodic hell because the kids who adored him and never get to go anywhere anymore don't ever forget and won't let you, either.

The sun warmed Mitch Russo's face, and he followed the progress of a festive bouquet of balloons as they drifted down the canyon of Franklin Street. "I'm not the hero type, you know what I mean."

"That's not the point, Mitch. Nobody's asking you to do noble battle. You know what you used to tell me? About how you made decisions about things? Well, you have to take your own good advice this time." Teresa Gallagher tugged at his sleeve, pointed south, guided him down the block. "Wait till you see this. It's amazing."

When they first started working together, eight years earlier, he'd outlined the simple tests he had for making decisions. The first question—what if my wife or my kid was the victim in this case?—was the one he'd asked himself most often. The second, the one that came up so seldom he could count the times on the eyes of his dead mother, made him ask what would he do if he knew the *New York Times* were writing a front-page article about him.

198

Which didn't say much, he'd admitted even then, for his moral or spiritual strength, but it helped him when nothing else did to see what was right.

"If I woke up tomorrow to this big spread in the papers, you know what I'd want it to say? I'd want to read that Mitch Russo made sure what he was doing before he turned a fellow officer in. What the lady carpenter said sounds damning, sure. But, hell, that's not my job. To judge? Not me. Holy shit!"

Laughing with surprise, Mitch Russo leaned closer to the window and met the glance of a bright green parrot the size of a schnauzer. The birds, some of them no bigger than a handful of flowers, made a kinetic painting in the window, soft grays contrasted against the raucous reds and greens, the yellow of buttercups. The words URBAN BIRD were reflected on the glass in bright neon letters.

"I find a reason to pass by here every day." Gallagher's grin spread her freckles over her face and she pulled her hands out of her pockets and tapped gently on the glass. Only one of the birds, a small puffy thing with a face like a fuchsia cloud, bothered to investigate. "I've been thinking of bringing this little guy home, except I don't know if Jay likes birds, can you believe that? I'm marrying the man and I don't know something as basic as whether or not he'd like to have a bird sharing his living room. You just came up with the solution, you know."

She was right, of course.

He had to talk to Rick Sarafino. He had to satisfy himself about the man's involvement without tipping him off to the reason for his curiosity.

"So, here's the first advantage to our being in separate precincts. You find out Sarafino's schedule and let me know when he'll be around. You set him up, start a conversation with him about some case. I come in to run a theory by you about how maybe these murders, you know, the Park Avenue Mummy and Montclair explosion and the Phoenix hot-wire and the Belt Parkway thing, are just the beginning of a long list. We watch him. If he doesn't bite, we have a problem. If he's straight, he's going to say something, some little thing about Claudia Miller and her list."

Gallagher glanced at her watch. "He's in the building. I saw him in the hall five minutes before I left to meet you. But he goes off duty in an hour. If we're going to do this, better to just get it over with." She looked longingly at the bird. "I'll be back later, sugar. Maybe I don't have to know if he likes birds, right? Maybe I can't be thinking I have to change who I am just because I'm getting married."

"And I can't change who I am just because Sarafino is in the homestretch to retirement. Forget all that crap about a setup, Teresa. I'm going to reach out, see what he has to say for himself. See what he knows about these murders."

Teresa Gallagher squinted up at him. "You're sure? You sure you want to give him time to hide evidence, cover his tracks, I don't know, find ways to retaliate? I set him up, you come along, that's better. He may feel threatened anyway, but he'll move slower."

"Hey, Teresa! The person I was looking for and here you are, my dream come true." Russo nodded at the big man before he planted a light kiss on his ex-partner's cheek. "You're looking pretty terrific."

Gallagher beamed back at him. "Now that I'm not working with you. Detective Mitch Russo, this is Rick Sarafino, one of the guys who's filling me in on the secrets of this neighborhood. Mitch was my partner when I was in Brooklyn. Evidently, he can't stand the separation."

Russo clasped Sarafino's meaty hand and shook it. "Listen, I only have a few minutes. I'm tracking down a hunch." He turned from Gallagher to Sarafino. "You know how that is, Rick?"

"Hey, you gotta go with what your gut tells you. The more you feel it, the more you can be sure you have it right." He started to edge away, as though he were trying not to intrude.

"You got that right." Russo moved closer, stopped short of throwing his arm around the man's shoulder. "So I have this case, see. It's one of the weird ones. The Park Avenue Mummy, right, where some old guy is wrapped in electrical tape, nothing's missing from this fancy apartment even though there's jewelry and paintings and silverware all over the joint. So I have to believe there's some kind of personal statement the killer is making, you know what I mean?" He maintained eye contact with Sarafino. "And then, because they think there's some connection, they put me on the task force after they find that guy in Brooklyn, the one hanging from the tree. And what do you know, he's got this extension cord wrapped around his neck. And I think, wait a minute, what do we have here, some nut with a long list of enemies, going around doing people with electrical equipment just for the hell of it?"

Enrico Sarafino did look like somebody's uncle, except that his brown eyes darted all over the place, never stopping on anything long enough to really see it. Talk about nervous—the guy kept licking his lips; it was painful to watch, as though his tongue were made of sandpaper.

"I mean, it sounds kind of stupid but, hey, if I can think of it, someone's already doing it maybe, right? So tell me, Teresa, Rick. You think somebody who knows how to wire up a lamp is working his way through a long list?"

Sarafino licked his lips again and broke the eye contact. With an elaborate shrug, he looked down at his watch and then backed away. "You know, that's probably why I never got my gold shield. First, I don't know shit about electricity, and second, I wouldn't connect those murders. Listen, I gotta go finish some paperwork so I can pick up my kid. *Hasta la vista,* buddy."

"You take care, Rick, okay?" Teresa shaded her eyes with her hand, as though a bright summer sun was glaring down on her in the middle of the police station. "See you tomorrow."

They watched the big man lumber toward the stairs, waited until he disappeared. "What do we do now?"

Gallagher's eyes widened. "We? You got a rat in your pocket, Russo?"

"You're right." He sighed. "I have never, in eighteen years, had to bring down a fellow cop. I don't even have hard proof here. My own eyes never saw this guy fuck up. I'll be going in with a civilian's far-out story, a cop who didn't rise to my bait, and my own gut feeling that he's holding back. If he is, if the guy sat on this and people died, then I'm doing the right thing. Shit, I wish I had more proof. Because I'm doing a really miserable thing if I get Sarafino in an Internal Affairs mess just before his retirement."

Gallagher took a step back and cocked her head. "It's not so complicated. He's involved or he's not. Period. If he's not, he's outta here on time and nothing's changed. If he is, he brought it on himself. End of moral dilemma."

Nothing to argue with in that neat package. Except that a little piece of Mitch Russo, the part that was a few years from his own retirement, wondered if anyone could ever really be considered blameless, wondered if something he had done to cover his back or his partner's would jump up and bite him one day.

"Maybe I have to tell him what's in my mind, you know? The thing I care about, first order of business, is to make sure the killings stop. Second, I want to close my cases. I mean, I'm no hero, I do want my numbers to look good, so that's the second thing."

"So?" Hands on hips, Gallagher cocked her head. "He's upstairs. Go play Grand Inquisitor, right? Go ahead. Find out what he knows."

It looked as though Enrico Sarafino had stopped breathing.

"Maybe I didn't say that clearly." Russo sat at the edge of the desk, one foot dangling, the other resting on the floor. "I asked where you were assigned when Kevin Mahoney's body was discovered in a burning building on Mercer Street sixteen years ago."

Sarafino moaned and rubbed a chapped hand over his mouth. "What's going on here, Russo? First you try to play with me about the Park Avenue Mummy case and the Miller murder and now you come asking about ancient history."

"Ah, yes, but current events have a past, am I right, Rick? You know what's going on. I'm going to be as straight with you as I possibly can. You have two weeks to go before retirement. Is that right?"

Sarafino stared at the wall.

"Is that right?" Russo slammed his fist on the desk and then stuck a single finger in the soft flesh under Sarafino's chin. The big man's head snapped up, and he nodded. "So, an investigation now into your covering up a couple, three, four murders would at the very least delay your pension, wouldn't it? An accusation of involvement would send the Internal Affairs Bureau poking around into all kinds of your business, wouldn't it? Wouldn't it?"

This time, Sarafino didn't wait for him to demand an answer. "What's your main point here, Russo? What do you want?"

"You stupid sonofabitch. My point is that people have died and I think you know something about it. You tell me or you tell Internal Affairs."

Sarafino's hand slipped toward his holster.

Automatically, Russo reached across his chest, drew his gun. "You're a dead man if you move." The cold barrel touched Sarafino's temple, and Russo was grateful to see that his hand was steady.

"Okay, okay." Great beads of sweat covered Sarafino's lined forehead. "I'm gonna put my hands right where you can see them. Get that thing off me, man."

Russo waited until both hands lay flat on the pitted surface of the desk. "All right, now you don't move. I'm going to take your gun and hold on to it until we finish talking." He reached across, slipped the gun from its leather holster, slid it into his jacket pocket.

"I don't know who's doing those people. Honest to God, on my kid's life, I don't know. I couldn'ta done a thing to stop it if I spoke up when that Miller broad talked to me the first time. Nothing."

The man was turning to jelly, his voice pitiful and pleading. Despite himself, Russo realized he was convinced that Enrico Sarafino was telling the truth as he understood it. "So why, then? Why didn't you pass the list along?"

His jaw jutting, Sarafino shook his head.

"Me or Internal Affairs," Russo said quietly.

"Shit. If I tell you, will you leave me alone? You can still be the big hero, but there's no reason to bring me into it. None," he whined.

"You have three minutes to convince me I shouldn't turn you in. Starting from now." Russo set his watch on the desk and folded his arms across his chest.

"Okay, all right. See, the thing was, that old fire? My friend Phil Lefkowitz was the first cop on the scene. And when Lefkowitz told me who burned up like that, I thought I was going to die right there with him. Kevin Mahoney—God, he was like a brother. We lived next door, his kids and my kids were like, I don't know, like cousins . . . My throat's dry. I get some water?"

Russo shook his head. "Two and a half minutes."

"Fuck you, Russo. I knew that if anyone found out Mahoney had set that frigging fire his widow wouldn't get the insurance money and even the union probably couldn'ta done a thing for her. So I found some drunk old lady on the second floor across the street and by the time I got through asking her questions, she was believing her own goddamn lies. See, this guy, some smart-ass carpenter, this Amos something, he'd kept me from making a big collar the month before. So I fed the drunken old bird his description, practically dictated it to her, and then she went down to the precinct and told Lefkowitz and he busted the carpenter. By the time he grabbed him, I rigged a receipt for a gasoline can, planted it in the carpenter's apartment, and that was that.

"So now someone comes along and starts killing people. People who are related to the plumber and the carpenter and God knows who else who worked that job. And when Claudia Miller came to me, I knew, I just goddamn *knew* that somehow, some way, I was gonna get nailed for setting up that guy. Christ, I'm not sure I even remember his goddamn name right. He disappeared after he was indicted.

"Look, all I want to do is retire, you know? I don't want to be a fucking hero and get my gold shield, not anymore. I just want to take my wife and go where there's no dirtbags and scumsuckers preying on old people, you know? So that's it, Russo. That's my story. That's why I didn't turn the list in. So what are you going to do now? Send in the cavalry and keep me from getting my pension?"

Mitch Russo nearly choked on his own contempt. "You're going to find a way to clear that carpenter's name. If it doesn't happen in forty-eight hours, I go to Internal Affairs. The other thing you have to know is that there's no way I can keep your name out of this investigation. Forty-eight hours, Sarafino."

The big man pushed his chair away and walked to the door, clenched fists held stiffly at his sides. "Well, that's clear enough. *Hasta la vista*, buddy. See you around."

Russo reached into his pocket and held up the miniature tape recorder. "Oh, yeah, I forgot to tell you. Your words were re-corded for posterity. I don't want to be worried about walking into dark alleys alone, you know what I mean? So my partner gets a copy and I keep a copy stashed in a safe deposit box. Forever, Sarafino. Some bullet finds me, this tape is right there with my will. So don't be a jerk and think you can get rid of your problem by getting rid of me."

He pocketed the recorder, tossed Sarafino's revolver on the desk, and walked out of the room.

Enrico Sarafino was one sad and desperate customer, but none of those things would buy him more than two days' grace.

Thirty-five

She felt as though she had embraced one of those rules in the twelve-step programs. She had finally admitted that she was dealing with something beyond her scope. She turned the case over, even in her heart, to the cops.

Still, she made sure elevators were empty before she got in.

She looked over her shoulder when she heard footsteps coming up behind her on the street. She made sure all the windows, even the ones that didn't open onto fire escapes, were securely locked.

She saw no one hiding in the shadows and taking her picture. For now, she had only the refuge of her work. As long as she kept working, and kept up a constant stream of chatter about anything and everything, she could get through the days. Today, while Bert was busy at the far end of the loft, Gary Bruno had steered the conversation to Ike Hitchens as a symbol of everything that was wrong with America.

As she measured the living room baseboards, Claudia recounted Ike's story. He'd told it so vividly that day in the park that she found herself engrossed in the details again, as though she were reliving a part of her own life. Her indignation grew with the telling.

"So you see how it goes if you're poor and black and trusting? Ike, who could have been a piano player or a piano tuner or even a piano *mover*, ends up on the street, and some sneaky bastard of a neighbor owns the family farm in North Carolina. Justice? I don't think so." Claudia bent over an oak board, examined the top face.

"So I decided to give justice a little nudge, to prove to myself it's not an illusion if only you work at it. I've got it set up for him to stay at that place on Houston and Third Avenue, the one that sells all the old chairs and doors and stuff, to work nights as a watchman. Give him a chance to catch his breath and figure out what's next."

Gary Bruno shrugged and reached for the bucket and his trowel. "Everybody has a sad story. Shit, I spent three months in a foster home because my mother was having problems and couldn't take care of me." He headed for the new wall of sheetrock at the rear of the loft, muttering as he stirred the soupy mass in the bucket. "But I'm working, paying taxes, not taking handouts. You train and you go into the ring and you win or lose, but you don't make excuses."

Claudia shook her head at his lack of charity, then set the board between two horses, pulled the metal tape from her belt, marked off nine feet and one inch, lifted the saw and checked the safety guard.

She'd forgotten how heavy the saw could feel in her tired arms. She set her feet, then braced against the board with her left knee and leaned into the wood. The blade whirred; she guided it along the mark, and the short end of the ten-footer fell onto the floor. The edge was true, and a satisfying little pile of sawdust fell to the floor, gold and fragrant, a festive mound she stopped to admire before she grabbed the next board.

The freedom to make her own rules had drawn her to construction all those years ago, but working with the materials was an unexpected bonus. Tile and brick, earth fired in ovens. Brass and chrome, molten ribbons cooled and polished. The silken smooth veins of marble and slate, rock transformed by heat and time. Wood swelling with years of sap that rose from wellsprings beneath the ground.

She lined up the shoe again, pressed the trigger, watched the blade spin into action.

"Oh, shit!" Bert's voice rang through the loft.

She pivoted, almost losing her balance. The saw came dangerously close to her thigh as she wrestled it away and let go of the trigger. Breathing hard, she set the saw on the floor and then gazed down the length of the loft to see Bert on one knee, head

207

bent, a piece of equipment rearing and jerking in his hands like a wild creature trying to escape capture.

"Turn it off!" she shouted.

By the time she reached him, Bert had managed to find the switch and set the thing on the floor beside him. A bright stream of blood snaked its way from his temple to his eyebrow as he looked up at her through dazed eyes. A trembling finger pointed to the sanding belt. "I was prepping that door to see how it was gonna take the new primer and the damn sander belt snapped . . ." His voice was barely audible.

"If this were a cartoon, you'd be seeing all those little birds tweeting around your head. Here," she said, holding out her hand and easing him to a sitting position, "just rest a minute and then we'll clean that cut."

Bert blinked, pushed himself up, and tottered to the bathroom sink, his face ashen. Claudia unrolled a fistful of toilet paper, stuck it under the cold water, and then dabbed at the wound, a neat slash less than an inch long.

Her electric sander: Bert was sitting on the edge of the tub bleeding and shaking because something went wrong with *her* electric sander.

Bruno appeared in the doorway. "I was mixing up some Durabond and I heard this crash. He all right?" He scowled, his chin thrust defensively forward.

"The sander belt was worn and it snapped. That's all." Bert leaned against the wall, color returning to his cheeks. He pressed a clean wad of toilet paper to his forehead, then balanced again on the edge of the tub and said with measured dignity, "I should have checked it. You've been using the sucker for years. When's the last time you replaced the belt? Anyway, no big thing."

Claudia moved Bert's hand away from the wound, grabbed the first aid kit from the shelf, and pulled out a large gauze pad, a roll of adhesive tape, and a tube of antibacterial ointment. As she unscrewed the cap, she felt Bruno's eyes following her. "What?" she demanded, annoyed.

"I never touched that sander," he said firmly.

"Fine. Nobody said you did." She spread a thin coating of gel on the gauze and leaned toward Bert. "Show's over, folks. Get back to work, Gary. Bert, you go home for the rest of the day. I don't want you bleeding on Mrs. Hockman's nice walls."

Bert pouted, arms folded across his chest. "I'm going to have a cup of tea. I'm going to Yaffa's and let all those nubile young things coo and hover and give me tea and sympathy for a little while. And then I'm coming back to finish my work. We said we'd have this job done in a week, remember? If we get the trim cut today and if Gary works fourteen hours getting the taping done and if I walk around behind him with the primer, then maybe we'll finish in time to get the floor guy in on time. Otherwise, forget it."

He was right, of course, but some things were more important than calling the floor man and putting him off for a while. The gauze pad was turning red; the bleeding hadn't stopped. "We're not children anymore, Bert. Sit down and let me change that before you go out. I'm going to apply pressure for a while."

"And here I've been thinking that's always been your role in my life. Okay, bad joke. I'll be all right after I get a little attention from one of my Marias. Go back to work, Claudia. I promise to take a whole hour off, okay? I should have married you," he said with a frown. "That way I could say no to you and not feel bad about it."

Bert sat still only long enough for her to replace the bandage before he shrugged into his jacket and disappeared. In the back of the loft, Gary Bruno picked up his trowel and bucket and got to work on the divider between the Hockman bedroom and Mrs. Hockman's studio, from which she'd conduct her movie-editing business.

Claudia stood in front of the lumber, staring at the stack, unable to concentrate.

That sander was meant for her.

That sander was the victim of deferred maintenance.

That sander was beside the point.

The real point was that there was still no answer to the question of who had killed her father. Nobody knew yet who had mailed those photographs to her. Russo still hadn't found out any more than they knew when Tommy's face was slashed. Some sneaky bastard had covered his tracks so well the entire New York City Police Department was unable to find him.

She still hadn't heard about the Sarafino business, either. Maybe Detective Mitch Russo had written her off as some ditzy broad who was so shaken by the events of the past month that she'd forget about a little matter of a crooked cop.

Angry, she dialed the number on the card he gave her.

"Russo here."

He sounded tired. Good, that would mean he was working long hours at least. "This is Claudia Miller. Listen, I'm getting pretty sick of waiting around. I wait and people get hurt or else they die. Did you resolve anything in that Sarafino thing? I'm not going to sit on this forever. If you don't do something, I'm going to tap into my other channels. I don't think you'll want me to do that, Russo. What's the news?"

After a long silence, Russo said, "I don't like being threatened, Mizz Miller. You do what you need to."

Maybe what she really needed to do was amass her ammunition, gather enough firepower to feel confident that standing alone in the middle of a field and sounding the alarm about a crooked cop wouldn't be her final, foolish act.

And she knew exactly who she could count on to help her find out as much as possible in the shortest possible time.

She dialed Laurette Lacroix's number. "Hi. It's Claudia Miller. You have some time to talk to me? Face to face?"

"You must read minds. You're a messenger sent to deliver me from this slough of tedium. How about we meet downtown? I need to get out of my office and out of my neighborhood and out of my routine," Laurette said. "You name it, I'll be there in thirty minutes."

Out of her routine—Claudia wished such a thing existed for her right now. "Riverrun. It's on Franklin between Hudson and Greenwich."

The funky, friendly, homage-to-James-Joyce bar would be a fine place to take the next step in her own investigation.

Thirty-six

Laurette Lacroix's beads shook as she swung her head. She held the door for two stockbroker types in wool topcoats, checked out the crowd seated in twos and fours in the banquettes along the brick walls and waved when she spotted Claudia leaning against the curved molding of the bar. Laurette slipped her arms out of her black down coat, her orange leggings and yellow tunic bobbing like bright dahlias in a summer breeze. Heads turned as she made her way to the end of the bar.

"Let's go sit over there in the corner." Claudia picked up her glass and made her way to a small, isolated table against the brick wall. Rows of paintings, all of shamrocks in violent, fluorescent colors, made their way nearly to the ceiling in their chrome frames.

She waited until Laurette settled into her chair. "Thanks for coming all the way down here to meet me."

"I'm the one who suggested it, remember? You saved me from committing mayhem against my computer. I couldn't stand sitting in front of that screen another second. That cut on your forehead must have been really nasty. It's looking pretty good now. Listen, I know I said it on the phone, but I really am sorry about your father." As though she knew she'd reached an unmarked border, she said, "I'm sure you heard plenty of that lately."

"What can I getcha, hon?" The waitress twisted one of the earrings in her right lobe and grinned.

"Hot tea, no milk or lemon, and an English muffin, no butter."

Laurette waited until the woman walked away. "Is this friendship or business?"

"I've been thinking about the information you put together about Charlie Pastor. You haven't come up with anything else, have you?"

Laurette shook her head. "You told me to stop. I did. Honestly, what I see in those reports is trouble, but maybe not the kind you thought he meant. Listen, I have to say this. You paid me good money because you're worried this Charlie might be connected with, you know, explosions, burnings, chokings. We're talking murder, remember? So you keep your distance." Laurette's eyes narrowed with doubt. "This is a job for the cops."

Claudia's laughter had a bitter edge—Laurette had provided her with a perfect opening. "You ever do any work on cops?"

"What, exactly, does that mean?" Laurette folded her hands, suddenly prim and attentive. "You're asking me if I ever investigated a cop, a working cop? Not yet. That's a whole different place I'm not sure I want to go."

Something in Laurette's posture, though, the way she sat a little taller, head tilted expectantly, contradicted her words.

"I want to know if one particular cop has a connection to Kevin Mahoney. Because I think he knows more than he's saying about these murders. He's hiding something, and it's driving me nuts trying to figure out what it is." She explained about the photographs and Charlie Pastor's book and the list, about the frustration of trying to get straight answers from Russo.

"You know something? I hate dirty cops almost as much as I hate guys who talk to my tits when we're doing business. You up for five more hours? I can get to his family history, his work records, and his financial status, you know, credit record, bank stuff, and a bunch of other information. And I'll make some inquiries with some of my pals."

"His name is Rick—Enrico—Sarafino. If you need ten hours, go ahead." Claudia swirled the beer to melt the last of the foam clinging to the sides of the glass. "You might as well see if there's a connection between Pastor and Sarafino, too."

"I was about to suggest that. You looking for a new job, come see me." Laurette waved a hand across the steaming surface of her tea and smiled.

"You never know." Her glass, nearly empty, left a ring on the paper coaster. "I don't want Charlie Pastor to be the one. Maybe that's foolish, but it's the truth."

"The picture I get is, this Charlie is a guy who's made a lot of mistakes and now he's trying to change things around. But I never had the pleasure of meeting him, you know, looking him in the eye. That strike you as a possibility?"

"It strikes me as what I'd most like to hear because it means my antennae are still working, I'll tell you that. Something about him makes me nervous."

Laurette's eyebrows rose. "I don't know what's going on here, but I have to say this. If you're afraid—now this is you I'm talking about, not some wispy little girl off the bus from Paducah—if you're afraid, which I'd bet doesn't happen to you but once or twice a decade, then you act smart. You don't trust this guy. Now this next is me talking, not my job. You're not the delicate type, you'll get over him."

"Information *and* personal validation." Smiling, Claudia toyed with her napkin. "Mikhail Chernin sang your praises but he didn't tell me just how good you are. What's your take on him? Mikhail, I mean."

"No how, no way, babycakes." When she laughed, Laurette looked more like a schoolgirl than a queen. "You're not really asking me to tell you about a client, right?"

"I don't mean professionally. You worked with him. He hired you. Which means you spent at least a little time together. Part of your job is to read people. So if you think it's over the line that I asked you, I'm sorry. I'm not asking you to be unethical. I just want your take on Mikhail Chernin, in case it might save me some time and some grief. I can't trust anyone anymore."

Laurette frowned. "I don't blame you. Look, Chernin's a smart man. He's ambitious and a quick study. That's about all I know, except for the vibe I get. I think I'd want him on my side."

"You *think*? Or are you sure?"

"I've been wrong once before. And I divorced *him*." Laurette looked at her watch. "I better get going."

"I'll pay you up front for the Sarafino work. Five hours, minimum. You'll bill me if you do the other five." Claudia grabbed her purse from between her feet and dug through it for her checkbook, fingers closing over her wallet, keys, pens, a roll of mints. The image of her red checkbook sitting on the counter came into clear focus. "Damn, I must have left my checkbook at home. It's only a couple of blocks away. If you wait I'll—"

"Whoa. Pay me later. You won't run out on my bill. I know where you live. As they say." When Laurette Lacroix laughed, tiny showers of light cascaded into the room; people turned to look for the source of the sound.

"Before you leave, I want you to tell me something." Glad to be allowed the pretense of normal conversation, Claudia poured out the rest of her Brooklyn Lager, watched the pale foam disappear into golden bubbles. You do that everywhere you go?"

"Do? Do what, give credit to my customers? Not all of them." Laurette leaned back and shrugged.

"No, not that. Command the attention of everyone in the room. Where'd you learn that?"

Laurette tossed her head and reached into her purse for a zebra-striped cigarette case. "You ever stay undercover for four months?" Her eyes narrowed as she blew a thin stream of blue smoke through burgundy lips. "You ever try being the wallpaper on the wall of a corporation that's being bled by one of its employees or the powder under the nails of a drug dealer? It's hard enough in everyday life being a black woman, but being a black woman who sometimes has to be invisible to do her job well, that really takes creative juice. But I do it. I pull it off when I have to. So, when I *don't* have to, I'm, like, pleased to be turning heads, you know what I mean?"

A blustery wind swirled down Franklin as she walked toward Hudson. Never in her life had she misplaced her checkbook. A sign of how preoccupied she'd become, her lapse would have been a great excuse for her father to deliver a lecture about the need to pay attention.

A creased black-and-white photograph caught an updraft and sailed drunkenly east. Eyes shining, a woman looked at the camera dead-on, a heart-shaped locket resting in the hollow of her throat. A type, devoured daily by the casting agency around the corner. Probably back home already, Cincinnati, Raritan—what was it about New Jersey that bred so many yearners who believed their own lies?—or serving osso bucco in a fresh-flower restaurant and praying for twenty percent tips from a clutch of arbitrageurs.

Claudia turned away from the hopeful, crumpled face.

That might have been me, she thought, except for the age, twenty years younger, and the Cleopatra eyes, and the trust in that other face. Nobody would mistake her for a dreamer; she hadn't been a person without a past for a long time. Besides, no one had ever taken Claudia Miller for a sweet, docile girl who followed the rules and hoped for the best.

She hurried south for one block, turned the corner at Harrison. A figure, tall and broad-shouldered, emerged from the dark overhang of the scaffolding in the Staple Street alley.

It was Ike, that was all. She almost cried with relief.

He had commandeered a couple of choice pieces of cardboard and had spread out his possessions under the scaffolding. He'd been stacking plastic containers one inside the other when she walked by. She thought briefly of the afternoon Tommy had arranged her spices during a burst of manic energy, understood that for Ike this activity was a much more complicated exercise, one that gave him the illusion his life hadn't disintegrated into total chaos.

"Looks like winter might actually be over sometime this year," she said as he approached. "You move in to that place on Houston yet?"

"Manager's away. I'll try again tomorrow." Ike nodded, rolled two shirts into a neat cylinder. His eyes seemed clearer today, less clouded with alcohol. "Nothing like a little spring cleaning to start things fresh. That scrape on your face is near gone. How you doing today? Your brother okay?"

"We're all doing fine." Ike wasn't much on keeping up with the daily news. He probably had no idea how much her life had changed since she saw him last. She pulled a ten from her wallet, pressed it into his hand. "They're serving an excellent meatloaf at the Square Diner today."

"You're a good heart, yes, you are. Mashed potatoes goes pretty fine with that." He stuffed the bill into the pocket of his thin trousers, then secured the bundle of shirts with a red striped tie and grinned. "My mama's mashed potatoes, mmm mmm, best in Mecklenburg County. Thanks."

As she rode up in the elevator she wondered what Ike Hitchens's mama would think if she could see her son so far from the steamy days and long Tarheel nights of his youth.

When the door slid open, she stepped into the loft and reached for the light switch on the wall beside the elevator door, fingers groping along the cold surface of the unpainted sheetrock. Her throat closed up and cold sweat beaded her flushed face. She opened her eyes wider, as though that would help her see any menace lurking in the darkness, listened like a feral creature wary of surprise attacks.

Her finger found the switch, flipped it up.

Light flooded the familiar space.

Head pounding with leftover adrenaline, she spotted the checkbook on the counter, tossed it into her purse. No need to make a searching and fearless emotional inventory. She was angry, frustrated, aware that it would be a while before she felt like her old self again.

Thirty-seven

Plugged in. He chuckled when he thought of those words, the way the magazines used them, the way the reporters on MTV or the other hipper-than-thou channels threw them around.

Ann Magursky Carleton wasn't going to feel connected to anything but the great beyond by the time someone else thought to use those words to describe her. After Ann, he'd let Claudia Miller stew for a little while and then it would be her turn.

That was going to be very special; he didn't want to mess that one up. How to do it? Something that would give her the opportunity to know exactly what was happening to her, to feel the terror of being unable to get away . . . to feel trapped, like Red Mahoney had been.

Not now. That plan required his complete concentration.

He'd think about it later, when he didn't need all his attention focused on that path twenty feet away.

The sun warmed his face as he reached into his jacket pocket. His fingers closed around the cold bowl of the pipe, then traced the length of the stem to the slightly flared mouthpiece. The dry grasses weren't great cover, but then no one much came around to this part of Staten Island. No one much except Ann, who trudged down the path every Wednesday all winter long to refill the bird-feeder in the marsh behind her house.

He wondered what people got out of it, sitting in a chair in their snug little houses with a pair of binoculars pressed up to their eyes, watching birds fly in and out of little wood houses on stilts. Some fun. Some damn fun. But at least it gave him a handle on her, on a place he could get to her where there would be no one to see, no one to hear her cries.

The wind picked up and he pulled the collar of his coat closer, wishing he'd brought a thermos of something hot this time because out here in the marsh he didn't have to worry about finding a bathroom. He ran his hand along the edge of the plug. It was good and sharp now, that was for sure. It had taken only an hour to make the points like little razors, and now his fingers couldn't stop running along the edges, along the points, knowing that when he hit home, the bright spurting blood would make the dry grass scarlet with color.

None of them was good enough to even wash Kevin Mahoney's socks. They would never understand what a difference a single person could make. How everything could be changed, lives thrown into the seventh circle of hell because the one person who could have made things different wasn't around. He closed his eyes and conjured up the face, flushed and smiling, the nose pushed over to one side, the scar that creased the bushy eyebrows. When he was young he used to like to rub those wiry eyebrows and watch them spring up in a hundred different directions. When he climbed down from the comfort of that lap, Kevin Mahoney would reach up and smooth them again and say nothing, but the smile would tell him everything. *You're safe here*, it said. *You can play and joke and I'll take care of you and love you, no matter what.*

What Kevin Mahoney had forgotten to say was that he wasn't going to be around forever.

A sudden movement at the edge of the marsh caught his eye and he whipped his head around. A small black and brown bird with a white cap disappeared into the round hole, then poked its head out. Did the stupid thing know she was coming? Was it going to warn her he was there waiting for her?

Eyes closed, he pulled the pipe from his pocket, inhaled the familiar aroma, the butterscotch perfume he found so comforting.

He held his breath, listened to the wind rustle the grasses. No, it wasn't the wind. She was coming. He glanced up, saw the bobbing figure approach, snugged the pipe into his pocket.

Her coat, the same tatty brown wool thing she'd worn every
afternoon to hang the wash or go to the Gristede's, was unbuttoned this afternoon, and she wore no gloves. A wool cap was
pulled down over her ears and he could tell even from half a block
away that she was smiling.

Maybe she was thinking of her husband, of how well things were
going for his restaurant equipment business. Maybe she was planning what she was going to make for dinner. A day that promised
spring, maybe she'd get a couple of lamb chops over on Hylan
Boulevard and splurge on asparagus and pretend it was Easter.
Whatever was making her so goddamn happy wasn't going to last
long, that was for sure.

Until Ann Magursky, it had been the survivors he wanted to
hurt. The ones who had to spend every day knowing they'd been
responsible for the death of a loved one. They were the ones who
would burn in their own private hell whenever they thought of
Kevin Mahoney and how they had contributed to his death, and
how that contribution meant one of *their* loved ones had to die.

Sure, he was going to burn right along with them, no question,
he knew that. But some shows were worth the price of admission.

The woman's step was plodding and regular, the bag of birdseed
swinging against her side with a rustle and swish. The path she'd
worn down for so many months still crackled with each step, a thin
layer of ice giving way beneath her muddied boots. She was almost
even with him now, ten feet to his left, and her brown eyes blinked
against the sudden sunlight that sparkled on the brackish waters.

She was talking to herself.

"Yes!" she said softly, nodding as she strode past his hiding place
in the weeds. "I'm coming. You're there waiting for me, I know
that. Even if I can't see you, I know you're there."

He shuddered, his bowels clenching in horror until he realized
she was talking to the damn birds.

Another couple of steps, and he tensed, ready to spring up from
his cover. But he would wait until she was no longer visible from
the street. He had watched her for weeks as she traversed the same
ground, had watched the top of her head sink lower and lower as
she marched down the incline, had calculated the exact point at
which she would become invisible from the street.

A bird peered out from the small hole in the feeder, and she stopped in her tracks. "See," she said merrily, "I knew you were there. Yes, I did. Nobody cares about you but me, so I have to feed you. Yes, it's Wednesday and I'm here and you're here. I wouldn't disappoint you, now you know that."

Was she afraid her movements would scare the stupid thing away? Was that why she froze, staring straight ahead, her breath even and loud? If she didn't stop saying all those creepy things, he'd howl. He bit his lip to keep from shouting at her to move along.

This is your last bird, your last cloud, the last piece of grass you'll ever see, he warned. He held his breath while she resumed her steady progress toward the bird feeder. She passed him, walked ten more feet, stopped at the spot where the grasses had been pressed flat from a whole winter of her standing out there, every Wednesday at exactly four o'clock. She was such a small thing, birdlike herself. He'd bet she twittered instead of laughing. No twittering after today.

She wheeled around, eyes wide when she saw him, arms flapping up as she tried to run. Her face was white, like the salt on the edge of the board that had washed up on the beach just a few feet away, and when her mouth opened, a tiny squawk came out.

He caught her from behind, her chin resting against the crook of his arm as he forced her head back. The sharp edges of the plug sank into her throat easily, and he pulled hard, up and across, until he reached her ear. Ann Magursky Carleton thrashed for a few seconds and then went limp, her eyes rolling back in her head, birdseed flying in the air.

When he reached the dirt path, he turned. Smiling, he noted that the air was suddenly dark with small bodies, the birds coming from God knew where to feast on the seed scattered on the ground.

Thirty-eight

They sat at the dining room table bathed in morning quiet, sun streaming in the windows. Reading the newspaper and drinking coffee had become standard morning procedure; Claudia smiled to herself. They slept on different floors of her duplex apartment and didn't have sex even occasionally, but she and Bert had fallen into an old-married-couple routine with ease.

Bert picked up a pen, folded the paper to the crossword puzzle, passed Claudia the front page.

When the buzzer sounded, Claudia frowned and padded to the monitor, sleepily focused on the figure on the screen.

"Shit," she whispered. "It's him."

Bert looked up, pen poised above the paper. "What?"

"Charlie Pastor. He's downstairs." The buzzer blared again. "I'm going to let him up. I'm going to find out about that list."

"Don't." Bert stood beside her, breathing hard. "Call Russo and tell him Pastor's back in town, but don't get involved."

"This is an opportunity, don't you see? Anyway, Russo and Laurette Lacroix put him in California when my father was murdered. Besides, he's not going to try anything with you here." She reached for the intercom, stumbled backward as Bert grabbed her wrist.

They glared at each other in silence, a flush rising up Bert's neck as he pressed his lips together. Finally she said, "Let go, Bert."

His hand fell to his side. She pressed the button to buzz Charlie Pastor in the front door, rang for the elevator, waited.

Wordlessly, Bert stalked back to the table, clicked his pen, and rattled the newspaper.

When the elevator door slid open, Bert didn't look up.

Hair windblown, leather flight bag slung over his shoulder, bright eyes pausing when he saw Bert, Charlie unleashed a smile that deepened the dimples alongside his mouth. He dropped his bag onto the floor and held her hands as he stood back and let his eyes travel from her black suede loafers to the shining fringe of her hair.

"Wow, you look so New York. God, it's good to be back in civilization. Eighteen people on the whole flight. How they make money on these red-eyes, I don't know." He slipped his arms out of his coat but left the bright blue scarf draped around his neck as he glanced at the dining room table. "Hey, I'm sorry. I didn't mean to intrude."

Bert glowered and picked up the newspaper again.

"Charlie, look, let's not play this game. This is not an ordinary Thursday morning breakfast, tra la."

He pushed his glasses up on his nose, his smile fading. "Right. No, it's surely not. How could you do that to me, Claudia? Those cops were sniffing around me like jackals around fresh carrion. I could practically see their teeth glinting in the desert sun, you know, getting ready to rip my flesh apart. And then I find out they actually went to the City Flickers people to verify that I was in a meeting with them ten days ago. You know what that does to my chances of working with them?"

Pretty Charlie's schoolboy cheeks glowed with color; Claudia kept her voice low when she said, "Perhaps that wouldn't have been necessary if you hadn't lied to me."

His turn.

She would wait. She bit off a piece of toast, chewed deliberately while his upper lip jumped with a twitch.

"Lied to you? Okay, so I wasn't as close to making a deal as I might have indicated. So, I really went back to California to finalize my divorce." He looked away, as though too embarrassed to meet her gaze. "She tricked me, you know. The old honey-I'm-

going-to-have-your-baby line. She seemed to be a sweet kid. I figured it wouldn't be the worst thing to give it a try. I'd end up supporting the child anyway so maybe we could make a family out of
the mess." He wagged his finger. "Dumb. And dumber than that,
I didn't ask for proof or anything. Because three months later,
when her figure hadn't changed and she still had this washboard
belly, she told me she lost the baby. Tears, sobbing, the whole
thing. And then she turned into a witch."

Claudia slathered strawberry preserves on her toast, set the knife
on the plate. "This isn't *Geraldo*. I don't care why you married
her. I care about why you lied to me."

"I didn't tell you," he said, reaching for her hand, frowning
when she pulled it out of his reach, "because the whole episode
made me feel like a jerk, and I really, *really* wanted you to think
well of me. To find me interesting and sophisticated. If you think
that's sinister, that's your privilege. Personally, looking back, I find
it endearingly human."

She couldn't swallow it. Couldn't swallow his story or his
attempt at humor, couldn't swallow the food in her mouth that
tasted like cardboard. "That's not the lie I'm concerned about.
Talk to me, Charlie. Tell me about the list."

He blanched. His hands shook and he took a tremulous breath,
bent down, unzipped a pocket of the bag that lay at his feet.

From the corner of her eye, she saw Bert rise, watchful, his body
tensed and ready.

But when Charlie straightened, he clutched a roll of antacid
tablets in his hand, peeled back the paper, popped two pink
lozenges into his mouth. "I found that book on the street," he
said. "Lying on the sidewalk, I'll tell you exactly where, right in
front of the bank on the corner of Hudson and Franklin. The day I
met you. About an hour before we bumped into each other. There
was no name or anything in it, and I just kept it, you know,
because I thought it meant that I'd read some poem that would
change my life, right? The owner was using a piece of paper as a
bookmark. Sure, I read it. Yes, I saw all those names, but they
meant nothing to me. Nothing. Until I literally ran into someone
named Claudia Miller an hour later. I took it as a sign that we were
meant to be together."

223

What was wrong with that picture? She couldn't tell. If she believed him, then Charlie was guilty only of the excessive romanticism to which he'd been pleading guilty since they'd met.

"Why didn't you tell me right then?"

He laughed. "I started to when we were talking there on the street but you interrupted me. Then, I was going to tell you the whole charming little story that day I brought the briefcase to your loft. And then again when I saw you in the park. But the opportunity just didn't come up. I didn't want to, I don't know, upset you. I could tell you had your own secrets, that you were edgy about something. I mean, more than the average permanently semiparanoid New Yorker. I didn't want to add to your problems with some stupid story about finding your name in a list in a book I picked up on the street." He shook his head. "Wrong."

Absolutely wrong. But whether or not that meant he was lying about the list and how he came to have it, she didn't know.

"Why does it matter, Claudia? What's so important about Robert Frost?" He stared at the brick wall behind her, like a student puzzling over an elusive point of logic.

"It was important to Big Red, wasn't it?"

"What? Big Red? I don't know what you're talking about. It really makes me feel bad to be so shut out."

"A while back I told someone else that whining was an unattractive quality. Grow up and stop making everything about you." If that didn't drive him away . . . "I think that's all we have to say to each other."

"What, you're expelling me from your life?" His face sagged, the fatigue now evident in his droopy eyes, the slackness in the corners of his mouth. "A book of poetry—you can have it. You can keep it to remind yourself of what you're missing or you can throw it in the trash so you don't have to go on thinking about how irrational you've been. I never wanted it. I just wanted you, Claudia. I wanted to be with you."

He grabbed up his bag and his coat and stepped into the elevator before she could set her empty coffee cup in the saucer.

Empty, empty—the word rolled around until the sounds started playing bumper cars in her brain.

"Maybe this is the wrong time to bring this up, but I'm sorry about what I said about his being young." Bert smiled and covered her hand with his. "Which doesn't change the fact that he is. I'm sorry."

She smiled back at him, acknowledging the truce. "That's been my line lately. I'm sorry, too, that I got on you about Ellie."

"That was some performance." Bert picked up his pen again. "His, I mean."

"You think he couldn't possibly mean what he said about wanting to be with me?" She felt a bubble of laughter rise up from her throat, knew it was relief that she'd gotten through the surprise of the past ten minutes.

Bert groaned. "There is no way I can answer that without getting into trouble again. Here, finish thirty-two across and twenty-eight down for me and pass me the Metro section." He slid the folded newspaper across the table.

"Finish the puzzle yourself. I'm calling Detective Russo. Charlie Pastor talks a good story, but I still need to let Russo know he's back in town."

He tilted back in his chair. "And while you're at it, you can tell him Pretty Boy is quite slick with the words so he shouldn't let himself get bamboozled. Although I'd guess the good detective is a little less susceptible than a certain—ow!"

He grinned when she pinched his arm and then walked to the window. As she peered down at the street, Charlie raised his arm to hail a passing cab. She waited until the cab was out of sight before she fished Russo's card from her pocket and started to dial the number, frowned when Bert approached and thrust the folded newspaper into her hand.

Pale and tight-lipped, he stood beside her, his scarred index finger pointing to a half column article on the front page of the Metro section of the *New York Times.*

She read the first paragraph. A corpse found the day before in a Staten Island swamp had been identified as Ann Magursky Carleton. Her throat had been slashed with a sharpened electrical plug embedded in the soft tissue of her neck.

Ann Magursky had married Somebody Carleton, and now she was dead.

"Ann," Claudia whispered. "Not her uncle or her mother or brother. Ann, herself."

She felt the way she used to when she had The Dream, as though she were pushing her way through a thick, damp fog as sticky as spiderwebs and the color of mealybugs. The Dream always left her with muscles that ached from clenching and a sense of foreboding that wouldn't go away even after she'd opened her eyes and saw that, beyond her window, the city was bathed in a golden sunrise.

"I feel sick, Bert. This one didn't have to happen. Maybe if I'd blown the whistle on Sarafino earlier, Ann would still be knitting those awful sweaters she used to make for some poor friend every Christmas. If I'd been more, I don't know, *dramatic* when I asked Benedetti to help me find her . . . I should have been able to stop this."

"I don't see how, sweetie. You did what you could. Besides, this one is different from the others. Looks like he's changing the rules."

Claudia sagged against the wall. "I wonder if *she* got pictures of herself."

"Ann Magursky Carleton is dead. This is another message, sweetie. You and me," Bert said gently, "we're next on the list. Go ahead and call Russo, and make sure you tell him about Pretty Boy."

She dialed the number and told Detective Russo that Charlie Pastor was back in town.

"He was carrying a suitcase and claimed that he just stepped off a red-eye from Los Angeles," she said, "which, if it's true, means that he probably didn't have anything to do with the murder on Staten Island."

"The dead woman was the Ann who worked with your Mercer Street crew, right? I was just about to call you," Russo said. "You be careful, you understand? Just be careful."

Thirty-nine

An earsplitting cacophony blared from the radio, and she stared at the dial, wondering who had made such an ungodly selection. Gary Bruno's noisy music. Bad musical taste—just another reason to look forward to the end of this job. She lowered the volume, hunted for classical music or reggae, wishing she'd brought her own tapes.

"I didn't hear you guys come in." Bruno stepped back, sponge and water pan in hand, and examined the plasterboard seam. When it was painted, no one would see the joint. He *was* as good as Bert had promised.

"You going to have enough of that stuff to finish the job or should I order more?" Bert rummaged among the slips of paper for his list of materials.

Bruno bent over a five-gallon container, peering into its depths. "This should be enough. I don't think I have but one, maybe one and a half days' work left. Unless there's something else you got for me to do."

"We'll talk tomorrow," Claudia said. "You go ahead and get the back walls taped." Not having to listen to Gary Bruno's grousing would be paradise, but he did good work and if Bert thought they should keep him on for other tasks, she'd go along.

Shrugging, Bruno said, "Yeah, sure. I'm going back to mix plaster into my Durabond. It dries out quick so don't call me for a while. You okay? You look a little tired or upset or something."

"Just tired. Go ahead and finish up."

Probably she wouldn't be using him again on this job. The shelves, thick slabs of oak designed to hold Mr. Hockman's record collection, still had to be notched into the wall. The closet had to be built so that, when fully open, it became a self-contained office, complete with ancient Moviola, storage for supplies, a filing system. She and Bert would do a fine job, just the two of them.

"You really want to keep that Chelsea appointment tomorrow morning?" Bert asked. "I can go over there if you want."

Claudia shook her head. "You know me—I'd rather have too much to do. They only want me to check out where the phone lines come in, and look at the second-floor fireplace. I can handle it. I'll take the shingler's hammer and maybe a nail puller. That's all I should need, pretty much, to get an idea about what it will take to do the job."

"You're sure you don't want me to go?" Bert set the sawhorses, selected a piece of three-inch trim from the stack, then looked up at her.

"I told you—I'm sure. I still remember how to swing a shingler's hammer. It might even make me feel better to smash something to tiny little splintery bits. If I don't keep busy I'll go nuts." Claudia dug through the carton, tossing hammers and screwdrivers and drills onto the floor. "Where is the damn thing?"

"In the basement storage locker, in the Knaack box," Bert said. "Where you put it with all the other tools we're not using because you said they were getting in the way. Remember?"

Grumbling, annoyed that she hadn't remembered and unwilling to ask Bruno or Bert to fetch and carry for her, Claudia snatched the basement key from the counter and stepped into the elevator.

If she allowed Ann Magursky's murder to throw her, she'd be letting him win. She had to get over this edginess. It was the only way she could reclaim her life.

When she reached the ground floor, a looming shape blocked the light and cast a wriggling shadow on the lobby tiles. Through the glass door she saw Mikhail Chernin, his arms waving.

"I thought you might be here," he said when she opened the

228

door and let him in. "I want to talk to you. Can you come and have coffee with me?" The stubble on his jaw was dark, as though he'd forgotten to shave, and his mouth was tight.

"I'm not ready to take a break yet. Come with me, talk while I get something out of the basement. What's on your mind, Mikhail?" The door to the basement swung open as she unlocked it; she found the light switch, flipped it on. The damp smell, a stew of mushrooms and wet wood, reminded her of spring gardens after a rain.

"I'm worried about you." He hung back on the top step, his shoulders hunched as though touching the walls would contaminate him. "I can't go down there. My father made us hide in the cellar one day. A long time ago, before all this new freedom, when I was four or five. You get what you need. I wait here."

She shrugged, continued down the stairs, until she was two steps from the bottom.

Was something waiting for her at the foot of the stairs, something Mikhail had prepared, an electrical surprise that would surge through her and crackle the hairs on her arms and sizzle her lungs? She looked over her shoulder at the silhouette filling the doorway. She was only imagining his dark eyes peering down at her. Perhaps Ann Magursky's last vision had been his smiling rictus mocking her fear.

She was acting like a goddamn girl.

Nothing had ever stopped her from riding the subways or going up to Harlem to order tin ductwork or walking home alone after a late supper at the Odeon. Now she was afraid to take one more step into a basement, and it made her angry.

Still, it wasn't very smart to continue moving toward what might be mortal danger just to prove to the dark-eyed man standing ten feet away how brave she was.

"I changed my mind. I'll get it later." She pivoted, started up to the landing, where Mikhail stood with a frown wrinkling his forehead. "I'll meet you in Yaffa's in half an hour. We can talk then."

He shrugged and let her pass, waited while she locked the basement door behind her. "Fine, whatever you want. I must tell you how much I appreciate your kind hospitality."

She answered his smile with one of her own. "You've learned a little American sarcasm, I see."

"You think Ukrainian sarcasm isn't good enough?" He shook his head, the smile fading. "I want to make the worry in your eyes go away. I want your mouth to not be so tight and angry."

"Wait, please. Stop trying to take care of me. I'm not a helpless creature who needs rescuing. Don't make this your business, Mikhail."

"I want you to be my business. I will learn how, if you give me a chance. I will let you take care of yourself, if that's what you want. But you need to know that to be an adult woman you don't stand all alone, like a rock in the middle of the sea. The sea eventually wears down the rock, you know." He brushed her cheek with his hand, then stepped back again. "I *am* worried about you. You look pale, thin, you jump at every noise. I know this is a hard time for you, and if you don't want my help, fine. But do something to take care of yourself, Claudia. I'll see you in half an hour."

"For a week you don't return my messages but I see you going to work every day, so I guess my friend Claudia must be feeling better." Irina planted her elbows on the table, her sculpted chin resting atop her crossed hands. "I have been worried about you. I didn't want to bother you, but I was going to send a telegram soon. You don't answer messages for a while, I can understand. But a week . . . I was worried, Claudia."

Claudia started to wave her hand, as though to dismiss her friend's concern, then pulled out a chair and sat down. "Sorry. It's taking longer than I expected to be ready to face the world again. I went back to work because I figured I was better off busy than remembering. And it does help. But I'm not really back to myself yet. Let's not talk about me anymore, all right? Did you do that job in Miami?"

Irina's fine white teeth flashed as she laughed. "The offer was only if I pay my airfare and my hotel. I said no. I was afraid when I said it. Maybe I would never have another job. But the agency finds more for me. I feel good I did that."

"Very brave." Claudia smiled at the victory, remembering the strength she'd felt turning down bad deals, wondering whether she'd lost her nerve permanently. Maybe it would regenerate, like some mended bone, stronger than before but less flexible. She sat up in her chair and pulled herself straight, hoping her body would help the rest of her find the necessary willfulness.

He was trying to cut her down with those photographs, maybe even Ann's murder, to chip away at her strength. Somehow, people survived decades of the kind of war in which buses and shopping centers blew up: Ireland, Israel, anywhere the terrorists waged battles away from what used to be neat official war zones.

People forgot, that was how they lived with it. They forgot, and kept the hard kernel of hate inside, so that it became impossible to dislodge, eventually becoming an essential part of their being.

When Maria from Prague set a pot of tea in front of her, Claudia looked up and Irina nodded at the door.

"Mikhail's here," Irina said softly, and for a moment, Claudia half expected to see a man dressed in black with a pipe bomb tucked under his arm.

Instead, she found herself peering into the dark eyes of Mikhail Chernin. He dipped his bearish head slightly, his silence an invitation for her to make an opening move.

She sipped her tea.

"Claudia," he said finally. His hand moved toward her face, then came to rest on the back of the empty chair beside her. Finally, he offered a slow smile, sat down, shrugged off his coat, opened the top button of his knitted shirt. "I don't want to rush things, so when you're ready to talk about a video store, I have some news."

Business—this she could handle, something direct and specific, with clear answers to comprehensible questions. "Good news or bad news?"

"I got my first American loan, so now I can say I'm really interested in the building you were talking about the night of Irina's party. I want to know if there will be a space for me."

"Nothing's changed. The building's not a done deal yet." Talking to Frieda Kurtz was one of the things she'd let slide. It had been so much easier to engage in simple tasks she could complete successfully—finishing door frames, painting walls. "And even if I work out the details, the renovation's going to take six months. If you want to move quickly, that Warren Street building isn't the way to go."

"Maybe you need money to speed things up. Maybe I have some to work with here. What kind of terms would I get?" He fussed with the sugar bowl, tracing the stamped silver design, cupping the fullness of the domed lid, his hands never still.

"Reduced rent for five years. Free utilities. The space divided to suit your needs." She and Murray had talked this out in the abstract months ago, but they'd never worked at finding a tenant. The words came easily, allowing her to wonder what Mikhail really wanted, and to watch his face, his gestures, his restless hands.

"In New York, I learn the best business is where each party believes he got the better deal. Okay, let's say you need two hundred thousand cash but you have hundred seventy. Let's say I give you thirty thousand dollars so you can do the fixing. I get a store on a street where people don't walk at low rent for five years. A risk."

"Well, the figures aren't exact," she said, "but keep talking."

Irina followed as though she were watching a tennis match.

"So, thirty thousand is fifteen percent of investment."

The rest of his plan was obvious; he'd learned his business lessons well. But Mikhail Chernin was about to find out that what was good for the gander wasn't necessarily what the goose would let him get away with. She didn't want a percentage investor. She wanted to repay a loan in space for a limited time, not in money she'd have to pay out forever. "No."

"No? You don't even let me finish and you say no? How do you do business if you don't hear the other side?"

She poured more tea from the pot, watched as he spooned sugar into his coffee. "Let's start again, Mikhail. We have an opportunity here to make this into something good."

His hand moved close to hers, but he stopped, fingers splayed on the table. "Good, yes. We can do it over. This is what I like about America, that you can always start again."

Not always. Not if you'd been wrapped in electrical tape, burned in an explosion caused by rigged wiring. Or hung by an extension cord. "Look, give me a while to think about how to structure this so we both feel good about it."

"Sure. I'll get my figures together and stop by. There's another project I'm interested in that maybe we could talk about then. Maybe over dinner or a drink."

"That's fine." As the words left her mouth, she wanted to take them back. She wasn't ready to drink with Mikhail Chernin or anyone else. But it was too late, and she'd live with it.

"In fact, maybe you will have dinner with me tonight?" Mikhail leaned close enough for her to smell his lemony aftershave. "Not business. Just dinner. Tonight, tomorrow, next week, whenever you say."

"I . . . Not yet. I'm just not ready yet."

"Okay." Mikhail grinned and reached into his pocket, drew out a business-size envelope and laid it on the table. "I'm going to Puerto Rico next month to talk to a friend about a *parador* in the mountains. It needs some work, interior renovation. You would do a good job on this little inn in the middle of an old coffee plantation. I have a ticket for you if you want to come. Strictly business, you understand." His grin widened. "Unless you think you might like to spend a day or two on the beach afterward, drinking piña coladas, dancing under the stars. If you come, I promise not to tell you how skinny you're getting."

Before she could respond, Mikhail Chernin rose and pulled his coat from the back of the chair. "We will talk soon."

He ambled to the counter and leaned toward Maria, nodding in the direction of their table. Her smile was shy as she looked down at her order pad, then up at him, trying unsuccessfully to avoid his gaze, finally grinning as she took the crisp bill he handed her, then watched him disappear behind the heavy folds of the velvet curtain.

Whether those talents were learned or inborn, Claudia mused, he knew how to use them. He spoke to every woman he met as if she were the only citron-and-teal cockatoo in a world of pigeons.

She sipped her tea, remembering Ted Stavros and the letters he wrote before they married, letters that should have been a warning, full of stories about his travels through the Sam Shepard west, the desert landscape and the clear nights and the women, always an epiphany about women, about the way they thought and moved and spoke. An epic admiration, and sadly for her, democratic and uncontainable. Mikhail Chernin seemed to be different; it was as though he had a talent for making women melt, a talent he wasn't quite sure how to use, except he kept it fired up and ready to go.

White sand beaches and gauzy curtains blowing in the trade winds—she could always give him back the envelope later.

Forty

Two young women whose dogs were leashed to the Duane Park fence chattered on a bench. A sprinkling of crocuses, white and buttery yellow, turned their faces to the sun in the cultivated strip around the perimeter of the triangle. Midway down the block, she recognized Ike Hitchens, watching the passing foot traffic as though he were surveying the neighborhood for its business potential.

"Hey, Claudia. Been waiting for you. I started that job on Houston so I won't be around so much. But I'll come by when I have time off. Maybe we'll have to make appointments to catch up with each other like real businessfolks do. Anyway, I want to tell you how grateful I am."

"You need help getting your stuff over there?" She peered behind him at the neat row of plastic bags that waited refilling with the items Ike was sorting.

"Nah, I'm giving a lot of this up. It don't seem right to clutter up a room, now that I have one. It don't seem necessary, neither." Ike reached back, picked up a blue baseball cap, passed it to Claudia. "I know your brother be wearing a hat sort of like this that night I seen you down by City Hall. And I know he lost it. So maybe he wants this one."

"Thanks. He's been missing his old beat-up number." She ran her finger along the brim of the hat. "You stay in touch, Ike, you hear?"

"Hold on." He dug through another pile, faced her again sporting a wide grin, his hands behind his back. He swung his arm out, held his closed fist in front of him. One finger at a time, he revealed a square of folded fabric. "This is for you."

Frowning, she took the square, opened it, gasped with delight. Three tiny blue and yellow hand-embroidered birds flitted among the swirls of a deeper blue ribbon in one corner of a lace-edged handkerchief. "This is beautiful. Thank you, Ike."

"It was my mama's," he said proudly. "She'd want you to have it for what you done for me."

"You keep in touch, hear? I better get to work." She hugged him, wondering how Ike Hitchens managed to smell like shampoo even though he'd lived on the street for over a year now.

"Whoever it is, I'm not back yet," Claudia said, unbuttoning her coat and glaring at the ringing telephone. "I need to—"

"Laurette Lacroix." Bert held out the phone to her. "She sounds like she used to play opposite Clark Gable in—"

Claudia took the phone and turned her back on Bert and Gary, who went on with their tasks. "Hi. I just got here. What's up?"

"I put my shovel in and came up with a tiny piece of gold. Sarafino used to live on the same street in Queens as Red Mahoney. They're not related, not by blood. But they certainly might have known each other. I'm going to keep digging, but this is a nugget I thought you should have right away."

Her head spun with the news, with the still-unrevealed meaning. "Thanks. Talk to you later."

She tried to work, but after she cut two lengths of baseboard half an inch too short, the prospects seemed dubious that she'd do anything more than ruin some perfectly good and very expensive material if she persisted.

Bert accompanied her to the basement, got the hammer and the nail puller, tossed them into the trunk of her car.

Then they went home. Bert disappeared down the spiral staircase, and Claudia Miller sat in a tub filled with scented oil, drank a glass of wine, cried when she thought about how long it had been since she'd spoken to Tommy.

236

Dry and dressed, she dialed the number, half expecting to hear her father's voice answering the phone. When was that going to stop? Someone had warned that every first would be difficult: the first Christmas, the first passage of her father's birthday, the first good news she wanted to share with him. But this, this every-day forgetting that he was gone—how long was that going to continue?

"Yes?" Nora sounded as though she'd been asleep.

"Hi, Nora." Claudia watched a man in the apartment across the street as he pushed a vacuum cleaner around his living room. "I'm sorry if I woke you. I want to talk to Tommy. Is he there?"

"You didn't wake me. He's here but he's the one who's asleep. Can I give him a message?"

Claudia bit her lip. Someday she'd stop feeling like every word Nora spoke was an accusation. "Just tell him I called, would you? How are you guys doing over there?"

"I'll tell him you called," Nora said, as though she hadn't heard the question. "Bye, Claudia."

She hung up and hunkered on the floor, head in her hands, rocking, as though the comfort of some childhood memory could take the pain away. The touch of a hand on her shoulder startled her. She looked up into Bert's concerned glance.

"Shit," she whispered. "If only I had called the cops. If only my father had stayed in London . . ."

Bert sank down beside her and clutched her shoulder, his grip tightening as his eyes narrowed. "Are you sure you didn't speak to your young Charlie and just happen to mention Evan's change of plans?"

She let her foot brush his, glad for his presence. "I'm sure. I'm sure I didn't tell *any*one. I was at Duane Street. I was alone in the loft when I spoke to Nora. I know I didn't tell Sarafino, so who does that leave? Charlie was in Los Angeles. Mikhail, Irina, Bruno, Ike? I'm sure I didn't say anything to any of them."

"Maybe you didn't. Maybe the trauma, I don't know, the smack on your head, made you forget someone was with you at the loft when you talked to Nora. You're sure you didn't say any-thing to Mikhail, maybe? Was someone in the loft when you

237

spoke to Nora? Close your eyes and take a deep breath and think, sweetie."

She did as he said, but her eyes flew open. When she tried to picture the scene, her father's face loomed larger.

"All right, try this. I'll talk you through that afternoon. I leave to go to the hardware store, Bruno's scooping his Durabond, leaning close to the wall with that squinty look of his. And then, what, the phone rings and it's Nora?"

"No. That's not how it happened. It was right after the cabinets were delivered that I spoke to Nora. Now I remember. Bruno took off just before the deliveryman left. He said something about going out to dinner. No, it was the movies. He left in a big hurry because he was going to be late for the movies . . . just before I called Nora and she told me my father was returning from London. I was alone in the loft. Nobody heard me."

"Unless the place is bugged." He scowled. "That would be one way to know what's going on with your family. And with mine. Someone might have tapped the phone or put a bug in a light fixture. It's not so hard to get hold of a listening device, right? Pastor wouldn't have to actually be in New York because he . . . oh, shit. This isn't getting us anywhere."

Someone had planted a listening device in the loft on Duane Street.

"Come with me to Duane Street. Oh, Bert, I'm not ready. I'm not ready for my father to be gone. We had so much to tell each other."

The key stuck in the front door. She jerked it out, tried again, nearly fell backward as she pulled the door open and waited for Bert to step inside. She stomped to the elevator, rode with him to the fourth floor in anxious silence.

The loft was dark and cold, and she stuffed her gloves in her pocket, groped on the counter for the flashlight, smiled when her fingers closed around it.

"You want to do this in the dark for some reason?" Arms folded, Bert leaned against the wall. "Can I turn the light on?"

"Sure. I didn't . . . Never mind. Where would someone put a bug in this place?" The apartment flooded with light when she flipped the switch.

"The telephone?" Bert found a Phillips screwdriver, removed the screws so the handset separated into two pieces of plastic. "Shine that in here."

She played the flashlight beam along the wires and chips, saw nothing that looked out of place. "What about the body? Take those screws out, too."

Bert moved quickly, confidently, but with the same result. Everything in place. Nothing that wasn't supposed to be there. He put the pieces back together, tightened the screws.

"The other phone, the one in the kitchen. Check that one."

He unhooked the wall phone, went through the same steps, replaced the telephone on the wall. "Nope. Not that I can tell."

"The light fixtures," she said through gritted teeth as she moved the ladder to the center of the room. The flashlight beam played along the copper wires, the black tape, the plastic cap that would be removed when it was time to hook up the fan. Nothing unusual. She pointed the beam at the long wall, lit up swaths of the ceiling, moved across to the south wall.

If it's not in the telephones, it's in the wiring, you dummy.

"The bug's not in the phones. Let's try the jacks." She scrambled down the ladder, crawled along the floor until she found the junction where the phone line ran to the living room wall, held out her hand for the screwdriver. Bert hunkered beside her and watched as she drew the screw out easily, yanked off the plastic cover, then knelt closer, her cheek almost resting on the dirty floor.

A copper square glinted in the light of her beam.

"You cowardly, lying, cheating, stupid, worthless, murdering bastard!" She smashed the butt end of the flashlight against the listening device again and again, her arm swinging wildly, the breath catching in her chest as she raised the flashlight and struck the jack box again, sending shards of plastic flying like scattershot into her face.

"Claudia." Bert touched her hand gently, then held her in a tight embrace. "Stop. You found it. It's done."

Her chest heaved and a hiss escaped between her teeth. "This is how they found out that my father was coming back early. But how—" She clapped a hand over her mouth. "Remember when I left that fire escape window open?"

Bert loosened his grip and stepped back. "Take a deep breath, sweetie. Calm down. You can't sit around second-guessing every move you ever made. Makes you crazy, that kind of thinking."

Forty-one

1981 / Mercer Street / The Aftermath

She recognized the expression. A bit of the peace she'd created for herself was about to be invaded, she could tell by the twist of the mouth that was more smirk than smile, the quirk of the head that let her know her intruder hoped to pry loose a juicy little morsel no one else had heard before.

She was having an afternoon cappuccino at a sidewalk table at Dante's, one of her favorite Greenwich Village cafés, flipping through a plumbing fixture catalog, enjoying the warmth of the late October sun, when she saw The Look on the face of the woman emerging from the dappled shade on the other side of MacDougal.

Libby something, a choreographer she'd built sets for, waved and headed across the street like a bomb seeking its target.

"I haven't seen you forever." Breathless, a coffee-stained script spilling from her hands onto the already crowded table, she brushed her long bangs out of her eyes and chattered about her latest theater project, working her way to her opening salvo. "So, yeah, we started blocking the staging last winter. About when, uh, everything must have been starting at Mercer Street. Can I ask you something? Didn't you see it coming? I mean, didn't you wake up one morning and realize you were in a mess?"

Claudia responded the way she always did when people asked her about Mercer Street, carefully, casually. "Not really. It didn't happen with captions running underneath. I was just living my life."

"I know what you mean. You have to believe you can turn things your way at will, create your own luck, so you don't feel co-opted by forces beyond your control." Libby dug into her backpack, pulled out a leather pouch and proceeded to roll a cigarette, tamping back the ends to seal in stray strands of tobacco. She went on at length about a seminar she was planning to take at a spiritual center in SoHo. "Firewalk for the Soul. Hey, you've already done your firewalk. So to speak."

"Look, someone burned to death at an apartment I was renovating. There was an investigation. The police concluded the man died under suspicious circumstances. They indicted a friend of mine despite my testimony that he was with me at the time of the fire. He's missing, and the cops still consider him their prime suspect. They tried to hold me as an accessory in his escape but they couldn't prove anything and they had to drop the charges. Finished. End of story."

"End of story? I thought you lost, like, ten thousand dollars on the deal."

Claudia sighed noisily. "Edward Molino's insurance paid him fifty thousand. The rebuilding cost sixty-six. I worked for three months without getting paid. Not because I was guilty of setting the fire. I didn't think it was right for Molino to have to put up that money when maybe I could have prevented the problem by going to the cops when Mahoney threatened me. I didn't. So I made up for my mistake."

A match flared. Libby held it and watched the flame flicker in the breeze before she moved it to her cigarette and sucked hard to get the tobacco burning. "If that elevator had stayed on the fifth floor, the electrician would have gotten out in time. Which left some of us wondering if you knew Kevin Mahoney was going to be in the building that night, so you changed the setting on the elevator so it automatically went down to the ground floor. But that's history, like you said, and nobody's talking about it anymore. So you must be feeling pretty good. Mother Hen took care of her chicks."

"What are you talking about, Mother Hen? I didn't have to protect anyone because nobody did anything wrong." Claudia started to gather her things, pushing papers and books into a manageable stack on the table.

Libby flicked a log of dry ash onto the sidewalk. "No, but really, isn't that what you were doing when you did that interview in the *Village Voice*, protecting your people? I mean, there's something admirable about that."

The reporter had been sly, so sly that Claudia Miller, in the quiet of her room, with the newspaper propped against the bowl of pop-corn and the newly opened bottle of Bud, had to give the woman points. Points for knowing what buttons to push, and points for seeming to capture even the inflections of her words, every one of them accurate. They had commiserated about how women had to work four times as hard as men to prove themselves, had celebrated the fact that they'd chosen fields where the finished product spoke for itself.

Cristiana DeLongi, that was her name. Her freckles and pulled-back frizzy hair and easy laugh had made Claudia relax, had caused her to forget for a moment that she was only fodder for the great media mill.

"When I gave that interview," she said, sending another mental curse in the direction of Cristiana DeLongi, "maybe I wasn't too tactful, but I knew if I was ever going to work in construction again I needed to tell the community I wasn't a criminal. The charges against me had been dropped, but a lot of prospective clients shied away. Maybe they thought I'd burn down their apart-ments, I don't know. Anyway, I'm doing work now for Murray Kurtz, so maybe my jinx is broken."

"You were just setting the record straight in the interview. That's why you said all that stuff about Mahoney, to protect your reputation?"

"I documented Mahoney's threats to me and to three other builders to Cristiana DeLongi because it was my only chance to let people know I had nothing to do with the fire. I told her about another fire at a job where the builder refused to hire union electri-cians. I also told that bitch reporter I had no proof Mahoney set the fire to punish me. That statement never made it into print."

"Yeah, so his wife never got to read that quote. Wow, that must have been hard for you, to read her letter, and then that picture.

The black veil and the two kids, like John-John and Caroline only without the expensive haircuts. I can understand, you know, how what you said hurt her."

The Widow Mahoney had adamantly misinterpreted her intent; it was what Claudia regretted most about the aftermath of the fire. "Well, I'm sorry his wife thought I was smearing his good name. It wasn't like that, so unless you have something new to say, leave it alone, all right?"

"Hey, I'm just saying that after all this, you have to get the concept that your ideas of self and safety, you know, the way you define your world, can be changed in a blink by people and events you haven't yet imagined." Libby exhaled a stream of blue smoke. "God, I hate it when I come to a turning point."

Calm again, Claudia's smile was agreeable, but she continued to send departure signals, folding her newspaper and slipping it into the canvas tote bag that rested near her feet. "I don't know about you, but when I'm in my life, I'm usually too busy to recognize a turning point. Maybe if you spent less time examining other people's warts and more time checking out your own, you'd understand what I'm talking about."

Libby frowned. "Hey, don't confuse curiosity with concern. I just wondered, that's all."

Forty-two

It was obvious the guy had no intention of contacting him.

Sarafino's wife, sounding more annoyed than worried, said he was on a fishing expedition with a buddy who had a cabin in West Virginia, no telephone, she didn't even know the friend's name or the name of the town. He'd be back tomorrow night, she said, and he would dump a load of smelly laundry on the bathroom floor and then take off for work after a quick shower—and wasn't that the way men behaved after all, her tone implied.

The gnawing questions in the pit of Mitch Russo's belly grew to a searing fireball of certainty: Enrico Sarafino was not going to do the right, the neat thing, and come forward with something about the Mahoney fire and the sixteen-year-old frame to exonerate Amos Fischer. And he was no closer to solving the multiple murders than he'd been the day he walked into that Park Avenue apartment.

"Whatever it is, will you tell me when it's over?" Cissie stirred sugar into her tea and watched his eyes. She set the spoon on the saucer and looked up at him.

"You know I will." He would honor the promise he'd made when they got married, to tell her about the troubling parts of the job. Not the gory specifics, not the way brains and guts glistened when they were freshly spattered on a living room wall, not the way a headless, armless, legless torso resembled a slab of beef. But to avoid the problems that busted up too many police marriages, they decided he'd find a way to talk about it.

Except sometimes, for reasons of safety or procedure, he chose to talk to her only after a case was over. Half a week he'd been silent. Three days didn't seem like much when you said it out loud, but it had been a cumulative agony, and Mitch Russo would be relieved when this Sarafino thing was out of his life.

"I'm going to call David, see if he's coming for the baby's christening. Mary Ellen really wants him to be there, but he keeps saying he doesn't know if he can take time off from work. I think he doesn't want to admit that his cousin is not his best buddy anymore. She's going on to a new phase in her life and he's feeling abandoned, you know?"

Mitch Russo could barely summon words to respond, was so preoccupied about what he was going to do about Sarafino that he merely nodded and drained his coffee and kissed his wife on the forehead before he left for work.

Murray Kurtz's apartment building stood among the others on the street like a piece of a child's construction set. Russo imagined yanking it out of place and watching the others tumble toward the middle of the block. Destruction and mayhem: it was a clue to what was going on in his head that he was thinking this way.

The doorman looked up from his newspaper and greeted him with a huge grin. "Okay, things are looking up. What can I do for you today, Detective Russo?"

Russo pulled a photograph from the manila envelope he carried under his arm. "Any of these people look familiar to you?" He pushed it across the fake marble counter and scanned the upside down image: five men hoisting plastic cups at a backyard barbecue, all laughing, all dressed in T-shirts and shorts, hairy legs exposed to the summer sun. In the background, four women sat at a long picnic table.

"Can't say they do. This guy, maybe." The doorman pointed to a tall, slender man, second from the left, whose smile revealed perfect teeth and a chin dimple. "But I think it's because he looks like my cousin Trevor from the Bronx."

"Use your imagination. Could one of these guys be the Therma-

Care man? Maybe this one, huh?" Russo pointed to another member of the group, watched the doorman shake his head. "Or this one?"

Squinting, the man leaned forward, the braid on his epaulets dangling. He held the photograph closer, then moved it back an arm's length and tried again. "Nah. Never saw any of these jokers before. The one in the middle, he looks like Frankie Fishcakes, someone I went to school with. We called him that because that was all he ever ate for lunch. Mayonnaise, cold fishcakes, and a pickle on white bread. I don't even know his real name. But this guy's nose is bigger, he's got more meat on him than Frankie. He looks like he could be a fireman or a cop, am I right?"

Russo stuffed the photograph back into the envelope. "Thanks for your time. If you think of anything—"

"I know. I got your number memorized. Hey, this guy a suspect or something? Was I right about him being a fireman?"

But Russo didn't want to talk about Enrico Sarafino, not until he made his decision final by taking the action he'd threatened. Two days had passed, and then one more. End of the line. As much as it pained him to do it, he had to drop the dime on the guy.

"So, that's it. I'm calling Internal Affairs. Unless you can give me one good reason not to." He shifted the phone on his shoulder, doodled Cissie's name on the pad on his desk.

"I think you should have done it day one," Gallagher said. "I'm not real big on protecting slime from their own stink, you know what I mean?"

"Thanks for the support, Teresa. You're a gem." But he knew she was only calling it as she saw it, and she was probably right. The guy's age, his twenty-plus years on the force, his family— Russo recognized the there-but-for-the-grace-of-God feeling for the lame excuse it was.

He didn't know who was doing the electrical murders. Enrico Sarafino had been telling him the truth when he said he was worried about getting snagged for the setup in the Mahoney fire, but Russo was convinced the man didn't have any idea who was killing all those people.

247

Sweat trickled down his neck. He slipped his arms into his jacket, straightened his tie, felt as though someone had poked a finger into his right eye when the phone rang.

"Russo," he managed to say.

"Yeah, I know what I'm talking about, so listen up. This is gonna make us square on everything. You go see a Mrs. Canelli on Mercer Street and say I sent you. She's ready to tell the truth about that night. That she was fast asleep when she supposedly saw Amos Fischer. Then you have a handwriting expert examine the gas can receipt and ask him if the top part, the date and the name of the buyer, are the same writing as the product name and the price. If he says yes, then fire him. I happen to know the date and the buyer's name were written by someone else, which you could probably figure out by reading some of my old reports but you only do that if you feel you really have to. Get that statement from Mrs. Canelli first, before she dries up and blows away. She's gotta be in her nineties by now." He rattled off an address. "*Hasta la vista,* buddy."

"Sarafino, where are you? Your wife said you were—" But the dial tone buzzed in his ear. Sarafino had delivered his information and hung up. Mitch Russo had no idea whether the man was in New York or West Virginia or someplace else entirely. Shit. He had to check out this Canelli information. But not without backup, not when someone like Sarafino, who had so much to protect, might be waiting for him.

His partner wouldn't be thrilled, but it was the only way to do it. He checked the locker room, looked in the interview room, saw the man staring at a solitaire layout, an upturned card in his hand. "Black ten to the red jack. Hey, Sully, I need you to go in with me to a Mercer Street address on a tip that may turn us onto something in this Belt Parkway case. Or it may be a setup of some kind. You be ready in five minutes?"

He waited patiently through the grumbling while his partner scooped up the cards and stuffed them into the box, waited until he said, "Eight minutes. Downstairs."

"That's great, Sully. See you." He patted his pockets to make sure he had his keys, remembered he'd left them in his coat. In his office.

He was not going to enjoy this, any of it. Getting a statement from an old lady who probably couldn't remember her own name, never mind what happened almost two decades ago, would be no picnic. How long was evidence held in a case that was never really closed? Maybe that receipt was still around somewhere, but finding it wouldn't be easy.

Suddenly, phones rang on three desks at once. Footsteps pounded down the hall; he heard a commotion of voices in one of the offices, and then silence. He ran into the hall toward the noise, realized the telephone on his own desk was ringing, dashed back and picked it up.

"Shit, Russo, you heard, right?"

"Teresa. What's going on? You're okay?"

"*I'm* okay. Enrico Sarafino got dead busting a dope house on the lower East Side. This just now happened. Shot maybe ten times, they're saying. Guy wasn't wearing his vest and now he's splattered all over a tenement hallway. Strangest thing. Someone across the hall heard him bang on the door and identify himself. Said he announced it was Officer Sarafino, that he was coming to settle a score. Then he kicked the door in and got shot dead, but not before he got the shooter, some small-potatoes smack dealer. Guy's gonna get a hero's burial. Honor guard, the works. Unless someone knows why he shouldn't. Unless someone is willing to say Sarafino's heroics were really how he committed suicide so he wouldn't have to face charges on the Mercer Street frame."

Without replying, Mitch Russo replaced the receiver in the cradle.

What was the point?

What was the goddamn point of getting up every day and going to work and being part of a system in which a basically good man deliberately walks into hell, ends his life so he won't have to face the shame of something he did when he was younger and not even a little wise? What was the goddamn point of it all?

He wasn't about to make this decision on his own. This wasn't something he could keep buried, the way Enrico Sarafino thought he could keep the past hidden away beneath years and years of pretending. He reached for the telephone, dialed.

"Yeah, Sully, this is Russo. Cancel the trip to SoHo for right now. I don't know how long it's going to take, but I need to do something else first."

Had to do it before the department got too deep in hero statements to the press about a cop who was killed in the line of duty, he thought sadly.

He tried to get out of his chair, realized that in the minutes since Gallagher's call, the weight pressing against his chest had doubled. But he pushed himself up and grabbed his coat and hat from the hook, made his way to the street, started downtown.

He knew what the point was, always had, just needed a few minutes to admit to himself that he had made a big mistake in trying to shield Enrico Sarafino in the first place.

Forty-three

She'd managed to get through the meeting at the Chelsea town-house without putting her fist through a wall, and now she had to figure out how to relax. Drinking wasn't an option; she'd discovered how much better she felt without the false solace of alcohol.

Which left the healing up to time, television, and Bert. But her good friend had taken his leave and gone off to meet Czech Maria for a nightcap. She pressed the button on the remote, shucked her wool slacks and white silk blouse, and settled onto the couch feeling a little like an actress in a commercial for some flavored instant coffee.

Images leapt across the screen, and she clicked the button, unable to focus, indifferent to the wrenching dramas and mindless comedies and ponderous recaps of Senate hearings on some environmental concern or other.

Murray shouldn't be dead. Her father shouldn't be dead. Evan Patrick Miller might have been a demanding father, but he still had lessons to teach, cases to try, so many moments to share with his family.

She stared at the vapid face of a painted doll, realized she'd been tuned to one of the shopping channels, jabbed at the button to change the channel.

Ann Magursky Carleton shouldn't be dead. And Claudia Miller didn't want to be next.

The television lit up with a display of Las Vegas fireworks and a story about a movie star making a comeback as a cabaret singer. She changed channels again, settled in with the news.

And then he was on the screen, filling it with his coarse features and dour smile. A posed shot, maybe for the Patrolmen's Benevolent Association yearbook.

Enrico Sarafino, dead at fifty-six, longtime veteran of the New York Police Department, killed while making an arrest in a lower East Side tenement, the reporter intoned solemnly. "Sarafino, who was to have retired in nine days, was killed in a hail of bullets that rained down on him from a known heroin dealer's place of business. No further details are available at this time."

When was it going to end? Rick Sarafino—neighborhood fixture for decades, family man, cop who let himself get all tangled up in murders connected to the Mercer Street fire, a man with a secret—dead.

Was this the last of it? With Enrico Sarafino's death, would the killing end? Or was this just a distraction, a sad detour?

She had to know. If anyone could help her figure out if it was really over, it was Deirdre Mahoney. The woman might wring her hands and bar the door and blame her anew, but she was the only one, Claudia was certain, who might help her understand.

Poking around. Probing the soft spots. Like a ghoul reporter haunting a family after a lurid tragedy has proven once again that pain sells newspapers, she was exploiting someone else's sorrow for her own purposes.

Claudia Miller parked the big white convertible under a streetlight as the night sky began to glitter with stars. She pushed open the iron gate, hurried up the walk, waited on the top step of the porch for Deirdre Mahoney to open the door.

"I just heard about Rick and I thought maybe you could use some company." It wasn't a total lie. She liked this plain-speaking woman and knew that Rick Sarafino's death would be difficult for her. "I am sorry, truly. I know how close your families were."

Deirdre Mahoney waved her inside, led her to a chair in the living room. "And you still in mourning yourself. I wanted to call you and say I was sorry to read about your father, but I just—" Deirdre shook her head, dabbed at her eyes with a white handkerchief, downed the rest of the tawny liquid in the glass she clutched in her hand. Her consolation had begun while the sun was still up.

"I understand. Listen, if this is a bad time . . ."

"You just stay right there. Can I get you a cup of tea? A whiskey?"

Claudia waited for the lump in her throat to subside. "Nothing, thanks. Do you mind if I ask you something? Did Rick Sarafino like to read poetry, too? Was he a fan of Frost's? He never said anything about—"

"No." Deirdre's hand reached out and grabbed her wrist. "No, please. Don't do this to me. He was in torment, poor man. He did what he thought he had to and when people started dying again he couldn't live with the knowledge. Don't ask me to shame him in his death. Don't ask me to soil his name. Let him rest in peace."

This had been a bad idea. She was no psychologist, but she knew if she pressed her point, the woman would only dig her heels in. Better to leave while both of them had some measure of their dignity intact.

"Of course," Claudia said. "I'm . . . upset. I want things to make sense and they don't. I came to express my sympathy, not make things more difficult for you. Do you mind if I use your bathroom before I go?"

The white handkerchief waved her toward the dark hall beyond the arch. "First door on the left," Deirdre murmured without rising.

Claudia made her way to the hall, squinting in the dim light, groping along the wall until she came to the first door on the left. She reached inside, felt around for a light switch, stepped back and slid her hand along the wall near the door. Her fingers traced the contours of the light switch, flipped it up.

She'd found the hall light; the bathroom switch was lower on the wall than she'd expected. She turned it on, examined herself in the mirror, ran the cold water to wash the smeared mascara from beneath her eyes. When she was done, she stepped out into the brightly lit hall.

Across from the door, scores of photographs filled a long wall from ceiling to floor. Kevin and Deirdre Mahoney and two children gathered around a Christmas tree. A formal, posed wedding portrait, Deirdre clear-eyed, glowing, Kevin proud and smiling. Unable to pull away, Claudia examined school photographs; a composite of the two small children, round-cheeked, hair neatly combed and shiny; family vacation snapshots. She traced the children's progress through school, the increasingly elaborate Christmas celebrations. Enrico Sarafino and his wife and son appeared in two holiday pictures.

Midway to the door at the end of the hall, through which she could see a four-poster bed covered with a white chenille spread, one of the family pictures included another child and a woman whose dark hair and eyes bore little resemblance to the Mahoney clan, or to the Sarafinos.

She studied the sad-eyed woman, put her face close to the glass covering the photo and squinted until the little boy's features became clearer. If she lengthened his nose, made his hair a little longer and a lot lighter, put glasses on him, gave his jaw a grown-up, squared-off definition . . . Was she looking at a young Charlie Pastor? She could round the face a little, darken the hair. He had the same broad-shouldered proportions, the same thick eyebrows. Was that Gary Bruno's picture on Deirdre Mahoney's wall? Or was that curling smile and the broad shoulders, that cocky tilt to his hips a picture of a young Mikhail Chernin?

The boy was beaming, looking with adoration into the face of Kevin Mahoney. His expression seemed to say that all was right with the world, that he felt secure as long as he could breathe the same air as Big Red Mahoney.

When she returned to the living room, Deirdre Mahoney was setting two glasses of whiskey on the table beside her.

She had to ask.

She couldn't leave without at least making the attempt. "That's quite a wall of photographs. My family hides all the pictures in albums and never takes them out."

"My own family is right here with me every day." Deirdre Mahoney sipped her whiskey, pointed to the other glass. "They were my life. I never had a job I cared about. I lived for them," she said. "A mistake, but there you are."

"Rick was a good-looking man when he was young. I never met his wife or his son. And that beautiful woman, the one with the long brown hair. Who's that?" Claudia poured a splash of whiskey into her untouched glass, added an inch to Deirdre's empty one.

"Ah, you must mean Cathleen. What a sad story that is. Her husband, John, was an accountant who worked his way through school running heavy construction equipment, those big bulldozer things. Cathleen, she was the delicate type, like a meringue, you know."

Easily, casually, Claudia said, "And the little boy in the striped shirt next to her? Is that her son?"

"Their only son was born when Cathleen was thirty-seven and John was forty. A surprise, since they were such good Catholics they thought the rhythm method was some system for teaching music. From the minute that child was born, Cathleen couldn't take her eyes off him, wouldn't stop kissing his little face. She doted completely on that baby. John started getting jealous, drinking, staying out. Over the years things only got worse. She would come here and visit and tell me about her husband's jealousy and his general bad temper after he'd been in his cups. And then one day I realized I hadn't seen her for a week. When I went over there, she tried to hide her bruises. All over her arms and her back, even the back of her legs."

The accountant beat his delicate wife. Not nice, but maybe this weepy little tale had something to do with her father's murder. Claudia held the whiskey glass in her hand, waited for Deirdre Mahoney to continue.

"One night, it was exactly twenty years ago this past winter, it was the Friday before Christmas and my sister had just arrived from Detroit and we were making the final shopping list for Christmas dinner—isn't it funny how you just remember some things? We were having an argument about whether to put oranges and nuts in with the cranberries—and there was this terrible pounding on the door and then we heard a shrieking, like the devil himself was after someone.

"Kevin went to the door in his bare feet and in flew Cathleen with the little boy in her arms. Back then, he was kind of a small lad, ten years old just, but short as some of the third-graders. And she all sobbing and shaking. Kevin took her inside to the kitchen and next thing I knew he told me to make up the sofa in the rec room and he pulled on his boots and went stomping out of the house. Came back an hour later, whispered something to the woman that set her to crying again, and then went straight up to bed."

In some alternate universe, all that pain and suffering might make the little boy grow up and take a vow never to add more sorrow to the world. Instead, Claudia was more and more certain she was about to hear why he became fixed on balancing the score he'd kept all these years.

"He never meant for it to happen, but Kevin became the father the child never really had. They played basketball in the yard and went to baseball games. Kevin taught him a little of the pugilistic arts, you know. They built a birdhouse from twigs they picked up in the yard. If Kevin had to work late, the boy would hang out on the steps waiting."

"So John stopped beating his wife because Kevin threatened him?"

Deirdre folded the handkerchief into a small rectangle. "John would disappear for months, come back and cause trouble, then go away. When the boy got to be grown, he made John stay away. Until two years ago. Just showed up one day and Cathleen let him come live in her house again. She died last year. John claimed someone broke into the house and beat Cathleen and him both. Had a broken nose to show for it. Cathleen . . . they couldn't have an open casket, she was that bad. Her son made a scene at the funeral, said it was John who killed her. That he would never have come near Cathleen if Kevin had been alive and—" She pressed the handkerchief to her mouth, eyes wide with understanding. "Oh, no," she moaned. "Oh, Lord help us all."

Cathleen's son's name.

She needed this sad, drunk woman to tell her who that boy was, because when Kevin Mahoney died in that fire on Mercer Street, everything the little boy counted on to make his world safe and decent died, too, and for months he had been exacting a horrible revenge.

"Deirdre." Now. Before she lost her nerve. "Tell me his name."

But Deirdre Mahoney shook her head and held out her hand to stop Claudia's words. "I watch the troubles in the old country. Sinn Fein denies the IRA blew up a bus, the Protestants shell a market, cousins kill each other. My priest's father came to this country to get rich enough to send gun money back to Dublin. It never stops, no one ever forgets, they sit around and talk and it looks good for about ten minutes and then the blood starts flowing again." The white handkerchief twisted in her hands, as though she could wring some sense from it if she tried really hard. "Someone's got to say enough. So I do. I say enough. But I have to do it my way. I have to give him the chance to do the right thing."

Claudia understood what the woman was asking. "One hour," she said evenly. "If he doesn't turn himself in in an hour, I go to the police."

"It's always up to the women to stop it, isn't it?" Deirdre Mahoney nodded her agreement. "One hour. I still have your card. I'll call you by ten-thirty."

Forty-four

When the telephone rang, he nearly hit his head on the edge of the dresser. Blinking, he saw from the bluish light seeping in under the window shade that it was night, that the street lamp on the corner was already on. The clock said 9:35. He'd been lying here, trying to decide what to do, trying to get calm after Claudia Miller almost broke his eardrums with her shouting and that terrible, deafening noise when she smashed the bug. He must have fallen asleep.

The phone rang again. He lifted the receiver, waited, finally said, "Yes?"

Her voice on the other end, soft and scratchy, whispered his name. She'd been crying, he could hear it. "Please," she said. "I know what you've been doing. It's not how he would have wanted you to honor his memory. Go to the police. You need help and they can get it for you."

She knew.

How did she find out?

"I'm doing fine without their help." Maybe she'd put it together from things she read in the newspaper.

"No, that's not what I call fine. Not what he would call fine. I know how much it hurt when your mother died. I know you think if Kevin was there it wouldn't have happened. But, dear boy, what you've been doing . . . It's not going to bring them back."

Three in a row near New York—he should have gone to California, Alabama, Chicago instead, should have made it harder for

258

Deirdre Mahoney or anyone else to see the threads connecting the events.

"But, see, I want them to know. They all should know how it is to see someone you love murdered." What he'd done had been for her, too, except he knew she wouldn't understand so he kept it from her. Until now.

"Claudia Miller knows."

That bitch figured it out and went to Deirdre Mahoney.

Big Red's wife went on. "She knows how it feels. But seeing Claudia Miller in pain doesn't give me my Kevin back. Please, you must stop. You must go to the police right now. You must turn yourself in. In one hour. I want you to call me from the police station. I'll come with you if you want me to. But if you don't do it in one hour, I'm going to call them myself. One hour. You have to—"

He hung up.

She shouldn't have done that. Claudia Miller should not have bothered Deirdre Mahoney. She should have left her alone, should never have told her about her suspicions.

Now he had to show that Miller bitch, finally, that she wasn't as smart as she thought.

Deirdre Mahoney shouldn't have given him an ultimatum. He was a man, and he needed to make decisions on his own.

She wanted him to give up.

Maybe it was the best thing. Turn himself in. Let it be over.

That's not what *he* would have done. *He* would keep fighting. No one would tell him when to eat, sleep, and piss. He'd make his own decisions.

He opened the drawer, pulled out the green box, pushed aside the folds of the handkerchief. Trembling, he drew the pipe out of its resting place, sucked on it, but it didn't help.

Beneath the bedroom a subway train rumbled by. The pity of it was that he hadn't finished. But maybe he didn't have to, maybe his real job was to make sure he taught Claudia Miller a lesson she'd never forget.

Excited, he bolted to the dresser and opened the red plush box, stared down at the watch resting on the folds of red satin. The sight of the rectangular face and leather band nearly brought tears to his eyes, and he reached in, laid the watch on his wrist, slipped the leather through the buckle, and inserted the prong into the well-worn third hole.

He opened the closet door, pushed past the shirts and pants and jackets and slid the garment bag along the pole. The zipper stuck. He wiped his sweaty hands on his jeans, gripped the bag and tried again, unclenched his teeth when the plastic seam gave way. That was just as good, it solved the problem, got him what he needed, which was to get the goddamn coveralls out of the bag. Because he needed those coveralls to finish this thing.

She shouldn't have gone to Deirdre.

Maybe, after he was done with her he would walk away, not into the arms of the police, but to New Jersey, where Aram Kossarian waited for him in a nursing home. Then he'd be done.

The pipe, still lying on the lace runner on the little table by the side of his bed, was the final item. Coveralls, watch, pipe: he could do anything now.

It had been so easy.

"I have information about who killed your father. Come to the southeast corner of Second Avenue and Sixty-eighth Street in five minutes. Don't call anyone. Don't tell anyone about this call. Don't leave a note. If you do, I'll know, and you won't like what happens when I really get mad. Just be there. Alone."

And then he'd hung up, stepped out of the coffee shop, zipped up his brown leather jacket, and waited in the doorway of the shoe store, where he could see the comings and goings of the people on the street. The night was full of stars, cold, but something sweet in the air alerted him that spring would arrive in a few days, that winter would finally give it up and go underground for nine months.

A bus belched and lurched down the river of traffic, and a woman stepped off the curb.

Tall, thin, short dark hair. Was it her?

But when he stepped out of the shelter of the doorway, he could see it was a boy, high school age, with a torn backpack. Besides, he was wearing glasses. It wasn't Thomas Miller, it wasn't Claudia Miller, it wasn't anyone he knew.

Would the boy recognize him? This would be a good game, to
see if the boy could look him in the eye and say, *So, it's you. I never
knew, you were so clever.*

His heart beat faster at the thought of one more little game.
There he was, coming down the block, his long legs running,
pounding on the pavement. Ice was gone, finally, so he could do
that without slipping.

Dig your heels in first so your feet don't go flying out, that's what *he*
said. He remembered now, that day they went to get the ashes
from the shed in the backyard. She would clean out the fireplace
twice each winter and then once again in the spring, when there
were no more fires to be made until Christmas Eve, the first official
fireplace lighting of the season. They did it together, as a family,
him and his mother included because, after all, they were connected by more than blood since *he* saved them.

And he would go with *him* to the shed when it was icy and *he*
had to get the car out of the driveway. They'd shovel the ash into a
bucket, cinders and all, and dump it along the ice so the car had
something to grip. And *he'd* say, "Dig your heels in first."

The boy had reached the corner, looking around as though he
was one of those rabbits caught in the headlights of a car. Eyes
wide—good, he was alone, no one seemed to be following him.
Weaving between the idling cars, he made his way toward the boy,
came at him straight on, saw him flinch when he got halfway
through the intersection. Even in the crowd, the boy's eyes followed him, picked him out, kept with him as he approached.

"Hey, Tom. You ready?"

The kid pulled his hand out of his pocket. Without warning, he
felt a burning pain searing his arm. The kid stared at him, then
started to run down Second Avenue. His torn jacket, the blood
seeping through the leather, made him furious.

In six steps, he was behind the boy, grabbed his arm, heard the
knife clatter to the sidewalk.

"You didn't believe me, did you? Now, if you don't want your
sister to get hurt, you just do what I say." He kept his grip on the
scrawny arm, grabbed a handful of the boy's hair, pulled his head
down and reached for the knife with his other hand, fingers scrab-
bling on the rough asphalt until they closed over the cold, slick

261

blade. He stood, knife pressed to the boy's side, maneuvering them into the shadows. "You and me and your little penknife, we're taking a subway ride downtown. You just pretend that I'm not about to break your arm, all right, because if you do anything else to make me angry, I'll make sure to hurt your sister even more. See, I need you to get to her. And I need her to be my insurance." He cackled. "That's what she is. My insurance."

"You're pathetic, you know that? And you're dripping blood all over the place."

The scorn in the boy's voice was like a second knife twisting in his gut. "Reach into my right-hand pocket and take out the handkerchief and tie it around the wound. You can do that, can't you, big guy? Because if you don't, I'll break your fucking arm."

Tommy Miller, the sharp point of the knife piercing the fabric of his jacket, did as he was told.

Forty-five

The drive from Queens had taken only twenty minutes. No traffic in the Midtown Tunnel, the streets as deserted as if it were the middle of a three-day weekend. She headed for the West Side Highway on 23rd Street, checked her watch again as she idled at the light at Eighth Avenue.

She'd given her word to Deirdre Mahoney, and she would give her the full hour she'd promised. She'd get through the next forty minutes somehow. And then she'd call Russo and this reign of terror would be over.

The light changed, and she waited for a cluster of kids who must have just come out of the movie to cross, then continued toward the river, glancing over at the huge London Terrace monolith as she drove past.

The river was a wide black ribbon tonight, like a somber bunting to mark her mourning. She drove south to Canal Street, turned onto Greenwich, bumped along the cobblestoned section until the street widened to a flat blacktop surface. At Harrison Street she turned left, so steeped in her own anger that she almost didn't see him as she pulled into the spot beyond the pump, set the alarm, got out and locked the doors.

Ike Hitchens lay curled around a plastic shopping bag, his shoes untied and his coat unbuttoned. He'd chosen the front step of her loft, as though he wanted to rub it in her face that she was wrong to try to reclaim his soul from the darkness. When she leaned down to see if he was breathing, the smell of alcohol sent her reeling back.

"I was waiting for you, Claudia." He rubbed his hand across his mouth and sat up.

"Aren't you supposed to be at work now, Ike?"

"I heard about your father and I wanted to make sure you're okay." He coughed, shook his head, closed his eyes. "My day off. I come around to see if you let me buy you a drink in your father's memory and I guess, you know, I started without you." He reached out for her, but she danced away. "I'm sorry. You have a drink with me?"

"Shit, Ike." She didn't have the energy to deliver a lecture, or to worry about hurt feelings and social niceties. "I can't. I have to make an important phone call. I'll talk to you another time. You can buy me a drink another time."

She let herself in to the lobby, trudged to the elevator, closed her eyes as she rode upstairs. Twenty more minutes before she could call Deirdre Mahoney.

The memory of the smashed telephone jack in the Hockmans' loft made her blood race with anger.

What a joke.

Russo had told her he'd try to track down where it was bought and when, but he hadn't seemed too hopeful. As she hung her coat in the closet, the telephone rang.

Deirdre Mahoney. Thank God. Breathing hard, she reached for the phone.

"Hello?"

No one answered.

"Hello? Deirdre? Bert? Shit." Furious, she slammed the phone down, emptied the dishwasher, wandered to the stove and filled the teakettle with water.

The buzzer sounded. When she checked the monitor, the tiny screen showed no one.

Frowning, she went to the window, looked down at the street, saw Ike Hitchens peering up at the sky, stumbling because he couldn't keep his balance.

She'd already done her bit for him, and if he chose to blow it, that was his business. No way would she stop to listen to his apologies now. She ignored the frantic bleat of the buzzer, poured Earl Grey leaves into the bottom of the teapot, almost knocked over the porcelain teacup because she was so angry with Ike. The buzzer blared again, boring into her like a dentist's drill.

She turned off the flame, grabbed her purse, rode downstairs ready to tell Ike that he had to leave her alone, that if he wanted to ruin his life he could do it without her.

"Claudia." Ike staggered down the sidewalk toward her, his eyes blinking lazily, a piece of paper fluttering in his fingers.

"Listen, Ike, I told you—I'm waiting for a phone call. Go sleep it off. I'll see you another time." *And maybe then I won't be too angry to talk to you,* she thought as she pulled her keys from her purse and stuck them in the lock.

"Wait. Don't go nowhere."

Heat rose from her throat to her cheeks as she watched Ike shake his head, a trickle of damp tears making their way down his dusty face.

"Your brother," he said, waving the paper as he stumbled and dropped heavily to one knee. "Your brother in trouble."

The keys fell from her hands and tumbled to the sidewalk.

She opened the paper Ike thrust into her hand. Before the words made any sense, the crabbed printing told her the note was written by the same person who wrote out the list she found in Charlie Pastor's book.

I'm watching you. If you want to see your brother again, do this now. Go to the bank and get three thousand dollars. Then meet me at the north end of the uptown platform of the Franklin Street station. If I see any cops, I will kill Tommy. Remember I am watching. You have fifteen minutes starting from now.

Her head whipped around.

No one on Harrison Street but Ike. She grabbed her keys and pivoted.

On Hudson, three people walked by, arms around each other, singing. He could be in a building, in the doorway of Chanterelle, in that parked car in front of Yaffa's. Ten-thirty exactly. The bank was a block and a half away on the corner of Hudson and Franklin.

The subway station was a block east of that. She could be there by twenty to eleven.

The hang-up call: someone had tracked her to her loft, someone who wanted to pin down exactly where she was.

"Ike, I need you to take this note to the police station for me. Hurry, you hear me? Ike?" She wasn't going to make the same mistake again and pay for it with another life. The cops had to be told. She held out her hand and pulled him to his feet, slipped the paper into his pocket.

"You don't go down there alone." He shook his head. "He's a mean bastard, Claudia. I'm no good for helping you, but you don't go down there alone, hear?"

Ten thirty-one.

She scanned the street behind her.

The tremor of anger that shook her almost made her strong enough, she thought, to protect herself.

No, it wouldn't work.

She needed to face her tormentor armed. She no longer had the gun. A knife could be turned against her. And she was running out of time.

It would take two minutes to get to the bank, two more to punch in her number at the ATM and collect the cash, another minute to get down the block to the subway station. Enough time. And then what?

No rules for this one, Dad. She would have to make this one up as she went along.

"Get that note to the police, Ike. Do it now. Hurry." She gave him a gentle shove, and he shuffled off to the corner, stumbling, reaching out for the fender of her car for support.

Was someone really watching her? She looked around again, peered into a taxi, squinted through the glass door into the lobby of the building across the street. Empty.

She would assume, for now, that he meant what he said in the note. If she did something to anger him, Tommy would be the one to pay.

Her car. She opened the trunk, pushed aside her briefcase, two sweatshirts, a handsaw, a paint sample book. She dug around and found a metal rule, her notebook, the goggles she'd worn to pro-

266

tect her eyes from fiberglass insulation. Finally, her fingers ran over the metal nubs on the curved head of the shingler's hammer, touched the claw-end of the nail puller.

That should be enough. And if it wasn't, she'd improvise. She slid the nail puller and the shingler's hammer into her briefcase, tossed her wallet and keys in the center section, dropped her purse in the trunk, slammed the door.

She ran to Hudson Street. A light went on above the nautical map shop. Steam rose in a white, ropy cloud from a taxi exhaust. If she were lucky, she'd be standing on the uptown platform of the Franklin Street subway station in time to meet his deadline.

In the next nine minutes, she'd figure out how she was going to pull Tommy out of this fire.

"You go fast," she panted as she pulled up beside Ike. "You tell someone at the police station I'm going to do what the note says. Now you do what *I* say." She patted his back. "Hurry, Ike. You make sure you cross at the light, okay?"

When she reached the corner, she looked back over her shoulder. Ike was dragging his feet a little faster, making his way north, his face tight with concentration. He'd do it. He had to. She surged forward, heading toward Franklin, flying past a couple walking a dog with ribbons in its hair, past a broad-shouldered man bobbing to the sounds of his Walkman.

Breathing hard, a pain stitching into her side, Claudia Miller ran on, dug through her briefcase for her wallet, fingers fumbling for the plastic card that would open the bank door and allow her to withdraw her money.

She stuck her card in the slot, watched the green light blink on, pulled the door open. Prayed that the TEMPORARILY OUT OF SERVICE sign would not be lit. Breathed a relieved sigh when she saw two people stuff bills into their wallets and walk away.

She went through the routine, touching the correct boxes on the screen, entering her number, listening to the beep and shuffle of the mechanism as it grabbed twenties and tens. She could withdraw no more than five hundred at a time. Surely he knew that no tellers were at work in the bank at this hour, that these machines had a limit. What did he think she was, superwoman or something?

Probably, he didn't think. Wouldn't have had the presence of mind to know that she wouldn't be able to meet his demands.

She glanced at her watch, shoved the money into her wallet, pulled the door open and stepped outside.

Even at this hour, the street pulsed with life. Couples headed home from late suppers, cars and taxis made their way uptown, young bean counters with their ties undone and their suit jackets thrown over their shoulders stumbled out of the sports bar. Alert, her gaze raking the shadows, she made her way to the subway station at Franklin and West Broadway.

Ike should have gotten to the First Precinct by now.

Unless he'd fallen into a drunken heap, a bundle of rags and sadness a passerby would step around, clucking about the meanness of a political system that had no compassion. Unless he'd forgotten where the First Precinct was.

She looked around, noticed that two men on the other side of West Broadway had stopped to watch her go down the stairs. If they followed her and grabbed her and pulled the briefcase from under her arm . . . She ran down the stairs, reached for her wallet. This was not the time for her MetroCard to be void; she hadn't used it in a while, preferred the token system.

She swiped the card, the green light blinked, and she swept through the turnstile and onto the platform.

Forty-six

The station was deserted. The note had said north end, uptown side, but the further she walked from the lighted waiting area, the more her throat closed up and her breath caught in her chest. Her steps echoed in the cavernous emptiness as she made her way toward the red light at the far end of the platform.

On one of the metal beams across the tracks, she noticed that a corner of the paper announcing that the area had been treated with rat poison had been torn away. Had the edge of the warning caught on a passing train? Maybe it had been snagged on some worker's equipment as he trudged between the rails.

Squinting into the darkness, Claudia spun around at the sound of the express train roaring out of the tunnel toward Fourteenth Street, watched the sparks under the metal wheels as the train picked up speed and rattled north. When she looked around again, two figures had emerged from the darkness at the end of the platform.

Tommy, his shoulders square and his head tilted, was being pushed along in front of Gary Bruno.

She sensed rather than saw the knife Bruno used to prod her brother toward her, and she picked up her pace.

Involuntarily, she turned her head at the rumble of the local pulling in behind her. Cold air rushed by. The first car of the train passed her and she started running as Bruno cackled, swerved to his right, and pushed Tommy toward the edge of the platform.

The train slowed. Bruno pulled back on Tommy's jacket, yanking him out of the way of the tons of steel rolling to a noisy stop along the track.

"You pretend we're talking about the goddamn weather." His eyes darted wildly along the platform. "Just stand there and talk to me and look like you want to be here."

From the middle of the train, the conductor leaned out his window, stared at them, shook his head. The doors rolled closed, and the train clattered out of the station. Two men in suits and raincoats made their way through the turnstiles and disappeared from view. On both sides of the tracks, the Franklin Street subway station was deserted again.

Bruno's eyes continued to dart to the south end of the platform and then back to her face. "You got my message, I see. Now, did you get my money?"

"I have five hundred dollars, but the machine wouldn't let me take more out." She was close enough now to see the pulsing vein at the side of his neck, and the lightning bolt dangling from his gold chain. Dressed for the occasion—Gary Bruno wasn't too crazy to remember not to wear his jewelry to work.

The muscles in Tommy's jaw clenched and again he tried to twist out of Bruno's grasp.

"I told you three thousand." He jerked Tommy's arm behind him. "You think you can pull this shit on me? You should know by now I don't like it when you underestimate me. It was so much fun helping this lad pull off the great escape to the country. It gave me the idea of how I could really make my point. I did come up with something much better, didn't I?"

She couldn't rise to his bait. "I can get the rest of your money as soon as the bank opens but the machine won't let me take out more than five hundred in twenty-four hours. I'm going to get my wallet so I can give you the cash." She lowered her hand slowly.

"Set that briefcase on the floor. Right here." Bruno tapped on the tiles with the toe of his work boot. "You think I'm dumb or something, you grab another nice little gun out of there maybe. Not tonight. You want to know something, this is even better than the other time. Because I get to see you up close and real personal. You think I don't see it in your eyes. You're afraid. Big sister standing here trying to be brave, but you're crapping your pants." His laughter bounced off the tile walls. "You think I'm here to get the money? That's not it. I want the pleasure of watching your face when you see what's going to happen next."

Ike. Where was Ike? "The wallet is in the zipper section in the middle. I keep it there so nobody can grab it." She bit down on her lip. The hammer lay at the bottom of one of the side sections. He might not see it, might not even feel it.

Still holding Tommy's arm, Bruno knelt, pulled the wallet out, kicked the briefcase to the edge of the platform.

Claudia stepped cautiously forward, hands open, and knelt to retrieve the briefcase. She stood slowly, watching Bruno as he followed every movement she made. "Deirdre Mahoney will be so sad about this," she said softly. Another step forward. Tommy looked as though he'd stopped breathing. "She told me she wanted it to stop, all the hating and the killing."

At the sound of Deirdre's name, Gary Bruno's shoulders sagged. A growl rose from his throat and he started muttering about traitors and ingrates.

Claudia reached into the briefcase, maneuvered the handle of the shingler's hammer so that it slipped up into the sleeve of her jacket, then closed her hand around the hammer's head.

Bruno ranted on and sidestepped again, closer to the edge of the platform, dragging Tommy with him. When he turned to check his footing, Claudia pulled her arm up and jammed her hand into her pocket, the hammer's shaft cold under her sleeve.

Bruno and Tommy stood inches from the edge, their shoes touching the warning strip set with glass beads that let passengers know they were too close to the five-foot drop. "You should have left her out of this," he shouted. "This is between you and me. All of you. All of you who set Kevin Mahoney up in that fire. All of you who killed him. And killed my mother. Toss me that briefcase again. I gotta make sure you're not carrying."

Jesus, he was going to find the nail puller. Claudia Miller didn't move.

"You got a gun in there, I shoot him with it, you understand? The briefcase, toss it here."

She slid the briefcase within his reach, waited as he knelt again and rummaged inside.

Another cautious step—she was ten feet away now, could see the wild movements of Gary Bruno's brown eyes, the slow and careful scanning of Tommy's lighter eyes. "Let my brother go, Bruno. He never did anything to you. Just let him go and I'll get you the rest of the money first thing in the morning. I keep my word, you know that."

Something moved in the shadows on the downtown side of the tracks.

"You bitch." He grabbed the nail puller out of the left-hand section of the briefcase, then kicked the leather case behind him. It slid two feet, hung on the edge of the platform, then fell onto the track. "You think I'm going to just set him loose now? You know why we're here? Your father, that didn't hurt you enough. This will. Watch this."

He looked down at the tracks, took careful aim, tossed the nail puller in a smooth, underhand pitch. The wedge end hit the third rail as the curved end clanged against a girder. A sizzling shower of sparks exploded and then died as the bar fell between the tracks.

"Next, we're going to fry little Tommy here." Bruno cackled. "Unless you want to go first. You gonna jump down there instead, Claudia?"

The figure was halfway across the tracks, crouched low. A woman with tumbled auburn curls, dancing her way between the metal beams.

Behind her, Claudia heard the rumble of a train, realized it was another northbound local.

"Come on, Bruno. That's enough." She jammed her hand in her pocket; her fingers ran over the nubs on the head of the hammer, closed around the thick shaft.

The sound of the train was louder, louder, and then the air began to change. The wind, the train's preceding breath, blew cold on her neck, but she didn't turn.

"Too many people know, Bruno. You're not going to get away with it." She was closer, closer, and he took a wary step back, dragging Tommy with him. "Leave him alone, okay? He's a kid who just lost his father. You should understand how that feels, Bruno."

Her words were drowned out as the train roared to a stop. She nodded, lifted her foot, kicked out hard at Gary Bruno's shin. Tommy stomped down with all his might on the top of Bruno's foot.

Startled and furious, Bruno screamed, wheeled, jerked his clenched fist back.

Claudia Miller pulled the shingler's hammer from her pocket and smashed it against Bruno's knee, hit him again on the other knee, shoved him away from Tommy.

Screaming, Bruno went down in a heap, and she grabbed Tommy's jacket and pulled him onto the train as the doors rolled shut. On the platform, his face contorted, Bruno had struggled to his feet and was hobbling desperately after the departing train. He stumbled, clutched his right knee, sprawled to the floor. The last thing she saw before the train disappeared into the tunnel was Gary Bruno's grotesque and angry face, a gargoyle lying on the cold tiles.

"You okay, Tommy?" The train rocked forward, and she looked at her brother, at his pale, wide-eyed fear.

"I will be," he told her quietly.

Every morning for a week, despite having to pay dearly on the first two days to have the *New York Times* delivered to her San Juan hotel room, despite having to spend the next five days reading in her halting Spanish the Ponce daily that was the only paper she could get in the mountains, she'd scoured the news diligently, convinced that she would find an item about a permanent truce in Northern Ireland or Bosnia or Somalia.

Today, finally, she wanted only to let the sun make her a little browner, to discover whether the birds sounded different in the *cordilleras* of this pretty island than in the city.

"We go home tomorrow." Across the terrace, the mountains emerged from a haze as the sun made its way to the middle of the sky. "Your brother will be glad to see you. Your policeman needs you to testify at Bruno's trial. Your friend Bert is patiently waiting for his turn to go, where? To Japan, yes? So we go back to the big city tomorrow. Too bad."

"This was good for me, Mikhail. I'm glad you persisted." She

273

reached into her glass for an ice cube, ran it along the inside of his arm, turned her face to the sun again.

"You still need a little meat on your skinny bones," he said, his fingers circling her wrist as he bent to kiss her neck. "And I still need you to tell me if this *parador* is a project you want to be involved with. But we'll keep working on both of them. Right now, let's see if we can find something to do to keep you busy while you're thinking about your decision."

"Watch out." She closed her eyes and leaned back against his warmth. "It may take me a very long time to decide."